Lyrics Alley

Also by Leila Aboulela

Minaret
The Translator
Coloured Lights (stories)

Leila Aboulela was born in Cairo and grew up in Khartoum. Both her previous novels, *The Translator* and *Minaret*, were longlisted for The Orange Prize and IMPAC Award. Her work has won the Caine Prize for African Writing, has been shortlisted for the Saltire Society Scottish First Book Award and the MacMillan Silver Pen Award, and has been adapted extensively for BBC Radio. She lives between Doha and Aberdeen.

Lyrics Alley

Leila Aboulela

Weidenfeld & Nicolson

LONDON

First published in Great Britain in 2010
by Weidenfeld & Nicolson
An imprint of the Orion Publishing Group Ltd
Orion House, 5 Upper St Martin's Lane
London WC2H 9EA
An Hachette UK Company

1 3 5 7 9 8 6 4 2

978 0 297 86314 4 (cased)
978 0 297 86009 9 (trade paperback)

A CIP catalogue record for this book is
available from the British Library.

Typeset by Input Data Services Ltd, Bridgwater, Somerset

Printed by Clays Ltd, St Ives plc

The Orion Publishing Group's policy is to use papers that
are natural, renewable and recyclable products and made
from wood grown in sustainable forests. The logging
and manufacturing processes are expected to conform to
the environmental regulations of the country of origin.

www.orionbooks.co.uk

For my father, Fuad Mustafa Aboulela (1928–2008)
in tribute to his love for his family.
And in memory of his cousin Hassan Awad Aboulela (1922–1962),
whom he spoke of often.
May Allah Almighty grant them mercy.

Principal Characters

Mahmoud Abuzeid (head of the Abuzeid family, married to two women)

1. **Hajjah Waheeba**, mother to his two elder sons, **Nassir** and **Nur**
2. **Nabilah**, his young Egyptian wife, mother to *Ferial*, his daughter, and *Farouk*, his youngest son. Nabilah's mother *Qadriyyah* and her stepfather *Mohsin* live in Cairo.

Idris Abuzeid (Mahmoud's younger brother, a widower with three daughters)

Halima

Fatma (married to her cousin Nassir) has two children, a daughter, *Zeinab*, and a son

Soraya (betrothed to her cousin Nur).

Ustaz Badr, an Egyptian, a teacher of Arabic and private tutor to the Abuzeids. He is married to *Hanniyah*, they have four young sons – *Osama*, *Bilal*, *Radwan* and *Ali*

Shukry, Ustaz Badr's cousin.

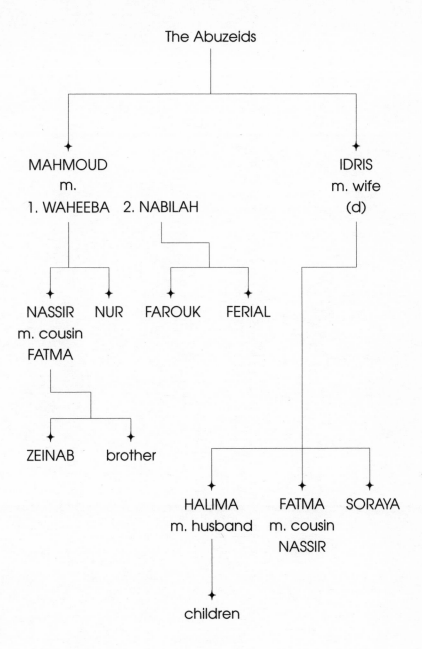

The Abuzeids

MAHMOUD
m.
1. WAHEEBA   2. NABILAH

IDRIS
m. wife
(d)

NASSIR   NUR   FAROUK   FERIAL
m. cousin
FATMA

ZEINAB   brother

HALIMA   FATMA   SORAYA
m. husband   m. cousin
NASSIR

children

m = married
d = deceased

I

Alhamdullilah, he was safe and the worst was over. Thank God, he was better today compared to yesterday – that was what everyone around her was saying, but Soraya was impatient. It was not enough that her beloved Uncle Mahmoud was recovering his appetite or talking to visitors about how the Korean War was likely to increase the price of cotton. Soraya wanted him as he was before, not weak and bedridden; she wanted him to be on his feet again, smiling and striding. Then they would slaughter sheep, or even a bull, to give thanks to his recovery, and beggars would crowd in through the gates of the saraya for their portion of cooked meat and bread. After that she would go back to school.

Soraya had been skipping school ever since the head of the family was taken ill; at a time like this she could not stay away. This evening, too, visitors were flowing in and out. Many of them had been before, and many would stay for supper. Today, Fatma and Nassir had come especially from Medani. It was Nassir's duty to be by his father's bedside; indeed, it was embarrassing that he had not come earlier. Soraya was delighted to see her older sister. They now sat on the steps of the garden, away from everyone else. Soon they would have to go and help prepare the supper trays for the men, but for now they could dawdle. The garden in front of them was shadowy and lush, and the warm air carried the repetitive croaking of frogs and the scents of jasmine and dust. Soraya glanced up and imagined that in the blur of stars and clouds there was the star she was named after; pretty, brilliant and poetic.

She turned to look at her sister, to gauge her mood. She wanted Fatma to be easy and generous when Nur came along. He would seek Soraya out as he always did, and tonight she wanted Fatma to be lax as a chaperone, neither serious nor grown-up. Soraya could remember when Fatma was unmarried and the two of them went to Sisters' School every day with the driver, crossing the Umdurman Bridge, passing by the Palace, then turning right at the church. She remembered Fatma in her senior uniform, neat and vivacious, spluttering with laughter, screeching with her friends, her thin hair tightly held down with pins of different colours. She also remembered Fatma crying when she had to leave school, and how Sister Josephine had visited them at home to try and stop the wedding.

Fatma said, 'We shouldn't be here; we should be back there with my aunt frying the fish.' But she did not move to get up.

'You're a guest. No one will expect you to help.'

'Since when have I become a guest? In 1950 alone I came three times and each time I stayed over a month.' She had taken offence.

Soraya tried to sound apologetic. 'Everyone knows you must be tired after your journey from Medani. You can help out tomorrow.'

They were silent for a while, then Fatma said, 'Has anyone been talking about me? About me and Nassir?'

'What about?'

'About us taking so long to get here. We should have been here days ago.'

'Well, why weren't you? The day Uncle Mahmoud fainted and the doctor came and said it was a diabetic coma – that was last Tuesday!' Her voice carried the edge of accusation and her older sister folded her arms defensively.

'So I'm right, everyone has been talking about us.'

'Well, they were wondering.'

'You know what Nassir is like. He wakes up at noon and everything is an effort for him. He dithered and dithered: tomorrow we will travel to Umdurman, tomorrow we will leave. He couldn't decide. He had to do this first, he had to do that. Should we bring the children or leave them behind . . .' She lowered her voice. 'We

2

had no idea how long we would need to be here. We could be stuck here if Uncle Mahmoud gets worse, and then what? So he hesitated and the days passed.' She sighed and then said more sharply, 'If I had left him and came alone, which I could have done, it would have looked even worse!'

Soraya regretted this turn in the conversation. She did not want Fatma to be sullen and grumpy when Nur came. So now she said, 'At least you're here now. Stay as long as you can even when Uncle Mahmoud gets better – don't leave.'

Fatma smiled. It was a sad smile. Soraya felt lucky she was not marrying a lazy, useless man like Nassir. It was said that he was an alcoholic and that people cheated him, that they borrowed from him and never paid him back. It was sometimes hard to believe that he was the son of Uncle Mahmoud, and Nur's older brother.

Fatma said, 'At first I used to think that Nassir would change, but now I am just glad that we are away in Medani. If he were here, Uncle Mahmoud would be critical of him and make his life miserable. And Hajjah Waheeba has such a sharp tongue!'

'Well, maybe this is what he deserves.'

'But I don't want that for him! Maybe it's because he's my cousin that I feel soft towards him, but no matter how many faults he has, I don't want anyone to rebuke him, even his father and mother.'

It was as if Fatma had said something profound and strange, because they both went quiet. It occurred to Soraya that Fatma had fallen in love with her husband. The idea was startling and disgusting. She could remember Fatma weeping because she had to leave school. She had seen her sleepwalk, passive and cool, into this marriage, and now she had become so protective of Nassir.

Soraya stood up, straightened her tobe around her and strained to look at the direction of the gate to see if Nur was coming.

She said, 'I am the same age as you were when you left school and got married.'

'Don't worry, Soraya. When Sister Josephine came that day, Father promised her he would let you finish school.'

Would a promise given by the Abuzeid family to a head-mistress be binding? But still, though she was a woman she was European, an Italian nun.

Soraya said, with a mischievous smile, 'But I did get a proposal of marriage.'

Fatma shrieked, 'And no one told me! I cannot believe it. It is as if Medani is at the end of the world, the way you people have forgotten me!'

This lively Fatma was the Fatma of long ago, the real young Fatma. Soraya laughed and put her arms around her sister.

'How can we forget you? How can *I* forget you? Don't you know how much I miss you?'

'You never visit me.' The reproach in her voice was sweet, without anger. She wanted reassurance, reassurance that marriage and distance had not changed anything between them.

Soraya understood this and her voice was loving, 'Because it's better for you to come here. You enjoy yourself, and there are more of us here.'

Every time Fatma was due to give birth, she came from Medani and stayed with their elder sister, Halima. In her first pregnancy, when her morning sickness was severe, she had stayed in Umdurman from her second month until forty days after giving birth.

'Anyway, anyway,' Fatma was impatient, 'tell me about this prospective bridegroom. He can't be from the family.'

Soraya smiled. 'You're right. His father is a friend of Uncle Mahmoud. His mother came and spoke to Halima. She said that her son is going away to study in London and then he wants to be an ambassador. When we get independence, he will be one of the first ambassadors of Sudan abroad. As if I want to travel!'

'You do, Soraya, you do.'

She did. Geography was a favourite subject. She gazed at maps and dreamt of the freshness and adventure of new cities. She loved travelling to Egypt, and how she didn't have to wear a tobe in Cairo. She wore modern dresses and skirts and so did

Fatma, and they went shopping in the evenings for sandals.

'You would make a good ambassador's wife,' Fatma said slowly, looking into a future, a possibility.

'Well, I have other commitments,' Soraya whispered as coquettishly as she could, making herself sound like an actress in a film.

Fatma laughed. 'What did Halima say to the mother of our future ambassador? How did she reject the proposal without offending her?'

'Guess!'

'She told her: "Soraya has already been spoken for by her cousin Nur".'

Fatma said the most beautiful words in a normal voice, without a smile. All the joy was her younger sister's and the anticipation that, within a few minutes, he would be here, sitting by her side under the stars.

Motherless child, too young to remember maternal love and milky warmth, too young to remember the anguish and strangeness of death ... Fatma remembered and told Soraya, made a mother myth for her. Halima, the eldest, put herself in the role of a mother to the two of them. Fatma resisted at first and was often awkward, but Soraya was docile. She was the pampered baby, loved, as Halima later told her, because while the women wailed over their mother's deathbed, she stood with a bit of hard bread in her hand, nappy sagging, her hair unkempt and her eyes innocent and wide. Over the years Soraya heard the story of their mother's premature death from an asthma attack over and over again. In her mind she saw their house burning with grief and loss while she, little and soft, toddled unscorched, like an angel passing through Hell.

A mother is a home, a hearth, a getting together. A wife is company and pleasurable details; expenditure and social contacts. Soraya's father, Idris Abuzeid, the younger brother of Mahmoud, quickly reverted to being a bachelor again. He was the agricultural expert, more comfortable in the countryside than in town. He was also responsible for the financial accounts of the family, a behind-the-scenes position that suited his reserved, untalkative personality. Unlike his flamboyant, visionary brother, Idris counted the pennies, knowing they would become pounds, which he valued not because of what they could purchase – he was austere by nature – but because the piling up, the stacking, the solidity of wealth, was in itself satisfying. He never allowed a tenant to get away with a late payment or a debtor to default. He disliked the English, not because they had invaded his country, but because of the effort required to understand their different language and customs. At the same time, he was in no hurry for them to leave, for he admired them, most of the time, not for the modernity they were establishing but for the business opportunities they brought with them. Prudent, some would say miserly, Idris calculated the cost of remarrying and decided to remain a widower. Sore? A little, like any man in his situation. Often lonely, too, but a good wife was expensive and, though he was a difficult, heavy-handed father, he did not want to saddle his daughters with half-brothers and half-sisters.

The result was a dry and hollow home, a house Soraya did not particularly like to spend time in. She became a nomad. At every family occasion: wedding, birth, illness or funeral she would pack up and move to where the company was. No Abuzeid family gathering was complete without her. She spent so much time at Halima's teeming, noisy house that her children grew jealous.

Her eldest son once pushed Soraya and said, 'You are not my sister. Get out of our house!'

Soraya did not cry. She pushed him back, strong in the knowledge that Halima would always take her side. Motherless child – but loved even more for it. A princess with glowing skin and beautiful features; that smile and liveliness which made her popular at school; the bubbling generosity that made her give time, energy and gifts to others. But no, she was not silly like

Fatma, who let them snatch her out of school and into the arms of the no-good Nassir, to be banished to Medani. *How I would have escaped marrying Nassir, had I been Fatma*, Soraya wrote in her diary, a present from her friend Nancy. She wrote in English, so that if anyone opened it they would not understand.

One. I would have insisted on finishing school and persuaded Sister Josephine to come home and speak to Father long before the engagement was made public and it was too late for him to back out.

Two. I would have refused to leave Father, Halima and the whole of Umdurman. I would have turned down Nassir on account of his work being so far away.

Three. I would have spoken to Nassir himself and told him I did not want him and challenged him that a gentleman would not marry a girl against her will. But is he a gentleman?

Four. I would have threatened to commit suicide.

Writing that last sentence conjured up anger and a deep sense of injustice. Number one and number two were her best option. Sister Josephine before, not after, an engagement announcement. But would she, on her own, have thought of Sister Josephine?

Sister Josephine, now in her late forties, lean and energetic, was formidable in her white habit, white clothes and black flat shoes. Wisps of auburn hair sometimes drifted from her habit, blowing away the rumour that all nuns were bald. When she had unexpectedly visited their house, Halima did not know where to seat her. A European woman requesting to meet their father? Should she be seated in the women's quarters or in the men's salon? Halima decided to treat her like an honorary man and that was the right thing to do, as everyone confirmed later.

Sister Josephine did not smile at Idris, but she had a soft spot for Muslim girls with rich fathers. Fatma and Soraya were easy to teach, and the generous donations made by the Abuzeid family to the school were essential for the nuns to pursue their mission of providing free education to the poorest of the Catholic community. On learning that Fatma had been pulled out of school to get married, Sister Josephine had taken the Bishop's

Ford Anglia and crossed the bridge to Umdurman. Despite the dramatic nature of that visit – she rarely left the convent and school grounds, and it was not easy to get the Bishop's car at such short notice – she was unable to save her student. Yet her strident, pleading voice, her protest, her confidence that she was right (which increased Fatma's misery) left a deep mark on Halima, Soraya and the other young girls in the neighbourhood. Halima, who had never been to school at all, vowed that her daughters would continue. Even Idris, ruffled and flattered by this visit, reluctantly and solemnly promised that Fatma would be the last girl in the Abuzeid family to drop out of school and get married. Soraya could safely, and with relish, complete her school education. She could, every day except Friday and Sunday, wear her beloved uniform, which suited her so well. She could write and make her handwriting beautiful, and she could look down to look at her book, and up to look at the board.

Although biology and chemistry were her favourite subjects, Soraya loved reading romantic novels in which the heroine was beautiful and high-spirited. She relished drama and action. Halima thought it insular to shut off the world and read.

'It's as if you are telling people you don't want to chat to them,' she said.

Idris shouted at her the day he saw her bent over his newspaper. He snatched it out of her hands, because newspapers were written for men. Her late mother had never read the newspaper; she was illiterate. Halima, who could read a little, never did and Fatma's favourite subject at school had been maths. But for Soraya, words on a page were seductive, free, inviting everyone, without distinction. She could not help it when she found words written down, taking them in, following them as if they were moving and she was in a trance, tagging along. A book was something to hide, the thick enchantment of it, the shame, almost. When everyone was asleep, she would creep indoors, into stifling, badly lit rooms, with cockroaches clicking, to open a book at a page she had marked and step into its pulsating pool of words.

Books were scarce and precious. Nur lent her books, English novels he bought from Alexandria and Cairo. He would talk about a book for so long that she would know the whole story before even starting to read it. She had never read an English novel that he hadn't previously read. He was her introduction, and it delighted her that he always remembered her. True, she could not read Shakespeare like him, for he went to the prestigious Victoria College in Alexandria, and in Sisters' School the Italian nuns did not teach Shakespeare, yet he would narrate to her all the plays, his enthusiasm infectious and appealing. Arabic novels were not much easier to get hold of. The colourful covers with heavy-featured, buxom women were enough provocation for the nuns, so that a great deal of stealth was needed to pass a novel from one girl to another. Soraya relished the times she visited Uncle Mahmoud's second wife, Nabilah, because of the shelf of books in her living room.

An Egyptian city lady, Nabilah was everything that Soraya considered modern. Nabilah's elegant clothes were modelled on the latest European fashions, and the way she held herself was like a cinema star, with her sweeping hair and formal manners. Soraya cherished childhood memories of Nabilah and Mahmoud's wedding in Cairo, the first and only white wedding she had ever attended. Whenever she visited Nabilah, she would pour over the wedding album or stare at the framed wedding photographs hanging on the wall. When the time came for her and Nur to get married, they would have the first white wedding evening Umdurman had ever seen. This was her dream, and it came alive and thickened in Nabilah's rooms, which were filled with flowers and ornaments, a gramophone and, even more delicious, books and magazines.

Once, Soraya had entered Nabilah's sitting room to find her walking straight and slow, with a big book balanced on the top of the head. Startled by Soraya's presence, the book fell with a thud on the floor and Nabilah refused to explain why she had been doing such an odd thing, even though Soraya asked her. Another time, she had walked in to find her reading to her daughter, both their heads bowed over a children's book. A surge of jealousy filled Soraya, flushing through her like fever. It was a sight she had never seen before, remarkably foreign and modern, something she wanted there and then with a deep, sick hunger.

The motherless child wanted Nabilah to befriend her and patronise her like everyone else did. Instead, that second wife, that other woman, was aloof and unwelcoming. Soraya, to some extent proud and sensitive, could be thick-skinned when it suited her.

'Can I take this novel?' she would ask, already drawing it to her chest.

Nabilah would pause and a blush would touch her cheeks, but before she could reply, Soraya would be heading to the door, pretending that permission had been granted. She would clutch the precious, lovely work and dart through the door.

A month ago, during chemistry, which Sister Josephine taught, Soraya's eyes had looked at the board and seen a blur of white chalk. Straining made her eyes water, and by the end of the lesson she was sniffing into a handkerchief.

'Maybe you need spectacles,' Sister Josephine said casually, even though only two girls in the whole school wore spectacles and they were both ugly. 'Ask your father to take you to the doctor for an examination.'

'I don't want to wear spectacles, Sister.'

'Your eyesight will get worse and worse and then you will not be able to read at all!'

This alarmed Soraya. She brooded on the matter, squinted and tested her vision on faraway objects. She developed a fear of blindness. *'Ask your father to take you to the doctor for an examination.'* But her father did not talk to her; most of the time he did not look at her, and to ask him for something, anything was preposterous. She asked Halima instead, but Halima trivialised the issue.

'Spectacles will make you look ugly. It's all that reading that's bad for your eyes.'

Soraya nagged like only she knew how to nag, confident that Halima would give in as she always did, and so Halima asked Idris for permission but he said no. No going to a doctor for an eyesight examination, no girl of mine will wear spectacles like a man.

'So hush about it . . .' Halima patted Soraya's back when she cried '. . . or else he will rise up against school itself and keep you at home. Hush now.'

The stars above were blurred and milky, but not Nur's face. He sat next to her on the steps of the veranda, so that she was in the middle, with Fatma on her right. It was nice to sit like that, surrounded and held by people she loved, the two who were away most of the time. She knew what it felt like to miss them, had bright, clear memories of the childhood they shared and was confident that one day they would return to Umdurman. Eventually, Nur would finish his studies and return to join the family business. Eventually, Uncle Mahmoud would give up on Nassir's agricultural efforts and recall him to Umdurman.

'I have so much to tell you about the poetry reading last night,' said Nur. 'It was so crowded that they ran out of chairs and made us younger ones sit on the grass!'

'You are wandering off while your father is ill,' scolded Fatma, 'and I am the one being criticised for arriving late from Medani.'

'Aunty Waheeba gave her a few words,' Soraya explained to Nur.

Fatma mimicked her mother-in-law's voice, 'Did you and your man come from Medani on foot?'

Nur laughed. 'She is occupied these days with all the people coming and going. It would have been worse if she had all the time for you!'

Fatma made a face at him and then became serious. 'How is Uncle Mahmoud this evening?'

'He's fine, almost his normal self. I am expecting him any minute to tell me that I should not delay my travel any longer and that I should set off for school. The autumn term has already started.'

Soraya tried to keep the disappointment to herself. Of course she wanted her uncle to get better, but it meant Nur would leave. It was nice that he had been delayed and it was exciting, too, that Fatma had come unplanned. Normal, day-to-day life could sometimes be boring and empty. She preferred the warmth of people around her, their voices and chatter.

'Tell us about the poetry reading.'

She smiled at Nur. How many times had he told her about discussion forums, poetry recitals and political lectures? He was her link to the outside world, that world that was not for girls.

'Abdallah Muhammad Zein read his new poem. It is the strongest of his work and the most melodious. I copied it down and memorised it last night. I couldn't sleep because his words were in my head. It's the time we're living in; everyone talking about self-determination and independence and then a poet says it in another way. Listen. *I am Umdurman.*'

'Who is Umdurman?' laughed Fatma.

'Shush and listen.' Soraya understood who Umdurman was.

'*I am Umdurman. I am the pearl that adorns my land. I am the one who nurtured you, and for you, my son, will ransom myself. I am Umdurman, the Nile watered me and sought my side. I am the one on the western bank and Gordon's head was my dowry. I am Umdurman, I am this nation. I am your tongue and your oasis . . .*'

The three of them were stirred by the patriotic sentiments that the poem aroused. Even though the ties of the family to Egypt were strong and, politically, Uncle Mahmoud supported the union with Egypt, the younger generation carried a strong sense of their Sudanese belonging. Their glittering future was here, here in this southern land where the potential was as huge and as mysterious as the darkness of its nights.

'It's a beautiful poem,' Soraya said.

She wanted to cry because Nur had heard the words from the poet's mouth and she hadn't, and because exciting, transforming things would happen and she would only hear about them and not be part of them, she who wanted to be at the centre of everything.

'It should become a song,' Fatma said, 'and then it would be easy to memorise. Even children could memorise it.'

'It's beautiful,' Soraya repeated.

'I wish I had composed it myself,' said Nur.

Soraya smiled. 'If you had written it or someone else did, what does it matter? The important thing is that it exists.'

'But it isn't mine.'

She remembered how, when he was younger, before going to Victoria College, he had loved to sing. He would sing at every family occasion, memorising poems and popular tunes, his voice sweet and hopeful. But when he sang at a wedding outside the family, the wrath of his elders descended upon him. He was shaming the Abuzeid family, they said, standing in front of strangers like a common singer; next, the audience would be tipping him! Soraya remembered him crying, when, as a consequence, his father punished him and forbade him from going out. She remembered his confusion and broken spirit, crying the way boys cry, with a lot of pain and little noise.

She said, gently, now, 'You will write your own poem. And it will be even better.'

'Come on you two, let's go,' said Fatma, standing up.

'Wait, I have something to give Soraya.' He took out a bulky packet from his pocket and opened it.

Fatma laughed as Soraya reached out her hand for the pair of spectacles.

'Where did you get them from?' Her voice was withdrawn because of Fatma's laugh and because Nur had acknowledged the imperfection in her.

'I had them made for you. Of course, you need to be tested yourself and you need a prescription that is especially for you but this will help for the time being.' For the time being. Until they got married and she would be free of her father's conservative restrictions. 'Try them,' Nur said.

13

'No.'

'Why not? Yalla!' Fatma adjusted her tobe, impatient to leave the garden and go back to the hoash.

'Later,' said Soraya. 'When I am alone I will try them on.' She touched the thick black rims. Later, in front of a mirror, she would try them on.

'She doesn't want you to see her wearing them,' said Fatma.

'Keep quiet!' said Soraya.

'Soraya's pretty,' Nur said to Fatma. 'The prettiest girl.' Fatma folded her arms and raised her eyebrows. He looked at Soraya, who sat with her head bowed, spectacles on her lap. 'Nothing can take away from her prettiness. And actually, the glass of the spectacles is going to make her eyes look even wider.'

Soraya could not help but smile.

'Yalla, try them.' His voice was warm with encouragement. 'Give them to me.'

He put them on her, his fingers playfully pinching her earlobes and brushing against her hair. The new heaviness on her face and a grip on her nose; everything seemed a step away and yet so much clearer. On the peripheries, sideways down and up, the familiar fuzziness, but in the centre everything was in focus. She looked across the garden and saw the bougainvillea, the camphor tree and closer, on the veranda, bright and clear, the huge pots of flowers. She looked up, and the stars were distinct and piercing. Oh, how she had missed this clarity! She turned and looked at Nur. He had a cut on his chin from shaving but she knew that smile and glowing eyes; that pride in her.

She turned to look at Fatma and asked, 'How do I look?'

'Ugly,' said her sister, 'plain ugly.'

The three of them were laughing as they walked back to the hoash. They could hear Waheeba's voice call out.

'Nur! Nur, your teacher is here.'

'I can smell the fish.' Fatma started to quicken her pace. 'She's started frying and I'm not there to help her!'

II

Allah Almighty will say on the Day of Resurrection: O Child of Adam, I fell ill and you did not visit me . . .

As he walked the dark narrow alleyways of Umdurman, on his way to the lighted saraya of Mahmoud Bey Abuzeid, Ustaz Badr assigned himself the task of reciting every verse from the Qur'an and every Hadith which pertained to the subject of illness. There were three benefits to this exercise. One, it refreshed his memory; two, it soothed the irritation triggered by the letter he had received this morning and three, it stopped his mind from wandering to the form and voice of his luscious wife, Hanniyah. He considered his obsessive desire for her unbecoming in a man of his profession and maturity. Their marriage was a constant challenge for him to maintain his dignity, as she devoted her talents – or so it seemed to him – to ruffle, tease, and provoke him. His ruse against himself worked, for when he reached the Qudsi Hadith that promised him that he would find his Lord in the company of the ill, his concentration was whole and his senses were steady to the extent that the words penetrated his being and tears filled his eyes.

Badr's eyes were large and protruding. In his spare, energetic body they looked a little out of proportion, as if they were a muscle overdeveloped from consistent training. And he had trained his eyes. He had trained them to read without effort, to suck in information, and then to act as a valve, preserving everything in his memory, keeping knowledge within and then letting it out at will, smoothly and professionally. Studious from an early age, he had been the only one of his brothers to complete secondary school and graduate from Teacher's College.

Now he was on a secondment to Sudan, to teach those less educated than himself, who needed his skills and were ready to pay extra money for his time. He was also being sought, more and more, to give lucrative private lessons. It was an opportunity to make the kind of savings he would never have made had he stayed in Upper Egypt.

'Doors have opened for you in this country,' he told himself. 'Thank your Lord and kiss the palm and back of your hand.'

Ahead was Mahmoud Bey's mansion, with the grounds and all three storeys lit up. It was elegant because of its fine design, and splendid because it decorated the entrance to Umdurman, positioned in such a way as if it guarded the secrets of this city so close to the Nile. Five fine motor cars were lined up on the broad asphalt road coming from Khartoum. They intimidated Badr, and so he bypassed the main entrance. He also hesitated in front of the gate that led to Madame Nabilah's extensive quarters. When he came in the afternoon to give her two young children their lessons, he usually banged on this gate, but tonight it was locked and this section of the saraya looked dark and unwelcoming. He therefore headed down the back alley, towards the gate from which he was used to entering, which was known as the women's entrance, but was also used by intimate family members, tradesmen, beggars and servants.

His clapping, his cries, 'Ya Satir', to announce himself so that unveiled women could either flee or cover their heads, went largely ignored. The wide, open-air hoash was lined with beds, little stools and tables. It was a massive kitchen, sitting room and bedroom in which women, servants and children cooked, slept, ate and socialised. Eyes lowered to avoid seeing anything forbidden, Badr waiting to be noticed.

Hajjah Waheeba, squatting on a stool frying fish, looked at him, at first vaguely, and then started to call out, 'Nur, son, your teacher is here!'

She shifted and settled her tobe around her stout body. She was more African in features than her husband, and on each side of her cheeks ran three tribal scars, like cracks on a dry riverbed, which made her face look broader and more open. With her wide eyes and excellent teeth, her colourful tobe and the bangles of gold that glittered from her wrist to her elbow, she was attractive in spite of her age.

'Nur, where are you? Someone go fetch Nur. Come in, Ustaz Badr. Welcome, come in.'

The hoash, always busy, was today over-filled with visiting women. The timing, just before serving the evening meal, added an excitement to the gathering. Large round trays were laid out, ready to be filled and sent to the men. The delicious smell of sausages mixed with the tart smell of fried fish ruffled Badr. He felt awkward, even though his presence did not bother the women. True, they covered their heads, some of them in earnest and others reluctantly, but they continued their chatting or with the repetitive task of laying out the trays with appetisers: little dishes of pickles, white cheese, boiled eggs, and red chilli mixed with lemon juice, salt and cumin.

'Come in Ustaz Badr,' Hajjah Waheeba insisted.

She was, Badr could not help thinking, the wife, or more precisely, the first wife of one of the richest men in the country, and yet she was content with the traditional semi-outdoors life of the hoash. His own Hanniyah had aspirations for a flat in a tall building, for a salon and a balcony. Why else had they left Egypt, if not to better themselves? She hated the Sudanese-style house they had been allocated by the school and complained about it day and night. It was something that rankled in their marriage.

He was rescued by Nur, who had been his pupil before he was sent to Victoria College. They had not seen each other for some time, and Badr noticed the changes in the boy. He had always been taller than his teacher, but now he was lean and muscular. Without the fat cheeks and unsteady, adolescent bearing, Nur had become more solid, more self-conscious and formal, but the quick, friendly smile was still there, as were the

17

intelligent eyes, which gave him an almost impish look. 'My best pupil,' Badr said and extended his hand.

Nur hugged him in return, a spontaneous gesture, cavalier and unexpected. He smelled of perfume, a scent fresher than his casual clothes suggested. Still holding Badr by the arm, Nur started to lead him indoors.

'You are here to see Father? Let me take you to him – we are so busy these days, with all the visitors.'

They walked through the small, familiar room with the white table where Badr used to give Nur his lessons, then under arches, through sitting rooms furnished in the French style, and a massive, breathtaking dining room. Nur asked politely about how his half-brother and sister were getting on in their Arabic lessons with Badr. Were they memorising their poems, were they sitting attentively for the whole hour?

Mahmoud Bey's suite was as large as Badr's house. Badr stood unnoticed at the door and tried to take it all in. It overwhelmed him, not only because of its opulence but because of its European character. The smell of cigar smoke and expensive perfume made him alternatively gasp and then hold his breath. He looked at the double bed where Mahmoud Bey reclined on large pillows and exquisite linen, but instead of concentrating on the patient, Badr's eyes wandered to the large mahogany desk, the two wardrobes, the sofas and armchairs that seated nearly twenty men, each two or three sharing a small table on which there was an ashtray, glasses of water, fruit juice and bowls of nuts. He heard the murmur of conversations, which were important because these were the country's most important men. And with his crumpled suit, his ink-stained fingernails and his haggard face, it was clear that he was not one of them. He was someone for whom the conversation need not pause, nor should anyone rise up to greet him.

Again Nur came to his rescue, attracting his father's attention, prodding his memory.

'Ah, yes ...' Mahmoud Bey removed the cigarette with its black, slim filter from his mouth, transferred it to his left hand and extended the right towards Badr. He was a handsome man, with a finely trimmed moustache, full lips and an open, steady look. He was wearing a wine-coloured silk dressing gown and his voice, when he spoke, was weakened by illness. 'Thank you for coming. How are you? How is your family?'

Badr launched into prayers for his speedy recovery, good wishes and praises, all the time standing up. It would be preposterous to sit down and join such a gathering. Unthinkable. A burst of laughter from the end of the room distracted the patient. Badr paused in mid-sentence when he caught the words 'building' and 'flats'. The word 'flat' in a city where everyone lived in houses – villas for the rich and mud houses for the poor – rang in the room, distinctly Egyptian, distinctly related to him, as if it was said for him and meant for him. He understood it as if it were the only Arabic word to be spoken in the midst of a foreign dialect. These men's world was so removed from his that he could not easily fathom the conversation he had walked into. Yet that word 'flat' was clear and right, a good place to live in, a proper home, Hanniyah's dream. He tried to follow the conversation but was distracted by what he was seeing all around him. He lost his sense of decorum and stared openly, his eyes darting around the room. This glimpse of Mahmoud Bey's bedroom would not be repeated. It was a one-off, something he would remember all his life, something that would enter his dreams. Not far from the head of the bed, he saw the door to another room, slightly ajar. It was a bathroom, all tiles and a modern toilet. To possess one's own bathroom! Badr's imagination could not stretch that far – to such a place, further even than the span of envy.

There was no longer any point in talking to Mahmoud Bey. Badr had lost his attention. Mahmoud Bey was listening to one of his friends, his face turned away. There was no good reason for Badr to linger, and again Nur was by his side, this time to accompany him in his exit. Outside the room both were silent until they reached the terrace, which overlooked the garden. A gust of wind blew; a promise of winter and Badr needed a cigarette. He rummaged in his pocket but Nur was quicker. He took out a packet of Peter Stuyvesant and they lit up.

'Does your father know that you smoke?'

Badr appreciated the good quality tobacco, a brand he could not afford.

Nur leaned against a pillar.

'No, and even if he did I would not dare light up in front of him.'

Badr chuckled. 'Tell me about Victoria College.'

Nur's eyes lit up.

'It is the best school in the world! I am now the captain of the football team. And we play against other schools. My swimming is getting better, too, because we go swimming in the sea, except when it's very cold. And oh, Alexandria is beautiful.'

Badr had never been to Alexandria, even though his province, Asyut, was not that far. But he only smiled, distracted by other thoughts and half-baked schemes. 'Do you still write poetry?' he asked.

Something in Nur changed, as if he was suddenly recalled to what was important and urgent. 'Yes, I do. But nothing I consider to be strong or, indeed, special. You were very kind to encourage me when I first started.'

'Because you have talent.' Badr took a long drag. 'And, with time, you will become more skilful and more in control of your poems' qafiyas and wazn.'

He remembered what was endearing and memorable about Nur as a student – the boy's genuine desire to learn, not just for the sake of school marks, not just out of fear of examinations. Perhaps Nur could be of help to him. Try, he urged himself, now that the boy is beaming with pride at the compliment you paid him. Try and persist, it just might work after all.

He took a breath. 'What was it they were talking about inside? An apartment block?'

'Yes, my father is building an apartment block.'

'Just like the ones in Cairo?'

Nur laughed. 'Yes, right in the middle of Khartoum. It will be the first high-rise in the city. In Newbold Street, next to Hoash Boulus. The ground floor will be leased to shops and offices and the top floors will be residential.'

'When will it be ready?'

'In eighteen months or more – I would say 1952, to be on the safe side. The work progresses steadily, but at times it can come to a halt if the materials are delivered late.'

Badr took a deep breath and blurted out, 'Would your father be so kind as to lease me a flat for my family and I to live in? A small flat with two rooms would be more than enough. I have, may Allah be praised, four children, and my elderly father is not well at all. We are in wretched housing now. My wife complains, and there is no privacy, it's not proper at all ... dreadful. And today I received a letter from my cousin. He wants to come to Sudan to look for work! Of course, he intends to stay with me and I am obliged to host him. But where am I going to put him? All I have is one room and we're all sitting on each other's laps as it is!'

Nur laughed at the choice of words.

Badr took a drag from his cigarette. It was humiliating to complain to this boy, this heir to a fortune. Yet pride was a luxury Badr could not afford.

'I'll ask him,' said Nur, smiling with confidence. 'He will surely lease you a flat. My father has great plans for this building. He wants Egyptian taste and expertise – itself borrowed from Europe – to be firmly placed in Sudan. Do you know how this saraya came to be built? Father was driving his motor car along a boulevard in Heliopolis and stopped to marvel at a Pasha's mansion. He then contacted the architect and said, "Design one like it for me in Umdurman." The materials, too, from the marble tiles to the garden lamps, were shipped from Italy via Egypt.'

On their way out, they passed the bustle and delicious smells of the hoash. Hajjah Waheeba was inspecting the laden trays, making sure that every dish was represented before being dispatched to the men.

She turned and said to Badr, 'Stay and have dinner.'

Nur repeated his mother's invitation. The huge round trays were too heavy for one servant to carry on their own, and family members swarmed around the trays, ready to lift them up. Nur was summoned to help and he excused himself. Even though he was hungry, Badr refused the invitation not only out of modesty, but for a genuine desire to go home. He wanted to be with Hanniyah tonight, to entertain her with descriptions of Mahmoud Bey's bedroom, and he needed to go back to put his father to bed. Also, Hanniyah could not be trusted to supervise the children's homework. He must do that himself, for it would be a disgrace if his children were not the top of their classes. The saying that the carpenter's door was unhinged must not apply to him. And, most of all, he wanted to eat with his family. He derived considerable satisfaction from watching his children eat. Every bite that rose from the plates to their mouths was halal, the result of his sweat and exertions all day.

Badr made his way back to the tram station with Nur's promise ringing in his ears: '*My father will surely lease you a flat in his new building.*' Out of habit, and too many instances of dashed hopes, cynicism gripped him. The boy was naïve. If Mahmoud Bey really did agree to lease him a flat, he would have to charge Badr below the market price. He would understand that Badr could not afford the high rent of the city centre and he would be obliged to do him a favour as the private teacher of the Abuzeid children. That was why Mahmoud Bey might not agree. But it was worth trying, and Badr was determined to petition Madame

Nabilah, too. As a fellow Egyptian, she might sympathise with his predicament and put in a good word for him with her husband.

As he narrowly avoided placing his foot on donkey manure, his mind drifted to the rumours that the British would thwart a union with Egypt. If the position of the Egyptian teaching mission were jeopardised to the extent that they had to pull out, how pointless his dream of moving house would be.

The sudden call to prayer from a nearby mosque jolted him out of his thoughts. It felt like a reprimand, a reminder of why he was alive. To struggle for the here and now but not lose sight of the end: to put meat in his children's small mouths and sweets in Hanniyah's enchanting mouth. To fulfil and pacify her, she who held his heart and was, so often, the cause of his disturbance. To act like a man and discipline her, so that she would keep on looking after his father and not complain. This was a considerable source of stress, as were the intrigues and rivalries of the school, the reluctant and stupid students, the darting to and fro from one private lesson to the next. And, above all, his horror at how his energetic, bellowing father had been reduced to confused, dependent blubber. It was a horror that was abating with time and being replaced by a grim, constant sadness. The kind of sadness that deserved no condolence and was too dispersed for sighs and platitudes. Badr's tumultuous, humdrum life. What was it all for, where was it heading? The answer peered at him now as it had done before and would do again. His life was a journey. A journey towards the day when Allah Almighty would look at him, really look at him, look through him, inside him, know him, and then would call him by his name. Ya Badr.

III

For Nabilah, the Sudan was like the bottom of the sea, an exotic wilderness, soporific and away from the momentum of history. It was amazing but constricting, threatening to suck her in, to hold her down and drown her. Sometimes she was able to hold her breath and accept, but on most days she struggled to rise up to the surface, working to recapture a routine like that of her mother in Cairo, a life of fresh air and energy, the natural bustle and order of civilised life. Nabilah knew that she should be more flexible, that she should adjust, but she was not easy-going enough, and too conscious of her status.

She had, with her husband's full approval and generous finances, designed her wing in the saraya like a modern, Egyptian home, not a Sudanese one. Instead of a hoash, there was a shaded terrace with a wicker table and chairs where, in winter, she could sit and enjoy her afternoon tea, while watching Ferial ride her tricycle and Farouk kick a ball in the garden. Instead of the traditional beds lining the four walls of the sitting room, she had spacious armchairs, a settee, and, in pride of place, her gramophone. It was a proper room, a room to be proud of. Guests reclining and sitting on beds, angharaibs made of rope being the only furniture in a room, the intimacy and privacy of a bed laid out for public eyes and use – was something that particularly infuriated her. It was, she believed, a sign of primitiveness, proof that the Sudanese had a long way to go. Meals too, in Nabilah's quarters, were served in the dining room, around a proper dining table, with knives, forks and serviettes, not clusters of people gathering with extended fingers around a large round tray, while sitting on those very same beds she had so many objections to. Her household staff, too, was all from Egypt – Chef Gaber, whose Turkish dishes inspired so much envy from her co-wife, as well as the children's nanny. Nabilah surrounded herself with the sights, accents and cooking smells of Egypt, closing the door on the heat, dust and sunlight of her husband's untamed land.

But she could not shut out his family. They came, invited or uninvited. And came casually, with friendly smiles, affection for the children and a staggering tolerance for her moodiness and indifference. She did not understand them. That boy, Nur, with his bright smile, so pleased and at ease with himself. She had explained to him once that he must ring the bell and not just barge in.

Instead of apologising, he had just giggled and said, 'Isn't this my father's house?'

And that girl, Soraya, with her lack of discipline, the sloppy way she carried herself, gum snapping in her mouth, her hands always moving, stroking the back of an armchair or playing with a doorknob in a way which irritated Nabilah. She would gaze dolefully at Nabilah's wedding photographs without saying a single word. Or she would lean, slouching, on this piece of furniture or that and drawl, 'how are you doing, Nabilah?' without addressing her as Madame, Abla, Hanim or even Aunty.

Soraya, too, floated in unannounced, to borrow books and never return them and to poke fun at how Ferial was covered in talcum powder and how Farouk's accent was Egyptian. How else did she expect the children to speak if not like their mother!

Nabilah kissed Farouk and Ferial the first of many goodnight kisses and prepared to tuck them into bed. They were the only children in the Abuzeid family who had bedtimes and a proper, decorated nursery, with beds of their own. The Sudanese did not understand about proper modern child-rearing, but she would teach them by example. Tonight, instead of a story, she was explaining to the children the origin of their names.

'You Farouk, were named after the King of Egypt and Sudan who granted Baba his bakawiyya. That's why Baba is Mahmoud Bey. Not everyone can be called Bey, even if they wanted to. Only the King can decide.'

Farouk smiled and slid deeper into his bed. Ferial was holding on to her mother's hand.

'And me, what about me?'

'Wait. Farouk wants to ask something.' He always needed encouragement. The boy opened his mouth, closed it again and then asked.

'But not everyone addresses Baba as Mahmoud Bey. Some people call him Sayyid Mahmoud.'

Nabilah sighed. 'Some of the Sudanese don't understand. They don't appreciate the title. Your father should correct them, but he doesn't.'

'So Sayyid is not as good as Bey.'

'Here in Sudan, Sayyid is the best way a man can be addressed. But your father—'

She was interrupted by Ferial who, not only satisfied with putting her hand on her mother's cheek, now pulled so that Nabilah had to turn and face her.

'Don't do that. It's not polite.'

The girl, whose hair was smooth in a ponytail, pressed her lips in annoyance.

'What about my name, *my* name?'

'Say sorry first, Ferial.'

'Sorry.'

'Say it like you mean it.'

'Sorry, Mama.'

'That's better.'

Nabilah kissed her cheek and smoothed her hair. What a blessing from God that her daughter did not have coarse hair! She had worried about this constantly during her pregnancy.

'You were named after a princess. Princess Ferial is the eldest

26

daughter of the King.' The girl squirmed with pleasure. 'Now into bed.'

She tucked her lively daughter in bed but Ferial was wide awake. 'When Grandma comes from Cairo will she be the one telling us bedtime stories?' The children knew that Nabilah had sent a telegram to Qadriyyah Hanim telling her about Mahmoud's illness and begging her for a visit.

Now she sighed.

'She won't be able to come. Next time I put a call to her, I will let you speak for a little while. Oh, if only we were in Cairo now! I am sure Baba would not have been so ill, for I am sure the doctors in Cairo are better than the ones here.'

It still did not feel right that they were in Sudan. This had not been the original arrangement when they first got married. The original arrangement was that she would live in the flat Mahmoud had set up for her in Cairo, and that he would spend lengthy visits with her. After all, his business required that he spend several months in Cairo and it made sense to have a home there instead of his suite in the Shepheard's Hotel. Nabilah would be his Egyptian wife in Cairo and Hajjah Waheeba his Sudanese wife in Umdurman. It had made perfect sense, and years passed that way, successfully, but suddenly he proposed to move her and the children here. Nabilah's mother encouraged her to accept and Mahmoud Bey assured them that Nabilah would have her own quarters; she would be independent of Hajjah Waheeba and the rest of the Abuzeid family. He promised that every summer she, Farouk and Ferial would return to Cairo. So Nabilah had gathered her courage, took a deep breath and with a friendly shove from her mother, plunged herself into Umdurman.

To banish the feeling of nostalgia, Nabilah turned to her serious son.

'Guess who visited Baba today?' She straightened the collar of his pyjamas. 'Your teacher, Ustaz Badr.'

Farouk stared into space. His skin was darker than his mother

27

and sister's, his hair more curly, his features more African.

'When will Baba come home?'

She stroked his cheek.

'Soon. He is better today. Tomorrow when we go see him he will come home with us.'

In his illness, Mahmoud Bey had chosen to go back to his old room in the central part of the saraya, near Hajjah Waheeba's hoash. He did not want his many guests to disturb Nabilah, he had said.

'Is he going to die?'

As if she had not just told him that his father was getting better! The boy was aloof, perhaps because of all the time they had spent alone in Cairo, without his father. Mahmoud Bey rarely addressed him and Farouk was stiff and uncomfortable in his father's presence.

She frowned.

'This is a very rude thing to say about your father. You must never say this word again. It is not a word to be said and it must not even cross your mind.'

Yet she thought it, too. She made peace with Farouk, for she did not want him to go to sleep weighed down by her disapproval, a situation which usually resulted in him wetting his bed. But after she put out the lights and walked to her own bedroom, she abandoned herself to the rudeness and anxiety she had denied him. The death of her husband would mean one thing for her. A return to Cairo.

She would be the same age as her mother had been when she was widowed. Nabilah's father had died when she was nine and her mother remarried within a year. But, if Mahmoud died, Nabilah would not need to marry again because she would have an income and an inheritance share in Mahmoud Bey's wealth. It was obscene to follow this line of thinking, yet her mind could not help but gallop in this direction. She saw herself wearing black, boarding a plane with the children, her eyes pink from crying, her face pale, without rouge. She imagined her mother meeting her at the airport and the drive home; the wide roads, the familiar sights and sounds. The doorman would stand up in greeting when they reached the building and carry her suitcase up the stairs. The door of the flat would be already open when they stepped out of the lift. Her mother's maid would be there, in her long patterned dress and kerchief.

'Alhamdullilah for your safe return, ya sett hanim.'

A feeling of shame passed through her and brought tears to her eyes. Mahmoud Bey was getting better, the English doctor had said that, and she could tell, too. There was no need for these morbid, perversely exciting thoughts. Her husband had been so generous to her, compensating for the father she had lost, for any sense of deprivation she had felt. She had experienced real joy when they were together in Cairo, the time after the wedding when their new flat was being decorated and they had stayed at his suite in the Shepheard's Hotel. There was the evening they had gone to see Um Khalthoum in concert, the nightclubs on Pyramid Road where they would go for dinner and a show. Oh, the fun she had had, watching the belly dancer and looking around at the other tables, comparing her clothes with those of the other ladies, her hair with their hair, and always feeling good about herself. In those days she had forgotten that she had married a Sudanese. Mahmoud was light-skinned enough to pass for an Egyptian, his clothes were as modern and as elegant as any other Bey, and she was his new wife, much younger than him, but that was not uncommon.

True, he had given her a lot, and he did not want much from her in return. Not much but to bear this exile, to tolerate his family, to decorate his new mansion in Umdurman simply by being herself. She was loved and cherished, and the fact that he was already married was not really a threat. He and Hajjah Waheeba no longer lived as husband and wife, not since they moved into the saraya. He had, long before his second marriage, separated himself from Waheeba and kept his own room. He would not divorce her, though, he had made that clear from the beginning. Waheeba was the mother of his sons and Nabilah must not feel threatened by her. Yet since he had taken ill, he had craved Hajjah Waheeba's food. In his exhaustion, his accent had become more heavily Sudanese, and when she saw him surrounded by his concerned family, he looked so much like them, was so unmistakably one of them, that their happy years in Cairo seemed distant and illusory.

When she was sure that the children were asleep, Nabilah put on her navy blue dotted dress and combed her hair, fixing the waves with a touch of cream. She put on her lipstick and used a tiny black brush to smooth her broad eyebrows, then she studied her reflection in the mirror and felt that something was missing. A handbag. She did not really need it because she was only going from one section of the saraya to another. But she picked up her handbag anyway. It completed her look and lifted her spirits, for the cloud of illness that was hanging over the saraya was depressing. It made Nabilah want escape, and her own circle of friends and acquaintances. Of course, propriety demanded that she stay at home. Only when her husband went back to work could she leave the house to resume her social activities among the community of Egyptian ladies – the wives of the engineers who worked on the irrigation projects, the wives of embassy staff, or the few transplants like herself, married to local men.

She expected Mahmoud Bey's guests to have gone by now. Nur had been spending each night with him, but he went and had supper at his mother's hoash before joining his father. It would be a good time to find her husband alone. She tiptoed downstairs and out the front door, then walked across the terrace past the huge clay flowerpots and down the garden steps. In Cairo, the nights were alive with the pleasures of leisurely walks, roasted peanuts and grilled corn, people chatting and shops that stayed open late – the liveliness and light of it all. Here, the heavy indigo sky was bearing down, the stars mysterious, and the clouds unnaturally large. As she walked around the garden to the other side of the saraya, she could hear frogs croaking and the hiss and breath of night creatures, as if this were a jungle. The huddle by the gate was a servant sleeping on a straw mat. They prayed Isha and slept as if this was the countryside not a city. In her fashionable dress and elegant high heels, she was wasted in this place, but she kept on walking to his room.

When she pushed open the door that had been slightly ajar, she saw Idris sitting on an armchair, toothpick in one hand, his face a snarl as he cleaned his teeth. He gave her his usual guarded greeting, but there was a hint of expectancy in the way he tilted his head and moved in his seat, adjusting his jellabiya. She turned towards the bed and saw the bulk of Hajjah Waheeba leaning over her husband. Mahmoud was lying on his stomach, head turned to one side, naked to the waist, and his wife was massaging his back. She was bearing down with her full weight, so that he was only able to grunt at Nabilah in recognition. She froze, not knowing what to do in the face of this unexpected intimacy. This was only her third time to be in the same room as Hajjah Waheeba. The first had been soon after her arrival in Umdurman, when many family members came round to take a good look at her. The women had made no attempts to hide their curiosity and had simply filed in, sat and stared at her, not bothering to introduce themselves or engage her in conversation. She had not even known which one of them was Hajjah Waheeba. They had all looked alike to her, these middle-aged Sudanese women swathed in tobes, their faces without make up and their hair in traditional tight braids close to the head. Later, she had come to know that Waheeba was the one with the tribal scars on her cheeks, those vertical scars that looked like cracks on a French loaf. The second time they had met, when Fatma gave birth, Nabilah took a good look at her co-wife and decided that she was neither interesting, nor worth competing with. They never exchanged words. Each avoided the other, marking her own territory, cautious and watching, as if they were assessing each other's strengths and weaknesses.

Now Hajjah Waheeba looked up and smiled at her, a genuine smile. There was a serenity in her face, as well as a warm flush of exertion. Her tobe was falling around her soft round stomach and slipping down to show her head and hennaed braids. Her large, plump hands were flat on Mahmoud's back, pressing. There was a pinch, like a bracelet around her elbow and above that the moving fat of her upper arms. She shifted her weight and, instead of pressing down on him again, began, with her thumb and fingers, to lightly smooth and iron out the tightness of his muscles.

He could talk now, and he said to Nabilah, 'My back has been giving me a lot of pain.'

This encouraged her to walk into the room and close the door behind her, just as Waheeba was saying to him.

'This will release it.'

She leaned down closer, propping her right elbow on his shoulder. She began to work a particular spot as Nabilah sat down in her regular armchair. It was impossible to ignore what was happening on the bed and she and Idris sat and watched.

'It's here isn't it?'

A grunt, a muffled, 'To the left a bit.'

'Here . . .' Waheeba smiled.

A groan and she laughed.

'But this is the bit you want. Be still!' Her laugh was hearty, coming from the throat. When it trailed off, she turned to look at Nabilah and pressed her lips, 'Of course, in Egypt they didn't teach you how to give a massage. But I can teach you.'

'No thank you, I don't wish to learn.'

Waheeba smiled, as if this was the exact reply she wanted. Her voice was soft and easy.

'And why don't you want to learn? Don't you want to please your husband? He brought you here to this good life and you don't want to serve him?'

Nabilah could not think of an able put down to what sounded like an accusation of ingratitude, to the insinuation that she had been needy or, at least, less well off before this marriage. She looked at her husband, but he turned his head so that she could not see his reaction. He did not come to her defence and, to make matters worse, Idris gave a chuckle. Nabilah looked at her husband's back, at the black-and-white of his hair. His neck and skin were smooth with oil, glistening, and his wife's dark hands, kneading now, her thumb moving, coaxing the sore muscles into calm suppleness. Nabilah knew she must control herself. She was well bred, she was cultivated; she must not overreact. She breathed and noticed, for the first time, Nur sitting at the desk in the far corner. He was writing in a notebook.

Mahmoud gave out a long, loud sigh of pain and Waheeba laughed in response, admonishing him to bear it. It was a laugh that was surprisingly attractive – but there is no competition, Nabilah reminded herself. How could she compete with me! She, who was obese, menopausal, illiterate. She, who had no concept of fashion or travel. She, who had never walked into a club or read a book or eaten with a knife and fork, or even been inside a hairdresser. Nabilah forced herself to smile, walked over to the desk and sat next to Nur.

'What are you writing?' Her voice was deliberately friendly. She was young, and she could read what her co-wife's son had written.

'I am making a list of all the guests who came to see Father. He asked me to do that.'

Idris called out, 'You should write each person's name as they come in. Now you are relying on your memory and you will miss someone out. Also, Ahmed Ismail and his son were here and I don't know where you were – so put their names down, too.'

This negativity was typical of Idris. Nabilah did not particularly like him. He was too Sudanese for her and, unlike his brother, rarely travelled abroad. She suspected that he had been against their marriage. But Idris knew his place and knew that he could not stand against his older brother.

'Let me see,' she said to Nur.

He put down his pen and handed her the notebook. His handwriting was neat. A few names were in English; Graham Westman, Colonel Freddie Hewgill . . . Colonel! She felt a surge of pride that her husband moved in such high circles and that even the English went out of their way to visit him . . . Mr Wavelry, Dr McCulloch.

'You even counted the doctor as a visitor!' This amused her, but Nur looked at her with the same steady gaze and did not share the joke. 'You wrote the English names in English,' she said loudly. She could read English, too.

'Yes. But the Armenians and Greeks I wrote in Arabic.'

There was also a list of those who sent telegrams from faraway provinces and from Cairo. Her stepfather's name was among them – she had always addressed him as Uncle Mohsin. He was a Senior Civil Servant and a prominent member of the Wafd party. Immaculately dressed and well-spoken, he did not have any children of his own and seemed to have enjoyed a carefree bachelorhood. Not many men would take on a widow with a daughter and he was conscious of this act of charity. You are my family now, he had said to the ten-year-old Nabilah, but everything she did seemed to irritate him. She ate too much, she laughed too loud, she disturbed his siesta and tired out his household staff. Qadriyyah took her husband's side. He was right and the girl must keep out of his way, out of his sight and hearing. Nabilah must become small, insignificant and inoffensive. She must tiptoe around the apartment, not use the bathroom for too long, not weep too loud, because, as her mother put it to her bluntly, she was a guest.

Nabilah held the notebook in her hand and turned its pages. She sensed that Nur wanted her to give it back, but the list of names was a welcome diversion. She searched for the Egyptian names she was familiar with, the husbands of her new friends.

She said to Nur, 'In Europe and even in Cairo, some families would have a guestbook and on special occasions visitors coming in would be asked to sign the guestbook. This guestbook would be a large, impressive album and it would be on a small table by itself.'

Nur did not seem to be interested in what she was saying. His eyes were on the notebook and when she turned a page she began to understand why. A loose sheet fell out. She picked it up and Nur's hand instinctively reached out, but politeness made him hold back. She started to read the sheet of paper. It was a poem, written in his handwriting. A poem of love and longing, of lovers separated by place. Nabilah was not familiar with Sudanese poetry, so she could not tell whether the author was Nur or someone else.

'Did you write this yourself?'

He hesitated before whispering, 'No.'

'Are you sure? I don't believe you,' she teased him. He was betrothed to Idris's daughter, Soraya. They were childhood sweethearts, Nabilah had heard. Perhaps he had written the poem for her. 'I think you wrote it. It's nice. You have talent.'

'A talent for what?' Idris called out.

'Poetry . . .' She raised her voice, smiling at Nur. The boy was looking more uncomfortable now, more wary than ever.

From the bed, Mahmoud grunted. He turned and sat up. Hajjah Waheeba handed him his pyjama top.

'Poetry, ya salaam!' he said. He sounded his old self again, high-spirited, a little amused.

'Wasting his time on this rubbish,' Idris said.

'Wasting his time indeed,' said Hajjah Waheeba, as she heaved herself onto the settee.

'No, he should be encouraged,' said Nabilah, keen to contradict.

Nur was not young enough to be her son and she felt an affinity with his youth. He was being educated in Egypt, at Victoria College, a school few could afford. She was proud of this further proof that her husband was truly enlightened. He was sparing no expense to give his son the best possible

35

education. And one day he would do the same for *her* son, Farouk.

Waheeba sucked her teeth.

'Encouraged?' She mimicked Nabilah's Egyptian accent. 'We are not that kind of family. We don't waste our time on jingles and silly words.'

'Read it and judge for yourself.' Nabilah walked over and, smiling, offered her co-wife the sheet of paper. 'Read it.' It gave her satisfaction and pleasure to underline Waheeba's illiteracy. 'Don't you know how to read? I can teach you.'

Waheeba turned her face and shoulder away towards her husband and said, 'Look at her! She gets up, she sits down, she walks backwards and forwards. What is wrong with her? Why doesn't she settle down?' She turned to Nabilah and said, 'Sit and have a rest. Don't trouble yourself with Nur and what Nur did and didn't do. What's in it for you?'

Before Nabilah could reply, Idris sprang from his seat and snatched the paper from her hand. He scanned it and tore it down the middle. He tore it once, twice, the noise slick and decisive in the silent room. A tall, dark man in a jellabiya with a set, impatient face taking action. He tore it again and dropped it in long, skinny strands on the floor. He sat down again and said to his brother, 'You are spending money on his education and what does he come back from Egypt with – silly songs!'

'Exactly,' murmured Waheeba, facing her son. 'Did you go to school, ya Nur-alhuda so you can write down shameful things?'

Nabilah looked at Nur, and the boy's face had that closed, shamed look she had seen before on the faces of servants when they were being told off. She wanted to come to his defence, but when their eyes met, the look she found there was one of hostility. The logic of youth – it was all her fault, she was the meddlesome one.

Mahmoud got up from his bed and put on his dressing gown.

He looked tired and thoughtful, his handsome face strained.

He said, 'Nur, you need to go back to Alexandria. The academic year has started and you've missed too many days of school already. I am better now – there is no need for you to stay any longer. Tomorrow morning I will give orders for your travel arrangements. Nabilah . . .'

'Yes . . .' She moved towards him.

'If you need to send anything to your mother, Nur will deliver it for you. He will stop in Cairo on the way. Also check with the Egyptian servants if they want to send anything to their families.' He put on his slippers and started to walk to the bathroom. The matter was settled, the subject closed.

After Idris left, Nabilah made a point of remaining in the room to outstay Waheeba. While Mahmoud Bey read the newspaper, she watched Nur pick up the torn pieces of paper from the floor. He crumpled them and threw them in the bin.

'Later on I will talk to your father about this,' she promised him, her voice low.

His response was an anxious look at his father's face, hidden behind the newspaper. She did not say anything more. Perhaps later, in private, Mahmoud would admit to her that he had been on her side, that Idris and Waheeba had over-reacted. Idris must have guessed that Nur's poem was addressed to Soraya and, as her father, taken offence. Later, Nabilah could convince Mahmoud that it was civilised and modern to allow young people to express their feelings through poetry, music or art. Now, though, she must bear this dull, metallic feeling of – not exactly defeat, but not exactly success, either.

Back in her quarters, she stayed up late, writing a letter to her mother, sharing every small detail of the evening's events. But she felt far away from Cairo, and somewhat excluded. Was it her fate to be always in the periphery? Her late father had been a provincial judge who toured the towns and cities of Egypt, and the years of Nabilah's childhood were spent adjusting to, and departing from, different schools where she was treated well because of her father's position. He had been an imposing, charismatic man, highly educated and liberal in his thinking. Had he lived, he would have risen high in the judiciary, and Nabilah remembered her mother tolerating the pettiness and deprivations of provincial life, struggling with packing, unpacking and setting up a new home; all in the hope of a brilliant future in Cairo. Yes, the Sudan was like a province of Egypt, and now she, Nabilah, like her mother before her, was yearning for the metropolitian centre.

Nabilah idolised her mother. She believed that she was less beautiful than Qadriyyah, though this was not true. She believed that her mother had the best clothes sense, the best hairstyle and that her cooking was superior. Nothing was good or real without her mother's acknowledgement. That was exactly why Nabilah's marriage had taken place and lasted for nine years. Her mother's faith in Mahmoud Bey transmuted itself to the daughter and Qadriyyah Hanim had wholeheartedly, and with utter conviction, engineered her daughter into this marriage. She had brushed aside Nabilah's protests: the twenty years age gap, his foreignness, his first wife and grown-up children.

'You don't want to marry an inexperienced youngster,' Qadriyyah had argued, 'who will wear you out and drag you around until he stands on his own two feet. You want someone established, mature, someone able to look after you and guide you. Mahmoud Bey will humour and indulge you; he will pamper and protect you. Wait and see, isn't Mama always right?'

Yes, Mama was always right. Nabilah waited and Nabilah saw. But there were other things, like this exile from the one she loved most. Nabilah's dissatisfaction, her low-grade unhappiness, was not entirely caused by this mismatched marriage, by this second-wife status or by this backward place. It was the banishment from her mother that was so hard to get used to.

IV

Usually, after a massage, he slept deeply, but tonight he was restless. It had been years since Waheeba massaged his back – he couldn't remember the last time, but it must have been before his second marriage. She was good at it, heavy-handed but effective. She might even have bruised him, and he would feel sore tomorrow, but after that the benefits of her treatment would be felt, significant and lasting. He shifted his weight and tried to find a more comfortable position. The room was airy because the windowpanes and shutters to the terrace were wide open. Without a full moon, the starlight was soft and untroubling and there was no reason for him not to sleep. He was not in pain; neither was he hungry or thirsty, nor was he lonely. His elder sons were spending the night in his room. Nassir, after his journey from Medani, was lying on his back, his hands folded on his belly, snoring loudly. Nur, on an extra angharaib, was lying on his side, the sheet as was his habit, pulled over his face. Mahmoud felt a surge of simultaneous fondness and grudge towards them. He was pleased that they were near him, but at the same time he envied how deeply they were sleeping. What were they dreaming of? He was not really interested, nor would he understand their generation's concerns. His children were an extension of him and he had hopes and plans for them, which he expected them to obey, but his core, his inner depth, was independent of them.

This sleeplessness, he realised, getting out of bed and walking out onto the terrace, was a good sign, a sign that his illness was coming to an end. Perhaps in a day or two he could go back to work. He had been going over things with Idris, but not everything could be done from home. It would be good to be back in the office again. The office. This word meant a great deal to him. He was not a merchant in the Souq Al-Arabi, as his grandfather had been. He was not the head of an agency, as his father had been. He was the director of Abuzeid Trading, a private limited liability company, one of the leading firms in the Sudanese private sector. There were British companies, of course – Gellaty and Hankey, Sear and Colley, Mitchell Cotts and Sudan Mercantile; there were the fabulous long-established Syrian-Christian families the Haggars and the Bittars but he, Sayyid Mahmoud Abuzeid, was indigenous. Let no one call *him* an immigrant! The immigrants came fifty-five years ago with the Anglo-Egyptian force, sent to avenge Gordon's death and recover the Sudan. Those newcomers were adventurers and opportunists who knew that the defeat of the Mahdiyyah and the new British administration would herald an era of prosperity. Instead, Mahmoud Abuzeid's grandfather had come in the early 1800s, fleeing conscription in the Egyptian army.

The Abuzeids had risen by a combination of financial sharpness and the drive to modernise. Unlike the Mahdi and the Mirghani family firms, who were supported by the British in order to distract them from politics and play them one against the other, the Abuzeids were independent. Mahmoud was proud of that. And he wanted to do more. He wanted to steer his family firm through the uncertainties of self-determination and stake a place in the new, independent country, whenever and whatever form this independence took. This was why he loved his office. The other burgeoning family businesses did not put so much emphasis on form. He, though, had an office, just like a British company, with secretaries, filing cabinets, qualified accountants, telegram operators, and everything was written down, filed in order. He needed to get back to work. A number of important meetings had been postponed because of his illness and too many things were now on hold.

Walking on the terrace tired him and he sat back on one

of the large metal chairs that made up the outdoor seating arrangement. The cushions were soft and cool underneath him, but by now he was bored with comfort. He wanted to be strong and energetic again. The doctor had assured him of a slow but complete recovery and Mahmoud wanted to forget these past days. He had not only been physically ill, but frightened, too, chastened in some way. Good health was a blessing, anything else a constraint. Being bedridden had made him feel morbid. Was he meant to think that death was around the corner? Should he start to put his affairs in order? He had seen the concern in his family's eyes. His death would affect their lives. Nabilah and the children would return to Cairo – she would have no place here, he was sure, but Farouk and Ferial would be deprived of their country and their Sudanese family. It was an unhappy thought, and though he trusted that Idris would not deprive them of their inheritance, his young, half-Sudanese family, would bear the brunt of being orphaned more than their elder brothers, Nassir and Nur. He listened to the breeze from the Nile and the sounds that came from the fields on the riverbank. A donkey brayed and pigeons cooed, even though dawn was a long way off.

His mind turned to the names and faces of the friends and business acquaintances who had visited him. He challenged himself to remember them all, knowing that he would be able to check the accuracy of his memory by looking at the list Nur had been writing. Some had come more than once, and those who esteemed him most had come immediately on hearing that he was ill. Their concern was gratifying. It filled him with affection for them and a desire to reciprocate. He, too, if Allah continued to give him life, would visit them in sickness, commiserate with them in death and celebrate their happy occasions.

And how had his family responded to his illness? Idris had risen to the occasion and could not be faulted. Nassir, on the other hand, had taken too long to arrive from Medani. People would talk of this – it was embarrassing. The boy resembled him physically, but was lazy and irresponsible, unlike Nur, who looked like his mother and yet held his father's sense of duty inside him. Mahmoud always compared the brothers and always found Nur to be superior. Even though he was not the eldest, Nur would be the next chairman of the Abuzeid group of companies, the next head of the family. But what to do about Nassir? Years ago, on the night of his wedding to Fatma, Nassir had been too drunk to consummate the marriage. Mahmoud had laughed along with everyone else at the story of the groom, henna on his hands and kohl in his eyes, passing out fully dressed on his marital bed, but Nassir's drinking was no longer a laughing matter. The reports that reached Mahmoud were damning. Nassir was never at the Medani office before eleven o'clock on any day of the week. It was clerks and employees who were running the Abuzeid Medani office, not the landowner's son. Cotton was yielding millions these days because the English couldn't get enough of it now that the war was over, but that was no excuse for Nassir to take things easy. It was the time to be aggressive, to develop and expand. Mahmoud resolved to confront him before his return to Medani, and if he didn't pull himself together, he would summon him back to Umdurman to keep a close watch over him.

As for Nur, the boy needed to complete his education. This evening's poetry episode was a phase he would get over. He was brilliant in his studies, outstanding in sports, especially football. An all-rounder, the English headmaster said, and how proud Mahmoud felt that his son was excelling at Victoria College. Every penny spent on the fees was worth this joy. It was especially gratifying to visit him in Alexandria. Mahmoud would park his car and visit the headmaster, Mr Waverley, in his office. With amazement – and a certain degree of alertness needed to follow English – he would listen to his son being praised. Such magical moments, sitting across the desk from the English gentleman who spoke loudly, slowly and clearly. Nur, his son was an all-rounder! After a few minutes – not long, for the English did not like to waste time – Nur would arrive at the office wearing his navy school blazer with the letters V and C embroidered in gold on the pocket, the C underneath the letter V. Nur's eyes would shine when he saw his father. He would rush forward and bend to kiss his hand before Mahmoud enveloped him in a brief hug. Then, obtaining special permission, Mahmoud would take Nur and his friends out for lunch. How those boys attacked their plates of kebab and kofta! As if they had been starving for weeks. They were not allowed such food in the dorms and they had to bribe the cleaning staff to buy them ful and falafel from outside. Poor boys, forced to eat English food every day: boiled potatoes, roast beef, and more tasteless boiled vegetables. Mahmoud chuckled.

Lulled by these pleasant images, he felt sleepy enough to go back to bed. As he stretched out, a niggling thought imposed itself. Something had happened this evening that he didn't approve of. Not only Nur's poem, but something else. What was it? Yes, it was the women, Waheeba and Nabilah. His two wives in the same room! It was a sight he had never seen before and never wished to see again. They belonged to different sides of the saraya, to different sides of him. He was the only one to negotiate between these two worlds, to glide between them, to come back and forth at will. It was his prerogative. This wretched illness had made him passive and given the two women space to bicker and make snide remarks at each other, without any respect for his presence. He remembered Idris's sneer. But this irritation would drive sleep out of his eyes. He pushed the image of his wives away and made himself ponder more pleasant thoughts. The concern and love in his friends' eyes, their good wishes and prayers for his recovery. In a few days, he would go back to the office and, after a full morning of work, drive to the site of his new building to see how the work was progressing.

Sheep were slaughtered to celebrate his recovery, and an ox, too. Their woolly, matted skins lay in piles on the floor of the hoash and the early-morning air smelt of fresh blood. The poor of Umdurman gathered at the door of the saraya. They were not given raw meat but instead chunks of boiled mutton, the fat soaking the kisra they were placed on. The household sighed with relief. The scorch and burden of ill health had been lifted and a feeling of renewal and purification filled both the hoash and the modern wing of the mansion. After days in bed, Mahmoud Abuzeid re-entered the world and fell in love with it again. The clean morning breeze, the fresh smell of other men's cologne, the thrust and satisfaction of business accomplished and the anticipation of more success to come. His laugh boomed again. He felt rejuvenated, touched by a miracle. It was good to bellow orders and send his staff scurrying. They had all gone lax while he was recuperating and it was time for them to be on their toes again. Not only in the office, but at home, too. He challenged Nabilah with a seated dinner party for thirty guests; that should keep her occupied and silence her complaints. And it was high time too, to deal with the problem of Nassir.

On his second day back at the office, he passed by Waheeba on his way home. At this time in the afternoon she was under the shade of the veranda having her siesta. His unexpected visit stirred the sleepy hoash. Waheeba's girls, Batool and the others, rose to greet him with smiles and hugs. They were the daughters of distant relatives sent to Umdurman for schooling and it was their voices that woke Waheeba. She sat up with difficulty, drawing her tobe around her and pulling down the edges of her dress. He sat on the angharaib perpendicular to hers while she coughed, wiped her face with her hands and settled herself upright. Her two legs stretched out straight from the bed, the calves pressed hard against the edge. She asked about his health and he asked her about the previous day's slaughter which had coincided with Nur's farewell. His friends and other members of the family had come to bid him farewell and today he was on his way to Alexandria, making the journey to Cairo by airplane for the first time instead of by train.

Batool brought him coffee and water.

'Shall I put sugar for you, Uncle?' she said, smiling. 'For Allah's sake, stay and have lunch with us.'

She was a pretty girl with smooth black skin and perfect teeth. Her father was poor and the girl had attached herself to Waheeba even though she had finished school. She was loyal and hard-working, entertaining and caring. Even though Batool was not his daughter, Mahmoud would spare no expense in getting her married and settled.

Waheeba did not repeat her girl's invitation. She knew that he would be having lunch and siesta with Nabilah. His days of lunching with her were over. Today, seeing the hoash quiet after what must have been the bustle of the past days, Mahmoud felt a faint pity for his wife. His illness had given her a role to play but now that he was better, she would recede to the background. In his mind, he associated her with decay and ignorance. He would never regret marrying Nabilah. It was not a difficult choice between the stagnant past and the glitter of the future, between crudeness and sophistication.

As if to confirm his thoughts, she asked now, 'Has Nur arrived safely?'

Stupid woman, ignorant of concepts of distance and time. He chuckled and said, 'No, Hajjah. It will be still a long time before his trip is over. I will let you know when I have news. The office in Cairo will send me a telegram as soon as Nur arrives.'

'Why does he have to travel so far away to study? Why couldn't he attend Comboni College like Nassir did?' It was a constant refrain.

He took a sip of his coffee.

'Because Victoria College is superior to any school we have here. It is based on the English public school system. And besides, next year when he finishes, I want him to continue his studies in Cambridge.'

'Is that in Egypt also?'

He sighed. 'No. In England.'

45

'Even further?'

'Yes, it is even further and I don't want any grumbling from you. I have already made a decision.'

She listened to him intently, her eyes never leaving his face. Behind the formality of respect and diffidence, he glimpsed a certain expression. She was looking at him as if he was a precocious child and she was curious to see what he would do or say next. She was only older than him by a few years but in their youth, this age difference had seemed like a decade. He had been shocked when his father ordered him to marry her. Waheeba was a distant relative, the only daughter of an established Umdurman merchant who had become wealthy by trading in Gum Arabic.

Waheeba came into the Abuzeid family with money and business connections. At twenty-one, she was considered a spinster and her family had no hesitation in marrying her off and financing a lavish wedding. Mahmoud, a youth of eighteen, his mind taken up with a fascination for commerce, had hated Waheeba at first sight; hated her because of her dullness and lack of beauty and, most of all, because she was forced on him. Their wedding night was a disaster, a humiliation he had buried deep and did not talk to his friends about. It was almost a miracle that Nassir and Nur were conceived, but their arrival, and the force of the years, eroded his distaste for her, so that on such an afternoon, after he had found fulfilment and success in another marriage, he could share with her the wish that Nur would arrive safely in Alexandria after a good trip. Nassir, though, was the reason he had come to visit her. Nassir, who had not yet returned to Medani.

'I am reducing his allowance,' he said to her, 'until he mends his ways.'

'But he has his house in Medani to support,' she protested. 'And he receives lots of guests. And Fatma will have more children. He said to me—'

Mahmoud didn't allow her to go further.

'He has to learn. He is my employee. He works for me, and he is not doing his job. And you know as well as I do how your son is squandering my money!'

She pulled her chin in so that the curves of fat were more pronounced.

'He is still young. He needs to learn.'

'No, he is not too young. Don't defend him. He is the reason I came here today, to tell you that while I am reducing his allowance on one side, I don't want you giving him money on the other side.'

She shrugged and looked down at her feet.

'Am I clear in what I am saying? You are not to give Nassir any money, either directly or through his wife or through anyone else. He gets nothing except what I give him and he gets nothing from you. Am I clear?'

Waheeba nodded and said faintly, 'Fine.'

'People are beginning to talk,' he confided in her. 'It's shameful. The family's good name will be affected by Nassir's delinquency!' This distressed him to the core. His position in society mattered to him.

Waheeba remained unmoved. She shifted her weight on the angharaib.

'Allow me just to pay for his daughter's circumcision. I want to celebrate it in style.'

'What?' he bellowed. 'I will not have such barbarity in this house. I forbid it.'

'Aji!' Waheeba slapped her hand on her chest and her voice rose. 'What kind of talk is this?'

'It's modern talk. We need to stop these old customs, which have no basis in our religion and are unhealthy. Besides, it's against the law.'

'What law? Are the English going to tell us what to do with this!' She pointed down to her lap. Batool snickered.

Mahmoud began to regret this turn in the conversation. 'What do the girl's parents have to say about this?'

'Nassir and Fatma are like everyone else. They want to do the right thing by their daughter. You are the only one protesting and I don't know why. Maybe your Egyptian woman has been putting ideas in your head. Is she not intending to circumcise her daughter, Ferial?'

'Of course not!'

'Shame on her. No man will want to marry her when she grows up.'

Dragging Nabilah and Ferial into the conversation was more than he could bear.

'I will speak to Nassir and Fatma about this,' he said, and rose to leave.

Idris was the other backward element in his life. When Idris returned from a business trip from Sennar, they had their morning tea together before setting out to meet the new manager of Barclays Bank. Mahmoud looked down and saw that his brother was wearing slippers.

'On a day like this! Slippers, in front of Mr Harrison?'

Idris smiled broadly. He slid his right foot out of his markoob and wiggled his toes.

'Is he going to listen to me or look at my feet?'

Mahmoud sighed. 'We have to make a good impression.'

'You think he hasn't heard about us? Our reputation will have preceded us.' Idris sucked his tea. He did this with too much noise, the kind of noise the English would not appreciate.

'We haven't done business with him yet and I don't know what he is like.'

But Mahmoud was an optimist. This was a result of his consistent good luck. However, he liked to play safe and be on more or less familiar ground. He was not happy that the previous bank manager had been replaced. Now he would have to start from scratch and win Nigel Harrison's trust. He would have to persuade him that the Abuzeid brothers were not only honest and with a good credit history, but that this new business venture of cotton ginning was going to bring in profits enough to repay any bank loan.

'You could have at least worn sandals,' he murmured. placing his empty glass on the table and standing up to leave.

Unlike Idris, who was in a jellabiya, he was wearing his best suit, purchased from Bond Street, and his Bally shoes. They pinched, and he was slightly hot, but personal comfort must be put aside. This meeting had been first postponed because Mr Harrison had not yet taken up his post, then again because of Mahmoud's illness and Idris's trip. Now Mahmoud was eager for it. He had hardly slept the night before, excited and going over the proposed figures in his head. He felt young and vigorous, eager for this new scheme.

In the car, he saw trees being planted in Kitchener Avenue. They would look beautiful, one day, overlooking the Nile. Two Englishmen and an English woman were on horseback, wearing broad-rimmed hats. The sight reminded him of his childhood when all the English rode horses. Now, most of them had cars, yet an eccentric few still preferred their horses. He turned his Daimler into Victoria Street and parked underneath the sign that said *Barclays Bank (Dominions, Colonies and Overseas)*. He switched the ignition off and they got out of the car.

'Maybe this will be the last English manager we will have to plead in front of. Imagine coming to meet a Sudanese like ourselves!'

Idris only grunted in reply. He was negative about Sud-anisation and self-government, whereas Mahmoud kept an open mind and a determination to go with the flow. Because of the Anglo-Egyptian Condominium, Sudan was not technically part of the British Empire. The Foreign Office, rather than the Colonial Office, ruled it, which resulted in a more graceful colonial experience and the British officials Mahmoud came into contact with were refined and educated, well-travelled and diplomatic. He knew that when the day came, he would not help but feel sorry to see them leave.

49

★

Mr Harrison, an Oxford graduate with solid credentials, was tall, with black hair and grey, watchful eyes. He rose from his desk to greet them and spent several minutes, as was the Sudanese custom, exchanging pleasantries in beginner's Arabic. It always irritated Mahmoud to hear his mother tongue grammatically distorted and heavily accented. There was no need for this, no need for the English to trouble themselves with a foreign language to try and gain favour with the Arabs. Especially when it was so clear who needed whom. Mahmoud was a man who appreciated hierarchy, the order and logic of it, and he had no problem ingratiating himself to this Englishman, young enough to be his son.

'What do you make of our country, Sir?' He sat on the edge of his armchair, eager to show off his English. He liked the roll of the words in his mouth, and the weight of the file with the proposal on his lap.

Thankfully, Mr Harrison stopped talking Arabic.

'It is a fascinating land. From what I have seen so far, it has great potential, and Khartoum is a pleasant city. I've been to several functions, social as well as business, and I'm staying at the Grand Hotel until my house is ready.'

'The best hotel in town,' Mahmoud murmured. 'An excellent introduction.'

'Yes, it is comfortable. I must say I am impressed by the architecture of the city; it is of a very high standard. Yesterday, I attended a session at the Legislative Assembly and that building was interesting too.'

'They voted to discuss the motion for self-government, I heard.'

'Yes, then in the middle of the session the electricity supply failed and a dozen flunkies walked in carrying hurricane lamps!' Mr Harrison smiled, clearly amused and Mahmoud laughed politely.

'Have you had the opportunity to travel outside Khartoum?'

'Not yet but it is something I look forward to.'

'Then you must come to our farm in Gezira and see for yourself the cotton fields!' Mahmoud raised his arms and turned to look at Idris to include him as a host. Idris nodded and re-affirmed the invitation. Mr Harrison must certainly enjoy their hospitality. He must partake of the celebrated Sudanese breakfast. He must bring his wife – no wife yet? Of course, he was too young for the shackles of matrimony. Laughter, and Mahmoud was liking this young man more and more, his wide-eyed inno-cence, his cotton suit slightly, only slightly, crumpled and his attractive modesty, because modesty in those with power and position was especially attractive.

Nigel Harrison looked and sounded his age now, his eyes bright with thoughts of leisure activities and a life outside work. 'I have always wanted to come to the Sudan,' his voice was more relaxed and confessional. 'My grandfather was with Lord Kitchener's army and often told me stories of the campaign. I grew up with a keen interest in the history of Sudan.'

'Your grandfather would have told you about the invasion, but those days of war are over now, Mr Harrison. We are now in the days of commerce, profitable commerce for you and for us. This country has vast potential but I need not tell you. You know already.'

'True, true . . .' Mr Harrison faltered slightly. He sat upright in his chair and became businesslike. 'And what can I do for you today, gentlemen?'

It was the cue they had been waiting for. Out came the proposal, the facts and figures carefully calculated and the large loan they were aspiring to. The cost of setting up the first cotton ginnery in the private sector. Abuzeid cotton would be ginned by the Abuzeids themselves. The proposed location would be Hamad Nall'ah in Sinnar. Yes, the governor of the Blue Nile province, Mr Peterson has welcomed the idea. Mahmoud explained that Idris was the farmer while he was the busi-nessman. Idris was the one who knew just how much more cotton the Gezira fields would be able to yield in the future. The future was promising and their business history was impressive. Two years ago, under the previous Barclays Bank manager they had been granted a loan to acquire the agency for Perkins motors, specifically the pumps for irrigation. The result was that the Abuzeid cotton fields were now irrigated by Abuzeid pumps. They no longer needed to buy or hire pumps from someone else. Idris explained the significant difference the pumps were making, their efficiency in irrigating the fields and how much acquiring the Perkins agency had cut costs. The Abuzeids were able to repay the loan in no time and it was with this confidence that they were now expanding into cotton ginning and asking for another loan.

Young though he might be, Nigel Harrison had done his homework and was canny enough to question his clients. 'There are capitalists in this country, some of them foreign and some of them local, who would be honoured to ally themselves with you. They have the finances you need and you have the base and experience they lack. Why aren't you allowing them to invest in your projects?'

The reply was confident. 'We are a family business, Sir. We do not want outsiders to come between us.'

'This possessiveness might do you harm in the long run.'

Mahmoud smiled. 'We do not need anyone else, only Barclay's Bank.'

Harrison responded with a small smile and went on, 'But given the more than healthy profit of last year's cotton yield, Sayyid Mahmoud, you cannot have any liquidity problem. Why are you seeking a loan?'

Mahmoud crossed his legs.

'I have invested my cash in a building, Sir. The very first high rise in Khartoum. It will be a big building on Newbold Street, a building similar to the ones in Cairo.'

Nigel Harrison, like every traveller from Europe, had passed through Cairo on his way to Khartoum and he knew what

Mahmoud meant. The brothers started to describe the building and its exact location.

'Next to Hoash Boulus,' said Idris.

Mahmoud rebuked him in Arabic, whispering, 'What would he know about Hoash Boulus!' Then he turned towards the desk, raised his voice and switched to English. 'I will take you to see it, Mr Harrison. It will be a fine piece of architecture when it is ready.'

A week later Mahmoud met Nigel Harrison at a reception in the palace. He introduced him to Nabilah, proud that she was next to him in her jewels and cocktail frock, her fair skin radiant in the lamp-lit garden. In his dinner jacket, with a drink in his hand, Mahmoud was satisfied that they made a favourable impression. But it seemed an inappropriate occasion to talk to Mr Harrison about the loan or to ask for a response.

'Is this a typical palace function, would you say?' It was Harrison's first.

Mahmoud was pleased to be asked this question.

'Everything is exactly the same as in previous occasions. Even the brass brand is as loud as ever.'

Harrison smiled and raised his voice, 'Perhaps it's a ploy to hamper any attempts to have a sensible conversation.'

Mahmoud did not understand the word 'ploy' and faltered a little. He changed the subject.

'Unless you have already met them, I will introduce you to my friends from the Chamber of Commerce.'

'I would appreciate that. I've noticed that formal introductions are not the norm here. Everyone of consequence expects to be known, but that can be puzzling for a newcomer.'

Mahmoud found this perspective interesting. It was true, he moved in circles where everyone knew everyone else. When in doubt, he was proud of his instinct to sort out who was influential and who was not. Sometimes he would sit in a gathering perplexed about the identity of another man and yet unable to place him. A whispered query to the most trusted person next to him would suffice, but usually he would have to trust his instinct. A name could be picked up later, but how Mahmoud greeted or treated a stranger could not be postponed and, of course, he had to get it right. Treating a man with less respect than was his due could be disastrous, but also flattering, and raising up a minor could raise eyebrows or even attract ridicule. Because he was, by nature, cautious, and by instinct generous, Mahmoud often erred on this side. Minor officials, irrelevant acquaintances, and struggling merchants would find themselves showered with his cordial attention, only to be cold-shouldered when their true identity was revealed.

Nabilah touched his arm and he leaned closer to listen.

'There are hardly any senior Egyptian officials. Very different from previous occasions.'

She was right. The government was keeping the Egyptian contingent at a distance. Instead, it was the aspiring Sudanese politicians who were milling close to the Governor-General. None of the conservative tribal sheikhs were here, though. They would shun such a gathering, which included women and alcohol. Here, with the garden lights and the waiters circling with trays of hors d' oeuvres, was the British and Levantine core of Khartoum: cosmopolitan and opportunistic, confident and only recently vulnerable. Mahmoud spotted a merchant who had expressed interest in leasing office space in the new building. It was too early to come to an agreement, but Mahmoud strode across the lawn to reassure him that the construction work was proceeding according to schedule.

V

Ustaz Badr stood in the busy Abuzeid office facing Mahmoud Bey's imposing desk. He took his time greeting the Bey, expressing with eloquence how grateful he was to Allah for restoring the gentleman's health and returning him to his place of business. But something was wrong. He could tell from Mahmoud's puzzled look and the way he frowned sideways at his brother and shook his head as if to ask, 'Who is this?' Before Badr could remind him that he was his children's private tutor, the door of the office was pushed open and, as it seemed to Badr, the sun itself blasted through. The Coptic secretary, who had a minute ago carelessly waved him in, was now standing upright with the utmost energy and expectation, to usher in a tall well-dressed Englishman. To Badr's astonishment, Mahmoud Abuzeid sprang to his feet and circled from behind his desk to greet his guest in the middle of the room.

'Mr Harrison, what a pleasure, what a pleasure! Welcome, Sir, to my office. What an honour!' He pumped the young man's hand and the Englishman smiled with appreciation.

It seemed to Badr that he was pushed aside. Metaphorically yes, he was discarded but physically, too, he was pushed aside, though afterwards, when he looked back on this scene, he was not sure who had actually touched him and shoved him out of the way. Was it the secretary, Victor, who had a few minutes ago in the reception area, casually asked him his name and occupation without leaving his desk? Or was it Mahmoud Abuzeid himself, or his brother, or the other attendants in the office who had sprung to their feet, not as fast as Mahmoud Bey, but immediately after him? Badr did what was expected of him. He moved out of the way. He shrunk himself, backed out, and slipped out the door, away from the enthusiasm between men who mattered and the exchange of these clipped, sparkling English words.

There was space for him in the streets of Khartoum. He blended with the pre-sunset liveliness when shops and offices re-opened after siesta. The December air was clean and invigorating and this should have been an afternoon of hope and new beginning, of action not delay. Subhan Allah, when something is not meant to happen, it will not happen, no matter what. Who would have thought that his mission would abort? Or that he would fail before even attempting?

'Go to him at his office,' Hanniyah had said. 'You have been relying on his son and his wife to ask him about the apartment but his son has gone away and Madame Nabilah must have forgotten. Go to him yourself.'

Her advice had seemed sound, remarkably solid for an uneducated village woman. But he should have followed his usual habit of doing the opposite of what she suggested. Here he was, now dislodged into the street, having not even mentioned the new building, let alone his request to rent an apartment. If he had gone in a couple of minutes earlier, he would have at least articulated his request before the Englishman blasted through the door. If. This 'if' would open the door to Satan. Quell your disappointment. Perhaps there would be another day, another opportunity. Badr felt tired. He had not really wanted to visit Mahmoud Bey in his office. The man could not even remember him! You have made a fool of yourself, Badr. But wallowing in self-pity and humiliation was a luxury he could not afford. What was next on his agenda of chores? Another private lesson? He must buy bread and olives . . . his mind was muddled.

He hurried down the road but the grocer closed the door in his face. Another door. No cheese and olives for the children's supper tonight. Hanniyah was newly pregnant and craving olives. Now he would have to deliver disappointment without even a pickle to quench her need. But a believer does not despair in

Allah's mercy. He needed to remind himself of that.

It was Shukry's visit that had aggravated the situation. His cousin had been true to his threat of coming to Sudan to search for work, relying on Badr's hospitality. But three weeks, one month, and Badr's patience was beginning to strain. Food was not the problem, space was. One cramped room and a narrow hoash was all they had. They had all been sleeping outdoors in the hoash but now the weather was cooler. Last night Radwan had started to cough and Hanniyah had to take him inside. What to do if a cold spell descended? Put the guest in the room as well as the children and his elderly father? But then Hanniyah would catch cold outside. It was an awkward situation, one that made him feel helpless and ashamed. This morning was the worst; he had caught Shukry stealing a lustful look at Hanniyah as she squatted over the stove to heat water. Cousin or not, Badr was willing to pull his eyes out, but in a hurry to get to school on time, he had controlled his anger and avoided a scene. Besides, if he confronted him, Shukry would go back to Egypt and spread nasty rumours about Badr. It was better to be patient and pray that, insha'Allah, the youth would find a job soon, a job that would provide him with accommodation. Badr couldn't wait to see the back of him.

One room and a hoash. The difficulty of being with his wife, alone. Always having to be careful, to lower their voices and hide from the children. Night was the best curtain, but even though his elderly father was senile and nearly blind, Badr still felt inhibited by his sleeping presence. Poor Hanniyah! She had no privacy to change her clothes or beautify herself like other women. Always his father and the children were in the way and now, worst of all, his cousin with the roving eyes.

He walked home, but his step had lost its earlier briskness. He took his time, conscious of the swift descent of the sun, the softness and birdsong that accompanied it. He heard the maghrib azan, but it came from random prayer zawias, rather than mosques. There was only one functioning mosque in the city; the other, the Old Mosque, built during Turco-Egyptian rule, had fallen into disrepair. King Farouk was now financing its refurbishment, but extensive work was needed and the project was taking too long. There should be more mosques, Badr thought. Khartoum had seven churches for its communities of Catholics, Greeks, Copts, Armenians and the Anglican British officials and their families. It was the Anglo-Egyptian invasion that had brought all these people in. They revived Khartoum after the Mahdi had neglected it and established his capital in Umdurman. Badr brought his mind to the present and joined a group of men washing themselves in preparation to pray. The water was still warm from the heat of the afternoon. His sons should have been with him. At home, Hanniyah would remind them to pray, but they would evade her and run out to play in the alley. He smiled, thinking of them, mischievous and lively, needing his guidance.

The men lined up in the garden on King Street, near the building site of the Farouk Mosque. Badr liked praying in Sudan. There was something spacious and welcoming about these prayers in the open air and it seemed to him as if they accommodated more of Allah's creatures. This feeling, when he first arrived in Sudan, had seemed to him fanciful, but he had grown used to it and accepted it. As a child in his village of Kafr el-Dawar, he had been terrified of the ghouls and djinns that inhabited the darkness of alleyways and the most deserted of fields. This fear had turned to caution when he was older, and whenever circumstances compelled him to take these haunted routes, he would arm himself with verses of the Qur'an and hurry to his destination. In Sudan, though, he had come to experience more benign spirits.

Today, as he walked forward to pray in the front row, his wet bare feet treading grass, he sensed the congregation swelling with invisible worshippers. So palatable was their presence that it was as if the barrier separating their world from that of mankind had thinned and become transparent. Were they angels, robust and pure, better than him because they never despaired and never tired? Badr felt himself slide into another dimension. It was unexpected and unasked for. A dip into an alternative state, where he was weightless and free, and his concerns, valid and pressing only minutes ago, slackened and moved away. They did not disappear, but receded to the back of his mind as if they were taking a rest. The imam, in his recitation, stumbled over a verse, and Badr, standing right behind him prompted the correct words. This gladdened him; he had made sure that Allah's words were recited in the correct order. He was a teacher, after all, and his role was to demonstrate and correct. He felt himself elevated, his presence appreciated by all who were present – men, angels and jinn.

Afterwards, he wanted to ask the men who had prayed with him if they, too, had noticed what he had noticed, if they, too, had experienced that thinning of the barriers. He wanted to confirm that this was not an ordinary maghrib prayer, but one in which one or more of Allah's powerful servants had participated. He was almost certain that inhuman creatures, who could neither be seen nor touched, had prayed too. And the reasons for this attendance, and the consequences of this attendance, he believed, were detached from ordinary day-to-day life. They were reasons and consequences of another realm that would not unsettle Badr's life or anyone else's. All that had happened was that two worlds, the spiritual and the material, had touched each other briefly before moving on, each faithful to its own orbit. It had been a privilege to bend in worship at this particular gathering. He was grateful. And it was this that finally restrained him from seeking con-firmation with the other worshippers. The villager's fear that flaunting good fortune, even if it were immaterial, would lead to envy. He kept his experience to himself and walked away from the garden and into the twilight.

If he had not visited Mahmoud Bey, he would have missed this; if Mahmoud Bey had spoken to him and given him good tidings about the flat, he would have dashed back home to Hanniyah. Everything happens for a reason. But Badr was an educated man and knew that coincidence existed too, randomness was created. It was one of the laws of the universe. Imagination existed, too. He could have been hallucinating or, Allah forbid, succumbing to a sickness of the mind. He could have conjured it all up to comfort himself after the disappointment he had experienced. No, his imagination was not that powerful, and he had never been prone to fancies before. It was this country. Something here was different. The twilight was thick with it, pungent and sensuous. He concluded that in Sudan, the barriers between the human and spirit worlds were thin, or that there were cracks and transparencies through which that other, unknown, world could, at times, be sensed.

In this heightened sense of awareness, he understood something of the events of seventy years ago. It was easy now to imagine how a man from the Jezira Abba, a place far west of Khartoum and even more backward than Umdurman, could imagine that he was the Mahdi himself, sent by Allah to fill the earth with justice and warn of an impending Judgment Day. In Badr's opinion, which was the position of the Azhar and the Sudanese tribes who were allied to Egypt, Muhammad Ahmad al Mahdi was a charismatic, powerful impostor, misguided at best and an apostate at worse. The British had done well to end his state. The Sudanese needed rescuing from superstition and deviation – this was why the Shariah judges were Egyptian and why it was so important for Badr to be here, to teach Arabic and Religious Education. The Sudanese were good people, they loved the prophet Muhammad, peace be upon him, but they needed to learn more about his sunna so that they would stay strong and not follow individuals who would lead them astray like the Mahdi had done. Yet now, walking in the twilight, Badr gained insight into that man's psyche and saw, all too clearly, that it was not only the oppression of Turkish-Egyptian rule that prompted the Mahdist rebellion, it was something in the very air and texture of Sudan itself. A place where reality was slippery and fantasy could take over the mind, a place of wayward spirituality, a place where the impossible and the romantic pulsed within reach. A place where intangible, inhuman, forces still prevailed, not yet tamed and restrained by the rules of religion and men.

His home was not far from the Egyptian school, but while the school was within the vicinity of downtown Khartoum, the houses allocated to the staff were on the muddy outskirts. There was no sewage system, only buckets that were collected and replaced at night by carts pulled by camels. The camel-cart must have passed and overturned not far from his door. He walked in, enveloped by the stench, jarred back to the feelings of disgust and injury. He opened the door onto the smallest of hoashs where four beds were arranged in a rectangle around a small table. He immediately looked for Shukry and was relieved not to find him. Hanniyah was preparing dinner in the strip of covered terrace that served as a kitchen. She was bent over, stirring something in a pot. His father sat cross-legged on one of the beds, hunched over, picking and fretting over his toenails. The children left their game of marbles and ran to greet Badr, three boys to shake his hand as they had been taught. He picked Radwan up, felt his forehead and tousled his hair, 'Are you still coughing, boy?'

'No, Father.'

There was mucous, dark green and thick, descending from his nose. Badr put him down. His suit had to last him all week, he could not go to school streaked with snot.

'Where did your Uncle Shukry go?'

'He went out to the prayer and didn't come back,' said Osama the eldest.

'He went back to Egypt,' said Bilal.

He was five, but spoke slowly, as if he were younger. Badr laughed and drew Bilal to him. The boys were stripped to their underwear – they only wore clothes when they went out. Osama was distracted by a blue and gold marble, which he tossed from one hand to the other. Badr had never seen it before.

'Where did you get this marble from?'

'I bought it from the shop.'

'Where did you get the money from?'

'Uncle Shukry gave me a piaster this morning.' Osama closed his fingers over the marble.

Bilal reached out and pressed his father's pockets to see if he had brought home anything. Sometimes he got them bubble gum or peanuts. Finding his pockets empty, the boys' interest cooled and they went back to their game by the light of the lamp. The baby was asleep on one of the beds. If he rolled over, he would fall off. Badr propped a pillow behind his back before turning to greet his father.

He bent down to kiss the old man's hand. 'How are you, Father? How are you today?' Whole days and nights would pass with the old man detached and confused. In this state, he even forgot he was in Sudan and spoke about feeding the water buffalos and milking the cow, as if the fields and canals of Kafr-el-Dawar were outside his door. He would also imagine that Badr's sons were his own sons, and often address Osama as 'Walla ya Badr' or 'Badr ya zeft'. This always sent Osama into a fit of harsh giggles, for it disturbed him to hear his father's name, the name of a venerable Ustaz of Arabic language and religion, abused in such a way. If Osama laughed in front of Badr, Badr would give his shaking shoulders a slap to restore order in the household. Behind his back, though, he was sure the boys, and even Hanniyah, had their fair share of laughter at his father's senility.

Badr never found it funny. His father had been a tough, imposing man in his younger days, a farmer and a fighter who inspired respect and even fear in others. Badr remembered him using his cane to beat petty thieves and highwaymen. He had a special talent with the stick, and at weddings and circumcisions he would dance, twirling it in his hand, a handsome, smiling man, strong and loud in his brown jellabiya. Loyally, Badr held this image in his head. This was his real father, not this mound of sagging flesh with the befuddled mind and naivety of a child.

'How are you, Father?'

In a flash the reply came, lucid and loud, as if it were being hurled from the healthy past. 'Isn't it time that this bastard cousin of yours found himself a job and got out of here?'

Surprise made Badr speechless. No one, in these past few days, had been sure if the old man was aware of the guest's presence. Badr felt as if he was meeting his father after a long absence and there was so much he wanted to talk to him about.

'What can I do, Father? I must honour my guest.'

'Enough! He's been here too long. And you have other responsibilities. You are busy working all day.'

Badr felt a surge of joy. His father sympathised, his father understood. He wanted to call out to Hanniyah so that she could share in the moment, and he glanced at her, at her moving, active body, but he could not catch her eyes. Her face was in the dark away from the lamplight.

'We are not in our village where everything is easy,' his father continued. 'We are in a foreign land.'

Amazing. Badr pressed his hand.

'Insha'Allah he'll find a job soon.'

'He won't get a job. He's no good. And is he looking for a job? Do you know why he's here? He's running from the police, that's why. He's committed a crime and now he's hiding where no one can find him.'

The old man's mind was wandering, or he knew something that Badr didn't.

'What crime, Father? What did Shukry do?'

His father looked caught out and his eyes, previously focused on Badr, lost their intensity. He started to mumble.

'I have to ask his father. He will know. Your uncle is disappointed in him.'

Shukry's father had died several years ago and Badr allowed the conversation to drop. It was healing enough to know that his father appreciated his daily struggles. He left him and walked over to Hanniyah.

Would she ask him about his meeting with Mahmoud Bey? He

started to gently chide her, 'I walk into this house and you don't come and greet me! At least have a sweet word for your man.'

She looked up at him and smiled.

'I have a sweet dish for you.'

She had flowing light brown hair and a ruddy complexion; her eyes shone, and her lips were beautiful.

He squatted next to her. 'What are you making?'

She paused in her stirring. 'Rice pudding.'

She herself was sweet and creamy as pudding. Her ample body was firm, a multitude of orbs, pliant, narrow, convex and intriguing. He was coarse and dreary next to her. It was a miracle that she belonged to him. Grateful for the darkness, he squeezed her thigh and his fingers dug at the back of her knees. She laughed.

'Don't get too close to the pot or you'll mess up your going-out clothes.' She went back to stirring. 'I ate feseakh today,' she said. 'Our neighbour, Salha, the wife of the post office clerk, came over for a visit and brought me some. She said to me, you have to taste our Sudanese dish and I said to her we have this same dish of salted fish but we only make it on Eid. I tasted it, and it was different – but tasty.'

He had not been able to buy pickles and olives for her today but alhamdullilah, she had received the saltiness she craved. He need not have worried. And now she said: 'You know I've been nagging you to move to a better place? Well, today when Salha was here and she was kind and friendly, I thought how can I move away from her and deliver all by myself? She promised to help me. Who knows what kind of neighbours we will have if we move! So I want to stay here in this house until after I give birth.'

A burden was lifted off his shoulders. Just like that. He need not tell her about today's visit to Mahmoud Bey's office, he need not say a thing. She prattled on, and he loved her best like this, when she was occupied with the concerns of the household or with some feminine matter, too busy to make demands of him. She had a sharp tongue and the potential to erupt when provoked. He had seen her haranguing women in the family, and she could spank the boys as hard as any man, yet with him she was soft-spoken and yielding, in awe of his teaching credentials and status. Even when they did quarrel, she was able to restrain her tongue and went so far, but not over the limit. He appreciated this. She was on his side and his fight was her fight.

He went indoors to change. The room was littered with their belonging, as well as their guest's suitcase, and in the dim light it looked untidy and squashed. There were no beds, now, because they were all out in the hoash. Badr put on his house clothes, which consisted of long johns and a vest. He tossed a pillow on the floor and stretched out. Stealing time, and stealing space. He could hear the children outside the door. Grandpa was trying to leave the house.

'Quick, stop him, Osama, or he will get lost like last time!'

Then Shukry's voice, 'Where are you going, Uncle Hajj? Come and sit with me.'

His father's voice, but he could not make out the words. Then Shukry, defending himself.

'Of course I am not escaping from Egypt!'

Badr got up and stepped out into the hoash. Shukry was sitting next to his father on the bed. He was tall compared to Badr, his body one solid, uniform bulk, his face large and tanned with a sunken, bleary look. Badr remembered him as a child in the village, in a striped jellabiya with filthy feet and hands, his face surrounded by buzzing flies. He had a clear memory of him deftly, and with glee, pulling off the sack that covered the face of a water buffalo. The buffalo were blindfolded to prevent them from becoming dizzy as they turned the saqqiya round and round. But a stressed and dizzy beast was what Shukry wanted. There was a cruel streak in him.

Now Badr greeted him and asked him about his day. He sat on the bed next to the baby, who sat up and started whimpering.

'I've been promised work, cousin. Insha'Allah, in the cotton fields in a place called Gezira.'

Elation. Not only would Shukry leave the house but the whole city too!

'Alhamdulilah, this is very good news. A thousand congratulations.' His voice rang out, 'Osama, come and carry your brother. Take him to his mother.'

After the crying baby was dispatched to Hanniyah, he turned to Shukry, 'Tell me, who exactly will you be working for? And how much are they going to pay you?'

'A family called Abuzeid. They favour Egyptians to work for them.'

It was a coincidence, but not particularly remarkable.

'I know them personally . . .' There was pride in Badr's voice, he wanted his father to hear, really hear. 'I teach Mahmoud Bey's youngest son and daughter. I am at their saraya two or three times a week.' He was boasting now. 'I taught Nur Abuzeid until he went to Victoria College and found himself the best student in Arabic!'

Shukry did not pick up on his enthusiasm. He slumped forward and put his elbows on his knees.

'But I am not sure I want to work as a farmer. I am thinking I should be patient and wait for another opportunity.'

Badr grunted with sarcasm. 'You want to be like me, an effendi in a suit? You don't want to get your hands dirty. But I have spent years studying. When did *you* learn? Did you finish school? No. Do you have a skill? No. You started to train as a nurse and then gave it up. You joined the army, and when you came back from Palestine, they dismissed you. So don't be proud. You arrived in Sudan thinking the streets are paved in gold. It's not so easy. Look at me.' He waved his hand to take in the hoash.

Shukry didn't look too happy with this lecture.

'I would rather work as a nurse,' he said. 'The pay would be better.'

'But you're not qualified as a nurse. The hospitals won't hire you.'

'Well, I could work privately.'

Badr started to worry that Shukry might turn the job down or had already turned it down. Would he continue to be their guest indefinitely?

His father startled all of them by saying, 'Don't be ungrateful.'

It was never clear whether he was following the conversation or merely repeating a random phrase.

Badr continued, 'You cannot just sit around doing nothing.' He stressed the word sit, making it sound unpleasant.

Shukry took the hint.

'I am a heavy guest, cousin. I should consider this farming job so that I can relieve you.'

Badr murmured the conventional, 'Don't say that, man. My home is your home.' But it was clear that he didn't mean any of it.

He stood up to get ready for the Isha prayer. It was getting late and Radwan had curled up on the bed next to him and slept. If Hanniyah didn't wake him up for supper, he would pass the night with an empty belly, waking up at dawn ravenous.

'Cousin,' Shukry said.

Badr turned around.

'Yesterday I had a twenty piaster note in my wallet. I left it with my belongings in the room and today I can't find it.'

The sentence felt heavy to Badr's ears. He turned stern, his schoolteacher self. 'You must have misplaced it or it's in one of your pockets.'

Shukry shook his head. 'I looked everywhere for it. Someone must have taken it.'

Badr bristled. 'You know very well that apart from us no one goes into the room. No strangers come here.'

Shukry looked him straight in the eye. 'I want my money back. I don't know who took it.'

Badr lost his temper. 'Be careful Shukry, in what you are insinuating.'

Shukry gave a little laugh. 'Why are you angry? Little boys can be naughty.'

Badr remembered the blue and gold marble in Osama's hand. He became even more angry, and bellowed, 'Osama, Osama, come here!'

The boy stood in front of them. In the lamplight, his skin was sallow and his rib cage stood out.

'Did you take money from Uncle's Shukry's wallet?'

'No, Father,' came the automatic response.

'Are you sure, Osama? Did Bilal or Radwan?'

'No, Father, they're too young.'

'Too young,' Shukry interrupted. 'But you're not too young. You could have shown them what to do. You could have set them up. If you did this, Osama, you had better own up.'

'I didn't do anything, Uncle.' Osama was looking scared now, caught between his father's glare and the guest's.

Badr grabbed his son by the shoulder. 'I will spank you hard, Osama.'

The boy burst into tears. 'I didn't do it! I didn't do anything. I swear.'

Hanniyah stepped into the lamplight, the baby propped on her hip. Strands of her hair hung loose from her kerchief and she radiated heat as if she had been sitting over the stove, not only stirring the pot, but rousing herself for battle.

'No one calls my son a thief!' she shouted. 'Do you hear me? No one!'

Badr surrendered to the realisation that the evening was not going to pass well. He should say, 'Shut up, woman!' but instead he let her speak her mind. He unleashed her, she who was his inner self, his unrestrained half; he let her loose on this burden of a guest.

VI

On the last day that Soraya loved the sea, she was wearing her new blue dress, a dress that was made by a Greek dressmaker in Alexandria. It was the perfect beach dress, fresh watery blue and white splashes and a crisp white bow pinching her waist. Everyone said she was pretty. On the beach, under an orange umbrella she sat squinting from the sun, alert to the crescendo and break of the waves. With her were Fatma, Nassir, and their two children. They were waiting for Nur to join them. The long academic year was over and he had excelled in his Cambridge entrance examinations. He was now with some of his Victoria College friends who had not yet dispersed for the summer. Nassir was dozing in his deckchair, the newspaper he had been reading collapsed on the bulge of his stomach. He was too large for the shirt he was wearing and perspiring in spite of the breeze. Fatma looked out of place wearing her pink tobe and annoyed that the children were kicking sand in her face. She preferred shopping to the beach. She would have been happier in Cairo, but Soraya adored the Alexandria lifestyle: the waking up late to the sound of the waves, and the aromas of a heavy breakfast. Waking up to the knowledge that all through the night Nur had been asleep on the couch in the living room, just outside the door, steps away from where she and the children slept. After coffee they would stroll across the Corniche, walk down the steps to the beach, hire an umbrella and some deckchairs, then settle down. Picking off from yesterday, the children were digging a canal. Zeinab, who was five, walked backwards and forwards filling her pail with seawater and dumping it in the hole. The sticky, pliant sand tempted even Fatma and Soraya to mould it into shapes.

'Don't spoil my canal,' said Zeinab, sounding serious and bossy like her grandmother Waheeba. Her baby brother toddled after her, panting a little, small and soft in this vast expanse of sun, sea and sky.

Waiting for Nur suited Soraya. The anticipation made her eyes bright and her skin radiant. This was the best summer ever, because Idris had stayed behind in Sudan. Even Uncle Mahmoud and Nabilah were held up in Cairo. So day and night, in this most wonderful of cities, Soraya and Nur were chaperoned by the most indulgent and inefficient of patriarchs – Nassir Abuzeid. Yesterday he had given them permission to go the cinema. Alone. Fatma had protested and nearly persuaded him to withdraw his consent, but Nur and Soraya made a dash for it and were out of the door before Nassir could change his mind.

In the silver darkness of the cinema, during the boring newscast before the film began, Nur whispered to Soraya and made her giggle.

'Baranah. I can't believe we are by ourselves! Baranah.'

The theme of this summer, its signature tune, were the lyrics: I love you, Soraya ... I love you, too.

'Will you marry me?'

This he said in English. It sounded formal and made her laugh. Who else would she marry? Who else *could* she marry? Her father, who in her eyes was a villain thwarting her every desire, would not dare, in his meanest of streaks, deny her the son of his eldest brother.

She put on her new glasses to watch the film. They were brand new and made her see as well as everyone else. The glasses were part of the summer. Away from her father and his disapproval, she had gone with Fatma to an eye doctor, chaperoned by the ever-generous Nassir, who paid all the bills and promised that he would never, drunk or sober, say a word to anyone lest it reached Idris. The prescription, tailored specially

70

for Soraya, was superior to that of the pair Nur had given her all those months ago in Umdurman and instead of heavy, thick frames, these were petal shaped, delicately feminine, with a slight point on each side and a dash of glamour provided by a gold stud in each corner. Nassir paid for this fancy pair of ladies' spectacles. He was in the best of positions – he was with funds. After months of reducing his allowance in Medani, his father had relented and given him his usual lavish holiday supplement. Nassir hired himself a motor car, made contacts with his friends who were also summering, and threw himself into the nightlife entertainment of downtown Alexandria. Fatma's protests were silenced with enough money to keep her shopping every day, and Soraya's glasses, too, were a bribe, to buy her goodwill and support. When she wore them she felt sophisticated, like a woman of twenty-eight, not a schoolgirl. They made her look intelligent, as if she had graduated from university and had opinions.

'I want to start smoking,' she whispered to Nur. 'I want a cigarette.'

'Now?'

He was taken aback. Sometimes she glimpsed a childish sweetness in him, a simplicity that was embedded and would not go away with time and age.

'Well, no. But one day.'

It was the glasses that made her crave a cigarette between her fingers. She wanted the sophisticated look, high heels . . .

'Shush and watch the film,' he said, squeezing her arm and guiding her mind back to the opening credits.

Fareed Al-Atrash's latest film was his best and they floated out of the cinema with the tunes playing in their heads, the lyrics jumbled and half memorised. The Corniche was lively with lights and street vendors, the waves a background rhythm with the frills of their white foam a decoration. It was as if no one was asleep. Even the children, odd in their clothes after the beach nakedness of the day, their faces shiny with sunburn, were

71

grabbing popcorn, candy floss and grilled corn as if they had not eaten all day. The breeze lifted dresses, and if Soraya had straight hair, it would have got tossed and tangled. Nur held her hand and they walked arm in arm like other couples did, unthinkable in Sudan or in the presence of anyone they knew. Here, husbands and wives linked arms, whereas back home they did not even walk side by side. This was what Soraya wanted for them, to be a modern couple, not to be like Fatma and Nassir each in their separate world.

She said to him, 'I wish we could stay here forever. When you graduate, ask Uncle Mahmoud to let you work in the Cairo office.'

'It's dull in the Cairo office,' he said. 'The real work is in Sudan.'

'But it is so much fun here!'

She was used to pleading for what she wanted, for her whims and passing fancies. And she knew the need to wait for what she wanted, while continuing with the gentle application of pressure. But she sensed a restlessness in Nur, even before he spoke.

'Let's go back home. If we're too late, there will be a row.'

There was something he wasn't telling her, but she would tease it out of him.

'What's the hurry?'

She stopped walking as if to make a point and sat on the low stone ledge that separated the Corniche from the beach below.

'You'd laugh,' he said, his hands in his pocket.

'I won't, I promise.'

People passed and left bits of their conversations; words in Greek and Arabic, French and English.

He looked down and said in a low voice, 'I want to write down the lyrics from the film's songs before I forget them.'

She had promised not to laugh and it was an easy promise to keep.

'I can help you. I can jog your memory.'

'No. I want to do it myself.'

There were corners in him that she didn't have access to. The part of him that wrote the poems, his masculinity, and a purity she did not share. Inside her was selfishness and impatience, unforgiveness and self-pity, all camouflaged by a wholehearted love for others and a delightful femininity. Her nature was immature and wobbly, faults that a mother's sound care would have corrected.

On the last afternoon that she loved the sea, she walked with Nur on the beach. She did not have her glasses on, but that was all right; there was nothing detailed she needed to focus on, nothing tricky. Nur had arrived without his friends, had left them behind in Sidi Bishr so that he could be with her. On the way he had gone to change and was now wearing his swimming trunks and a white shirt. They walked along the edge of the water because Soraya had seen other couples do that and she wanted to imitate them. Her arm brushed against Nur's arm. They were the same height, the same build, the same colour. Their feet pushed into the wet sand and once in a while the froth of a wave would encircle their ankles. The beach was not flat. It dipped gradually to the water and, in other places, steeply, yet the stronger waves reached up higher and further. The beach was scattered with umbrellas. Each had a different design but they were all colourful and gay. Rainbow stripes, polka dots, bright greens and the orange Abuzeid umbrella they were walking away from had different shades like the segments of an orange.

He said, 'Why don't you swim?'

The red flag was hoisted today, which meant that the sea was boisterous but swimming was still allowed. A black flag meant keep away, and when the white flag fluttered, the sea was calm as a carpet.

She lifted her dress up to her knee as a wave splashed up and reached them.

'I don't have a bathing suit.'

'We'll go and buy you one.'

She laughed and dropped her dress. Their feet were imprinted in the wet sand and the imprint would last until the next strong wave.

'I don't know how to swim.'

'I'll teach you.' He held her hand, which meant they were out of sight of Fatma and Nassir.

'I knew you'd say this.'

'Say what?'

'Say you'd teach me.' She had to raise her voice above the sound of the waves.

'I am sure you will learn in no time.'

'I don't know any girls who swim.'

'Not a single one?'

'Not one.' But she did not sound so certain. 'Apart from Nabilah.' Every summer Nabilah shocked the Abuzeid women by donning her striped navy swimsuit, pushing her hair in a white cap and striding into the waves. But Nabilah was Egyptian. 'I wouldn't be allowed to swim,' said Soraya. She stopped walking and waved her hand towards the orange umbrella. 'Have you seen Fatma this summer? She's refusing even to wear a dress. Every summer since I can remember we come here and wear dresses. This time she's saying she's married, so she shouldn't take off her tobe!'

'She was married last year and the year before. What got into her?' He started to walk again.

She followed him. 'Fatma would never allow me to wear a swimsuit.'

'I'll talk her into it.'

She believed him. He could do that.

'My father would have a heart attack,' she said with a giggle.

'He's not here. Tonight we'll buy you the swimsuit and tomorrow your lessons start.'

She imagined a dazzling white swimsuit, her long legs bare on the sand, his eyes on them. She held his hand tight.

74

'Is it difficult to swim?'

'No, it's easy. Diving is harder. I'll teach you to dive too.'

She gasped and laughed at the same time. 'Even Nabilah doesn't dive.'

'Why do you talk about her so much?'

'Do I?'

'Yes, you're always going on – Nabilah does this, Nabilah said that.'

Soraya was taken aback. She did not want her admiration for Nabilah to be questioned, because it was not reciprocated. Nabilah had no time or sympathy for her, but Soraya was confident that she could win her over in time.

'You're still against her! You just don't like her, do you?'

He raised his eyebrows. 'Am I supposed to, when she causes my mother so much grief?'

'She doesn't mean to.'

'She knew my father was married. She knew he had grown-up children so why did she marry him? Because of his money, that's why!'

He was blaming Nabilah to avoid blaming his father, but Soraya understood why her uncle had married Nabilah. She could imagine clearly his desperation to move from the hoash to a salon with a pretty, cultured wife by his side. Everyone loved Uncle Mahmoud, even though they were in awe of him. It made her say, 'I would trade you my father for Uncle Mahmoud and Nabilah any day.'

He laughed. 'Uncle Idris? Keep him.'

'Do you hate him because he tore up your poem?'

'And the things he said.' He wasn't smiling any more. 'He certainly knew how to stop it in me.'

His bitterness did not surprise her.

'Just ignore him and keep writing.'

He sat down on the sand and looked out at the sea.

'It doesn't come to me any more. As if it's all gone dull inside. I read collections, I memorise whole poems, and I copy down the lyrics of songs that I like, but that poem he tore up was the last one I composed.'

She tucked her dress behind her knees and sat next to him.

'Can't you make yourself do it? Like homework?'

'No, it's not like that. Besides, I don't care for it any more. No, that's not true, I *do* care but I don't have hope that I can amount to anything as a poet. After university, I am going to join the family business; I am not going to become a poet, so there is no point in wasting my time on it. Every family has a vocation. We are traders, not scholars or army men. We are men of the souq, not rulers or judges or engineers. Our great-grandfather started with one dingy shop in the Souq Al-Arabi and look how far we've come. Father has invested so much in my education and Nassir is not pulling his weight. I can't deviate and be something else.'

He sounded grown-up and realistic, pushing back childish dreams. But it still seemed sad and she did not know what to say to him. Should she console him or applaud him? His words were heavy, too serious for this golden beach and holiday breeze.

'Come on, let's walk back.'

He stood up and they turned, retracing their footsteps, surprised that in many places the smudged imprints of their feet were unruffled by the reach of the waves. She felt him soften next to her, settle back to his normal, easy mood.

'I have big feet for a girl, nearly as big as yours! Sometimes in shops I can't find my size.'

They measured their feet against each other. He dug his right foot in the sand and then she nestled hers in the imprint. His feet, they concluded, were slightly but definitely larger.

Nur picked up a shell. He brushed away the damp sand from it and made it look like ivory. It was flatter and wider than the shells the fortune tellers used back in Umdurman.

'Have you ever had your fortune told?' she asked.

'Yes. It was all nonsense. I didn't like it.'

'Oh, I love to have my fortune told. It's exciting.'

He smiled and put the shell in her hand, closed her fingers over it. They were quiet for a while, facing the direction of the orange umbrella and the moss-covered rocks, reluctant to traverse the distance.

'Do you know what time Nassir came home last night?' He was smiling. 'Three in the morning. I know because he made such a clatter and woke me up.'

She laughed. She had started to feel kinder towards Nassir this summer, especially after he had purchased her glasses.

'Next week Uncle Mahmoud will come and he'll have to behave himself.'

'Yes.' Nur smiled. 'No more parties and no more belly dancers.'

'Belly dancers!' Her eyes widened.

'What did you think – that his nights were men only?'

She shrugged. 'I didn't really think about it.'

'Maybe he'll take us with him one night.'

'Us?'

'Yes. You and I. We'll go to a cabaret. You'll like the show.'

A cabaret. Did she have anything to wear for that? She imagined wine-coloured chairs and laughter, cigarette smoke and English soldiers, Greek girls dancing and, at the end of the evening, the voluptuous belly dancer. No! It would be one prank too many. They would never get away with it. Nur had a mischievous look on his face and she responded to his delight, his sense of adventure. He started to tell her about a night he and his schoolmates had gone to the Petit Trianon. Behind the sweet counter was a ballroom where a band played and couples danced. She listened, enraptured, and he put his arm around her waist as if they were dancing in the European way. It made her laugh out loud, but they were close enough to see Fatma waving at them to come back. Soraya couldn't make out the expression on her face.

77

'I wish she was the short-sighted sister,' said Nur and this made her laugh in a different way.

They quickened their footsteps towards the umbrella.

'If we had walked in the other direction, we could have sat on the rocks,' said Nur.

The rocks were covered with slippery green moss, a lurid green in contrast to the beige sand and pale blue water. It was not a colour Soraya favoured and she was glad they had not sat on the rocks. Perhaps the moss and the seaweed would have stained her new dress.

'Tomorrow,' she said to him. Tomorrow, when she would be wearing her new bathing suit.

Nassir woke up when they ducked under the umbrella and threw themselves on the sand.

'Zeinab, come and give me a kiss,' said Soraya. 'These cheeks of yours, I just have to pinch them.' She cuddled her niece while Nur grabbed the newspaper off Nassir's belly and started to read it.

Fatma, as expected, was annoyed. She whispered to Soraya, 'Every day you two get more ridiculous than the day before. Behave, girl.'

'Tell him, don't tell me.' She wanted to tease Fatma. It was amusing to see her angry.

'I will tell him. You think I won't? He shouldn't be spending so much time with you alone.'

'Why not? There's nothing wrong with it.'

'Soraya, behave or I will send you back.'

'Back where?'

'Back to Cairo. Back to Umdurman.'

This was so far-fetched that it didn't have a sting to it.

Soraya laughed and gave her sister a hug. 'When Uncle Mahmoud and Nabilah come every single one of us will be behaving properly.' This was a reference to Nassir, and Fatma made a face.

'Go play with them,' Nassir was saying to Nur. 'Why not? Go join them.'

Soraya turned to see that a football game had started further back in the beach where the sand was completely dry. Three men were kicking a ball; they were in their bathing trunks with their hair cut short.

'Don't you know they're English soldiers?' Nur didn't look up and turned to a new page.

'So what?' Nassir said. 'You're the captain of the football team at Victoria. Tell them that.'

'Nassir, you go and play with them,' said Soraya and Nur chuckled.

'Me!' Nassir heaved himself up to an upright position. 'Can't you see I am out of shape?'

Nur folded the newspaper. 'You used to be a fair player.'

'Back then . . .' Nassir reclined back and folded his hands on his stomach.

'Baba, look. The fresca man is coming. I want some,' Zeinab pointed to the man with the white hat and large glass box balanced on his shoulders. He was loping towards them, making his way at the edge of the water.

Nassir hailed him and he came over and knelt on the sand, balancing the box on one knee. They all leaned forward to see what he was offering.

'I want the coconut,' said Soraya.

'I want the flat one with the honey,' said Zeinab.

'Give us a mixture,' said Fatma.

Nassir reached for his leather pouch. It was a characteristically slow gesture. He prized the pouch open and, with care, started to take the coins out. He was enjoying the process, enjoying paying for something, giving up money to get something in return. He had looked like that when he had paid for her glasses, generous, not questioning the amount. Soraya felt a fondness for him.

They munched in silence. Soraya enjoyed the sweetness of

79

the coconut and the delicate crunch of the wafer. Nur had the one with the sticky peanuts. He bit half of one and gave her the rest. She dug her teeth in the honeyed peanuts and felt a surge of joy. This was his saliva she was tasting, and his lips.

The football rolled towards them. Nur was quick to stand up, place his foot on it and dribble away from the umbrella in the direction of the game. With one kick, he joined the game. He did not have to announce that he was captain of the school team; his footwork was enough for the soldiers to welcome him.

Nassir turned his deckchair, giving his back to the sea and his full concentration to the game. He shouted out comments in English, jovial and witty, to endear himself to the soldiers. Soraya could sense Nur showing off, conscious of the expectations of his older brother. He put all his energy into the game and was soon enjoying himself.

Soraya chatted with Fatma and played with the children. The football didn't interest her, but watching Nur run was a pleasure, and she liked the English she was hearing from the soldiers, natural and fluent, not like the sentences in school books. The one who was called Stan had an accent she had not heard before; he was stocky and had freckles. Eddie was handsome, like an actor in a film. His hair was black and his nose was sharp. The third, who ended up in goal, looked older and more muscular, and she did not catch his name. Later, when she went over everything, when she spoke about that day – again and again – she would remember the game and see the players clearly in her mind. How they grunted and Stan became red in the face. How often Eddie swore and how Nur started to perspire.

Another group of players joined in. The newcomers, young Egyptians, challenged Nur and the soldiers. This was how a friendly languorous kicking of the ball turned into a serious match. A masculine dedication she could not share, though in the pit of her stomach she wanted Nur's team to win and she wanted Nur to score again.

'Clap for your uncle, children!'

Even Fatma clapped and laughed. Nassir was beside himself with excitement. He raised his arms up in the air every time there was a goal, and when the other team had the ball, he made kicking gestures with his feet, tossing up gusts of sand. Soraya sensed the sun change position and start to mellow into mid-afternoon. They should head home for lunch now. The baby had started to whine and Fatma was getting restless.

'We won!' Nassir raised his arm in the air for one last time. Nur came towards them drenched in sweat. He took off his shirt and said, 'I'm going into the water to cool off.' He ran towards the sea before they could detain him.

'Don't be long,' Fatma called after him.

'It's lunchtime,' said Nassir.

Nur swivelled around and, trotting backwards, waved to them and mouthed, 'Just a few minutes.'

There was an anti-climax after that, a drop after the game and Nur not being present to talk about it. The soldiers drifted past their umbrella and sat at the edge of the water on the damp sand, Eddie sat with his legs straight in the water. He scooped handfuls of water and wet his hair and shoulders. Stan lay on his back and, when a strong wave reached him, he let the water pull him closer to the sea, laughing out loud.

Soraya watched Nur climb the moss-covered rock and dive in the sea. Next to her Nassir rubbed his stomach.

'I'm hungry.'

She was hungry, too. Their late breakfast of sausages, fried eggs and ta'miyyah had long been digested, the fresca too miniscule a snack to go far. Come on, Nur. Fatma started to gather their things together. Soraya didn't want to help her; she wanted to watch Nur dive again. She saw him, blurred and brown, climb the low cliff again and dive. Could she really learn to dive like that? Her mind wandered to buying her new and very first swimsuit. Would she try it on in the shop or just take it home?

She looked back at the sea and couldn't see Nur. She blinked and narrowed her eyes, which always made her see better but he was not there. She stood up and untangled her handbag from the spokes of the umbrella. She took her glasses out of their case and put them on. There he was! He was floating, his body straight and bobbing, the waves moving him around. He disappeared from sight as the sea dipped and, beneath him, a wave swept forward and rolled upwards. He was playing a game, she guessed, seeing how long he could hold his breath. She moved towards the sea, magnetised by the oddity of his pose. Something was not right. He should be swimming again now. She started to run; behind her, the surprise in Fatma's voice, calling out. Stan and Eddie looked up and watched her run directly towards them. They kept watching her instead of looking out to the sea. She wanted to shout but the waves were too loud. When she stopped running, her voice came back. In English, that was important, so that they would understand. Help. Help was the word. She pointed and screamed.

Stan and Eddie ran into the sea. She walked forward until her calves were deep in the water, the hem of her dress soaked and heavy. Eddie and Stan lifted Nur's arms and put them round their shoulders. He wouldn't pull a prank on them. Not on them. They half-dragged, half-swam, half-carried him towards the shore and he wasn't helping them in any way. His head was lolling to one side. She felt ashamed for him, because he looked bad and was so needy of help. The shame was visceral, as if it was hers, not his. When they laid him down on the wet sand, he spluttered and spat, raising his head but not sitting up or rolling sideways. He opened his eyes and closed them. Nassir was next to her now.

'What happened?' His voice was soft with concern. 'What's wrong with him?'

Eddie and Stan crouched on either side of Nur, pumping his chest, talking to one another over him. Their bodies dripped with water. Soraya and Nassir stayed back. When she heard Nur's voice, when Stan sat back on his heels and Eddie stood up, she rushed forward, flooded with relief.

'Nur, get up. Nur, let's go home.'

She wanted the soldiers to go away, she wanted the day to be normal again.

Behind her Nassir was full of effusive thanks. The English words tumbled out of him. He was generous in his praise and his manners pleased the soldiers. They moved away from Nur. Stan smiled broadly; Eddie shook Nassir's outstretched hand. Nassir moved next to Soraya and sank to his knees. He lunged forward, embracing his brother. Nur didn't raise his arms to hug him back. One arm lay outstretched, entwined with seaweed; the other, motionless too, was at an awkward angle, the fingers grazing the sand.

'Nur,' she said. 'Come on.'

'He's resting,' Nassir said. 'Let him rest.'

But she insisted, 'Nur.'

He looked up at her as if he was distracted by a supreme heaviness that bewildered and absorbed him.

'I can't,' he said. 'I can't move.'

VII

This was the day Nabilah, empowered by her native Cairo, started to contemplate divorce and the right to stay here forever, not go back with Mahmoud to Sudan at the end of summer. The day she started to contemplate the right to a normal life like that of her mother, the girls she had gone to school with, and the neighbour's daughters. Enough of this African adventure, of being there while thinking of here, of being here and knowing it was temporary; enough of the dust, the squalor and the stupidity. Enough of buildings that were too low, gardens that were too lush and skies that were too close. Enough of his large family, his acres of land, and his connections, of money without culture, prestige among the primitive. She would put an end to it all: an end to being inferior because she was the second wife, and of being superior because she was Egyptian. Enough of these contradictions! Life should be simple: a man who goes to work and comes back the same time every day; a good climate and uncomplicated children; outings on Friday; a picnic or a walk – everything proper and understandable. Why did she not deserve this? Why had she, in the first place, been married off to a foreigner, a man old enough to be her father? Was something wrong with her? Did she have a defect?

These questions inflamed her with a sense of injustice. There was no defect in her. This was a fact. She was beautiful. She came from a good home. She was well brought up. If she was not beautiful, he would have not have stopped dead in his tracks that first time he saw her sepia-coloured portrait displayed in the window of the photographer. Indeed, that photographer himself, on Midan Soliman Pasha, would not have chosen her portrait out of so many, had she not been outstanding. A man looks into a shop window and catches sight of something that is useful, special or visually pleasing. He says to himself, 'I must have that.' Perhaps other men, too, walking in downtown Cairo had also stopped and gazed at her picture. Other men too might have desired and thought, 'That's the kind of girl for me.' But Mahmoud Abuzeid had gone further; he had put desire into action, had tracked down the name to match the pretty face, an address, a family history. He had engineered an introduction to her stepfather, endeared himself to her mother, and made his move.

Years ago, when they had first got engaged, she had loved that story, the search for the girl in the portrait. What girl wouldn't be proud of such a story?

'He just had to have her. He couldn't get her out of his mind. Would you believe how much he offered the photographer for that portrait? Based on this, you can extrapolate how much he paid for her dowry!' It was the stuff of dreams and gossip, as magical as the cinema. She had, her eighteen-year-old eyes shining, swelled with a new sense of self-worth, the pride that she had made her mother happy. In those heady days of courtship and gifts, Qadriyyah would embrace her and say, 'Look at the pearl necklace he bought you! Look at the diamond ring. You will be the most beautiful bride. To think that I felt you were a burden when your father died. To think that I was anxious day and night about your prospects as an orphan!'

When Nabilah said the word 'divorce', she was in her mother's kitchen with its smell of fresh mint and coriander. All year in Sudan, she had missed this kitchen, with its little balcony cluttered with baskets of onions and potatoes. On the shutters, garlic hung from a net and the bird cage was there, too, a large one with two parrots. From where she was sitting at the kitchen table, Nabilah could see the neighbour's balcony and their washing hanging on the line. A young boy in his pyjamas was leaning over the edge as if he were talking to someone in the street below.

Qadriyyah, in her navy blue dressing gown, was kneading dough. She had taken off her rings and was pressing down on the pastry mix, folding it, and pressing again. Her hands were small and plump, but strong, the nails manicured. She was a solid, compact woman who looked as if she was wearing a corset even when she wasn't. Her hair, which she dyed, was a glistening, unnatural black. It was thick and wavy and she considered it her best feature. Nabilah expected her mother to be alarmed at the mention of the word divorce. She wanted her to be concerned.

'Why?' Qadriyyah did not look up. 'What has he done to upset you?'

'Haven't I explained in my letters? It is everything about my life there, and nothing specific.'

'Do you think marriage is a game? Have you forgotten you have two children?'

'Our life there is not like here,' Nabilah replied. 'He is so much a part of his family, of his wife and all the customs. He is Sudanese like them and I'm just not happy with that.'

'Not happy!' She slapped the dough back in the bowl. 'You live in a palace, waited upon by a drove of servants. You said that Mahmoud Bey entertains a lot and you wanted a chef from here, so we got you one. You said you want a nanny from here, and we sent you one. Every single summer, you come here and spend three months. All of this and you are complaining?'

Nabilah did not know how to answer. Sometimes unhappiness seemed like the symptom of a malady that had no name, but flared up and calmed down on its own accord.

Qadriyyah looked her in the eye.

'Does he hit you?'

'Of course not!'

'Are there other women?'

'No, nothing like that.'

'Well, what is it then? Because he certainly isn't being stingy with you!'

'He is more than generous, Mama,' she sighed.

'Then shut up and thank your Lord! Look around you and see what other wives are enduring. If he divorces you, who will support you and your children at the high standard your highness is used to? Do you think your stepfather and I will take you in? Think again.'

Nabilah didn't reply and there was a tense silence between them.

Qadriyyah pushed the dough into a ball and turned to look for the roller.

'You will make me ill with your complaints.'

'I'm sorry, Mama. I just want to be with you all the time, to see you all year round.'

'Grow up, Nabilah,' Qadriyyah sighed. 'You are not a little girl any more. It disgusts me how ungrateful you are.'

When Nabilah walked out of the kitchen, she felt chastened and unsteady. But she also knew that she had not been given a fair trial and that she had not said everything she wanted to say. This was not Qadriyyah's fault; it was hers, for not having the right words, for not presenting a convincing grievance or sufficient evidence.

Entertaining the English couple was hardly a burden she could complain of. They were staying in the Semiramis and not with Nabilah and Mahmoud in their Garden City apartment, yet she regarded them as an intrusion on her precious summer in Cairo. She still hadn't visited her grand-mother and was longing to see her. She had not taken the children for cakes at Groppi's, and she had not seen an Egyptian film in the cinema.

'Why must we be with them every day?' she asked Mahmoud when they first arrived.

'Because,' he finished combing his moustache in front of the mirror, 'he is the manager of Barclays Bank.'

'But we never go out by ourselves, just you, me, and the children. We could go to the zoo.'

He made a face. 'The zoo? Be reasonable. It would be dull.'

'My father always used to take me for outings. He didn't think it beneath him.'

Mahmoud grunted as he tucked his handkerchief into the breast pocket of his jacket. 'We're all going to Alexandria next week. The children will have all the enjoyment at the beach. Come on, let's go. We mustn't keep them waiting.'

For days it had been the same. She had watched him fawn on Mr and Mrs Harrison, wine and dine Mr and Mrs Harrison, chauffeur and amuse Nigel and Sue Harrison. When she questioned the amount of money he was spending on them, Mahmoud laughed and said, 'This is nothing compared to the loan he granted me. I need to be on excellent terms with this man, and I want you to take good care of his wife.'

Sue Harrison, according to Nabilah's assessment, was lacking in sophistication and beauty. The short hair was unbecoming, the clothes austere and the shoes too sensible. However, Sue's enthusiasm, her *oohs* and *aahs*, her *darling* this and *darling* that, made her captivating. Her complexion was gorgeous, too; milky white, with the rosiest of cheeks. The young woman was optimistic about her future in the Sudan to an extent that made Nabilah spiteful. Her warnings of perpetual dust, infernal heat and a host of creepy crawlies fell on deaf ears. Sue was in love and happy that she was going to Sudan. The couple was on an extension of their honeymoon. They had already spent a fortnight in Devon and, en route to Sudan, were lingering in Cairo before a cruise down the Nile and a stay in Luxor and Abu Simbel. How fortunate it was that Mahmoud Abuzeid was in Cairo at the same time! What a charming and generous host!

Nabilah struggled to match her husband's goodwill. Yesterday morning had been spent visiting the Pyramids, and Sue and Nigel wanted to climb the Great Pyramid. Although Mahmoud had long recovered from his illness of last autumn, he felt it prudent not to exert himself and, out of politeness, Nabilah accompanied the couple. The women did not get very far, each stone was too large to surmount and the wind was dusty and irritating, so they sat together, waving down to Mahmoud and up to Nigel who was attempting to reach the top. Nabilah watched the other groups below, haggling with the photographers and those who offered donkey and camel rides. As a hostess, she must offer her guests the opportunity to have their photograph taken astride a camel with the pyramid in the background . . .

Afterwards, they strolled down to the Sphinx and she saved Nigel from buying an overpriced fake scarab. By then they were hungry and it was time to drive in Mahmoud's Buick for lunch at Mena House. They could gaze at the pyramids while they ate, and Nabilah felt proud of her country in the company of the three foreigners. She even smiled when Mahmoud inevitably told the Harrisons the anecdote she heard every time they came to the Mena House.

'When Roosevelt and Churchill met here at the end of the war, the RAF had an observation post above the Cheops pyramid.'

In the afternoon, back in the apartment, Mahmoud had his siesta while she punished the children for throwing their toys out of the window. Accustomed to the saraya in Umdurman, they did not understand that they were now in an apartment overlooking the street. However, their ignorance only increased her disappointment that they were not normal, well bred Cairo children, but half-castes, stigmatised by the boorish, backward Sudan.

In the evening it was time to meet up again with the Harrisons, this time for dinner at St James. While eating, they watched a cinema show, this being a specialty of the venue. Nabilah felt a pang of guilt that she had been so harsh with the children. She wished she were at home, putting them to bed and making amends. Now they would go to sleep believing she was still angry with them. She visualised her daughter's arms around her neck. Ferial had thin arms, but a firm grasp. She heard her son's voice calling out to her. Farouk's voice was like no one else's; it had a warble and she could never mistake it. But *Samson and*

Delilah soon absorbed her and she began to enjoy her excellent dish of Nile Perch and asparagus.

After dessert, they went to the Auberge des Pyramids. It was the first time Nabilah had walked through the red and gilt interior, and this made her feel close to Sue, sharing the same first experience. The band was outdoors and they sat in the garden close to the dance floor where a French singer crooned and made flippant remarks that amused the audience. Mahmoud, the only one who had been to the Auberge before, was pleased to point out the luminaries at the other tables. Over there was a Pasha, a confidante of King Farouk, and at the next table was Major Fitzgerald who owned an extensive collection of Islamic Art. Nabilah ran her eyes over the gowns of the ladies. Her heart skipped a beat when she recognised a House of Dior, and she began to talk to Sue about fashion, sharing her speculations and appraisals. It surprised and flattered her to discover that she knew the names of the famous fashion houses and their creations better than Sue.

'I have never heard so many champagne corks popping,' remarked Sue, and her husband laughed and looked at her fondly.

They got up to dance, clearly in love, clearly happy. It made Nabilah envious but also confused. She was not sure what she was longing for, what it was she wanted and didn't want.

The entertainment's highlight was the belly dancer Samia Gamal.

'She is superior!' Mahmoud proclaimed, delighted to be the one to introduce Mr and Mrs Harrison to their first experience of oriental dance. 'She danced at our wedding, didn't she, Nabilah?'

'Yes, she was a new star then.'

Nabilah was feeling sleepy because she had missed her siesta. She would have liked Mahmoud to wrap up the evening, but he was just beginning an anecdote.

'During the war, King Farouk freighted one hundred kilos of

Groppi chocolates to Princesses Elizabeth and Margaret. I am not exaggerating. I know about this because the airplane came to Khartoum.' He moved his wineglass out of the way and jabbed an imaginary map on the tablecloth. 'This was the route the airplane took, a roundabout route because of the necessities of the war: Cairo – Khartoum – Entebbe, then Dakar, Lisbon and finally Dublin.'

The conversation started to seem to Nabilah like splotches of paint; bright colours of similar shape that didn't connect or make a whole. She made an effort to keep her eyes open. Mr Harrison mentioned something he had read. Sue made an observation.

'Our room has an absolutely marvellous view of the Nile.'

'He has been exiled, is living comfortably, very comfortably if I may say so, while his family back home are destitute.'

'Life here is not as good for the British as it is in the Sudan. There are too many restrictions regarding their post and their travel.'

In contact with this couple every day, doing things and going places, eating and laughing, would they draw closer and become intimate friends? Would they build a liaison that would last? Nabilah sensed in herself a loneliness, a fractured spirit that no one could share or understand. And early the next morning, in a hurried visit to her mother before taking the Harrisons to the museum, she sat in that kitchen she was fond of and for the first time said out loud the word divorce.

The Cairo museum was even more of a success with their guests than the Pyramids. Their main interest was the treasures found in the tomb of Tutankhamen.

'We have read so much about these relics,' said Nigel Harrison. 'How extraordinary that all this wealth was unearthed by accident!'

The four of them gazed at the solid gold coffin, the heavily decorated throne, the vases, alabaster and gems, at the beauty of the golden mask that had covered the head of the mummy. Tutankhamen, a boy king, not more than nineteen: such a short, tragic life, yet his name would live forever. They stood, awed by the sight of so much wealth, craft and hard beauty. Afterwards, Nabilah felt drained, and it seemed that she was not alone for the others, too, were subdued over their lunch on the Shepheard's roof garden.

'What would they have done without you?' she praised her husband as they drove home. 'They would have been quite limited in their activities and restricted in their movement without a car.'

She had said the right thing. He was pleased, even though he didn't say so. She ventured to share her observations with him.

'There are two things I've learnt these past days about the English. They have a long breath.' He smiled and this encouraged her to elaborate. 'They could go on and on, without breaking down or even resting. It is not excessive energy or greed but an innate, steady longevity, a lasting strength. Secondly, and that was more surprising, they believe everything they are told. Their style is to ask a direct question and expect an honest reply.'

'Whatever you say, they are better than many.'

If he were less proud, he would have said 'better than us'. If he were less diplomatic, he would have said 'better than you'.

When they walked into the flat, the telephone rang. It was clear from the extended ring that it was a long distance call. Mahmoud picked up the receiver and spoke to the operator.

'It's Alexandria,' he said to her with a smile. He liked receiving telephone calls. Connecting with people was vital to him.

He greeted Nassir in a loud voice and then listened. His face became grave.

'When did this happen? Has he been seen by a doctor? Yes, I will come now.'

She packed a suitcase for him and watched as he opened the safe and took from it a huge wad of cash. He gave her more than enough for the household expenditure and put the rest in his pocket. For the next hour she was absorbed in the drama of his hurried departure. The unplanned journey, the many instructions and tasks he set her, overshadowed in her mind Nur's accident at the seaside. She was excited by the unexpectedness of the day's events, and how they would impact on her. When he finally left, she found herself alone, and it was as if a prayer had been answered, a gift bestowed on her, the responsibility lifted from her shoulders. She was here, in Cairo, and she could do whatever she wanted.

She was out of breath when she reached the bus station. She had been walking fast, clutching her purse, aware of the swish of her dress and the tap of her high heels. Now she felt at ease because she was just another Egyptian lady, attractive and elegant, waiting for the bus like everyone else. A truck full of English soldiers passed and several of them waved; one blew her a kiss. When she was younger, she used to giggle and wave back. Now she only smiled and looked away.

A familiar sight, the bedraggled seller – it couldn't be the same man – who stood at bus stops and sold all sorts of little delights – hairpins, sweets, marbles and matches. She opened her purse. Yes, she had enough money, more than enough. Mahmoud had taught her this. Sometimes he didn't carry enough change and he depended on her.

'Give me a shilling,' he would say or, 'Give me a franc.' The first time he made this request, her purse had been empty. 'Never, ever leave the house without money,' he reprimanded her. 'You never know when you will need it.'

She needed crystal sugar from the street-seller now, a little bag of it. How much sweeter it tasted than any of the fancy desserts she had shared with the Harrisons.

The bus came and she boarded it. Anticipation. This was *her* outing, *her* treat. Why didn't she say to Mahmoud days ago, 'Take me to see my grandmother'? It had not even occurred to her to ask him, as if he and her grandmother lived in different cities. Her grandmother was a link to her father, a link to the past. She had fallen out with Qadriyyah when she remarried. They were no longer on speaking terms, which was why Nabilah visited her grandmother behind Qadriyyah's back. These were precious visits, stolen moments, because her mother always wanted to know her whereabouts.

Nabilah sucked a lump of sugar and, from the bus window, watched the people in the street. It was a quiet time of day, the streets almost empty with so many families away in Alexandria for the summer holidays. Some employees were heading home. So few wore their fez these days, keeping it for formal occasions, not as it was in her father's time. How different her life would have been, had he been alive. They would not have moved to Cairo so soon, for he would have continued to be a provincial judge for some years. And she had loved Cairo, even before she came to live in it. When she was young, all the vacations were spent with her grandmother; joyful days when her father was no longer solemn and important but a cheerful, boastful son. Qadriyyah always spoke of Cairo and wherever they were posted, whatever location or status, Qadriyyah would remind her daughter that Cairo was better. Cairo was bigger; the mother of the world.

She spotted the green curtain billowing in the balcony of the second floor. It was time to get off. This was her stop. She crossed King Street and entered the side road. The grocer with the strong smell of Rumi cheese and the pails of olives, the butcher with the meat swinging on hooks, and her favourite, the juice shop with pyramids of fruit displayed in its window and sticks of sugarcane propped against the doorway. How often had she stood in her grandmother's balcony, pushing away the heavy green curtain and gazing down at this row of shops? Why, right now her grandmother might be sitting behind the curtain, not knowing that in a few minutes Nabilah would ring the bell! She quickened her pace. The staircase was stone-cool after the heat of outdoors. Each landing had two flats, arranged around a central gallery. The gallery was a perfect, wide circle, so that, looking up, she saw circles upon circles bathed in sunlight. This had fascinated her as a child, and she would skip around the gallery, completing the circle and returning to her beloved Nenah's flat.

The maid opened the door for her, a new maid who did not recognise her, but this did not dampen Nabilah's spirits. She strode across the hall and the sitting room to the balcony, and in the shade of the green canvas curtain, in her grandmother's arms, it was the fulfilment of a dream, the sweetness of a long separation coming to an end. Nabilah did not cry – she was not prone to sentimental tears, but she brimmed with pleasure, kissing her grandmother's cheeks, breathing her scent of lavender as if scooping back her childhood.

Her grandmother was tall and thin, with wavy grey hair that she held back in a kerchief. She had a worldly air and yet a light-hearted disposition. Her late husband had been a police officer who had regularly confided, and sometimes even consulted her, in matters of his work. Although she rarely went out, she held an active interest in the affairs of the country and was an avid listener of the radio. Her talent for befriending the young and acting as their confidante ensured that she was never out of touch with modern times. She was delighted to see her granddaughter.

'I did not even know you were in Cairo! How pretty you look! What elegance, what style!'

Nabilah would never hear such compliments back in Sudan. In Umdurman, her clothes highlighted her position as an out-sider, and Khartoum high society was too competitive and capricious to ever voice its admiration.

'I've missed you so much, Nenah!'

'Alhamdulillah, you look well. But where are your children, Nabilah? Why didn't you bring them with you?'

'So that I could have you all to myself, my love. That's why.'

Her grandmother laughed and leaned over to twist the knob

of the radio until it was switched off. They exchanged news and more talk of Nabilah's fashionable blouse. The balcony was furnished with wicker chairs and a matching table; there was a woven rug on the floor, plant pots and jasmine trellises arranged on the wall. It was more luxurious than a typical balcony and more casual than indoors. Now, with the curtain drawn, it was cool and completely secluded from the street as well as the neighbour's range of vision. The bustle reached them, though. A seller cried out 'fresh tomatoes' while another wanted everyone's bric-a-brac. Nabilah walked over and drew the curtain open. Late afternoon sunlight streamed in and she could now see the tomato cart, and the donkey pulling the cart piled with all sorts of bric-a-brac. She picked up the wicker basket that was tied by rope to the ledge.

'Do you want something from the shops, Nabilah?' her grandmother asked.

She smiled and shook her head.

'I just miss this basket. We don't have anything like it in Sudan and here we don't live near shops.'

The basket had fascinated her as a child. How her grandmother, from behind the green curtain, would call down to the grocer, the butcher or passing vegetable sellers. She would tell them what she wanted and lower the basket with the rope. They would place her order in the basket and she would hoist it up. Then she would put money in the empty basket and lower it again. The basket was so sturdy that Nabilah, as a child, would often plead to be placed in it and hoisted up and down.

'You were a lively little girl,' her grandmother said, 'always wanting an adventure or plotting some mischief.'

'Ferial is naughty too,' Nabilah said. 'Farouk is quiet and mostly well-behaved, but he can get up to lots of mischief, too, when everyone's back is turned.'

'May Allah protect them for you, my dear. You will find that the years fly and in no time they will grow up. Then they will

96

be like friends to you and you won't feel lonely or bored because of their company.'

It was easy to talk to her grandmother. Thoughts that were complicated and suppressed took wing and became spoken grievances against the Sudan.

'They have no sewage system and I am disgusted with the buckets and the men coming to empty them at night!'

'The Sudanese circumcise their little girls in the most brutal and severe of ways. Waheeba wanted to circumcise her grand-daughter, Zeinab, but Mahmoud explicitly forbade it.'

'There are no hairdressers in Umdurman, I have to go all the way to Khartoum!'

'Everyone is serious. They don't laugh or joke. They take offence at the slightest rebuke.'

'I get heat rash. If I don't put on talcum powder my skin goes all red. I have to put chamomile lotion on the children, all over their arms and legs.'

'There are things I can't understand. There is no privacy. His eldest son, Nassir, once strolled into our bedroom! And the endless social obligations – they are continuous, really, so that there is no time to do anything else. You know how much I like to sew? It should be a simple pleasure to spread a pattern on the dining table and cut it with scissors or to sit at my sewing machine, but I am always being interrupted by visitors, who come without warning, and if they arrive at mealtimes, they stay and eat. So I must always be dressed for company, I can never stay long in my dressing gown. It is irksome. And how the windows and doors are open all the time! To let in air, but they let in dust as well, and the glaring sun. I feel as if I am roughing it up in a chalet on the beach!

'And it is so hot for so long, like an oven. The winters are not cold enough for winter clothes; a cardigan over a summer frock is all that's needed. I do miss my fur coat. I do miss knitting and crocheting.'

She lowered her voice.

'I am afraid of his wife. The Sudanese practise black magic and she might harm me or the children. She is jealous of me and, of course, she has every reason to be.'

The balcony was enveloped in the soft glow of sunset now. Her grandmother sighed.

'This is the only thing that troubles me about your marriage – his wife. He is a lot older than you, but for many couples that is normal and successful. I don't think of you as being far away; Sudan and Egypt are one country, so you are not like the girls who married Turkish men and moved to Istanbul, you are much closer. But Mahmoud Bey should have divorced his wife before marrying you. He is neither being fair to her or you. I should not say this, but your mother rushed and said yes to his proposal straight away. Qadriyyah was influenced by your stepfather – and you are not his flesh and blood. If your father had been alive, he would not have given his consent.'

This was poignant for Nabilah, but at the same time reassuring. Her father would have protected her. She told her grandmother about this morning's conversation with Qadriyyah.

Her grandmother looked sad and sounded angry.

'What does she mean, you will have nowhere to go? Shame on her! This house is your house, your father's home. My door will be open to you – whatever happens.'

These words, spoken in the gold and green of the balcony, bolstered and pacified Nabilah.

Then, as if she had been paving the ground for a request, her grandmother's voice grew soft and coaxing, 'But why don't you love your husband, my child? Why is your heart hard towards him?'

She could answer now. 'There is a wide distance between us. I am something, and he is something else.'

'Then try and get closer to him,' was the advice. 'Involve yourself in his affairs and concerns. Change, Nabilah, become different. Do it for your children's sake. Do you want them to be without a father, too? You, of all people, who know this deprivation, should not want it for them.'

They went indoors, and while her grandmother prayed maghreb, Nabilah gazed at her father's portraits. In one he was standing, wearing his fez and his judge's robes. He looked large and healthy, with a steady, confident gaze. In another, less formal, portrait, he was sitting down and she, a child of six in a pinafore and felt hat, was standing next to him. She could still remember the handkerchief protruding from the pocket of his jacket. It had a navy border and on that day, after the session with the photographer, she ate candyfloss and used that same hand-kerchief to wipe the pink sugar off her hands.

When her grandmother finished praying, they had tea and cakes. Nabilah caught up with all the news of her paternal family and she had to wrench herself away, knowing she had left the children too long.

'Next time bring them with you. Or, better still, bring them and spend a few days with me. Now that your husband is away, why should you be by yourself?' Such possibilities!

At night she had the luxury and space of a double bed all to herself. She stretched and turned to lie on her side, tucking the pillow under her chin. Her grandmother's kindness had soothed her and given her hope. For weeks now, ever since they had arrived from Khartoum, she had longed to visit her. Every day there was an obstacle, and duties that had to be done. First, she had to quench her thirst for her mother, which was under-standable. Then the Harrisons arrived and she was caught up in a whirl of daily outings and engagements. For Mahmoud, her grandmother was not a priority, many other people came first, but she did not want to think bitter thoughts about him now. She wanted the joy of the afternoon, the green curtain and wicker basket, and her grandmother's support. She wanted this feeling of home to settle inside her until it gave her the sweetest of dreams.

VIII

He walked into a nightmare – the military hospital in Alexandria, with its disinfectant smell and muted atmosphere. There were Nassir, Fatma and Soraya, standing in the corridor, looking anxious and out of place. They were relieved to see him, Nassir not hiding his gratitude at being able to hand over the responsibility. He explained that Nur had been admitted here because Victoria College students were entitled to the same amenities as the British staff and Army personnel.

'It was an accident, Father,' Nassir blurted out. 'It was no one's fault. No one did anything wrong. No one was negligent.' Then, remembering his manners, he offered his father a seat. 'You must be tired after your journey. Have a rest.'

Mahmoud refused to sit down and wanted to see Nur straight away. But . . . enter a room and your son does not spring up to greet you. Walk to the bed and he does not even raise his hand to shake yours.

'Is he asleep?' Mahmoud's voice was loud because he hoped to wake Nur.

He wanted to reassure himself that the boy was well, that nothing serious or drastic had happened to him. His head was lolling to one side and his neck was bandaged. The rest of his body, including his arms, was under the stiff sheets. He looked peaceful, only his hair was uncombed.

'The doctors gave him painkillers,' Nassir explained. 'When we moved him here he was in pain.'

Mahmoud walked over to the window. The orange sun was halfway into the sea. He was lucky to have arrived before dark. The fatigue of the journey was catching up on him, and the siesta he had given up to drive north. He slumped in an armchair near the window and looked round. The room was spacious and immaculate, the bed looked new and modern. Yes, his boy was in a good place, in safe hands; the English doctors would make him better. Here was one now, as evidenced by his white coat and stethoscope, entering the room followed by a nurse. Mahmoud stood up and introduced himself. He found the words slow to conjure; his English was sluggish today, his accent more pronounced.

Dr Hempster was a large man with spectacles and fair hair and his blue eyes reminded Mahmoud of descriptions of General Gordon.

'Your son is lucky to be alive.' He said each word clearly and sounded confident and calm. 'When Mr Abuzeid dived, he must have hit his head either against a sandbank or a rock. Several vertebrae in his lower neck and upper back have been smashed. This is why he is unable to move his limbs. We will need to operate.'

Mahmoud felt confused between the doctor's matter-of-fact tone and the words he was hearing. He wanted to slump back into the armchair, but had to keep standing because it would not be polite. 'If we operate, we can save his life, but it is major, high-risk surgery.'

The room darkened and Mahmoud sank back into the chair, apologising in a faint stream of Arabic. The boundaries of his vision shifted. This situation was new and repulsive; he was in unfamiliar territory, grappling with strange rules and different consequences. Someone held out a glass of water . . . Fatma. He gulped, and immediately felt better. When he looked up, Dr Hempster was not there. Instead, there was Nassir's frightened face and Fatma's anxiety. Soraya was crying; the tears streaking her face, her handkerchief covering her mouth. It distressed him to see her like that. He held out his hand. She took it and burst into fresh tears.

'Why are you crying?' He pretended to scold her, but his

tone was gentle. 'Stop it. Insha'Allah he is going to be all right.'

His words made a visible impact on her. She gulped, took a deep breath, and wiped her face with her handkerchief.

'Good girl,' he said. 'Let's go outside so as not to disturb him.'

Both the Cecil and the Windsor were full. There was not a single suite or even a room available – it was the height of summer and the peak season, after all. This irritated him, and he shouted at Nassir to *do something*, meaning find a place for him to stay. Naturally, he did not want to join them in the flat. It would be noisy with the children and the service not up to his standards. After an hour's search, he settled for a pension in Gleem, across from the Paradise Casino. Its Greek proprietor, Madame Marika, recognised him, despite the fact that he hadn't stayed with her for many years. She was respectful and solicitous. Yes, she had a suite for Mahmoud Bey on the second floor, with a bedroom overlooking the sea. Her smiles and golden hair raised his spirits. He did not negotiate the rent with her – whatever she asked for he would pay. She would overcharge him, most likely, but on a day like this, he was not in the mood to barter.

Madame Marika showed him to his rooms. She waddled over to the window, her satin dress tight against her hips and her plump feet overflowing from her slippers. She drew open the violet curtains to prove to him that he had a view of the Corniche. He glimpsed the sea, dark and brooding, a backdrop to the glamour of Alexandria by night; the young dressed up after a day at the beach making their way to the cafés and the cinemas. He told her about Nur's accident. Her green eyes clouded with pity and she offered him a glass of whisky. How thoughtful of her! How well he would be looked after!

'If I were in your place,' she said, pouring cold water from a pitcher, 'I wouldn't let these army doctors operate on him. Take your son abroad, Mahmoud Bey. Take him to Athens or London or Switzerland. There they will make him stand on his feet again.'

He reckoned her hostility to the doctors was nothing more than Alexandria's impatience with the lingering British army, but he still warmed to her optimism. Yes, Nur would recover. Dr Hempster, perhaps, was too pessimistic.

He slept deeply but woke up too early. He started to think about Nur and could not go back to sleep again, so he dressed and left the pension, stepping into the morning light and noise of the sea. The Corniche was deserted and so was the beach. The salty air was bracing and his stomach rumbled. He had not had dinner the previous night – his last solid meal had been lunch at the Shepheard's, with the Harrisons. That was only yesterday, but Cairo and Nabilah seemed far away. It was as if he had turned a corner, all by himself, and was not certain where to go next.

He crossed over to the Paradise Casino and walked down the steps to the entrance. The restaurant was as empty as he expected. Two waiters were cleaning the floor and most of the chairs were stacked upside down on top of the tables. He made his way to the terrace and sat under an umbrella. The cash he had taken out of the safe in Cairo was intended to pay for what those in the building industry named the 'erasure' of the new building, materials that were unavailable in Khartoum, which included the tiles on all the floors, and the paint as well as the bathroom and kitchen fittings. He had already struck a deal with the agent and the next step was to pay the first half of the instalment; the second he would pay on delivery. But now he would not be able to part with the money. He needed it to finance this crisis. It was impossible, now, to gauge Nur's medical expenses, and he must, at the very least, be with funds. The building would just have to wait until he was liquid again. This was annoying, not just the delay, but the fact that he had given his word to the agent; he had shaken hands on an agreement and now he would break his word. It had never happened before. He lit his first cigarette of the day. How empty and stale the casino was. At night it would be lively with music and dancing; with young people and pretty girls. He had had his fair share of enjoyment; he had lived life to the full. Nur was too young to suffer. The first tears came to his eyes. He blinked them away and ordered a full breakfast as a long day lay ahead of him. He would make decisions and set wheels in motion, but, first of all, the family in Umdurman must be informed.

He touched Nur's hair and the boy opened his eyes.

'I didn't do anything wrong, Father . . .' He sounded drugged and distant. 'A big wave knocked me over.'

'Don't worry, Nur. It was an accident. Everyone knows you didn't do anything wrong. I am here, now, and your mother is on the way.'

Nur's eyes brightened. 'When will she arrive?'

'In a few days. Your Uncle Idris is bringing her, and Halima is coming, too, to join her sisters.'

The stillness in the boy's body was excessive and odd. He did not fidget, he did not raise his hand to scratch his chin or touch his nose, he did not bend his long legs under the sheet. It was as if an invisible power had pinned him down to the bed.

The following days were full and empty at the same time: static and busy, monotonous but edgy. Visitors started to appear; other Sudanese in Alexandria – their numbers swollen because it was the holiday season; Nur's friends from Victoria College as well as those members of staff who had not gone away for the summer; Mahmoud's Egyptian friends and business acquaintances. The news spread, and there were telephone calls from Sudan and Cairo, a few from London and Switzerland, as well as several telegrams. Some visitors travelled up from Cairo – they included the staff from the Abuzeid office – spent the day, and returned by train in the evening. Some of them needed to be met at the station, given lunch and refreshments and another lift back to the station. These tasks became Nassir's responsibility, and he started to look haggard, deprived of the beach and the nightlife, but he seemed excited, too, roused by the number of friends and acquaintances he was meeting every day.

At the hospital itself, the Abuzeid family took over the waiting room and ordered extra chairs in Nur's room. They befriended the nurses, cleaners, and kitchen staff deliberately, giving them gifts and extra tips. Nur's room filled with flowers, with chocolates from Groppi's and lively conversation. This generosity flowed over to the patients in the adjacent rooms and total strangers received chocolates and pastries, cigars if they were men, and visits from Mahmoud Bey.

Waheeba came straight from the train station, her tobe incongruous in this most cosmopolitan of cities. She threw herself on Nur's bed and made a scene. Fatma and Halima had to restrain her while Mahmoud turned his back in disgust and stared out at the sea. Her wails and anguish grated on his nerves. She turned on him.

'Do something! You can't leave him like this. Spare no expense. I want my son well again.'

She had never left Sudan, except for the time she went to Mecca and returned a Hajjah. Now she was traumatised as much by the journey as by the cause of it. At the end, after she had worked herself into a state, slapping her face and gnashing her teeth, he managed to get a nurse to give her a sedative and he ordered a spare bed to be brought into the room so that she could lie down opposite Nur.

After she had rested and calmed down, he said to her, 'They are going to operate on him. We were waiting for you. I would not let them perform surgery on him until you arrived.'

This gratified Waheeba. She became her usual alert self, scolding Fatma for not bringing enough food from the flat, and snapping at Nassir for bringing the wrong suitcase to the hospital, not the one she had requested. When she made a sarcastic remark about Soraya's bare arms, Mahmoud knew that the worst was over. His wife was no longer in shock. She had accepted Nur's accident and was ready to play her part.

'I am not afraid of any operation,' she said. 'Everything is in Allah's hands. Yes, let them go ahead with the surgery. I want my son well again, and I want him back with me in Umdurman.'

Nur, himself, became more communicative. His appetite revived as his mother fed him. It was as if he was a baby again.

'Open your mouth. Take another sip of milk.'

She was not awkward or reserved, popping grapes in his mouth with gusto, and combing his hair with care. In contrast, Mahmoud found himself embarrassed in the face of his son's helplessness. He would bolt out of the room every time the nurse came to change Nur or give him a bath and was more comfortable greeting the visitors and keeping them company. Their good wishes comforted him, and he did not mind the pity in their eyes. And now Idris was by his side, a steady, mostly silent companion, but Mahmoud drew strength from the sheer physical presence of his brother. Nur's schoolmates spent time with him in the room, but Mahmoud's friends would only stand for a few minutes exchanging formal greetings with the patient before joining the gathering in the waiting room outside. The conversation would drift from the state of the patient to the state of the world, and Mahmoud found this soothing as his mind followed the sequence of another story or a gripping piece of gossip. Several times he laughed out loud when one of his friends cracked a joke.

On the day of the operation, they all gathered at the hospital early in the morning. Today Nur might die – but no one said these words out loud. Mahmoud felt heavy with the responsibility of the risk he was taking with his own flesh and blood. Dr Hempster had explained to him that the neck was a sensitive area; that all the nerves that went from the brain to the limbs passed through the neck. Mahmoud tried to understand. He was not a scientific man and he only held a preparatory school certificate. He knew the ways of the market, but the human body was a mystery.

Hours of waiting, one cigarette after the other. The room felt odd without Nur. They were gathering around someone who was not present, who dangled between life and death. Soraya sat on Nur's bed, hunched forward and biting her nails. Waheeba, stretched out on the extra bed, was muttering prayers. Idris dozed in an armchair, while Nassir flicked through the pages of a magazine then took to leaving the room and coming back in again. Mahmoud gave them his back and stared out the window. He watched waves approach, with varying strengths but one destination, to curve and unfurl against the shore. The white froth was attractive, decorating the endless blue. He wanted what Waheeba wanted – the boy to live and return home to Umdurman. They all wanted Umdurman now. Alexandria was not a place for the unhealthy. The holiday season wrapped itself around them like an unsuitable costume. The young ones no longer went to the beach, the cinemas, or the fun fairs. They were inside this glumness together, absorbed and waiting. He turned and spoke to Nassir, his voice odd in the hush and anxiety.

'I want to contact the English soldiers who pulled Nur out of the sea.'

Soraya stopped biting her nails.

'One was called Stan and the other was Eddie.'

'Eddie is Edward and Stan is Stanley,' said Nassir.

'I want to meet them,' said Mahmoud.

He would thank them for saving Nur's life. Would a gift be in good taste? What kind of gift? Would they take money? How much? These questions of etiquette occupied his mind until the nurse came in to say that the operation was finished. They crowded the corridor until Nur was rolled out of the operating theatre.

Relief that he was alive, and unspoken dismay that there was no movement, no movement or sensation in either his legs or arms. 'The operation was a success. Nur is making good progress.' This was the wording of the telegram Mahmoud ordered Nassir to send out. In reality, the only progress was from the grogginess of the operation to the boy becoming alert and responsive. The nurses cranked up the bed, propped him up on pillows and his bright eyes roamed the room, as if doing the moving for him. He chatted to his family and visitors, cracked the occasional joke, and asked of news of the outside world. Often he would seek his father's eyes and ask the silent question: what next? Hope. Hope was the nourishment, the drug, the saving grace. After the anticipation of the operation and the acute days following it, there came a lull. Nur and the hospital were enmeshed in the fabric of the family's Alexandria life. The patient was in a stable condition. No one needed to hold their breath any more. They could let their gaze wander, could surreptitiously, but not without restraint, start to live their lives again.

Mahmoud took Idris out to lunch at Abu Qir for a change. They tucked into grilled fish and shrimps, fried boulti and tahina. The restaurant was surrounded by cliffs, and there were mossy hard rocks instead of a sandy beach. Drinking mint tea after their meal, they discussed business – all the things that had been put on hold, all the transactions awaiting approval, and how to make the most of their temporary presence in Egypt. Then Idris asked, 'Did you manage to contact the two soldiers who pulled Nur out of the water?'

'I found out their names, but they are no longer in Alexandria. They've been transferred to the Canal Zone.'

'I've heard from more than one source,' said Idris, 'that more and more forces are being stationed in Suez.'

'I will write to them,' said Mahmoud. 'I would have preferred to meet them, but a letter of thanks should suffice.'

Idris had to be his negative self. He had to sigh and say, 'Young people are nothing but trouble. Why did Nur have to go swimming? What connection do we have with the sea? Nothing! We are neither sailors nor divers. Who taught him to swim anyway?'

'The English. At school they taught him. All the students were taken to Sidi Bishr where they would camp at night and swim during the day.'

'What kind of school is that? Instead of lessons, taking them for outings!'

'Victoria College is the Eton of the Middle East.'

'What is this Eton?' Idris stuck a toothpick in his mouth.

Mahmoud didn't bother to answer. After such a meal, he needed his siesta.

With the cream of Cairo holidaying in Alexandria, and Nur's accident a high-profile event, Mahmoud's social life continued to flourish. Loose ties were strengthened and old alliances were cemented. Even strangers, brothers of so-and-so, and friends of so-and-so, were taking time away from the beach to drop in at the hospital or at least telephone. Mahmoud pushed his personal sadness down – he had had such hopes for the boy – and presented his usual amiable self to society. It touched him that so many important people were standing by him in his hour of need. Best of all was when they said, 'You are an upstanding, generous man, and you do not deserve this.' Or, 'Nur is a fine young man, he doesn't deserve this.'

Mahmoud knew that such personal warmth was excellent for business, and even though no one spoke of work, he could sense, not without irony, that in these solemn hospital corridors, seeds were being sown for a profitable, thriving future. However, sometimes, when guests probed him excessively about Nur's condition or offered conflicting advice, he would become defensive and insecure. It was important to save face. He must be seen to be doing the best for his son. He must be seen to be sparing no expense. No one would esteem him and he would not forgive himself if he cut corners, or was negligent or impatient, too rash or too cautious. Or worse, simply did not care enough. Never had he loved his son more, and never had he been more uncertain of the future. At the end of each day, which always

109

seemed long and stifling in the hospital, he would need Madame Marika's platitudes and Cyprus wine; need the cool, shady interior of the pension to soothe his ragged nerves.

Waheeba, everyone agreed, was spending too much time at the hospital. They persuaded her to go home on the pretext that she, and only she, could cook Nur's favourite dish of assida. Mahmoud drove her to the flat because Nassir was not yet at the hospital. They were silent on the way. He sensed her reluctance to leave Nur – she was as attached to him now as she had been when he was an infant.

'Look around you,' he said. 'Look out the window at this magnificent city.'

She obeyed him, but quickly returned to staring straight ahead, fidgeting with the gold bangles on her arms.

'Ignorant woman,' he sighed. 'What is the point of your travelling anywhere?'

'Travel hurt my son,' she said. 'If he had stayed in Sudan, none of this would have happened. He would have been well.'

Did she want to blame him for the accident? His fault for insisting that Nur studies at Victoria College.

'All the Sudanese boys studying in Alexandria, all the ones swimming and holidaying – have they been injured?'

She didn't reply and, as he turned the corner, he said to her, 'Answer me. Why don't you have an answer for that?'

'I should have stayed at the hospital. Talk to the administration and get me permission to use the hospital kitchen. Then I can cook Nur's meals there for him.'

He went up to the flat with her. She did not know where it was and could not be trusted to read the number on the door. Nassir was still in bed when they walked in. Mahmoud walked into his bedroom and opened the curtain.

'It's noon,' he bellowed. 'Noon! And you're still asleep!'

Nassir sat up. He was bleary-eyed and downcast and looked like he had a hangover.

'Where were you last night?'

'I went out with some friends.' He avoided meeting his father's eyes.

'Well, that's fine behaviour! Your brother in hospital and you are out gallivanting till the small hours! I am mighty proud of you.'

Nassir shifted from one foot to the other. His daughter, Zeinab, walked into the room, shook hands with her grandfather, and walked out again.

Mahmoud pulled the chair from the dresser and sat down. The flat was not to his taste. It was disorganised and basic, typical holiday accommodation. He had bought it for the family and it fulfilled its function, while he always opted for a hotel.

'Listen, Nassir, you have to become more responsible. Stop this staying out late. Is this what you want your reputation to be? A drunkard? A womaniser? And at a time like this, the circumstances we are going through!'

Waheeba walked into the room. Seeing Nassir sitting unkempt on the bed she exclaimed,

'What's wrong? Are you sick?'

'No, he is not sick,' said Mahmoud. 'Nor does he have any respect for the one who *is* sick.'

'Every day since the accident, I have been at the hospital,' said Nassir, emboldened by the presence of his mother. 'Every single day, all day. For how long is this going to continue? When is Nur going to get better? They don't know how to cure him, do they? The operation wasn't a success. He is still as he is.'

'Don't talk like that!' snapped Waheeba.

'But I can't bear to see him like this.' Nassir was getting more heated. 'All the time, he's just lying down. How is he going to go to university? How is he going to get married? I would rather not live if I couldn't get up to take a piss. I'd rather die.'

Waheeba slapped him.

'Don't you dare!' Her lips quivered and her tobe fell and hung low. 'Don't you dare wish your brother dead.' She straightened her tobe, turned and walked out of the room.

Mahmoud felt sorry for Nassir. He was taller than Waheeba and his little children were milling around the flat. That crazy woman. Nassir put his head down in his hands and Mahmoud moved to sit next to him. He patted him on the back. In the silence, he could overhear Waheeba talking to Halima in the kitchen. She was saying she wanted to get Nur to Umdurman so that she could take him to a faqih. Someone, for sure, had given the boy the evil eye. Vulgar, stupid woman. Mahmoud squeezed Nassir's shoulder.

'There are other operations that can be done. I am considering taking him abroad for treatment. I've been making enquiries. Don't lose hope. He can be cured, I am sure.'

On the way out, he looked in at the women in the kitchen. It was good that Halima had come from Umdurman. She had a calming, matronly presence, and was a restraining influence on the younger ones.

'Greet your grandfather, Zeinab,' she said, turning from the sink.

The little girl walked towards him and he said, 'She already did. She came especially into the room and greeted me.' He put his hand into his pocket and bought out a piece of bubble gum. 'Here, this is for you, Zeinab.'

It was his habit to carry sweets for the children who came his way. When he didn't have sweets, he gave them coins.

Waheeba was sitting at the kitchen table, occupied in some task that held her attention.

'You should rest, Hajjah,' he said to her. 'You are tiring yourself these days.' Then he lowered his voice and continued, 'No respectable woman raises her hand against a grown-up man, even if he is her son. Your nerves have been under a lot of strain these past days. Take care of your health and rest.'

Instead of the expected conciliatory response, she flared up.

'We are all tired. I am working day and night to tend to your son and serve your guests, and where is your Egyptian wife? Sitting comfortably in Cairo with her mother, spending your money—'

He interrupted her and his voice was cool, 'Nur is your son. It's your duty to be with him.'

'Yes, he is my son, and I know what is good for him. I was just telling Halima. The English doctor had got it all wrong; there was no connection between Nur's neck and his limbs. This is black magic, believe me, I know it when I see it. And no one can lift this curse except certain faqirs in Umdurman!'

'Superstitious nonsense,' retorted Mahmoud. 'I am going to take him to London, and you will go back to Umdurman where you belong.'

She shook her head. 'No, I go where my son goes. He will need me on the journey.'

It was as good a time as any to break the news.

'Nabilah is travelling with us. She will see to his needs.'

Waheeba's mouth fell open. She put her palms on the top of her head and started to wail.

'Oh, have you heard this! Have you heard what he's doing to me? Nassir, come and hear what your father is intending to do!'

Halima came over to comfort her aunt and Nassir shuffled into the kitchen.

'Oh, she is the cause of all this!' Waheeba swayed from side to side. 'I tell you, she is the cause of evil. I wish to God the same thing will happen to *her* son! Let her heart burn like mine is burning.' Her eyes bulged and spit blew from her mouth.

Halima drew in her breath. 'I seek refuge in Allah. Is this a thing to say?'

Without a word, Mahmoud left the flat. He should have divorced the bitch a long time ago. Not only was she ugly and ignorant, she was chock full of venom, too!

At the Central Post Office, he parked his car and went in to put a call through to Cairo. Nabilah always said the right things. She was refined and polite and her wording was pleasing, too.

She placed her hope in Nur's age and would say, 'Young bones heal quickly' or 'The young can withstand blows and stand up again.'

She had offered to come to Alexandria and bring the children as planned, but he had preferred that they stay away in Cairo.

'I am taking Nur to London and I want you to come with us.'

She paused, and then said, 'Of course I want to come with you and I can leave Farouk and Ferial with Mama, but don't you think Hajjah Waheeba will take offence?'

'London is not a place for her. I will be meeting people there and making new contacts. I want *you* with me.'

He sensed her smile. If she was triumphant, she deserved it.

'But Mahmoud,' she said, 'Nur will naturally be more comfortable with his mother.'

'My decision is final,' he said. 'I can't stand her, Nabilah. I am on the verge of losing my temper and divorcing her. Believe me, any minute I am. I should have done it a long time ago.'

'Yes, I wish you had.'

'Now I am in the middle of a crisis. I have to think of Nur. I can't inflict this on him as well. The day he stands on his feet again, I promise you, will be the end of my marriage to Waheeba.'

She started to repeat her warm wishes for Nur, the conventional words that soothed him, 'It is but a setback that will pass. Every illness has a remedy, insha'Allah,' until the operator informed them that the call was coming to an end.

It was time to hurry back to the hospital in case any visitors were waiting for him. Today he would be able to meet the boy's eyes; meet his silent, brooding and persistent plea for help.

IX

London is an interrupted dream. A tall ship docks and his fortnight's journey from Alexandria is over. Dark skies, even though it is late summer. Englishmen mill around his stretcher with coarse accents and rough hands, doing heavy manual work. They are not like the English he is used to seeing, his teachers at Victoria and his father's friends. They unload him from the ship like they unload the luggage. He used to walk everywhere by himself, and now his movements are someone else's achievement.

London is not unknown to Nur, even though this is his first visit. Mr Dickens had told him about it and there were the films he had watched at the Blue Nile Cinema. But even though it is 1951, what Nur sees is war-damaged, dented buildings, glimpses of a ruin waiting to be rebuilt. The city is in rehabilitation, poised between peace and construction, between austerity and boom, between rationing and plenty. He understands, because he is injured, too. He wants to mend; he wants to be normal again.

It is not meant to be like this – his first visit to London. He should have been among a batch of new Sudanese students. They would have arrived by ship together, to be met by a Sudan Student Office representative who would whisk them off to Sudan House where they would stare around them with wide grins, conscious of their new clothes, their accents, their skin. They would be tense with the sense of adventure, shy, but too excited to be truly shy.

'Let's go dancing tonight,' they'd laugh, their first allowance warm in their pockets.

And in a few days' time, when all the paperwork was sorted, they would hug each other and disperse. Some to Oxford, Nur to Cambridge, others to Edinburgh and Dublin. This is what it should have been like: his hands in the pocket of a new jacket, buying a newspaper from a vendor, a jaunty step on the train at King's Cross.

The hospital ward reminds Nur of the dormitory at school. It is spacious, with a high ceiling. The man in the next bed is called Jack. A wall had fallen on him during the Blitz and he is now in hospital because of a urinary complication. Nur tries to start a conversation, but Jack is busy reading the paper. With a device like a thin metal rod clasped between his teeth, he can flip over the pages of a newspaper. Jack cannot walk, but he can light his own cigarettes. His teeth are strong and clever. Nur admires him.

But *he* will not end up like Jack. He will get better and everything will go back to how it was before. He will go to Cambridge as planned. He will ride a bicycle and go rowing and dancing. He will reach high in the library for thick, heavy books. He will be free from this stay in one place, from this keep still against your will. And if the operation doesn't succeed? No! It will, it must. Because all this good future is just around the corner, he can see it.

Nur feels as if he is wrapped tight in a bandage, a mummy who is alive and seeing. This inertia is a new kind of physical pain, not intense but constant. His body clamours for movement. It is a fight – this struggle to be free – it is an effort. Awkward, too, to want to reach out, to be straining all the time, awkward and frustrating. He wants to pull the sheet up. He wants to scratch his chin, to rub his eyes, to pick his nose. He wants to draw the curtain around his bed. He wants to push his feet in slippers, to adjust the collar of his shirt. He wants to hold a pen. He wants to hold a pen and write. And he wants to walk the pavements of London like everyone else.

He can move his head from side to side, he can nod and

clutch his upper arms closer to his body. Chicken wings, says the nurse. She is young and flirty and there is another nurse, older, like Matron, who looked after the boys at school. Nur likes their accents.

'Judy Garland's singin' at the Theatre Royal . . .'

He copies how they talk, practising by himself. It shames him that English ladies are changing and washing him, sticking the enema in the morning, shaving his chin. They should not be doing such menial work, and it makes his face hot and his eyes moist with anger. Dressed and clean, he would like to chat to them, be nice to them, but they are busy. Most of the men in the ward are war heroes with ongoing complications. They don't look triumphant or strong, and they shout in their sleep, but they are heroes all the same. Even though parts of them are missing, even though they are spastic and scarred, they have medals to their name. He is different. He was on a day out at the beach.

Although he does not like Nabilah, she is someone familiar and she speaks to him in Arabic. He can tell that she does not like the hospital and is unsettled by the men with missing limbs. One winked at her, and she blushed and frowned. The man's left arm had been amputated and his left eye was missing but he could wink with the right. Nabilah comes to visit more than his father.

'He is busy,' she says. 'Guess who he was introduced to yesterday? A duke! And this duke has a huge aviary full of amazing birds from all over the world. Your father has agreed to ship monkey nuts from Sudan for these birds. He is arranging the shipment now. Of course, the Duke is delighted to have met him.' She is lively with pride and a sense of adventure. She describes the first television she has seen. 'In the hotel lounge,' she says. 'How long do you think it will be before we have television sets in Egypt and Sudan?'

Nur likes the story of the caged birds that will eat nuts from the Sudan. He misses his mother and her food. The food at the hospital is even more horrible than at school, except for the puddings. He loves custard and jelly, but they are scarce and the portions minuscule. At night he dreams of Soraya. They are walking on the beach and she is smiling and beautiful. They lie down together and she doesn't push him away. In the morning when the nurse comes to change his clothes, she rolls her eyes at the stains and shakes her head. A part of him is still working, is still free and moving, after all.

At last, Jack from the next bed, is talking to him. He wants to know about Alexandria during the war. Nur was in elementary school in Umdurman then, but not wanting to disappoint his new friend, he makes up a story based on experiences he had heard from older VC students. It is easy, he discovers, to put himself in a different place and time. He says that the school buildings were used as a military hospital and that the masters, pupils and books were moved to the San Stefano hotel, which had its own beach. There were air raid shelters dug on the side of the hotel and most of the bombing raids were at night. In the summer, when Rommel threatened Alexandria, the school was closed and Nur was in Sudan. By the time the October term started, the emergency had passed. He talks about his friends; Tuf Tuf, Ramzy, Joe and Yacoub. He explains that Tuf Tuf's real name is Fuad and how he got into trouble with Ahmed Saad, the prefect, until Jack says, 'Steady on, lad, you're a chatterbox!'

Nur has more to say about the role of the Sudan Defence Force in the Abyssinian Campaign. They served with distinction again the Italians on the eastern border. Then, to entertain Jack, Nur sings Sudanese songs. He gets carried away, enjoying the sound of the Arabic words and the simple sadness of the melodies. *Oh come to me. Why are you dry towards me, my love?* At first Jack is amused and then he is bored.

'Shut the fuck up,' he says and Nur laughs out loud, delighted to hear an Englishman swearing.

With the clever metal rod between his teeth, Jack flips over the newspaper and Nur twists his neck to read about Clement Atlee opening the largest oil refinery in Europe. Jack mutters under his breath. Inside him is bitterness, small and hard, like bullets inside a gun. He is also tired. Tired of the war and how what happened to him will never go away. He looks handsome but unkempt. No matter how well someone else washes you, Nur learns, no matter how well they shave you, groom you, dress you and comb your hair – they can never get it right. They will never do it exactly like you would have done it yourself. The constant, constant irritation. Jack knows more than Nur. It is not only being in a wheelchair and having useless arms, but the things that go wrong inside; infections and minor complications that keep him in and out of hospital.

There is an operation scheduled. Nur does not like the neurologist Mr Copeland. Mr Copeland sticks a needle in his thumb and knocks his knees with a hammer. He has hairy arms and hunched shoulders. He does not look pleased with this case from overseas, but he will operate. So, no dinner or pudding the night before and nil by mouth, and in the morning his father kisses him. He smells of aftershave and days in a London hotel. His face seems larger, pumped up with anticipation. Next to him, Nabilah, in a new hat, smiles. Everyone has hope. Everyone wishes him well. They roll him away, down unfamiliar corridors and up in a huge lift. The anaesthetist asks him to count. Nur counts out loud and finds it hard to believe that he will ever stop counting. But the darkness does come.

He is back at school on the playing field. Tuf Tuf passes him the ball and he flies with it, on and on, knowing he can score, knowing he will score. Ramzy tackles him; he is well built, but Nur is lean and light. Tuf Tuf is shouting and the referee blows his whistle. A light shines on Nur's face and there is the ugly clang of metal on metal. Someone is saying his name, insistent, irritating. They want him to wake up but he wants to continue sleeping. They insist, and he has to obey. He opens his eyes and the brightness hurts. It stabs his eyes and the back of his throat.

Nausea makes him groan. He leans forward to retch but he is still lying on his back when the bile comes out.

They give him something for the pain and it makes him light-headed; it makes him float, not sink into sleep. Sensations and dimensions are out of proportion. Soraya's skin is incredibly smooth and there is more and more of her to kiss. She is not slender or coy as in real life, but abundant and overflowing; accessible and generous. His mother's hoash, too, is vast, bigger than a football field and it is full of people who love him and love each other. There are fruit trees and colourful, chirping birds. The Nile flows through with vigour. The wind carries the scent of fresh grass and everyone knows that it has been raining in the provinces. There are swings, there are tents and music and songs. Batool is dancing, her back arched, her breasts high. Someone is playing the oud and children kick a ball; yet all of these people and all of these things – turtle doves and laughter, canaries and incense, henna and lyrics – are in that one hoash in Umdurman.

Then the nightmares blast through. A giant thumb pushes him to the ground; he feels the weight of it on his chest, the insistent pressure. The thumb, meaty and human, grotesque with a brittle purple nail, pins him down, and no matter how much he wriggles and crunches, he cannot break free. Soraya is smiling at another man, older and more established, a man who is loathsome and cunning. They are standing close together, too close and the man puts his arm around her waist. Nur must rescue her. He must drag her away, but first he wants to punch that man's face. Anger rises. He shouts out loud and the sound makes him open his eyes. It is grey night in the dormitory. Someone is weeping; it must be the new boy. The new boy is homesick, he doesn't understand the rules of this new school and his English is rudimentary. He thinks he can leave. Well, home is a long way away, in another country. Nur can explain all this to him, patronise him, enjoying the feeling that he is older and knows more. Here are your new friends; here are the masters who will teach you. Here are the prefects; you have to obey them and address them as Captain. You are a boarder; you are not a day boy. You will be called by your last name, everyone is. Do you know how to play cricket? Are you good at football? Dodge, tackle, dribble, and pass. Score. Score again. And remember, 'English is the language of the school. Anyone caught speaking other languages will be severely punished.'

Nur is the new boy. He speaks Arabic and the prefect has gone to report him. Nur is bewildered by the new rules. No underwear to be worn at night, only pyjamas, cold showers first thing in the morning, grey flannels. Two types of boys fail in Victoria College – those who are religious and those who are poor at sports. It doesn't matter if you're a Muslim, Christian or Jew. It doesn't matter if you're Russian, Palestinian, Sudanese or Greek. Maybe Nur will succeed. Maybe he will crawl his way through this first term, but the more he struggles, the more he is bullied; the more the masters despair of him, the more his schoolmates despise him. At the end of the term, it is time to return to Umdurman and never be seen again. Nur is being punished. He has to sit down in the empty classroom and copy out five hundred lines from the telephone directory. He copies and copies, stopping to count the lines but still they are not enough. Tedious. Tedious.

'Alhamdulillah for your safe recovery,' Nabilah peers down at him. What is she doing in London? He remembers as his father touches his forehead and hair. 'How are you feeling? The anaesthetic troubled you.'

Nur is not sure how he is feeling. He should be better; he should be able to get up. He is still wrapped in a cocoon.

'Squeeze my hand,' his father says but Nur doesn't know where his father's hand is. He turns his head and sees that his father is holding his hand.

Mr Copeland appears with his needle and trusty hammer. He goes away and then returns. He addresses his father, who stands up straight and deferential. Mr Copeland pushes his glasses up his nose and talks in a steady voice. He says that, unfortunately, there is no significant progress. The likelihood of any recovery at this point is remote. We can offer an extensive programme of rehabilitation. It normally takes eighteen months. A progress from bed to wheelchair. The patient will learn how to feed himself. His father's face darkens and he interrupts in a mixture of Arabic and English.

'With what, Doctor?' Mahmoud sounds angry. 'Feed himself with what? No sir, I can hire tens of people to serve him day and night.'

His father is being rude to an Englishman. Mr Copeland is unsettled, and now Mahmoud gives him his back. He turns to the wall, cradles his head in his hands and sobs. Nur has never seen his father crying. Nabilah touches Mahmoud's arm and murmurs things Nur cannot hear. He can only hear his father's sobs.

Mr Copeland turns to Nur, blinks and speaks again of re-habilitation and gaining some degree of independence. Nur can't listen any more. The words pour out of him.

'I want to use my arms. It doesn't matter about my legs, but I want to hold a pen.' He has seen the patients in crutches and wheelchairs and he could live like that, but ... please Sir, he needs his arms. Nur is bartering and negotiating. Swapping his legs for his arms, his feet for his hands. He is begging, but Mr Copeland is powerless. He looks at Nur as if Nur is speaking a foreign language.

'I need my hands to do simple things like turning over the pages of a book. Please, Sir!'

X

Summers in Khartoum were dry, shimmering heat, with the sun's lashing rays and not a single breeze, not a breath. This would intensify to an unbearable stillness when even the nights and dawns became hot. Such tightness had to give, had to break; it did, not gently, but through dust clouds, reddish brown formations gathering on the horizon. They would advance, looking innocent and colourful, then, closer, they revealed their menace and crushed the city in an embrace of grit and sand. Visibility diminished and the wind would blow and howl, churning dust and ripping loose garbage and bushes. Branches fell off trees and chicken pens were ripped apart, and hours later, when the air cleared and became fresh, there would be ripples of sand on the ground, swirls and patterns as if the desert had visited and left its tracks.

Badr was not entitled to paid leave this summer. His contract gave him this privilege only once every two years. To go home to Egypt he would have had to finance the trip himself, and after calculating the travel expenses for himself, Haniyyah, his father and the four boys, it became clear that this was not an option. So, even with the school closed, he remained in Khartoum and Haniyyah, in the late stages of pregnancy, had to endure the Sudanese weather. When the dust storms came, they huddled in their one room, hot and restless. When it rained, and it started to rain in July, usually at dawn or at night, as if the water feared the sun, Osama, Bilal and Radwan stripped to their underpants and ran out to splash and laugh, opening their mouths up to the sky. Little Ali, toddling proficiently now, would join them – and then retreat back to cover because the rain alarmed him, and his puzzled face made them all laugh. Prayers made when it's raining are accepted, Badr would remind his family, and he prayed that Haniyyah would have a safe and easy delivery.

Ramadan came in the middle of the summer. Badr welcomed it and made a schedule for himself. Every day he would read a section of the Qur'an, one thirtieth or more. He would wake up a couple of hours before dawn for the tahajud prayers and at night he would go to the mosque for isha and taraweeh. At the hottest time of the day, he had a nap, and his plan was that he would spend the last ten days of Ramadan in seclusion at the mosque. He made time, too, to read his favourite books; the tafseer of Ibn Kathir, and Imam Ghazali's *The Revival of the Sciences of Religions*. There were the household chores, too, for Haniyyah was becoming increasingly heavy and tired. He told her to stop fasting but she didn't listen.

'I don't want to miss out,' she said.

She was involved in an exchange of dishes and drinks with their Sudanese neighbours, noting their love of sweet drinks and how they drank more than they ate when it was time to break the fast. Helu Mur and Abre, the children, sipped and made faces, but grew to like them before long and they were fascinated by the cannon that was fired from the barracks at precisely the time of the iftar. Osama and Bilal were fasting, and during the day they were quiet and thirsty, becoming boisterous and energetic after the evening meal and late into the night. This was part of the charm of Ramadan, turning day into night, treats of mixed nuts, dried apricots and dates. Badr did not begrudge his family any delicacies. Every day he went to the souq and every day Haniyyah cooked delicious meals and satisfying puddings. It was a month of plenty, and he marvelled at how rigorous it was, and at the same time buoyant; solemn, and at the same time merry, with the children playing football in the street by the light of Ramadan lanterns.

He felt a surge of love for his family that month. Often, he would draw the boys into his arms and kiss them, enjoying their smell and childish skin. Little Ali would sit on his lap, listening and lulled as Badr recited the Qur'an, going over the suras he had memorised. He taught Osama Surat Yasin, Bilal completed Juzu'Aama and Radwan learnt Surat Al-Borooj. This was joy; his sons loving him and wanting to please him, strong in body and in faith.

Badr revelled, too, in the closure of the school. No need to wake up early and rush with the boys to catch the tram, no need to be punctual, no need to scurry around from one private lesson to the next, and no need to dress formally. He felt relaxed and free. At home he would wear his underwear of long johns and vest, and when he went out to the mosque or the souq he wore his jellabiya. His father, seeing him in the clothes of the Egyptian peasant, mistook him for his older brother, Abdel-Salaam.

'It's me, Badr,' he repeated, but the old man looked at him as if he were a trickster or Abdel-Salaam trying to pull his leg.

Abdel-Salaam had died years ago, of dysentery. If he were still alive, their father would not have needed to travel with Badr to Khartoum, he would have lived at Kafr-el-Dawar. Abdel-Salaam had been the reason Badr was able to continue his studies and go to Teachers' College. Abdel-Salaam was the older brother who looked after the farm and followed in their father's foot-steps. He was the one who devoted his early life to family duty and gave Badr the luxury of time off for education. But humans plan, yet Allah has different plans for them.

'Father, Abdel-Salaam died seven years ago,' Badr spoke gently.

'Ah, yes, I remember now,' roused grief and fresh tears.

How soft and small he had become. He used to be rough; he used to be strong. He used to be cheerful, too, or at least good-natured. He used to be brown from the sun; now his skin was pale from sitting in the shade all day. Badr chided himself for insisting that Abdel-Salaam had died. He was never sure whether to fix his father's mind to the present, humour him, or just leave him to his delusions and meanderings.

'Today is the middle of Ramadan, Father.'

'Yes, of course. I am fasting.'

But he was not fasting, nor was he required to. His body was too frail and his mind could not distinguish between day and night. Often he would skip meals, insisting to Haniyyah that he had already eaten, and sometimes he would demand breakfast as soon as his dish was cleared away, forgetting completely the ful he had just minutes earlier consumed.

On a soft cool morning, blue grey with dawn's rain, Badr stood in front of the construction site of the Abuzeid building. Ramadan seemed to have brought the work to a standstill and the building was far from complete. The entrance was a gaping hole, strewn with bricks and piles of sand. There were sacks of cement, wheelbarrows, and discarded spades. All of these things were soaked with rain, the ground covered in puddles. Badr counted five storeys and chose a flat for himself, the second floor on the right. Not the left, which overlooked the main road. Haniyyah would need to go out on the balcony to hang out the washing, and he did not want any man watching her. The balcony on the right was more secluded. His own flat indeed! Wishful thinking. The flat was as distant to him now as a glass of tea to his fasting lips. He smiled to himself at the likeness. He was not hungry now; the pre-dawn meal was comfortable in his lower belly, nor was he longing desperately for the flat.

He looked at the building dispassionately, surprised that it was so incomplete. But perhaps, now that it was up, it was in the last stages, and these last stages didn't take long. What would he know? He was an Arabic and Religious Studies teacher with a farming background.

The guard of the building suddenly emerged from a flimsy shack which Badr hadn't noticed. The man's cheeks were etched with tribal scars and his eyes were bleary, as if he had just woken up. They exchanged greetings and Badr asked about the building.

'Sayyid Mahmoud is away travelling, that's why the work is on hold. He's been away a long time. His son is ill and he took him to the land of the English for treatment.'

'Which son?'

The guard shrugged. 'I don't know.'

'Once Mahmoud Bey gets back, how long will it be before the building is complete?'

'Soon, insha'Allah,' the guard replied. 'But the materials from abroad have to arrive first, otherwise the work can't go on.'

Badr still had hope of moving into a flat. Earlier today, after the heavy rain, his hoash had flooded and he had spent hours with his long johns rolled up, sweeping water into the street, and on his hands and knees, mopping up the concrete strip of terrace. He occupied his mind and made the task lighter and even pleasurable by reciting every verse from the Qur'an on the subject of rain. The skies opening, the water pouring to carry Noah's ark to safety, heavy clouds, lightning splitting the sky and the anticipation of rain, the longing for goodness and moisture. Water from the sky to give life to the earth after it is dead. It is Allah who sends the winds and they raise the clouds. He spreads the clouds in the sky and then breaks them into fragments until you see the raindrops. Badr was jolted from the stream of his thoughts by Haniyyah's voice, praying out loud that they could be delivered from this wretched housing. She had been, these past weeks, lulled by fasting and her heavy stomach, but the state of the hoash after this morning's rain triggered her old refrain of moving. Badr knew fellow teachers who had to share their hoash with other families. He was paying extra to have his own hoash, but Haniyyah had aspirations.

If he loved her less, he would have kept her, his father and the children back home in Kafr-el-Dawar and he would have lived in Khartoum as a bachelor. Many of his colleagues had opted for this arrangement because it saved money and was less of a hassle. But Badr needed his wife. He knew he had a weakness and a love for women. If the devil were going to tempt him, he would tempt him with adultery. So Haniyyah had to be close to him, protecting him and, at the same time, making day-to-day life sweet. He would be bored and miserable without his boys and he had hated being a bachelor: the constant pressure to avoid temptation, the dreams, the loneliness and frustration. He was proud that he had remained chaste until his wedding night. It was like an examination he had passed with flying colours. Now, caring for his elderly father was an examination, too, a responsibility and a duty. He must look after him because the reward of serving one's parents was great. And the punishment for begrudging them and shunning them was great too.

He took the tram to Sirdar Street where the shops were stacked with items from England and Egypt, Greece and Lebanon. In a grocery run by an Armenian and his wife, Badr surveyed the numerous packets of biscuits, cold meats, pastries, and even, shamelessly, in this holy month, bottles of wine! He examined the boxes of sweets to see which ones were both value for money and Hanniyah's favourites. The well-dressed man next to him, hair slicked back with Brylcream and a box of shortbread in his hand, looked familiar. Yes! He was the secretary of Mahmoud Bey, proof that this shop indeed was upmarket and reputable.

'Good morning, Sir,' said Badr.

Victor turned to look at him. It took him a second to place Badr, then they shook hands. Badr asked about Mahmoud Bey, then, 'Which one of his sons has been taken ill?'

Victor spoke with the superiority of a man who enjoyed being privy to the intimate details of an important family. His words had the weight of accuracy and the two men shared a solemn moment. A sigh from Badr.

'There is no strength or will, except from Allah. An excellent student, one of my best.'

'Naturally, rumours are circulating,' said Victor in his soft voice. 'The business community of Khartoum and the hoashs of

Umdurman are making up their own stories. They say the boy picked a fight with a group of drunken English soldiers and they beat him senseless and threw him in the sea.'

'Well, the English broke their promise that the troops would withdraw once the war was over,' said Badr. 'No wonder no one wants to credit them for saving the boy.'

'Another rumour,' said Victor, 'is that his English school was at fault. He dived in the school's swimming pool and hit his head against the side. They say he became an imbecile and his father whisked him away to London to hide him in an asylum ...'

Even the rich were vulnerable to tragedy. This observation satisfied Badr; it was definitive and interesting. He listened as Victor became more animated and less guarded. He concluded with a heated whisper.

'The boy is as good as finished!'

'Poor child,' Badr mourned. 'To be the victim of such an accident! May the Lord protect us all.'

'Between you and me, I wish him death. Tell me, what value does life have, when one is completely helpless and dependent on others? In a case like this, death is a mercy and a dignity.'

Victor didn't wait for a response, but looked away, back at the shelves. Badr reached out for a box of Turkish Delights, a treat for Hanniyah. It was not cheap, not cheap at all. On the way out he stopped in front of the sacks of loose sweets. A quarter of a kilo of nougats to delight the children, so that they would hug him and cover him with spontaneous kisses, blurting out 'thank you' from the bottom of their hearts, not out of duty or habit.

He presented the sweets after they had broken their fast and eaten a meal of lentils and rice, radishes and beetroot, dried wheat and milk. The moon shone down on them and they didn't need a lantern. Badr placed the box on the low table and the children reached out for a piece. Because his father showed no interest, Badr placed a piece in the old man's right hand and pushed it up to his mouth. Toothless gums mashed the sweet softness.

'You liked it, Uncle Hajj?' smiled Hanniyah, licking her own lips. 'Have another piece.'

She stood up and leaned to offer him the box. Her shape was like that of a goose; the large, taut belly, the thin neck and arch in her back. In her first pregnancy, when she was carrying Osama, her huge size had alarmed Badr. With each successive pregnancy, however, his wariness had abated and now he was amused and titillated by her fullness. She was massive, and yet, at the end, a very tiny baby would emerge.

She continued, her voice gentle and coaxing, 'Have another sweet, Uncle Hajj. You haven't been eating well. Today you've hardly eaten anything. Have a piece.'

To everyone's surprise, the old man took the whole box and put it in his lap. He started to eat from it. One piece of Turkish Delight after the other, shoved into a mouth half-full; the flabby lips drooling, the sagging cheeks bulging and squeezing. His fingers and face were soon covered with white smudges of sugar. He was sitting cross-legged on the bed, and soon his lap was covered with half-chewed bits that looked pale and disgusting. The children stared at the diminishing sweets with dismay. Bilal put his thumb in his mouth and sat back on his heels away from the table. Radwan started to cry. Osama looked up at Badr, pleading silently for him to act, waiting for him to act. Badr reached out to take the box from his father. But the old man held on to it with all his strength. His fingernails were cracked with dust and filth and his eyes took a cunning look.

'Thief,' he hissed. 'Get away from me, you son of a dog. You want to take what's mine? I won't let you, you son of a bitch!'

It was not the first time he had cursed Badr in front of the children. A man who had been fasting all day should not break his fast with anger, but anger flushed through Badr, the pure sense of injustice. He could not afford a whole box of Turkish Delights for his father and another for his children. He just could not afford it. And why should his children be deprived, eyeing the sweets and not being able to eat them? The look in their eyes! He grabbed the box and pulled. His father's body was jerked forward with the box and he lost his balance and fell over, collapsing on the floor and hitting his head on the edge of the table. Hanniyah cried out and Osama jumped to his feet, but Badr didn't pull his father off the floor, didn't respond to his cry of pain. Instead, he carried what was left of the Turkish Delight and hid it in the bedroom cupboard. He heard himself breathing out, in the height of tension, in the grip of anger, disgusted with his own impatience.

He left the house and walked in the darkness. The streets were empty because people were in their houses, still finishing off their iftar. He felt thirsty and stopped at a zeer to have a drink. He lit a cigarette, appreciated the rush of nicotine, and continued to walk. Life was better during the school year. He was at work all day and tutoring in the evening – this reduced his contact with his father. But his father had deteriorated, these past few months. There was no doubt about that. He was becoming more senile and troublesome and it was becoming difficult to keep him clothed, clean and well fed. It took more effort and vigilance to keep him from wandering out of the house and getting lost in the city. Perhaps if they were home in Kafr-el-Dawar it would have been easier. Village life would have been more accommodating, and his father would have been surrounded by faces and places he had known all his life. Badr's mind darkened with foreboding, with a sense of being compressed. He walked to get away, to clear his mind, to regain his peace and balance. For as long as he could remember, he had wanted to be a model son, a model father, exemplary in the eyes of his sons. Educate by example. Let them imitate in order to learn. His behaviour today was ignoble and his boys had witnessed it all.

He found himself in front of the Farouk Mosque. The promise that the refurbishment would be complete in time for Ramadan had not been fulfilled and worshippers were still not allowed inside the building, which was bereft of electricity and flooring. The men sat on their rugs in the gardens and the spacious courtyards, drinking cardamom tea and chatting while waiting for the isha prayer. Badr sat by himself under a lubukh tree. A breeze blew the branches and he heard, through his anger, the movement of the leaves and the sounds of the night birds. The mosque was dark in front of him and its doors were closed. It was an old mosque, neglected by the Mahdi when he set up his court in Umdurman. Only a few years ago had interest in the mosque been revived and the refurbishment project started. Sitting staring at the building, Badr felt that he was shut out and excluded. It was as if he and the men around him were deprived, waiting for permission to go in and worship.

It was a quick decision. He strode to the Central Station and boarded the tram for Umdurman. The tram ambled towards the river and began crossing the White Nile Bridge. On Badr's right was the moonlit water, its depths dark, and its surface light blue and shimmering yellow. The breeze raised the smell of fish and pasture. Badr started to feel better. The movement of the tram, the distance he was covering, and the clear night air all reassured him. He could see the farms on the shores and the heavy, pulsing Nile heading north to Egypt. Above him were the metal arches of the bridge, its design of connecting semi-circles as simple as a drawing made by a child. There had been many humiliations in his life; his father's condition would not be the first or the last. Badr had always been the son with aspirations, because he could hold a book in his hand and memorise forty hadiths, because he could deliver a Friday sermon and teach Arabic poetics. The train reached the shores of Umdurman and, soon after Al-Mouradah, rose the Abuzeid saraya. Even though the family was away, the lights over the gates and a few lamps in the garden were switched on. The mansion itself was in grey darkness, the moon illuminating the wide balcony, silver mixing with the beige of the pillars, arches and arabesque design.

Badr walked the alleys of Wad Nubawi, heading towards the mosque. It was in a compound, and to one side was the tomb of Sheikh Gharieballah, while the spacious courtyard in the middle was covered in sand. They were already praying when he joined in. He stood in the last row, which, due to the congestion, was outside the mosque. His feet on coarse sand and above him the benign sky, he entered the long, drawn-out prayers of taraweeh. Keeping the Ramadan nights alive, standing up, reciting, and moving down, it felt like a journey with its own hardships and elation; its anxieties and weakness, its greed for God's mercy, its yearning for blessings, its departure point and graceful arrival. There were breaks between every four rakahs, when the men would drink water, renew their wudu or wander off. Most of them, though, sat in rows chanting *La illaha illa Allah*. The chorus of the chant was random at first, but quickly it settled into one rhythm, one movement with the beat. As Badr said the words, he sensed a speeding up. Some men, in their white jellabiyas, stood swaying backwards and forwards; the words became more emphatic, the definite no, starting with no, and ending with the grandest word, Allah. No god except Allah, no god other than Allah. And again the *La* drawn out, the relief of it, setting out by a pushing away and then moving in to the destination, Allah, and needing to repeat it over again. Repeat it until it was time to stand and pray again.

Another break and three munshideen started to recite Sufi poetry. Through the Sudanese accent, Badr recognised the words of his compatriot Umar Ibn al-Farid.

Compared to my dawn,
the long day's light is like a flash;
next to my drinking place,
the wide ocean is a drop.

Didn't he know all this? In a day of suffering in the world, an hour was nothing in the long run. Must he need reminding, time and time again? Like the Sudanese sun drying wet cotton, bleaching it with its rays, he felt his sluggish mood evaporating, his irritation and anger giving way to lightness. He would go home now refreshed, his energy replenished, his armour strengthened. After the taraweeh, the men ate their dinner. Large basins appeared and were placed on the sand. Ten to fifteen men squatted around each one, their arms stretched out, grabbing handfuls of kisra soaked in a watery stew. In minutes, the basins were wiped clean and dripping fingers were sucked and licked. Hanniyah cooked food that was more appetising and nutritious, but Badr felt satiated after this meal, in this company. It was time to head home, body and spirit bolstered. In a few hours it would be dawn and time to fast again.

His father was standing by the door – another of his sleepless nights, his delusions and restless wanderings. There was a lump on his forehead, a swollen, aggrieved wedge of redness. It hurt Badr, and he hugged his father, determined to be good, determined to be patient, to tolerate every insult and withstand every humiliation. His father looked agitated and stern.

'Badr,' he said and it was a pleasure that he remembered his name, that he got it right this time. 'Son, I have something very serious to tell you.'

Badr smiled in the darkness. Yes, he must humour and love him, be generous with his mercy and time.

'Tell me, Father.'

'This is bad, something very bad.' His hands were scrunched into fists and he banged his knees, which were slightly bent, as if he wanted to sit down and was tired of standing up. He looked Badr in the eyes and whispered with anguish and disbelief. 'Today something abominable happened in this house. Your wife turned out to be a bad woman, Badr. She deceived you Badr. Yes, she did. Your wife is a whore!'

The word pierced through the armour he had built up, an odious word that compressed his lungs and turned his insides cold. He gasped from the shock, even though he knew that what he was hearing wasn't true. He knew his father's mind had deteriorated, but a part of him bore the brunt of the accusation as if it were true or could be, in a twisted dream-state, Fate's fiercest blow.

He steeled himself to be calm, to sound normal.

'Don't upset yourself, Father.' He put his hand on his elbow to lead him back into the house. 'I will deal with this. I will make things right again.'

'She brought a man into the house. Look for yourself – he is here.'

They were in the hoash now. In the moonlight, Badr could see the children sprawled asleep, each two sharing a bed. Hanniyah was nowhere to be seen. From the shadows near the wall, something moved, and, to Badr's horror, the shape of a man rose. Badr lunged at him, crying out. He punched him with all his strength. There was a roar in his ears now. And nothing existed but the power of anger and the need to destroy. The man protested, but Badr couldn't hear. His fingers encircled the stranger's throat.

'Cousin, it's me it's me. What's got into you?' Shukry struggled away from his grasp.

Badr's hands fell down to his sides. He could see now, Shukry's long face, even his protruding Adam's apple. 'What are you doing back here?'

'I came by train. We started out at midday but there was a technical problem and we were delayed for hours.'

Badr's father was by his side.

'Get out of here, you thief!'

'It's your nephew, Father. Shukry. He is not a stranger. He is our relative. Remember,' Badr swallowed and caught his breath. 'Remember, Shukry came from Egypt looking for a job and he was staying with us until he went to Gezira.'

Shukry took his uncle's hand.

'I am sorry I disturbed you so late at night.'

There was no response except for a bewildered, vacant stare. He stooped even more than usual and his face looked drained.

'Father, come and get some rest.' Badr led him to one of the beds and helped him to lie down. He sat next to him.

Shukry pushed away Radwan's legs and made room for himself to sit on the opposite bed. The gesture irritated Badr. Why should this unwanted guest disturb his little boy's sleep?

'Badr, your father's condition is deteriorating,' Shukry whispered. 'He hit Hanniyah and hurled abuse at her ... for no reason at all.'

Badr became even more annoyed.

'What are *you* doing here? How did they give you a holiday when you just started work six months ago?'

Shukry dropped his head.

'Well, you see, they kept finding fault with me ...'

'They fired you, didn't they? What an idiot! What a lost opportunity!'

'Let me explain, Cousin.'

'Enough! I don't have patience for your excuses. You are nothing but trouble, arriving in the middle of the night and disturbing us.'

'But where else could I have gone? I don't have any money.'

'Shut up! Shut up and we'll talk in the morning.'

He left him, knowing he would be unable to continue the conversation without seriously abusing the youth. Again! Again they would have to put up with his presence until he found a job!

He went inside the room to find Haniyyah. She was lying on her side on the floor, facing the wall and crying. The room was hot, even though the window was open. Moonlight came in, but not enough air. He knelt next to her. She was perspiring and swollen, her belly nestled on the floor, her beautiful hair, her beautiful skin, her cracked feet and callused hands.

'Come on, girl, don't be silly. You're not going to be upset over what a daft old man said.' He kissed her cheek and rubbed her arm. She wept, her fists pushing into her mouth. He stroked her hair. It smelt of Naboulsi soap. 'Come on, stop crying. No one believes anything he says. He's lost his mind.'

Her distress oozed into him despite his emphatic words. He stretched out and lay behind her, his stomach pressed against her buttocks. Her skin smelled of cloves, sweat and cooking.

'What have I done to deserve this?' Her voice was muffled and broken. 'I swear by Allah. I swear . . .'

'I know, I know. You don't need to say anything.'

He felt queasy and angry. She was hurting him with these affirmations of innocence. At the core of every man was a dormant distrust, a fear that his woman, wayward and tricky, clever and teasing, could deceive him with ease. Badr did not want to inflame his own jealousy, to admit that his father's words had shaken him, even though he knew they were untrue. He must stand by her now, must not let her down.

'You're a silly girl, you are,' he made himself say. He tried to sound light and calm; he gave her hips a playful squeeze. 'You're a silly girl to worry over such a thing.'

'I heard the knocking at the door,' she said between sobs. 'Uncle Hajj was awake but the boys were asleep. I started to wake up Osama. I said to him, Osama go see who is at the door, but he was fast asleep. He wouldn't move and I felt sorry for him. Poor boy, he's been fasting all day in the heat. I went myself to open the door and your father followed me.' Her voice broke and she took a gulp of air. 'He didn't recognise your cousin at all and he started abusing and hitting me. I got frightened and came here in the room.'

Badr experienced a blankness of mind, a stillness in which the only sound he could hear was her weeping. He must get rid of Shukry; either by finding him a job with accommodation or sending him back to Egypt. Enough was enough. I could have killed him, my own flesh and blood, in my own house. I could have killed him and ruined my own life, but for the grace of God.

'Come on, girl, stop this fussing. It's not good for your condition. Come on, turn over and give me a smile. For my sake, if I am truly dear to you.'

He sensed that his words were making an impact on her. Her sobs halted, she gave a small hiccup and rolled round to face him. Her round, taut stomach was between them. Her face was red and her lips were swollen. He bent and kissed her neck and she buried her face in his shoulder.

'He will be staying here again? For how long?'

Oh, the anguish in her voice. It made him realise that this wretched house was her centre, her every day and every night. While he went out and invigorated himself with school, souq and mosque, she was home all the time and he had not been able to fulfil her dreams of a balcony, privacy, an apartment up a flight of stairs.

She was whispering to herself now, drowsy almost, but too roused to fall asleep.

'Why, Uncle Hajj? How can you say this about me, your daughter-in-law? How?'

It moved Badr to see her dispirited. Even the pain of childbirth had not crushed her like this. Simple, good-natured woman, her honour precious to her – why must she suffer like this? Why, my Lord?

XI

She loved Christmas, its gaiety and difference. She knew it from the English novels she read – snow, mistletoe and evergreen – but she also had access to the Sudan version through her Christian schoolfriends. Every year on Christmas day, with a gift in her hand, Soraya visited Nancy in Khartoum. Her Uncle Mahmoud took her, because Nancy's father was his friend and Mahmoud always visited his Christian friends, one by one, on Christmas Day, in the same way that they visited him in Eid. He would leave Soraya at Nancy's house, do his rounds, and then pick her up several hours later. Nancy's mother was Armenian and her father Irish and she often complained to Soraya about the hostility her parents' marriage encountered from their respective communities, but Nancy's house was always crowded and happy on Christmas Day, and Aunty Valeria was so glamorous and fulfilled that Soraya never took her friend's complaints seriously. This was Christmas in Khartoum: perfect weather, cool enough for a cardigan, peals of laughter, the cake with white icing, the tree with golden baubles and silver fairy dust. Then Father Christmas, his face puckered in the midst of cotton wool, his black belt suppressing the red pillow of his belly, his amazing black boots and sack in which he carried a gift for Soraya, too. When she was young, she was thrilled with the wrapped gift, and when she was older and could guess Santa's true identity, the occasion was delightful and amusing. Standing back, watching Nancy's younger brothers and their friends, aware of her cosmopolitan surroundings, being in the same room as boys her age, animated and happy to be in a party, as if this was what she was born for, she lost her Umdurman bashfulness and was drawn out by a phrase or a smile, to be her real self in public – witty, generous, and with a capacity for enjoyment that generated the equivalent in others and drew them towards her.

'What do you mean, you can't come to the bazaar?' Nancy faced her in the school yard. Both of them were in their short-sleeved white blouses and the low V-neck of the navy pinafore that marked them as senior girls. It was mid-December, and the air was cool and made school feel clean. 'It's on Sunday, this Sunday!' Nancy had plucked the hair from over her lips for the very first time and the area was red. It made her look aggrieved. 'We *always* go together to the Christmas Bazaar at Clergy House. Everyone goes!' This was another characteristic of Christmas, the anticipation, the build-up. 'And I will be in the choir.' Nancy wasn't giving up. She was an only girl and strong-willed. 'You said you would hear me sing. You promised.'

Soraya reached out and nudged one of Nancy's ringlets; thick golden-brown, just like the pictures of Goldilocks. The curls bounced over her fingers then sprang upwards again. Nancy had beautiful hair, just like her mother. Aunty Valeria's, though, was a deep, dark brown. Aunty Valeria wore glasses and still looked glamorous; her eyebrows and lips like those of a cinema star.

'Answer me,' said Nancy. 'Don't you want to buy things from the bazaar?'

'Yes, I do.'

Secondhand books and magazines were the most popular items on sale, almost as popular as the cakes and knitwear. Soraya usually bought as many novels as she could, and a few copies of *Vogue* and *Women's World*. She would be almost breathless as she surveyed the tables where the books were laid out, and choosing absorbed her to the extent that she forgot her surroundings. She would pick up the books whose covers she liked, flick the pages, look closely at the illustrations if any, and then discover that the stack she was carrying was too heavy. Time to trim her purchases – and that would vex her, for she must make the right choice. To discard a potentially wonderful novel would be a significant loss and, who knows, it might never come her way again. After she paid for her pile, she would experience a feeling of peace, an awareness of the plenty she was carrying. Often she would sit on the steps and start reading a novel while waiting for the car to pick her up.

'So why can't you come?'

They were standing in front of their classroom, under the little statue of the Madonna carrying baby Jesus. The figures were moulded on the wall itself, in a small alcove high above the white walls and the large blue shutters of the classrooms. It was shady in this part of the school and in the summer this dimness was a haven of coolness. Now, Soraya put her arms in the sleeves of her cardigan.

'Sunday is a good day to visit Nur. All the men are at the office and when I go to him in the morning, he is usually alone.'

'It's just one Sunday out of a thousand Sundays,' insisted Nancy. 'You'll feel wretched if you miss the bazaar.'

'Well, how does *he* feel missing out on everything?' She sounded sharper than she felt. The anger, heavy within her, was not yet fully aroused.

Nancy, who was kind and tender, who nursed her puppy when he was sick and adopted stray cats, said, 'How hard it must be for him! Can he not come to our house on Christmas Day? He can be carried in the car and then he can lie on the sofa and be part of the celebrations.'

Soraya was touched.

'Thank you, Nancy.' She hugged her friend and felt the questions within her start to stir. How could the world go on as if nothing had happened? As if nothing happened to Nur? 'I will tell him that you invited him. It would be wonderful if he could come to your house. He's been back from London a month and he's never been out! He's been lying in the hoash day and night.'

'He's not getting better, is he?' Nancy's voice was soft and her heavy eyebrows knitted. She put her arm around Soraya's shoulder. 'My mother said he is going to be bedridden all his life.'

Soraya jerked herself away.

'What does your mother know? Is she a doctor?' Her voice rose, 'Of course he's going to get better! If anyone breaks their arms or legs it takes months for them to mend. So it's the same for his neck and back. The doctors in London wanted him to stay much much longer than three months, but Uncle Mahmoud brought him back straight after the operation. Sometimes, Nancy, you say stupid things.'

A few girls turned their heads to look at them. Soraya turned away from Nancy. While Nur was in London, she had fretted and every day walked over to Aunt Waheeba's hoash to wait for news.

'Why doesn't he write to me?' she had whined, and remembering that he couldn't made her feel even worse. There had been anxiety over the operation, wild hope that he would become as perfect as he was before, joy that he was, at last, on his way back home, relief to see his smile again and hear his voice, then the horrible, unspoken disappointment. But it was treachery to lose hope, to say these things that Nancy and her mother were saying. Soraya needed to believe. People stayed in bed and got up again. So would he. She walked into the sunshine and the girls who were skipping rope.

'I'll join you,' she said to them, and they nodded, the two girls turning the long rope to slap the sandy floor.

Soraya watched the rope, raised her arm, and the moment before the rope rose up in the air, she lunged in, jumped right in time and picked up the rhythm. Confident now, she skipped from one end of the rope to the other. It was a green plastic rope, the kind used for hanging out the clothes. It brushed against Soraya's hair.

'Higher,' she called out.

'You're the one who's too tall!' came the reply.

'Helena! Helena, come and skip with me,' Soraya called out

to the tallest Southern girl in the school. Helena was playing netball. She turned and waved.

'Come and annoy these two who are saying I am too tall!'

It felt funny to call out and skip at the same time. She and Helena sat next to each other at the back of the classroom, both of them too tall for the front-row desks, where they would block out the blackboard for the other girls. Helena was a good four inches taller than Soraya, with a perfect posture and a long, beautiful neck. She was athletic, too, and took playing netball during the break seriously. So it was Amal, petite and vivacious, who joined in the skipping, and the two of them started to pass each other, coming closer then moving apart, facing the group who had gathered to watch them, then twirling to give them their backs.

Amal and Soraya held hands, jumping simultaneously until one of them missed the beat; the rope thudded to the ground and didn't come up again.

'Again,' said Amal.

'No, I want to drink.'

Soraya took off her cardigan and walked with Amal to the zeer. She dipped the tin mug in the water and lifted it to drink and then let water wash over her face. Cool water over her eyes, her hot cheeks, her dry lips. She filled the mug and drank again, feeling the water touching her teeth, rolling on her tongue and down her throat. She gulped; the courtyard was a blur of navy, white, and beige sand, the clamour of the girls, their laughter and the thud of the ball on the cement of the court.

'I want to invite you to my sister's wedding,' said Amal, a little out of breath from skipping. She had dimples in her cheeks, which deepened even when she was talking normally and not smiling. 'It's next week. You must come every day. Also, if you come to our house today, after school, you could help her practise her dancing.'

Soraya's eyes shone; there was nothing more exciting than a bride learning to dance, to watch her practise, to listen to the advice she was given by recently married women, to watch a new step demonstrated. Soraya would absorb it all, and when it was time for her wedding she would dance better than any other bride. The whole of Khartoum and Umdurman would talk about her.

Buoyed by the after-school outing that awaited her, she sought out Nancy to apologise and make amends. She found her with the bell in her hands.

'You know how much I admire your mother, but Aunty Valeria is wrong about Nur. He *is* going to get better.'

Nancy looked confused.

'Look, I have to go and ring the bell.'

She moved away and Soraya called after her.

'Give us a few more minutes!'

She was joking, but Nancy didn't smile. She just turned and called back.

'I can't.'

Standing in the middle of the hallway overlooking the court-yard, her strong, hairy arms lifted the heavy bell and shook it. The clamour made Soraya put her hands over her ears. Nancy's expression was resolute, her lips pressed together, her legs hip-distance apart. She was serious and responsible, which was why Sister Josephine had charged her with ringing the bell. Soraya might be better at her studies, but she would have cheated with that bell, added a few minutes to the break, sent everyone home a little bit earlier.

There was Sister Josephine now, her habit billowing behind her as she swept down the hallway ushering the girls from the yard to line up in front of their classrooms.

'Soraya, where are your spectacles?'

'In my bag, Sister.'

She fell in step with her teacher and noted the dark hair escaping from Sister Josephine's habit. She was definitely not bald, whatever anyone else said. Just had short, unkempt hair. And she would never marry and have children. She would stay as she was; a virgin, celibate. It seemed too cruel to contemplate, but it was true, and it was her choice, too. Sister Josephine did not inspire pity, but she made Soraya feel privileged. *She* was going to get married; *she* was going to have a bride's trousseau, *she* was going to experience a man's love and a man's body.

'Take care of your spectacles, Soraya. I'm pleased that you are now seeing the blackboard clearly, because I can't have you sitting in the front row! Besides, you have external examinations at the end of the school year. You must do well so that you can go to university.'

University. It sounded distant and awesome.

'Do you think they will accept me, Sister?'

'Yes,' Sister Josephine said without a smile. 'You and Amal are our strongest science contenders. Perhaps you can be accepted into medicine.'

Ambition stirred in Soraya. It would swell and take hold.

'But my father,' she began.

'Oh, I knew he would eventually relent about the spectacles,' Sister Josephine interrupted. 'Now you have no excuse. Work hard, my girl!'

Soraya started to explain that Idris didn't even know she was wearing glasses, that she had got them secretly in Alexandria, but Sister Josephine was away, rounding up the rest of the girls. The yard started to empty and it was the halls that were now crowded with navy and white.

It was as if every girl in the neighbourhood was in Amal's housh to watch the bride practise her dance routine. When Soraya walked in, the dallooka was already beating. There was the smell of sandalwood and perfume, the joyful lyrics of the song, and the breathless, expectant atmosphere of parties yet to come. Then ululations would break out and dates and sweets would be tossed in the air for the guests to catch. Soraya remembered Nur, lying propped up in bed listening to the radio. She remembered her vow not to attend any celebrations until he recovered. But this was only a practice session; she would not come to the wedding party. She would keep away. Now all eyes were on Amal's sister, standing in the middle of the gathering. Bare feet on the palm-fibre mat, she arched her back, swaying from side to side, and her neck was tilted so that her chin pointed to the sky. This was the difficult Neck dance, with all the movements concentrated on the chest and head. Reaching up and, again like a bird, craning in stylised slow motion to peck at a fruit dangling from the branch above. All the dances were designed to mimic the movement of birds, arms held back like wings, spine curved, breasts pushed out and upwards in seduction and pride.

In Soraya's assessment, this bride-to-be was doing well, stretching out with her chin further and further away. She could arch her back more and perhaps with practice she would become more flexible. Every day now, until the wedding, she would be wrapped in a blanket and hunched over the smouldering fire for the 'smoke treatment'. The herbs and perfumed wood would not only beautify her skin, but the heat would make her back muscles toned and supple.

Soraya found a better place to sit, just as the bride stopped dancing and covered her face with her hands. The dallooka ceased. In the wedding, with the bridegroom in attendance, she would continue to stand, covering her face until he moved each hand away, revealing her face with its closed eyelids and the gold ring on her nose. In some families the bride danced naked, with nothing but a belt around her waist, the bridegroom holding onto it as she moved and swayed, her skin glistening with oil and every part of her body in full view. But neither Soraya nor Amal's families supported such tribal customs.

The wazira, a jolly, hefty woman, started to talk about the fall.

'On the day of the wedding, we'll see if that bridegroom of yours is paying attention or not.' The girls laughed. 'You must reach the ground before he catches you. Then we will jeer at him and you would have scored a point. So take him unawares, don't give him any sign. Dance as you will, and then abruptly let go and fall to the ground.'

The girls started talking among themselves. Most bridegrooms were dazed and easily tricked. But there were sharp and quick men, who would be sensitive to the faintest facial expression, watchful for the slightest shift in movement so that they would reach out and grab their bride just in the nick of time. If the bride succeeded in reaching the ground, she would be covered in a large, bright coloured cloth and there would be a pause in the dancing. Soraya imagined herself enveloped in this silk, unable to see. Nur would remove it, fold it and put it on his shoulder. Only then would she stand up to dance again.

But now the beat of the dallooka quickened and Amal was pulling her to the centre of the circle. This was the energetic dance Soraya excelled in, and the bride could do well to learn from her. First position, both hands covering her face, and then she removed one and left the other. Arching her back, but not too much, because the focus of this dance was on the hips. She pushed her right buttock out while shifting her feet on the rug, heels pressed hard on the ground. Pulsing, quivering, flicking her behind ... In her own wedding – when Nur got better – she would be in a sleeveless red dress, her head covered in gold, coins on her forehead, kohl in her eyes, a bracelet high on her arm, henna on her hands and feet. She would swing her braids, which, on that day, would be extended with fine black silk, made long enough to almost touch the back of her knees. Nur would stand tall in front of her, a sword in his hand, his eyes watching her every movement, her supple back, her breasts and bare arms. She would heave towards him, again and again, wanting him and offering herself. Don't take your eyes off me. Catch me when I fall ...

'There is no reason why you can't go to both the wedding and the bazaar,' said Fatma. 'Actually, we are obliged to return Amal's invitation because, remember, she came to my wedding.'

'She and her mother came to see Nur when he returned,' added Soraya.

She had taken to dividing people into two camps; those who came to visit Nur, and those who didn't. The first group were true comrades. The second earned themselves a place on her black list. She shunned them, and had no qualms talking about why she shunned them. Girls she had been friendly with found their greetings unreturned because they and their families had not paid their respects to Nur Abuzeid. Soraya had self-righteously recorded every visitor when Nur first arrived from London, those first days when the saraya was as busy as it had been the previous year, when Uncle Mahmoud was ill. At that time, Fatma and Nassir had come especially from Medani. This time they moved permanently to Umdurman, and were now living with Idris. Nassir said he would not leave his brother.

'Nur needs his family and friends around him. We must not leave him alone to brood and become sad.'

Soraya approved of Nassir's stance, and she was delighted with Fatma's presence; her sister and the children all with her, under one roof.

Now Fatma said, as she bent down to cut her toenails,

'We can't sit in Aunt Waheeba's hoash day and night any more, waiting for people to call on us. Everyone did already. People were gracious to the extreme.'

'Not all of them!' Malice shot from Soraya's heart towards those negligent ones. She had no forgiveness.

'Most of them,' said Fatma, emphatically. 'We really can't complain. Now we need to go out and fulfil our social obligations.'

'I don't have the inclination to go to a wedding.' Soraya, lying on the opposite bed, was staring up at the ceiling. '*No* celebration feels right while Nur is ill.'

She had forgone her birthday last month, so there was no party, no gathering of girls and no cake from Papa Costa's. Such a contrast to last year, on her sixteenth birthday, when she invited all her friends from school and Uncle Mahmoud hired a magician who proved himself to be the most marvellous of entertainers.

The sound of the scissors ceased, and she sensed Fatma looking at her.

'Soraya, there is nothing we can do more for Nur. We are with him, we keep him company, but Nassir has to go to the office, you have to go to school and Nur's friends are either studying or working.'

'I know all this,' said Soraya. 'But I'm still not convinced that I should go to Amal's house.'

Fatma took a big breath.

'Batool is going to be married next month. We need to prepare for her wedding. So you see in Nur's household itself—'

Soraya sat up. 'I don't believe you!'

Fatma sighed and turned her attention back to her toenails. She was pregnant, but it was early days and her stomach was not big enough to prevent her from bending over.

'Yes, it's confirmed. Uncle Mahmoud wants a good wedding for her. He is marrying her to one of his office boys, and Aunt Waheeba promised her a full trousseau, from a double bed to a sewing needle. Batool is delighted, and so are her parents who will be coming especially from Sinja for the celebrations.'

'I will have nothing to do with this!' Soraya folded her arms across her chest. 'The wedding needs to be postponed till Nur is better.'

'Aunt Waheeba is not happy, either, but she has no choice. Uncle Mahmoud has already given his word. Besides, Batool is like a daughter to Aunt Waheeba and we are not in mourning. There is no justification for denying the girl her happiness.'

'I will not take part,' repeated Soraya.

'Batool would be heartbroken if you keep away. She will think it is because she is a poor relation.'

'Don't be silly. I love her, and I have always treated her like a sister.'

'Well, then, you have to stand by her at her happy hour.'

Soraya frowned. 'And where is Nur going to go while the hoash throbs with wedding celebrations? How is *he* going to feel?'

'I don't know,' said Fatma. 'And I can't argue with you forever.' She put the scissors on the side-table and stretched out on the bed. 'I am tired today. I am really not well and oh, the pain in my back.'

'You shouldn't have been hunched over like that.' Soraya was still in a combative mood. 'I would have cut your nails for you if you'd asked.'

Fatma didn't reply. She looked queasy, and later that night, before Nassir returned from his evening outing, she woke the whole household with her cries of pain. Only when she expelled her four-month-old foetus, did the pain finally cease.

It was a frightening experience for Soraya, even though she was shielded from seeing the worst of it. Halima came over promptly and took over the situation, and Idris stayed awake and was uncharacteristically tender and helpful to his daughters. For a long time he had resisted installing a telephone, but now it proved to be valuable. In addition to summoning the midwife, the telephone also conveyed the news to Nassir. He came home, drunk as usual but still able to absorb the shock and console his wife.

The following day Soraya stayed home from school. It felt odd to see Fatma lying in bed ill. It felt odd that now everyone visited them in their hoash instead of Aunt Waheeba's. The news spread. Fatma has had a miscarriage. Nassir Abuzeid's wife miscarried. Uncle Mahmoud stopped by on his way to the office and Nabilah came later on in the morning, in a new frock, on her way to coffee with the Egyptian Minister's wife. The neighbours trooped in and out. One brought soup and another a jug of fresh orange juice. Batool came over and stayed to help with serving the guests. Every woman relation was gathered, and yet, when Soraya saw Waheeba walking in, she cried, 'How could you leave Nur alone, Aunty!'

'Girl, on a day like this I have to be with my son's wife. How can I not?'

She had not set foot outside her hoash since Nur returned from London, would not leave his side for any occasion or obligation. Which is why it shocked Soraya to see her. And Waheeba did not just come for a quick, dutiful visit; instead, she stretched out on the bed perpendicular to Fatma's and made herself comfortable. Soraya overheard the women gossip about Waheeba, as she handed them out glasses of tea. They were whispering, 'It's good that she has finally started to go out. Now that she has visited Fatma, she will visit others as well.'

These words scorched Soraya. She wanted her aunt to be always with Nur. Life should not be normal until Nur was standing on his feet again.

At night, she was woken by Fatma's heavy movements in the bathroom and Halima's voice checking on her. Batool was spending the night with them to help with the children and she left her bed, next to Soraya's, and went to fetch water for Fatma. They were all indoors because it was too cold to sleep outside. In the darkness, Soraya remembered that she had not congratulated Batool on her engagement. She should have, but there was a bad feeling, a grudge incubating inside her. It was uncharacteristic of her to be ungenerous, and she herself felt uncomfortable, unused to these new feelings that were lodged in her stomach like an undigested meal. She drifted back to sleep and, before she was even deeply asleep, the nightmare came back.

In the twilight between illusion and sleep, an evil pocket claimed her with authority and strength. The pocket held her snug, caught up in a single, jumbled thought, churning with no release; situations, conversations and dilemmas repeating themselves with no outlet or resolution. The sides of the pocket, meaty and crimson, prodded and squashed her. She was pinned down, unable to move her legs, unable to wave her arms, like the day she was six years old, when she was tricked with sweets and new clothes before the slash and tear of the midwife's knife.

Fear made her scream. Then she could turn over, she could move. The sounds of sobs from the next bed were real. Fatma was crying out for her mother, the mother Soraya could not remember. *Yumma, Yumma.* Soraya cried about Nur, not understanding why he wasn't getting better, or why the accident happened in the first place. Stand up, Nur! Run and play football again. Hold a book in your hands. Write with a pen. Go to poetry readings and debates, which girls can't attend, and come back and tell me about them.

His voice was clear on the telephone, surprising and precious. She knew it was him, straight away. He knew it was her, straight away. He said her name and she forgot last night's bad dreams, forgot even that he was ill. She forgot the accident and the hospital in Alexandria, the months he went to London and left her all alone. She smiled and said, 'This is the first time ever that we've spoken on the phone.'

'It's good that my Uncle Idris finally relented and installed one.'

'We must be the last house in the country to be connected.'

He laughed. 'You are exaggerating. But yes, Idris Abuzeid is a conservative man.'

'But believe it or not, Nur . . .' She spoke quickly. They would not have privacy for long, someone or another, family members, guest or a servant, would come in and bring the conversation to an end. 'Today, of course, I didn't go to school, and my father surprisingly said, "You must go tomorrow. You can't miss too many days of school."' She mimicked her father's voice, his coarse accent.

Nur chuckled. He, too, adopted her father's accent to do an even better impersonation.

'My daughter, I have become an enlightened man. Education is a priority. We are on the brink of a new dawn of self–determination and independent rule. I read this in the papers.'

She giggled. 'Does he read the papers?' The hostility to her father was always around the corner, ready to pounce.

'Soraya, my dear you are being too harsh.'

She liked him saying 'My dear.' It softened her.

'I miss you so much and there is no way I can come and see you. I can't leave Fatma.'

'I know. How is she now?'

'She's fine. The doctor came to see her and said not to worry. Is that why you telephoned, to ask about Fatma?'

'Of course, she's my sister-in-law. If I could, I would have come to see her. Tell her I was asking after her.'

She put her hand on her hips.

'And here I am thinking you called to speak to me.'

He laughed. 'Yes, I want to complain that I don't see you enough. And when I do, you sit all quiet and not inclined to chat.'

'Only because we're never alone. You are always surrounded by visitors.'

She felt a sense of urgency, a fear that if her father overheard this conversation, he would be furious.

'I get bored when I'm alone.' Nur's voice was higher, thinner.

'Soon you will get better.' Her voice didn't waver, it trilled with confidence. 'While we're speaking now, a scientist in America is in his laboratory working out a cure for you. I just know it.'

She sensed him snatch the hope she was offering, his unspoken thanks.

'An American scientist, you think?'

'Yes, Nur.'

'He would look like Errol Flynn?'

'Oh no! He would be bald and grumpy but exceedingly clever.'

'He would have a degree from Harvard?'

'Definitely.'

'Come and see me.'

'I will. As soon as I can.'

'Soraya . . .'

'Yes?'

'Every song I hear on the radio reminds me of you.'

When the euphoria of that conversation subsided, she repeated his words to herself time and again, treasuring the memory of his warm voice, the hint of a smile, the lilt and playfulness with which he had said her name. After she hummed the tunes he had hummed and dwelt on the lyrics he had quoted, she asked herself, 'Who dialled our number for him? Who held the receiver to his ear while he talked?'

Someone else had done all that, she realised, another pair of hands, another's body, another's movements. One of the servants did all that.

She turned to novels for comfort. Nancy brought her a selection from the Christmas bazaar and Soraya would make sure her father was out of the house, then safely put on her glasses and lie down in bed to read. Outside, she could hear the distant sound of a radio and Fatma talking to the servants. She was back on her feet now and getting stronger every day. Soraya propped another pillow under her head. She took a bite off her pink mawlid doll, from the cone-like base; it was as sweet as candy floss. Of course, Soraya had refused to attend the celebration for the Prophet's birthday; the colourful tent that was erected in the square behind Uncle Mahmoud's saraya, where horses pranced and singers chanted, but she could not resist the traditional mawlid doll, with its colourful paper-tissue dress and its delicious body made of solid pink candy. She read while chewing. *Lorna Doone*, *Rebecca*, *Liza of Lambeth*, *Emma* and *The Woman in White* – these she all enjoyed, but a novel about a woman whose husband returned crippled from the war, disturbed her. She abandoned it, but then went back to it, fascinated and, at the same time, repelled. She wanted happy endings, she wanted things to work out, she wanted Fate to comply with human desires.

She heard her father's voice and her blood froze. Fear made her unable to move. As he opened the door she sprang up, shocked that he was home from the office so early.

'What are you doing?' He stood in his long jellabiya, his eyes wide, incredulous. 'What's this? You're wearing glasses! Who do you think you are?'

He walked forward and slapped her. The glasses crashed to the floor. She screamed and covered her face.

'Do I have no say in this house?' Idris bellowed. 'I forbade you from wearing glasses, which means no wearing glasses. Can you hear me?' He hit her again, a blow that landed on her shoulder.

'Yes, I can hear you. Yes!' she bawled.

Pain throbbed on the side of her head and that other, inner pain, that she was of no worth, insignificant, dirty and small.

'Keep silent! I don't want to hear your voice.' His voice was level now, as if he had rid himself of most of his anger.

Fatma hurried into the room. She did not need to ask any questions, but stood helplessly at the door with her hands down her sides. Soraya could not see the expression on her face. Her vision was blurred. She couldn't see where the glasses had fallen.

'Do you think you are a boy? Answer me!' He gripped her arm.

'No. No I don't think that.' Her voice was flat. 'These glasses are especially designed for women.'

'Keep quiet, Soraya. Enough,' said Fatma coming closer.

'You dare defy me?' His face was close to hers now and the spit that flew from his mouth smacked her forehead.

It occurred to Soraya that he would forbid her from going to school, that any minute now the penalty would fall. But Fatma's presence must have restrained him. He turned to her and said,

'You, her older sister, should guide her, instead of leaving her to do what she likes.'

'I will, Father.' She gently pulled Soraya away from him.

He walked out of the room hissing, 'You disgust me!'

'You disgust me, too,' Soraya mumbled to herself.

She ignored Fatma's platitudes and refused to cry. She picked up her glasses; one of the lenses was broken and she still refused to cry. She checked her face in the mirror to make sure there were no marks, bruises or cuts, then she curled up in bed and closed her eyes. Fatma sat next to her and stroked her arm.

'Don't worry about the glasses, Nassir will get them fixed. In the meantime, wear the pair Nur got you, we still have them. Didn't you realise that with all the strikes this week, he's been leaving work early? Today the police had to break up a demonstration with tear-gas. Gordon's College's been closed and the shopkeepers are afraid to open for fear of looting. And it's good father didn't confiscate your book; you can finish reading it later.'

Fatma's voice reached her from far away. She was already sinking into a state close to sleep, being sucked back into the pocket, that place where she could not move her body. Red flesh was closing upon her. What was this small, mean world of the pocket? Madness? Or empathy with Nur? Or was it being buried alive? In Alexandria, on the beach, they used to bury each other in the sand, the whole body underground and only the head sticking out free. Was this how Nur felt? Perpetually restrained by heavy sand. Someone was calling her name. It was Fatma of course.

'Soraya my love, did you fall asleep?'

She rolled over. The movement felt good. She stretched her legs and arms out. There was an ache on the side of her head from where her father had hit her. It will go away. She was wide awake now, and could make out the details of the room. Her schoolbooks were on the dressing table, reflected in the mirror.

This was where she did her homework, looking up to make faces at herself in the mirror.

'I have to leave this house,' she said to Fatma. 'I have to get away from him. I will marry Nur and then I will be free to do what I want. I will have a husband and Father will not have any say over my life.'

Fatma sighed. 'This is not a time to talk of Nur and marriage.'

'You mean because he is ill? He will get better.' She stood up and said, 'I am going now to Uncle Mahmoud. I am going to complain to him about Father.'

Fatma gasped, 'Have you gone mad, girl?'

'Tell me, what other choice do I have?' She was already finding her slippers and smoothing her hair. She wrapped her tobe around her and headed for the door. 'There is no one in the world Father will pay heed to except his elder brother.'

She found herself navigating lunch with a knife and fork. Her uncle and Nabilah were having veal escallops, stuffed vine leaves and yoghurt salad. An extra plate was set for Soraya next to the two children. A family sitting around a dining table sharing a meal – it was like walking into a film or stepping into a novel! The servants, in embroidered blue jellabiyas, with red sashes around their waists, collected the main course and brought in dessert, a creamy trifle as well as a selection of apples, oranges and pears.

After the meal, sitting sipping mint tea with her uncle, she told him what happened.

'I need those glasses, Uncle. I have exams in a few months' time, final exams. I have to see the blackboard properly, I have to be able to read with ease.'

Uncle Mahmoud looked grave but not surprised. He smoked his cigarette with its black, slim filter. There were crinkles of white in his hair and he looked solid and important. Now he spoke slowly.

'If Idris finds out that you have complained to me, most likely he will be even harsher with you. I will have to proceed with tact. I do support you, Soraya. I want you to sit for the Cambridge School Certificate and I want you to go to university. There is nothing wrong with a girl wearing glasses. If you need them, then you must have them.'

'Thank you, Uncle, I knew you would not let me down.' She leaned and kissed his forehead. 'I am sorry if I disturbed your siesta.'

'Don't worry. I only need a brief rest today, as I'm not going back to Khartoum. I decided it would be safer to close the office this evening.'

'Did you hear, Uncle, about the girls in Umdurman who left their school and went out in a demonstration?'

'Yes, and now the whole school has been shut down.'

'Oh no! All this because Egypt abrogated the Condominium Treaty!'

He smiled at her instinctive response.

'The move shouldn't have come from the Egyptians. It's humiliating for our national movement, and it's put those of us who support a unity with Egypt in an awkward position.' He took a draw on his cigarette. 'And, naturally, the British are angry; they claim Egypt wants to swallow the Sudan!'

'Maybe she does, Uncle?'

He smiled. 'My, my! You are questioning me, too! Idris is not going to subdue you as he subdued your sisters.'

She flushed, wishing that he would talk to her more about politics, about trade, about the ways of the world. His opinion would be the right one, his information the most accurate.

'Look,' he said. 'I have something for you.' He stood up and from a cabinet brought out a box of chocolates. 'Have a piece.'

She reached for the diamond shape, wrapped in a purple foil when suddenly there was a vivid flash and a whizzing noise. She squealed and started to laugh. It was a trick, and the thrill revived her spirit and dispelled what was left of her earlier gloom.

'I thought they were real chocolates, I did!' she squealed.

He chuckled. 'I am taking this trick, as well as a real box of Groppi chocolates, to my friends Mr and Mrs Harrison, who are having a Christmas party. You must come with me, Soraya.'

Her instinct was to wrap her arms around him in joy. Gone was her stance of not attending any celebrations until Nur recovered. It was swamped by the magnitude of the opportunity, the unexpectedness of the invitation. Mr and Mrs Harrison were newly married and romantic. It would be a proper grown-up party, not one for children.

'Thank you, Uncle. Thank you!'

'Can you speak English well and impress these people?'

She answered him in English.

'Of course, Uncle, of course I can.' She tried to sound as proper as she could. 'I graciously accept this invitation.'

She would wear a new dress that day, something glamorous and ladylike; she would have it specially made, there was still time.

Pleased with her reaction, Mahmoud switched to English.

'You are not only my niece, Soraya, you are like a daughter to me.'

She giggled. 'Your future daughter-*in-law*, Sir.'

But as soon as she said those words, there was an odd, cold pause. He looked taken aback; in his eyes a mixture of dis-approval, sorrow and apology. Her exuberance faltered. She had said the wrong thing but did not understand why.

'I will not do it,' he said, his voice hoarse with emotion. 'Never. I will not shackle you to an invalid.'

XII

So Nur goes on strike. He will not eat. He will not drink. He will not talk, even. His demands are death or a miraculous recovery that will restore Soraya to him. The latter, of course, is preferable but he no longer believes it can happen and neither does anyone around him. Therefore the former is more realistic. Death, a violent death, because every door of reprieve has shut down and left him in darkness. His sentence has barely started and he will not serve his time. He is innocent and does not deserve this punishment, this life which is not a life. Rebellion fizzes in him. They want him to be sweet; they want him to smile and chat. They want him, against all odds, not to look at what they have and what he has lost, without feeling bitter. Yesterday, his mother, who will not give up hope, brought him a spiritual healer. He read verses from the Qur'an in a rasping voice, mumbling the words, oblivious to their beauty. Nur, who loved rhythm and appreciated metaphor, whose intellect thrived on eloquence, took offence. The faqih leaned over him, squeezed his rigid arms and motionless legs, and the man's breath stank and his eyes were bloodshot and yellow. He poured water over Nur's body, as if it were a wilting plant that could be brought back to life. He made Nur drink water in which he had soaked pieces of paper and ink. It was the last thing he drank before he went on strike . . .

His mother is weeping. If he starts to feel sorry for her, he will soften and give in. He is seeing too much of her and this is part of the problem. The men go to work in the mornings, and again after their lunch and midday siesta, while he is stuck at home with the babble of women. At first he had taken an interest in their activities; curious to see rituals he had been excluded from – the woman squatting to pat henna on his mother's feet, the mashata braiding her hair, the fuss over Batool's wedding. Hours spent grooming and hours spent cooking, the sideways, quirky ways they chat. But this voyeuristic streak hadn't lasted long. He wants to be the hero of his own life. He wants to do, to reach, to contribute.

The weather dictates his movements – if they can be called such. In the late afternoon, when it starts to get pleasant, he is carried outside to the hoash. His bed is placed as far away as possible from the cooking area, but the other angharaibs are arranged around him and he becomes a natural part of the gathering. When the women are not cooking, they come and lounge adjacent to him, sipping their coffee and gossiping. They move back again to their pots and stoves when male visitors arrive. At night, everyone sleeps outside. This is Nur's favourite time, the most normal and familiar, staring up at the stars as he had done all his life, waiting for sleep to come, listening to the night sounds of the alley or the ululations and beat of the dallooka that mark a bridegroom's procession to the home of his future wife. In the morning, when the sun becomes too hot and the flies start to annoy him, he asks to be moved to his room. This is where the radio stands, taking up the whole corner. There is the telephone and the fan, as well as all the things that are his – clothes, watch, comb – which he must ask someone to fetch. He has lost all sense of privacy. There is no bathroom he can lock himself in, rub his own body with a towel, pull, scratch, wipe, fiddle. He hates. There is nothing, now, he does not hate. Anger is solid and opaque; it blocks his way and is insurmountable. There is nothing for him, so he should gracefully leave. Broken spine, broken engagement, broken heart – they should put him out of his misery. Prisoners sentenced to twenty-five years of hard labour are better off than him.

He closes his eyes. They think he is asleep and start to talk among themselves.

'What's wrong with him today?' they drawl.

There is a creeping tediousness in their voices for the drama of his accident had been played out. People's shock, indignation and pity had gushed forth in this particular order, but now they are drifting away. Now everyone is inclined to move on to another challenge, another crisis, or, better still, a cause for celebration – something cheerful, or even just the swing of ordinary life. They will leave him behind – for what?

His new nurse, Shukry, offers him soup, but Nur clenches his teeth and purses his lips. He does not particularly like this cousin of Ustaz Badr, who is unlike him in every way. But Nur's refusal to eat is a matter of principle, unrelated to the performance and disposition of this reluctant nurse.

Nassir comes in. He leans and whispers, 'What you need is to get drunk! Drunk out of your mind so that you can't think any more. Leave it to me, I'll come tonight and make you oblivious.'

This is disingenuous of Nassir. He knows that drink makes Nur weepy and querulous, intoxicated with self-pity. It eventually provides the convulsion of migraine and the stillness of exhaustion, but neither a deep nor lasting release. Nassir suggests drink as a remedy because he, himself, wants to drink (always) and if he can convince Waheeba that liquor is beneficial to her ill son, she will fish for her leather wallet which hangs on a string around her neck and start funding. Nassir is a buffoon, and Nur looks straight at his brother, at his flaccid face, his shifty, bleary eyes and thinks, 'Why wasn't it you instead?'

His father comes in.

'I will call the doctor.'

His father can't stand the sight of him, he never meets his eye. Politeness urges Nur to greet his father, to reply to his questions, but still he resists. Even if Soraya were standing in front of him, he would not speak to her or smile, because looking at her is like nourishment, and he will not cross that picket line yet.

Fatma says, 'He is upset because of all the preparations for Batool's wedding.'

She is completely wrong. His mother wails and says, 'His father broke off his engagement to Soraya. Now he wants to die and leave me.'

She is right, of course.

When he first came back from London, he was happy to be home. Umdurman wrapped itself around him like satin and wiped his tears away. Love was everywhere: in the visitors who came to welcome him, in the sound of the birds, the smells of the hoash, the very texture of the wind, which, at night, carried snatches of songs and wedding drums. He relished the early morning coolness, the shady coolness, the dewy, supple air that was as fresh as young skin. He inhaled the smells of cardamom with coffee, incense with sandalwood, cumin with cooking, luxuriated in the sounds of water being poured on the ground, a donkey braying, the birds riotous, knowing, hopeful and small; loud and fragile. His senses were sharpened, as if by not walking or touching with his hands, his skin had become more sensitive, his vision, hearing and sense of smell sharper than ever before.

Then, after the first two months, people drifted away. The occasion of his return was over and he must get on with his new life. But what to do with himself? When a fly hovers around his face, irritating him by scratching his eyelashes, flurrying in front of his nostrils, he cannot brush it away. Someone else must do that. So many are at his service day and night, it is disgusting. It makes no sense. People are labouring away just so that he can exist. The English shoot injured horses. They lay them down to rest. And that makes perfect sense.

Second morning of the strike: the fresh, gentle sun. When he was young, he used to run around this hoash, his bare feet on the uneven floor, his arms flapping against the sheets of the angharaibs. He used to pick guava from that tree in the corner and eat it raw. He used to take pieces of coal from the kitchen

163

area and scribble on the wall. And when he was a little older and outgrew the hoash, the whole alley became his playground, to kick ball with the neighbourhood boys or follow the donkey that delivered milk from hoash to hoash.

Another dinner uneaten, and the crescendo of concern rises.

'Perhaps he has malaria. Has the doctor seen him?'

'He likes the radio. Put it on for him, to amuse him.'

'Prop him up with pillows.'

'Lie him flat on his back, it's more comfortable.'

'Call the English doctor from Khartoum.'

'Make him something tasty to eat, something special. Send for some sponge cake from Papa Costa's, or those Groppi chocolates his father saves for guests.'

'Instead of kirsa and mullah, stuff a sandwich for him.'

'Nassir, take him out for a drive. The fresh air will do him good and it will be a change of scene.'

'Poor lad.'

He wants to spit in the face of pity. He wants to end it all, not with pills and a deep sleep. No, he wants a dagger plunged in his heart, or the whirling ceiling fan dropping straight down at him, the blades ripping through his useless long limbs. Or his neck sliced like that of a bull. He wants blood, anger and bile erupting.

His mother says, 'Cry, my son. Don't keep things to yourself. Talk and cry so that you can relieve yourself.'

Can he really cry? His heart is hard and bitterness blocks the tear ducts. Soraya will marry someone else. In a year or two she will be a bride and there is nothing he can do about it. He will not take his place at the Abuzeid office; he is finished in that respect. He will not go to Cambridge University, even though he excelled in his exams. He will not play football again, he will not drive a car. He will not, he will not, he will not. It is wave upon wave of anger, and not a single drop of tears.

Nassir bounces in, waving a letter.

'It's for you, from Dublin. I didn't know you had a friend called Fuad?'

Tuf Tuf is what everyone called him in Victoria College, the best of the 'Old Boys'. Nur yearns to tear open the envelope, to draw Tuf Tuf close. But he will not have Nassir's voice reading out his friend's words of comfort and well wishes. He stares past his brother, to the swaying branch of an alley tree that yields only thorns. Receiving no response, Nassir gets bored and goes away.

Finding Nur alone, Fatma sits by his side.

'Please eat something, Nur, you are making your father and mother very anxious. All of us are worried about you. Please, for our sake. Are you upset with Uncle Mahmoud because he broke off your engagement to Soraya? She is sad, too, but Nur, Uncle Mahmoud is the head of the family. You know that when he makes a decision we have to obey, because he knows what is best for us. You and Soraya will always be cousins. She will come and see you.' Fatma pauses. 'On occasions, of course, not like before. It's only that she needs to keep away these days. It was never an official betrothal, and now it has to be made clear to Umdurman society that she is free. Do you understand what I mean?'

Nur closes his eyes and pretends to doze. Hunger and thirst give vivid dreams. He dreams of a sensation, singular, focused and distilled. He dreams of his foot touching the floor, of the weight of his body bearing down. He dreams of gravity.

Day three of the strike. He is weak from hunger. He drinks milk but will not talk.

'Look,' his mother says. 'Look who has come to stay with us. All the way from Sinja.'

Another trick to make him perk up, to get him to speak? A new face. He gazes at a boy of about ten years old. He has an earnest, trustful face, a tranquillity.

His mother prattles on, explaining the boy's lineage; a son of a distant cousin.

'Zaki's been sent here to go to school. There are no junior schools in Sinja and he's been crying to continue after elementary school, he's that clever.'

Nur remembers his relations in Sinja but doesn't remember this particular boy. It's been years since he was there, and Zaki must have been very young. Nur used to feel sorry for that branch of the family, because they were poor; now he doesn't any more. Why should he, when his misfortune is greater than theirs?

Zaki looks at Nur with curiosity. There is no pity in his eyes. Zaki accepts Nur as he is, because he has no concept of what he was like before the accident. He extends his hand to shake his, and when he finds no response, cups his palm around Nur's elbow. Nur can move his elbow if he wants, in a jabbing, upward flutter. He remembers that he is on strike. He closes his eyes, and speaks for the first time in two days.

'Get out of my room.'

He also answers Ustaz Badr's greeting when he walks in.

'How is my star pupil?'

Nur shakes his head.

'I am the most useless of your students.' It feels strange to talk again.

'Don't say that, man, say alhamdullilah instead.'

'For what?'

Badr is taken aback but moves his seat closer.

'Well, for one you can be thankful for your eyesight.'

'I would rather be blind.'

'Really?'

Never seeing Soraya's face again. If he was blind and mobile, walking towards the unseen, touching, pushing, carrying. Would he be good enough for her then?

'And your mind,' says Badr.

'What do you mean?'

'I mean your intellect, your reason, your ability to recognise. Losing one's mind is one of the saddest of fates. It is an exile.'

Nur recognises the fleeting pain in Badr's eyes and wants him to keep talking.

'You are with us, Nur, in our company. You are among your

166

family and friends. You are blessed with love and care.'

'I am a burden on them. I have no future.' His voice is thick, but he needs to say these ugly words.

'Only Allah knows our future.'

Nur looks away and the question comes out in a whisper, 'Why did He do this to me? I don't deserve it. I am not a bad person. I shouldn't be punished.'

Badr sighs.

'The Prophet Muhammad, peace be upon him, said, *When Allah loves a people, He tries them*. This is a trial, son, not a punishment. You are being drawn into the company of the Lord.'

Tears come to Nur's eyes.

'But it doesn't feel good! I just want to be ordinary. To be like everyone else.'

'Remember at school we set you examinations to see which one of you would excel and which one of you would fail? It is the same in life. Allah tests our patience and our fortitude. He tests our strength of faith. Be patient and there will be endless rewards for you, insha'Allah.'

'You mean I will die and go to Paradise. Well, let it happen now and get it over with.'

'No, no don't say that, Nur. You are young and you don't know what the future has in store for you.'

'I don't believe that I will get better. This miracle won't happen.'

'But there are other exits, a release of some kind. Maybe none of us can see it now or imagine it, but we have to pray for it and wait. Trust in Allah's mercy, be reassured that you are safely in His hands.'

Nur feels like a child who has been taken seriously by an adult. Badr had looked him in the eye and had talked, really talked, about what happened.

'Come and see me again,' he says.

His teacher's words stay with him. They blend with a line of a poem he had studied at school. *The winds don't blow in the direction the ships favour.*

Day four of the strike. He drinks soup, but will not have anything solid. He answers in monosyllables when questions are put to him. Zaki, thick skinned and unsmiling, comes home from school and barges into his room. He is wearing his school uniform and carrying a satchel. He reeks of the outside world, of sweat and the sweets schoolboys buy from the women who squat with their wares outside the school gates. Zaki clutches a paper cone full of peanuts and greets Nur the way he did the day before, grubby hand cupping elbow. Today Nur lifts his elbow in response, the little that he can, and Zaki does not expect more. To Nur he appears brave, away from home in a new city; his first day at school, and his presence in the room is not overbearing. There is no irritation radiating from the boy, or a desire to impose. He is blunt and matter of fact, but light, not weighed down by awkwardness and confusion.

'Here take this . . .' He pops a peanut in Nur's mouth.

Nur should spit it out, but his teeth crush the fresh nut and the taste is strange on his fasting tongue. Zaki pops another one in.

'Enough,' Nur protests, and Zaki obeys, neither meekly nor grudgingly but as if it is natural to move on and do something else.

He takes his reading book out of his satchel and holds it up in front of Nur's face.

'Can you help me with my homework?'

Nur could tell him to get out of the room. He could taunt him and say, 'Are you stupid? Your folks have sent you all this way to get an education and you can't do your homework by yourself?'

But, despite his age, Zaki commands respect, and Nur does not want to be mean. Besides, the words 'help me' rally his inherent sense of honour. Somewhere deep inside, beneath the crushed body, 'help me' reaches his real self, it chimes with his true voice, it touches his essence.

From across the room, Zaki collects three pillows from the other beds and arranges them on Nur's lap in such a way that when he places the book on top of them, the words are in perfect line with Nur's vision.

He opens the book to the first page.

'See, now I don't have to hold it up! When you finish reading this page, I will turn the page for you. Now read!'

Nur reads. He reads, and there is a reason not to die. This is an activity he had forgotten, a pleasure he can take up again. The boy, Zaki, has solved the problem of raising a book to eye level and he is willing to turn the pages. In a few days' time, Ustaz Badr walks in, carrying a wooden easel dislodged from an unwanted desk in his school. He props it up in front of Nur like a table and other books, not just schoolbooks, are placed on it. Nur's old books to read again, and now that his appetite is whetted he wants more, more words, more stories, more poems. Hajjah Waheeba gives Ustaz Badr money and Nur dictates the titles that he wants from the bookshop. Ustaz Badr recommends this author and reminds him of another. Nur is occupied; Nur is busy. Why has no one thought of this before? Why has the obvious taken so long? When he reads, he floats in a current of thoughts and images; he swims as if he is moving his arms and legs. This is a kind of movement, this is a momentum, a build-up, starting, strolling, wandering, exploring. He is blessed with literacy. Something has not been taken away from him. Something, like his family's love and his family's prosperity, is there to buffer him. The words on the page are like a breath that muffles his thoughts, tousles his sentiments, plays havoc with the arguments in his head. The words on the page are a mirror. They reflect his secrets and his beauty. He is more than an invalid; he is more than a tragedy.

He is Nur Abuzeid and he is reading again.

XIII

'He was doing well for a while, busying himself with his books and then suddenly he deteriorated again.' Waheeba addressed herself to the ladies sitting with her in the hoash, but deliberately ignored Nabilah. She had received her co-wife coolly but her agitation at this unprecedented visit was obvious.

Nabilah sat on the opposite bed, with her children at either side. She felt them pressing against her, both sullen in their best clothes and with their hair brushed and neat. She, too, had taken special care with her appearance. She was dressed modestly, for why should she put on a show when she was only walking down a dusty alley to sit in Waheeba's courtyard? But she had made a point of wearing a new cotton dress and having her hair done. A visit to the hairdresser in Khartoum always uplifted her spirits and increased her confidence, while a new dress, however simple, was gratifying in its very newness; crisp, uncreased and smelling of fresh cotton. The children stared at Nur. He was asleep, sedated as Waheeba had explained, but it was a restless sleep for he moved his head from side to side and occasionally mumbled. Was he ever going to stabilise or were these migraines psychological? Did Mahmoud want Farouk and Ferial to see their half-brother before it was too late or was this too dramatic an assumption? It was not something to be proud of, but actually the children had never been to see Nur since the accident.

This morning over breakfast Mahmoud had confronted her.

'How could you, Madame, have overlooked this! How could you not have taken them all these past months?'

'You didn't tell me,' she snapped back.

'Must I tell you everything? Can you not think for yourself?

Such a simple social obligation – is it not obvious to you?'

Nabilah was unruffled by this criticism.

'You told me I need never set foot in Waheeba's quarters. So how, then, can I accompany the children? You are their father. *You* are the one who should have taken them.'

He frowned and pushed away his plate. He never took the children out unless Nabilah was with him.

'Send them with the nanny.'

'The nanny won't be able to protect them if Waheeba pulls any tricks.'

'Nonsense! You are being fanciful. Today,' he insisted, standing up to leave to the office. 'Today they must go to him. We've left it too long, and now he's had another setback. Either send them with the nanny or go with them yourself.'

Now that she was actually sitting in Waheeba's hoash, curiosity gripped her. She had always wanted to see Waheeba's quarters. Not that she had any doubt that they were inferior to hers, but still, she craved the small details. The hoash was large, with the string beds arranged in a large rectangle. Nur's bed was one of them, but his was a proper hospital bed with wheels. Coffee tables of various sizes were arranged in the middle of the rectangle, and the smallest of them were pulled near the beds, within arm's reach. It was as traditional, and as crude, as expected. Yet Nabilah could not help but admire the linen, the embroidered pillowcases, and the charming tablecloths. This was where, in addition to the gold bangles gripping her arm, Waheeba's wealth manifested itself. The level of cleanliness was high, too. Nabilah sat on fresh-smelling, ironed sheets and the glass she drank from sparkled, though it smelt faintly of clay from the zeer where the water was stored. The tea glass smelt of incense and the tea itself was spiced with cardamom. It was sunset, and the floor of the hoash had been watered. A cool, gentle breeze carried the earthy, cloying scents of Umdurman, these scents that Nabilah could never get used to.

Apart from a neighbour and some family members, the hoash

was busy with servants and those poor relations who helped out, even though their status was above that of the servants. Nur's nurse Shukry, the cousin of Ustaz Badr, came over specially to greet Nabilah, thereby acknowledging that it was through her that he had obtained his post. He then kept at a distance, and it was the young boy, Zaki, who sat on Nur's bed. Batool, newly married and living with her husband, was, nevertheless, in close attendance, as she was the one who had offered Nabilah the tea and water. There were children, too, running around, and there was certainly enough room for that. Nabilah recognised Zeinab, Fatma's daughter. She was the same age as Ferial, but while Ferial was sitting politely next to her mother, the other girl was roaming around, her hair unkempt and her feet bare. All this chaos around Nur, with no respect for his condition! He should be alone in his room, entitled to peace and quiet.

'I don't know what happened to Nur today,' whined Waheeba, addressing Fatma and Halima. 'Yesterday he was chatting with me and laughing, just like his old self. He was in his room reading, and I said to him, "My boy, you will hurt your eyes. Besides, there are no pictures in these books. What is grabbing your attention so much?"'

Nabilah smiled at this admission of ignorance. Only an illiterate woman could harbour such a thought, only a stupid one would voice it.

'So he started reading out loud,' Waheeba continued. 'I liked his voice, sweet and lifting, but I couldn't understand a single word. He said "It's English poetry, Yumma!"'

Nabilah laughed. It was the wrong thing to do, for no one else had even smiled. Fatma and Halima looked sombre, while the neighbour was listening avidly, as if there were more to come.

Waheeba glared at Nabilah, and then turned to her audience.

'Look at that Egyptian woman! She is coming here to laugh at my misfortune.'

'Oh no, Hajjah,' replied Nabilah, but still she did not sense danger, still she felt safe. 'Your misfortune is mine as well. We are all one family. I was just admiring Nur's wit and intelligence. He is a fine, educated boy. His father is proud of him.'

'Don't fool me with your clever tongue. You! What can I say about you? The truth is out. You yourself have exposed yourself. Months, months after Nur's return you are bringing his little brother and sister to visit him!'

Nabilah protested, 'Their father, Mahmoud Bey—'

'Don't blame anyone else! You deliberately keep your children away from their relatives. They don't know anyone. You, girl.' She glared at Ferial. The girl shrank closer to her mother. 'You, Ferial, do you know that girl who is playing here? She is the same age as you!' Waheeba pointed at Zeinab, who twisted to look at them. Her arm hung on the headboard of Nur's bed. 'Speak up, Ferial, can't you speak? Don't you have a tongue to speak with?'

Nabilah whispered to her daughter, 'You must answer Tante Waheeba.'

Children must be polite. When addressed by adults they must respond.

Ferial and Zeinab stared at each other. Two six-year-olds assessing each other. The distance that separated them was defined by cultures, constructed by adults.

'I don't know what her name is,' said Ferial. Her Egyptian accent was pronounced, foreign in this setting.

Waheeba mimicked Ferial's accent, 'I don't know her name.'

Mocking laughter from the neighbour, and even Fatma and Halima smiled. Nabilah held her daughter's hand. Zeinab's face lit up and she moved closer to Ferial. Waheeba continued, 'Her name is Zeinab and she is very closely related to you, but maybe you don't even know who her father is? If Nur is bedridden for months before you come and see him, then maybe you don't even know your older brother, Nassir?'

There was so much hostility in her voice that Nabilah

173

intervened, 'Hajjah Waheeba, the girls go to different schools, that's why they don't see each other.'

'Oh no! *You* are the one to blame. You are the one keeping them apart, as if your children are better than ours.'

The accusation startled Nabilah, not because it was true, but because such fierce pride was unexpected.

Waheeba looked more aggressive now, leaning forward, her hands on her knees.

'You yourself, how have you behaved? What have you done for Nur?'

'I did as my husband commanded,' said Nabilah, provocatively. 'I went with him and Nur to London—'

The word 'London' infuriated Waheeba even more.

'God curse London and London's useless doctors! Did they help us in any way? Sucking our money, the thieves! What was the use of that journey? Did you want to have a vacation? Did you want to see the sights? I heard all about it. You were out and about. You spent the nights in my husband's arms in a fancy hotel, not at the hospital.'

Nabilah was taken aback.

'Every day I visited the hospital, every single day.'

'Only for a few hours. Sitting in a chair like a guest. Did you lift a finger to nurse my son?'

'For a fortnight on the ship, I nursed Nur. Day and night I did the best for him that I could. When we returned here, I was the one who found him the nurse he now has. I asked around and Ustaz Badr said his cousin, Shukry, had nursing experience. And *I* was the one who asked Ustaz Badr to come and see Nur on a regular basis. I explained to him that Mahmoud Bey didn't expect Nur to sit formal examinations, but that literature was something he had always been keen on, and he could do with some mental stimulation. Hasn't Ustaz Badr been coming regularly?'

Waheeba didn't reply but Fatma nodded.

'He comes after he goes to your place to give Farouk and

Ferial their lessons. I've also spoken to him about giving Zeinab lessons.'

'That's good. He is an excellent tutor.' Nabilah turned to Waheeba. 'You see? I am always looking out for Nur's welfare.'

Waheeba snorted. 'You don't fool me. Let us look back, let us see what you did on the day of the accident.' Spittle flew from her mouth. The neighbour sat up straight in anticipation.

'Where were *you* on the day of the accident?'

'I was in Cairo.'

'Yes, you were in Cairo, and when you heard the news what did you do? You didn't budge! You didn't accompany Mahmoud to Alexandria. He travelled as soon as he heard the news on that same day. And you didn't follow him, not the day after, or even the week after. You did not get on that train and visit Nur in hospital. The staff from the office made the trip. Friends, business acquaintances, people I didn't even know made that trip. But did you show your face? No. You stayed in Cairo with your mother. Shame on you. Shame, shame.'

There was a hush in the hoash. Neither Fatma nor Halima extended a word in Nabilah's favour. If this were a showdown, they would close ranks with Waheeba.

'I acted according to my husband's wishes,' said Nabilah. 'I stayed in Cairo because he told me to stay. I went to London because he asked me to go. This is exactly how an exemplary wife would behave. A wife who knows how to please her husband and hold on to him. And if you don't know how to please your husband, learn from me!'

'Learn from you!' Waheeba cried out. 'If I learned from you I would learn to be hard-hearted. You are without tenderness. You live with us, but you have no sympathy for us. Your heart is as black as can be and your eyes are hot and envious. You don't wish us any good! We were living well before you came from your country; we had nothing to complain of. I ask myself, who gave Nur the evil eye? Who would wish me, and my son, harm? It's you! And you're not even hiding it. You come in here smiling and gloating!'

'I will not sit here another minute to be insulted, not another minute!'

Nabilah stood up and yanked the children up by their arms. But instead of marching out, she paused. It was a cue for one of the other women to intervene, to put in a good word, a sweet phrase to calm the atmosphere, to placate the two of them and restore peace. Nabilah did not want to flounce off; she wanted Fatma to beg her to stay, to plead with her not to take offence. But Fatma kept silent because Waheeba was her mother-in-law. Halima, then, should play that conciliatory note, but she merely looked down at the floor. The neighbour was an amused spectator, a collector of gossip. She watched with a grin on her face to see what Nabilah would do next.

Nabilah grabbed each of her children by the hand and tottered out of the hoash. The floor was uneven underneath her, not the smooth surface needed for her high-heeled sandals.

'Who is Zeinab?' Ferial asked, as Nabilah tucked her into bed.

She felt great tenderness towards her daughter tonight. Ferial was clearly and irrevocably a piece of her, though vulnerable and somewhat contaminated by Sudanese blood. This made her imperfect, in need of guidance and rescue.

'Zeinab is the daughter of your half-brother, Nassir. Her mother, Fatma, is your cousin, Uncle Idris's daughter.

'So Zeinab is my niece and I am her aunt.'

'Yes.' She kissed her cheek.

'So she should call me Aunty.' Ferial giggled.

'She won't.'

'Why not?'

'Because she is the same age as you, and because they don't respect titles here. Now go to sleep. Enough of this, enough of them for one day.'

Yet Nabilah did not leave. She stretched out and lay next to her daughter, smelling her hair and the talcum powder on her neck. Ferial's breathing became steadier. She was falling asleep, happy because her mother was close. How trusting she was! Everything Nabilah told her she would believe, every place she would take her, she would go. A surge of love filled Nabilah. There were only two people in the world she loved equally and as much as her children; her mother and grandmother in Cairo. She ached to tell them about her visit to Waheeba, to rally them to her side. Her words would rouse their indignation. How lonely she was, how far away from home. She could tell Mahmoud all that happened today and he would not sympathise. 'Women bickering,' he would say, or something along those lines.

Last summer in Cairo her grandmother had reproached her.

'Why don't you love your husband? Why is your heart hard towards him?'

It was not hard any more. Seeing him struggle to help Nur, seeing him weep at the hospital in London, had softened Nabilah. She felt sorry for him, that rich, powerful man who could not buy a cure for his son. She fell in love with his vulnerability, his chivalry and eagerness to succeed. London drew them together, those three months in the Ritz that might well be the happiest period of their marriage. Free from their respective countries, the two of them became buoyant; they turned to face each other unrestricted by the demands of Egyptian versus Sudanese culture, equalised on imperial soil. Charming London, atmospheric London, solid and looking forward; it made them a couple, a 'Mr and Mrs', as was the English expression. This brought out the best in Nabilah, and she returned to Umdurman with high hopes, resolved to tolerate the Sudanese side of her husband. His marriage to Waheeba and his closeness to Idris was a shell, she decided, unrelated to his true progressive personality, the one she had discovered in London and cherished.

For this reason, Nabilah brushed aside the incident at Waheeba's hoash and deliberately belittled the antagonism that increasingly wafted from her co-wife's side. Waheeba would never forgive her for usurping her rightful place by Nur's bedside in London and there was nothing Nabilah could do about that. She had obeyed Mahmoud, and he was the important one. How could Waheeba ever be a true rival? How could Nabilah's position ever be threatened when Mahmoud publicly and privately, in no uncertain terms, favoured his younger wife?

The news from Egypt distracted Nabilah, too, funnelling from the public sphere to the private. In Suez, Mahmoud told her, the English commander, besieged by guerrilla fighters, demanded that the Egyptian police and paramilitary officers lay down their arms and leave the city. Of course they refused! How could they not? They were punished with open fire and the numbers killed appalled the whole country. Then Cairo burning, places she had visited; the downtown that held memories – Groppi, Cinema Metro, shops and businesses with foreign connections – were targeted in retaliation for the massacre at the Canal Zone. Nabilah did not have to strain or go out of her way to get the news, Mahmoud always had the latest developments, and he was as avid as she was, if not more. Dispatches of a more personal matter reached her through her mother's letters. Nabilah's stepfather had lost his job. His party, the Wafd, had fallen out of favour. There had been a government shake-up and Uncle Mohsin was summoned to stand before the Purge Committee, accused of corruption and pensioned off.

'He is sitting at home,' wrote Qadriyyah. 'He doesn't know what to do with himself. We go for walks or he meets his friends in the café. I do my best to amuse and distract him but I cannot compensate him. He is pining for his old job and highly irritable most of the time. No one knows how long this crisis will last.'

When Nabilah showed Mahmoud this letter he said, 'Let them come here. The travel will do them good and I can find your Uncle Mohsin a position in Khartoum.'

Nabilah was overjoyed. She flung her arms around him and thanked him in a gush of words and kisses that made him laugh.

Her mother here! In the same country! Nabilah's life would be enhanced, it would be shared, and the loneliness so long inside her would finally be cured. Such joy and optimism! She set out immediately to redecorate the guest room, with new beds, new curtains and a fresh layer of paint on the wall.

There was, too, another dimension to Nabilah's excitement. Her mother had never visited her before. This would be the first time. Now Nabilah would see her own Umdurman life through Qadriyyah's eyes. Her position as Mahmoud Bey's wife would be inspected and assessed. Now that he was intent on helping her stepfather, Nabilah felt honoured to have such a powerful, generous husband. But what about other things? She was never quite certain whether she was in an enviable position, or a wretched one. She wanted, naturally, to be in an enviable position; that was what she aspired to, that was what she worked for from morning to night. But a side of her felt that she had been wronged, that her marriage was unjust, hastily arranged, even a mistake. Qadriyyah's visit would lay the matter to rest. Her mother would be the judge.

Walking down the steps of the airplane, both her mother and stepfather looked considerably older and less steady. It was not only the fatigue of the journey; Uncle Mohsin was tired from deep within. His once athletic body seemed frail, and over the next few weeks he was often absent-minded, as if he could not stop mulling over the upheaval that Egypt was going through, the demise of his party and the rise of his adversaries. Qadriyyah was solicitous towards him, engineering every situation to meet his comfort, possessive about his new fragility and mindful of his new prospects in Sudan. It was not the situation Nabilah had envisaged. She wanted her mother's full attention, more intimacy, more analysis, but she hid her disappointment even from herself and threw herself into the role of the perfect hostess.

Mahmoud gave a dinner party for his in-laws to which every high-ranking Egyptian official, including the Minister, was invited. There was a picnic in the Abuzeid ranch in Kadaro, and another in Burri, where they sat under the trees in a charming boathouse overlooking the Blue Nile. Qadriyyah met all of Nabilah's friends, and she visited the children's school and studied every corner of the saraya. A visit to Nur was scheduled as part of the visitors' itinerary because Qadriyyah and Mohsin felt that they could not possibly be in Sudan, in the adjacent house, without visiting their host's invalid son. Mahmoud accompanied them himself, and they made a substantial party: Mohsin and Qadriyyah, Mahmoud and Nabilah with their children.

It was the first time the Cairo couple had seen a traditional Sudanese hoash, and although Waheeba was their hostess, she remained a silent figure in the background. She stared at the visitors, but apart from exchanging simple greetings, said nothing. Nur was in good form, sitting propped up and chatty. He seemed to enjoy seeing new faces and hearing all the news from Cairo. He charmed his half-brother and sister, whom he rarely saw, and, in general, showed himself to be a witty conversationalist. Nabilah felt a surge of fondness for him. They had become close, in London, and she missed him when they returned to Umdurman. But Waheeba was a barrier in their relationship. Nur's loyalty to his mother made him keep Nabilah at a distance, and Nabilah's need to avoid Waheeba's hoash prevented her from visiting him.

Afterwards, on the way home, Ferial whispered to her mother, 'Hajjah Waheeba pinched my shoulder.'

'Maybe she was just being playful.' Nabilah held the children at arm's length these days. She was straining, instead, to have her mother all to herself.

'No, she was being nasty. She's a beast!'

'Shush. Don't be rude about grown-ups.' But Nabilah's reprimand was mild. She was eager to hear Qadriyyah's assessment of Mahmoud's first wife.

They talked that night, staying up late on the terrace after

Uncle Mohsin had gone to bed and Mahmoud left for a dinner engagement in Khartoum. By Sudanese standards the night was cool, but both women were in summer nightgowns, enjoying the breeze, the slight chill in the air and the heavy disc of the moon. It was the talk Nabilah had ached for, and it started with Nur.

Qadriyyah said, 'They treat him very casually, I couldn't help but notice. That little girl, Zeinab, climbed onto his bed and slotted a cigarette in his mouth!'

Nabilah laughed. 'He never used to smoke in front of his father, now he has no qualms.'

'But it's in such poor taste for a child to light cigarettes! And is he always surrounded by all and sundry? Invalids need their peace and quiet.'

'I told them this, and they said he loves company. They are spoiling him. It took months for them to realise that he can read on his own if someone turns the pages for him, and it's only now that they're using the wheelchair! In London the doctors stressed the importance of independence, but his mother wants him waited upon. No wonder he has his ups and downs!'

'Poor boy! Your Uncle Mohsin said to me, "When I see the tragedy of others, my own seems small in comparison". He is not himself at all. Mahmoud Bey is going out of his way to secure him a suitable position here, but Mohsin is not interested.'

Nabilah did not want the conversation to drift yet again to her stepfather. She spoke sharply, 'What did you think of Waheeba, Mama?'

'She is nothing next to you, of course. Your fingernail is more valuable than the whole of her. Everyone knows this, and Mahmoud Bey more than anyone else.'

'So why doesn't he divorce her?'

'Oh Nabilah,' Qadriyyah sighed, 'you should not even think about her. She doesn't threaten you in any way. She will come round, you'll see. She will be on your side, eager to serve you and your children.'

'But it is not only her that is the problem. It's the whole country!'

'Don't start again. Don't start complaining.'

'I just want to know what you think, now that you are here, seeing my life and my house for the first time. Is this what you imagined when you married me to him?'

Qadriyyah lit a cigarette and inhaled. She was bringing her attention round to a serious subject.

'When I saw Mahmoud Bey for the first time,' she began, 'I saw an Egyptian man wearing a suit and a fez, speaking as we do. He was a little dark, but not too dark, and he was in his prime. We heard that he was wealthy, that he was well-known, and that he had been received by the King. All positive credentials. Yes, he was married and he had grown-up sons – he didn't hide these facts – but he was no longer living with Waheeba, and no bridegroom is perfect.'

'Didn't I have other options?'

'Oh, you did. A pretty girl like you had her suitors, but they were all young and struggling. No one could compete with Mahmoud. No one could match him. I didn't hesitate, Nabilah, not once.'

'You didn't care that I would be so far away? You didn't care that I would be alone?'

Qadriyyah sounded defensive. 'I did not think of this country, Sudan. I did not visualise it. For me it was like a southern province, an extension of Egypt. And Mahmoud is not a foreigner.'

'He is, Mama. He loves Egypt, but he is Sudanese.'

'But that's not how I saw him first. His automobile, his accent, his favourite dishes – he was one of us. And if he *was* truly Sudanese, he would want you to dress in a tobe like every other Sudanese woman. He would insist that Farouk and Ferial speak with a Sudanese accent. But he doesn't!'

'When he was ill, he spoke all the time with a Sudanese accent.' Tears welled up in Nabilah's eyes, but she held them in check. 'At work, he is inseparable from Idris, and I am sure he loves Nassir and Nur more than he loves Farouk and Ferial!'

'Nonsense, Nabilah. He doesn't deny you or your children anything.'

'Oh I used to be more confident,' she admitted. 'He hardly ever used to visit Waheeba, and at the mention of her name he would make all sorts of expressions of disgust. But now, every day, every single day, he is at her hoash!'

'To visit his invalid son,' argued Qadriyyah. 'He goes there for Nur, not for Waheeba.'

'I know,' sighed Nabilah. 'It's the accident that changed the situation, to *her* advantage. The other day I went to see her and she frightened me. I am afraid she might harm me or the children.'

'Well, you made a mistake that day. You should not have gone to see her alone. Mahmoud Bey should have accompanied you. In his presence she would not dare say a word against you. Look how she was today, a shadow in the background, as unobtrusive as a servant!'

'You are right, Mama.' Nabilah smiled and kissed her mother.

'Remember how contented you were in the early years of your marriage when you were living in Cairo? And last summer, when you were together in London. Keep your husband close to you, my girl.' Qadriyyah stood up to retire to bed. 'No one, no matter how wicked or clever, would be able to drive a wedge between you.'

When Mahmoud came home, Nabilah was sitting up in bed reading a magazine.

'Look what I got for you,' he laughed.

It was a small black top hat. He sat next to her on the bed and took out his lighter. She put the magazine down and prepared herself for one of those party tricks he was so fond of. He set light to the top of the hat, and out slithered a black snake.

She squealed when the warm rubber caressed her neck. The snake's skin felt real and its length increased.

'Take it away from me!' She was breathless and flustered, but it was precisely her agitation that Mahmoud was enjoying, the excitement in her eyes and voice. He laughed out loud when she crawled to the other end of the bed, silk nightdress riding up her thighs.

After bidding Qadriyyah and Mohsin farewell at the airport, Mahmoud remained in Khartoum on business and Nabilah set off with the driver back to Umdurman. She found the separation from her mother even more painful than she had expected, and immediately began to count the months until summer when it would be her turn to travel with the children to Cairo. Although Mahmoud had secured more than one position for Uncle Mohsin, her stepfather had turned them all down. He was unable to pull himself away from Cairo and was too weary, he said, to start afresh. It was a severe disappointment to Nabilah and she had to content herself with Qadriyyah's gratitude that the couple had, at least, gained an intermission from the political climate in Egypt and enjoyed a rejuvenating change.

Just before the bridge, the car thudded to a halt and broke Nabilah's reverie. The problem was a punctured tyre And she had to stand in the sun while the driver replaced the wheel. In Cairo there would be a vender selling cool drinks, there would be other ladies walking about and she would entertain herself by studying their dresses, hairstyles and shoes. There would be buses and trams. There would be, at the very least, a bit of shade. But here it was nothing stretching out into nothing. It was a harsh country, a harsh climate. She took her compact out of her handbag and powdered her nose.

Subdued and thirsty, she returned home and headed straight for the ice box. As she was getting herself a cold glass of water, Farouk came running in.

'Ferial's hurt,' he said.

'Did she hurt herself playing in the garden?'

Before he could reply she turned to see Batool and the nanny carrying Ferial into the room. It was strange to see Batool here. Usually, she never came to this side of the saraya and was constantly with Waheeba. This raised Nabilah's suspicions. Ferial looked dazed and in shock and she was wrapped in a light cotton sheet. The nanny and Batool laid her down on the sofa and Batool put a pillow under her head.

'What happened? What have you done to her, Batool?' Nabilah knelt next to Ferial. 'What's wrong, my darling, what's hurting you?'

Tears ran down the girl's face and Nabilah's anxiety rose.

'Aren't you going to tell me?'

Ferial's face was unharmed, no bruises. Her arms were fine. She pulled away the sheet.

'She's been circumcised,' Batool said. 'Today was Zeinab's circumcision and Aunt Waheeba said Ferial should be circumcised, too.'

At first Nabilah's mind couldn't absorb this information. She stared at her daughter. Under the sheet, Ferial was naked from the waist down. The wound was raw, fresh, the soft vulnerable folds removed, and in their place, the flesh stitched up. Nabilah cried out. It was as if her own body had been punctured, her insides sucked out.

'Farouk, go to your room,' she whispered.

He must not see his sister like this. She gathered her strength to stand up and face Batool. She slapped her. She hit her once, twice with all her fury. Batool screamed. She raised her arms to shield herself and her tobe collapsed.

'Why are you hitting me? Didn't you know? I thought they told you!'

'Liar!' shouted Nabilah. 'How dare you! How dare you touch my child!'

She grabbed Batool's long braids and pushed her against the wall.

Batool let out a wail.

'You are cruel, cruel. You hate me, but I am just a poor girl. I was just doing as I was told.'

Faced with such obtuseness, Nabilah's anger began to subside. She now wanted to know details, wanted Batool to speak instead of scream. She wanted Ferial to stop crying. Already the child was distraught, not only from the ordeal she had endured, but now the sight of her mother attacking Batool.

The facts were revealed, piece by piece, through Batool's hiccups and sobs. While Nabilah was at the airport, Ferial was lured over to Waheeba's quarters. She was told that Zeinab was having a party and that there would be sweets and many girls her age to play with. Indeed, it *was* a celebration of sorts for Zeinab, though it was kept low-key because Mahmoud had forbidden circumcision in his household ever since the procedure was declared illegal by the Anglo-Egyptian government. Clearly, his authority had been overridden by Waheeba, who insisted that her granddaughter must follow tradition. Zeinab was dressed in a new red satin dress and the women of the neighbourhood were invited. They sang wedding songs, and the older girls danced, miming the bridal pigeon dance. Only the best midwife was summoned for the Abuzeid girls. She injected them first with procaine and the instruments she used were sterilised. Afterwards, to prevent infection, she administered penicillin.

Batool reassured Nabilah that the stitches would be removed after two days, then Ferial would be up and about. She would be like other Sudanese girls, girls like Soraya and Fatma. If Ferial was now in pain, Zeinab was in pain, too. If Ferial was now traumatised, Zeinab was traumatised, too. Waheeba herself had held the girls down one by one, gripping their knees apart. The deed was done and the procedure was irreversible. The slice of a knife, the tug and cutting away of flesh, and Ferial was someone else, one of *them*. She could never ever be like her mother again.

Nabilah surrendered to the nightmare. It held her in a vice.

Such unnecessary pain, such stupidity and malice. She dismissed Batool.

'Don't ever set foot in my house again. I don't want to see your face.' She fired the nanny for not protecting Ferial. 'Pack your belongings. First thing tomorrow morning I want you on that train back to Egypt.'

The girl started to cry. Farouk, caught in the middle of this, was also reprimanded for not looking after his sister, and yelled at even more for wanting to see her wound. Nabilah wanted to summon a doctor to check on Ferial. Yes, she would bring in an English doctor, scandal or no scandal, and expose Waheeba's crime. However, the telephone lines were down. She ran to catch the driver but it was too late. He had already gone back to Khartoum to pump the punctured tyre with air and wait on Mahmoud.

Ferial would not allow Nabilah out of her sight. Her light-skinned, smooth-haired daughter brought so low, whimpering and clinging. She needed help to drink, to eat, to change into her nightdress. She needed help to pass urine – and that was the most difficult process of all, because the fear of burning her wound made her hold herself back. So much did Nabilah empathise with her, so much was her reaction visceral, that she herself, when her bladder felt full, could not pass water. She sat on the toilet seat, trembling and crying, but not for long, because Ferial called out to her and she scrambled to her feet again. In the end, the two of them lay down on the bed. The power failed and the ceiling fan came to a halt. Darkness and heat: this ghastly accursed country. Nabilah moved the children out to the terrace. A bit of fresh air, but Ferial would not settle.

'My feet hurt,' she whined.

Her feet! What now? Nabilah lit a candle and examined her daughter's feet. True enough, there were red welts running sideways on the bridge of each foot. She washed them down and applied mercurochrome, struggling to identify the cause. She came to understand that during the circumcision Ferial had been placed on an angharaib without a mattress. Waheeba held down her upper body while her heels were tucked through the strings of the bed so that she wouldn't kick the midwife. That was why there were now marks on her feet from the ropes that made up the base of the angharaib.

'Where were you, Mummy? Why did you go out and leave me? Why did you let them do this to me?'

The reproach grated on Nabilah's nerves. She kissed Ferial, she wept and mumbled apologies. She smoothed her daughter's hair and promised everything from candyfloss to ice cream to a trip to the zoo. Rage still pulsed inside her, and she began to fret over the consequences. In the short term, the risk of haemorrhage, septicaemia, urinary and genital infections. Time and again, she checked Ferial's temperature. She encouraged her to drink more liquids and pass more urine. But even if all went well in the next few days, until the stitches were removed, there would still be long-term consequences. She recalled the horror stories she had heard since arriving in Sudan. Brides, whose wedding nights were a disaster because of too tight an infibulation; the story of a baby's head damaged during labour, endless complications.

When Nabilah had first heard these stories, they had sounded abstract and distant, folklorist tales of backward women. Now her own flesh and blood was incriminated. In the future, when Ferial got married, she would suffer pain and alienation from pleasure. A progressive, liberal man might not even want to marry her in the first place. He would have to be Sudanese, one of *them*, and Nabilah, casting her vision to the future, had always wished that her children would marry Egyptians. Even more consequences: every time Ferial had a baby, it would be necessary to slit the circumcision skin fold during labour and stitch it up again afterwards. Nabilah could visualise the future scene in a modern Cairo hospital, the obstetrician shaking his head, disgusted to come across such barbarity, the kind of barbarity only found among peasants and the uneducated. Nabilah's face burnt with shame. She dragged herself away from Ferial's side, stumbling in the dark until she reached the bathroom and retched in disgust. A pulse beat in her head. Why? Why all this? Waheeba had struck her a terrible blow, but she must be strong for Ferial's sake.

There was no one Nabilah could talk to until Mahmoud came home. Farouk, after she had made amends with him, was fast asleep. This was a blessing, as she had neither the energy nor the peace of mind to answer his questions. Ferial continued to cling and whimper, reproachful and unforgiving. But who could blame the poor child?

'Go to sleep, my love. Close your eyes so that your body can rest and be better again.'

She herself was wide awake and alert. She stared up at the sky and the twinkling stars were mocking and cunning. What should she do next? Would she ever be able to get back at Waheeba? Ferial sighed and started to doze off. In turn, Nabilah relaxed a little. Mahmoud would surely be furious; Waheeba had done something he had explicitly forbidden. In his own house, she had flaunted his wishes, let alone the deviousness of taking Ferial behind her mother's back. He will divorce her, Nabilah thought. He must. Waheeba would be cast out in disgrace. And that would be the ultimate retribution.

XIV

Earlier that same evening, after bidding his in-laws farewell at the airport, Mahmoud went smiling to Barclays Bank *(Dominions, Colonies and Overseas)*. The news was official. Earlier this morning, the Financial Secretary had called for a special meeting of the Legislative Assembly to reveal a budget surplus of twenty million pounds. Due to the Korean War and increased demand from post-war Britain, cotton prices had risen to unprecedented heights – prosperous times for the government, and prosperous times for the man whose name was synonymous with the private sector. With the backing of the bank, Mahmoud had established almost all of the private cotton schemes. The trade figures for 1951 were published today. Nigel Harrison had the details and the two men beamed over the results.

'Exports from Cotton Ginned,' Mr Harrison read out, 'forty-seven million, four hundred and forty-nine thousand and six hundred and six pounds.'

'Nearly one third of that,' smiled Mahmoud, 'came from Abuzeid Ginning. Excellent.'

'The country now has no national debt, no fear of insolvency, and the government's reservations regarding the private sector will finally be laid to rest.'

'Oh yes,' said Mahmoud, 'the government will be freer with its licences and concessions, now. I will start to have competitors – but you will have more clients!'

'Indeed I hope so.' Mr Harrison closed the folder in front of him. 'But you and I will continue to do business together. With your credit history, you are in a fortunate position well ahead of the competition. Any new projects on your mind?'

'Industry,' Mahmoud replied. Nigel Harrison made a sceptical face but Mahmoud continued, 'During the war, when imports were halted, I set up a glass factory in order to meet local demand. I would like to venture into ice as well as vegetable oils and canned food stuffs.'

'But my good man, these are modest projects, not worthy of your stature. The Sudan is an agricultural country and it will remain so. The government has just approved a five-year plan to develop alternative cash crops to cotton. This is the direction I urge you to take. Industry is not lucrative, certainly not in comparison. Nor is it suited to a developing country with such a poor infrastructure.'

'But our thinkers and politicians are directing us towards industry. An independent Sudan will need its industries and I want to serve my country. True, the Gezira Scheme has been a spectacular success and the Sudan is now a model for other African countries to follow. But industry is vital, too. However, I shall consider the alternative cash crops you recommend. Meanwhile we can congratulate ourselves for championing the cause of private enterprise and making a success of it!'

Nigel Harrison laughed and stood up.

'This calls for a celebration. Let's go for a drink!'

The terrace of the Grand Hotel was busy this time in the evening. Both men came across acquaintances who would greet them from afar with a nod, or come over to their table for brief hellos and introductions. In a typical Sudanese fashion, shaped by a society where word of mouth mattered and everyone's background was known, Mahmoud gave Nigel Harrison a detailed biography of the man he had just shaken hands with as they made their way to their table.

'I knew him from the mid-thirties,' he said. 'He was with me on the committee which formally received the first Egyptian Economic Delegation headed by Fuad Bey Abaza. Our committee was set up by the Sudan Chamber of Commerce and they made me head and gave me the responsibility of receiving the Egyptians and touring the Sudan with them. Here's an anecdote for you: the delegation was invited to his base in Gezira Abba by the leader of the Ansar, Sayyid Abdel-Rahman Al-Mahdi. You English call him SAR, don't you?'

'Yes,' smiled Nigel Harrison, 'and we call his rival Sayyid Ali El Mirghani, SAM.'

'Well, this is what happened. We came down the river on a steamer. Just as we were nearing our destination, the steamer had a technical failure and came to a complete standstill. Our host could see us from the shore, and we could see him, too, surrounded by about five thousand of his men. But how were we to reach him? Attempts to fix the steamer failed. So what did SAR do? He picked up a handful of sand ...' Mahmoud mimicked the action, '... and threw it in the river. His men went and picked up their shovels. In the course of an hour, they turned the water into land! It was an incredible sight. In a few hours of continuous work they built a road and we embarked from the steamer and into motor cars that drove us straight to our host.'

It was now Nigel Harrison's turn.

'The one sitting on the left is Sir Christopher Cox. He used to be Director of Education, but now he's with the Colonial Office. He's been doing the rounds ever since his visit started. Sue and I met him at a dinner given in his honour by Sayyid Shingitti. We were told it was going to be a small dinner, but when we arrived at the house there were five policemen in charge of the car parking! Every leader of the Independence Front was invited, as were the whole of the Electoral Commission. It was quite an affair!'

'No, he is Greek,' said Mahmoud about the gentleman who had just greeted them on his way out. 'He is the head of accounts at Mitchell Cotts and has been for years. His brother owns the GMH cabaret. Between them they own the most expensive, spacious villas in Khartoum, which they rent out.'

'That young man,' said Nigel Harrison, 'graduated from Oxford University. He was on a Sudan Government Scholarship. Now he's joined the Department of Finance as one of the first Sudanese graduate recruits.'

Mahmoud looked at the young man. He seemed vaguely familiar and had, in fact, addressed him as Uncle Mahmoud when he came over to their table. He looked not much older than Nur.

'Was he at Victoria College by any chance?'

'Yes, I dare say he was.'

Victoria. Whenever Mahmoud had visited Nur, he would take him and his friends, as well as every Sudanese student, out for lunch. Maybe that young man with the bright prospects had been one of them. How these boys used to devour their kebabs and koftas! Fond memories. Nur running across the field with the ball; Nur, all in white, playing cricket. Mahmoud felt a sudden shame. This was how he was coming to regard Nur's condition: as a blight on the tapestry of the family's life. The more Mahmoud threw himself into work, into daily life, the more Nur, on his bed, seemed unnatural, an aberration that was almost impossible to get used to. Every day, every single day after the morning session at the office and before lunch, Mahmoud went to see him. It was his duty to do so. Just to sit for a few minutes and ask, 'Is there anything you need, son?' Mahmoud's consolation was doing practical things for Nur: summoning the doctor, buying him a bigger radio, encouraging his friends to visit him. He had no words of explanation or comfort for the boy, only diversions. He had promised that he would take him to London and cure him. They went and came back. Life was random blotches of misery and bliss, Fate lapping up good fortune and humans wrestling bad luck. How was it that he was always blessed where money was concerned? Even in London, in the midst of all the disappointments and expenditure, there came that commission from the Duke of Bedford.

'Did I tell you,' he now said to Nigel Harrison, 'about the

monkey nuts I shipped to Liverpool for the Duke of Bedford's aviary?'

At Mahmoud's age, there could be no turnaround, no starting fresh. He was reaping what he had sown; he was living a time of achievements, a time of outcomes. At this moment, for example, as he sipped his drink and appreciated the murmur of voices around him, he was proud that he was sitting in the Grand Hotel with an Englishman. This was a situation he had worked for. Every time he stayed at the Ritz in London, on his very first day, as soon as he walked in he would tip the doorman, the bellboy, the concierge and the chambermaids. What was the point of tipping them on the way out (although he did that too)? He tipped them on arrival so that they could treat him well, so that they would overlook his colour and his nationality and give him the respect he deserved. Money talks. A coin pressed into that white palm to hear the sweet word 'Sir'.

'He is politically anti-British,' Nigel Harrison was saying about one of the Sudanese gentlemen at Sir Christopher Cox's table, 'but, on a social level, very charming, and with a great sense of humour.'

'In this country politics are shaped by tribal affiliations and everyone's allegiances are those of his ancestors and family.'

'This is true for the older generation, but the young are different,' Harrison protested. 'The Sudan Student Office in London sent out a circular requesting students to provide information on their age, tribe etc. Hardly any of them wrote down their specific tribe. They all described themselves as Sudanese.'

'This is Britain's aspiration, but I tell you, ethnic divisions run deep in this country.'

'Not to the extent that it would hamper a Sudan free of Egyptian influence.'

'Well, to be frank, I would not mind a unity with Egypt. This, as I said to you before, is a natural consequence of my family's background.'

'Do you sincerely believe that a union is in the interests of the Sudan? I do not.'

'We are historically, geographically and culturally tied.'

'Only the North.'

'It was Egypt which financed Kitchener's force.'

'My grandfather served under Lord Kitchener. He said it was a campaign that was left far too long. By the time they arrived in Khartoum, there was nothing worth saving.'

'Oh, the chaos of the Mahdists!' Mahmoud sat back in his chair. 'To the extent that it has become an expression. Here's an anecdote for you. When General Gordon was killed and the Mahdi's army took over Umdurman, my mother was a young girl. Because she was fair-skinned, her parents hid her in the cellar. They were afraid she would be captured by one of these hooligans. No one trusted them. My mother stayed in that cellar for days. She hated it, and insisted that it was haunted by jinn! Whereas the jinn were out there, raping and looting Umdurman to their hearts' content! When things settled down, the Mahdi himself moved to Umdurman and made it his capital. Every notable man lined up to swear allegiance to him. They had no choice. My father was one of them. He bent down on the floor and kissed the Mahdi's hand. If he hadn't done that his shops and land would have been confiscated and his precious agency would have been razed to the ground. I applaud him for this. He grovelled on his knees so that I could be the man I am today, so that I could have an inheritance. He was pragmatic in that way.'

'Did he immigrate from Egypt?'

'No, his father did. In 1801 my grandfather walked to the Sudan, yes, all this way on foot. Why? To escape recruitment into Muhammad Ali Pasha's army, even though that army was actually heading here!'

'I read that the Viceroy of Egypt invaded the Sudan to find gold and to capture slaves.'

'There was hardly any gold – a little in the Red Sea Hills –

but the slave trade flourished. That's how our Nubian women found themselves in the harems of the Ottoman sultans!' Mahmoud chuckled. 'That was the mission my grandfather absconded from. He had an aversion to cruelty and injustice and he didn't want to kill or loot or kidnap. He wanted to trade. He wanted to buy and sell, to exchange and barter and strike a deal. You know, Mr Harrison, I consider commerce to be a noble profession, whatever anyone else might say. While other men fight and hate, we give and take. We negotiate with everyone, Christian, Jew and pagan. Money and goods are what makes men equal. That is my creed. And true righteousness is not in taking a political stance or on serving slogans. It is in fair trade. I am not a religious man by any means, but there is one saying of the Prophet Muhammad that I cling to. He said: "The truthful and honest merchant will be with the prophets, affirmers of truth and martyrs." I am not a perfect Muslim ...' Mahmoud picked up his glass of whiskey and held it up in the air, '... but when I die and meet my Maker I will say to Him, this is what I have done: I have never cheated and I have never defaulted. I have helped those who came to me asking for help, and I have spent my charity on widows and orphans. And I will say to God Almighty, yes, I disobeyed you at times, and I was lazy when it came to acts of worship, but I am that honest merchant which your Messenger talked about.'

Shortly before midnight, the driver drove him home. In the darkness, lulled by the movement of the car, his early cheer subsided. He dozed, and the image of Nur settled before him; supine and good for nothing, his body dead but his mind and soul young and alert. How strange it was, how strange! Questions sprang like rebellion to his mind: if Fate was intent on striking one of his sons, why Nur? Why not Nassir who was already a disappointment? Why not Farouk who, as a young child with a foreign mother, seemed distant and insubstantial? And if Mahmoud was meant to lose Nur, why didn't the sea take him once and for all? Death would have been devastating, but sharper and infinitely more decisive. Instead of this daily, hourly, lingering suffering. And the boy's eyes, with their hot pain and bewilderment, waiting patiently for what – a cure or just oblivion? Mahmoud sighed and lit a cigarette. There was no benefit to these unanswerable questions. The English were right in keeping their stiff upper lip; that was the civilised way. Everyone had cried enough over Nur, even his fiancée, Soraya. Young men would queue to ask for her hand, now; she would be married off in no time. And Mahmoud would smile at her wedding and throw parties such as the country hadn't seen before. Let no one say he was sour because she was marrying another man's son!

He tapped his ash in the car's ashtray and shifted in his seat. Thinking of Nassir was no consolation either. His brother's accident hadn't sobered him in the least. True, he rounded a good crowd of friends to keep Nur company, but he still came into the office late every morning, and he was listless and inept. The move from Medani to Khartoum had not straightened him out. Instead, there were new rumours which Mahmoud would have to confront; hints that Nassir was keeping a mistress in Khartoum. He sighed. Nabilah was good at getting him to forget his worries. Looking at her youth, her outfits, her mannerisms, lightened his temper and eased him into a brighter, frivolous mood. With her he became an image he favoured, the dashing Bey, a man of the world, sophisticated and dynamic. But he was to return home that night to discord and aggravation; a traumatised daughter and a furious wife.

The next day at the office he could scarcely concentrate on the details of the tender that was spread open on his desk. Ferial in pain, butchered for no reason, no reason at all. He winced as he pictured the mutilation and her screams. He blinked and took a sip of his Turkish coffee. The small cup rattled against the saucer. Even if he were to call a reputable surgeon, nothing could be done to restore her to what she was before. He took another sip of coffee.

'Your hands are shaking.' Idris, too, was having his morning coffee.

'I hardly slept last night.' He sat back in his chair, elbows on the arm rests.

'How is Ferial this morning?'

'She ate and is looking much better. She has no fever and so far no complications.'

'Once the stitches are out, she'll be fine. Zeinab is doing well, too. What's done is done. It can't be reversed and there is no point even talking about it.'

Mahmoud felt bolstered by Idris's pragmatism. He got his voice back. 'Midnight, and Nabilah was demanding that I go over to Waheeba, not only to shout at her but to divorce her there and then!'

Idris folded open his newspaper. 'Buy her a gift. On your way home get her a piece of expensive jewellery. That should placate her.'

Mahmoud snorted and put his face in his hands. It had been a terrible night. He had tossed and turned while Nabilah kept vigil in Ferial's room. What a scene she had made! He was still reeling.

'Would you believe it,' he said, 'she even dismissed the nanny. I found the poor girl wailing, with her belongings all packed up. I told her to stay put. Are people's livelihood a game?'

'You did right,' his brother said, without looking up. 'In a day or two Nabilah will simmer down and she'll be relieved that the nanny didn't go.'

'I strictly forbade Waheeba from going ahead with this business!' He banged his desk. 'She just doesn't listen. And where were my son and your daughter in all of this? Is this what Nassir and Fatma wanted for their girl? They're the younger generation, they should be more enlightened.'

Idris looked up.

'As if you don't know this society! Fatma and Nassir can't stand up to Waheeba – I bet you they didn't even try. And listen to you talking. You might be progressive, but the rest of the country isn't. Who cares if the British outlawed female circumcision? The practice has just gone underground, that's all. Consider it a patriotic act of resistance.' He smirked.

'Nonsense,' said Mahmoud. 'It's barbaric. I have said time and time again that I would not have this procedure done in my house and Waheeba had no right to disobey me. Besides, she took Ferial without her mother's consent, knowing full well that Nabilah would not give her consent. She's deliberately malicious, that woman, chock full of envy. It's disgusting.'

'What happened to Nur has made Waheeba aggressive.' Idris folded his newspaper. 'She wasn't like that before.'

'Speaking of Nur, his nurse, what's his name ... Shukry ... absconded after making off with Waheeba's gold!'

'When did this happen?'

'Early this morning. I drank my tea and went over to tell her off about yesterday and found the whole hoash in an uproar. The theft must have happened during the night, but they only discovered it at dawn. They all slept outside yesterday because it was hot and the nurse went into Waheeba's room, broke open the cupboard and took her jewellery.'

'Did you tell the police?'

'Of course. And Waheeba is blaming Nabilah for bringing a thief to our house. She has the audacity to do so! Just because Shukry is Egyptian and Nabilah is the one who asked me to hire him for Nur.'

They were interrupted by a knock on the door and in came a short, dishevelled Egyptian man, who launched into lengthy greetings. He was clearly in awe of the office, the presence and the reason he was paying this call. Although Mahmoud could not remember his name, he recognised him as the Arabic teacher, cousin of that thief of a nurse. The teacher had recently taken to visiting Nur and conversing with him on literature. No harm in that, was Mahmoud's verdict. Anything to keep the poor boy amused and out of the pit of despondency.

'Mahmoud Bey,' the teacher was saying, 'perhaps Master Nur has already mentioned this to you, or perhaps Madame Nabilah did. Sir, I am in dire straits with regards to my accommodation. I live with my family and my aged father in pitiful conditions. And I am here to solicit you, Sir, if you can be so kind as to rent out to me one of your apartments?'

Before Mahmoud could reply, Idris leapt to his feet and threw his newspaper to the ground.

'Is it possible? After what your cousin did to us? How dare you show your face here and ask for help.'

'My . . . my cousin?' the man stammered. 'What has he done, God forbid?'

'Shukry the nurse is your cousin. Isn't that how he got his employment, through you?'

'Yes – yes!' his eyes bulged large with anxiety.

'Ustaz Badr doesn't know.' The teacher's name suddenly came to Mahmoud's mind. 'He has no idea what happened this morning.'

'Well, I'll tell him,' bellowed Idris, towering over Badr, who was by now almost trembling. 'Your cousin turned out to be a thief! He stole Hajjah Waheeba's gold and now the police are after him.'

Badr turned pale and rigid. He mumbled incoherently and Mahmoud began to feel sorry for him.

'Get out!' shouted Idris. 'Go and retrieve our belongings for us. Discipline that relation of yours. Once the police get their hands on him, he'll curse the day he reached out for what wasn't his!'

Badr found his voice. He wanted them to know that he condemned his cousin's action. Shukry was no good; he had never held one job for long. He was a scoundrel and now, even worse, a thief! He was a burden on Badr and a scourge. He should have stayed in Egypt and never come here looking for work.

'Go, go,' repeated Idris. 'Enough of all this!'

Mahmoud, too, wanted to see the back of Badr. A replacement for Shukry had to be found. Was there no end to these domestic trials? And still there was Nassir to confront.

The meeting with Nassir had to be conducted in private – it could not take place in front of Idris. Nassir squirmed in his seat as Mahmoud placed his pen in the ink stand.

'Where were you yesterday when your crazy mother decided to circumcise your daughter Zeinab and dragged Ferial into it as well? Why didn't you prevent her?'

Nassir looked relieved, as if he had been expecting a different topic of conversation.

'Oh, Father, these are women's issues, what does it have to do with me?'

'Shame on you!' Mahmoud snapped. 'Your own daughter's wellbeing and you don't want to shoulder the responsibility for it?'

'It's Fatma who's to blame. She must have known about it.'

'You know Fatma is weak in front of her mother-in-law. You should have put your foot down.'

'To tell you the truth,' Nassir smiled, 'Mother sweetened me up with a little something.'

Mahmoud banged his desk and Nassir jumped.

'How dare you! Your mother goes against my wishes and you allow her to buy your silence. You are disgusting, Nassir. You sicken me!'

Nassir stood up.

'Sit down! I am not finished with you. This morning a Greek gentleman came here, claiming that we, as a company, owe him rent on one of his villas in Khartoum.'

There was a silence in the room. Now Nassir started to look anxious. He looked down at the ground. Mahmoud continued,

'Why should we, as a company, lease a villa in Khartoum! Naturally I asked to see the contract and I am waiting for him to get back to me. Do you, by any chance, know anything about this?'

'Yes,' Nassir swallowed. 'I took out this lease.'

'For a villa in Khartoum? Whatever for?'

'Well, it's tedious to return to Umdurman for lunch and siesta then back again for the evening office session. It is convenient to have a place in town.'

'Presumably you furnished and staffed it.'

'Yes, of course.'

'And you signed the lease in the company's name?'

'I had no choice. It put me in a favourable position. And—'

'How dare you!' Mahmoud interrupted. 'How dare you use my name without my permission?'

Nassir's voice was sharp with resentment.

'You would not have granted me permission. I am so often short of funds, but you have little compassion towards me.'

'Listen,' Mahmoud glared at him, 'what you're doing is dishonest. You want to cheat on your wife? You want to keep a mistress? Then be a man and do it at your own expense. Don't drag my name into this.' Mahmoud lowered his voice and spoke more slowly, 'What havoc would this wreak if Fatma found out and complained to her father? Believe me, your Uncle Idris taking offence is not pleasant!'

'Oh no, no!' protested Nassir. 'It is nothing like that, I swear.'

'Don't swear. I detest liars and I abhor cheats. And, on top of this, you are not even capable of financing your own sins. You expect me to bail you out? Well, here's a surprise for you. I will not do so. Let that Greek kick you and your lady-friend out of that villa. I will not lift a finger to help you. When you leave this office now, you will go and change the lease to your name and face that landlord yourself. You're a grown man, Nassir. I would like to slap you but I can't.' His voice became soft, almost pleading. 'You have a son and a daughter – when are you going to take your life seriously? Think of our forefathers and their accomplishments. Think of the family's name and our reputation.' His voice almost broke. These sentiments came from his core.

At Louisinian's the jeweller's, Mahmoud relaxed. Mr Louisinian's warm welcome was gratifying and Mahmoud took a seat, wiping his brow with his handkerchief and sipping a glass of cold lemonade. He liked Mr Louisinian's restrained professionalism and his immaculate appearance. On trays of red velvet, the jewellery was placed in his view.

'I see that the construction work is progressing in your new building,' said Mr Louisinian.

'Yes, indeed.' Mahmoud took another sip of lemonade.

He had recently purchased all the materials needed for the finishing. Things were going well indeed. If he had not been in a hurry today he would have passed by the building to check on the progress. It gave him such pride to see it standing strong and tall, the first high-rise in the city, a symbol of modernity and prosperity.

He chatted with Mr Lousinian about the businesses that were now applying to lease units in the building. The conversation became more interesting than the jewellery he was selecting! In the end, he bought Nabilah a necklace on which beads made of solid gold were strung together. It was expensive and unusual, too.

'Unique,' as Mr Louisinian put it, 'distinguished.'

For Ferial, he bought a brooch in the shape of a flower. There was a diamond in place of the centre and the stem and the petals were in gold. He felt refreshed. Now he could face his daily, dutiful visit to Nur.

Before he stepped into Nur's room he heard him admonishing his mother.

'You knew you were doing something wrong. That's why

you hid it from me and left me in this room. I kept calling out for someone to take me out to the hoash but you wouldn't let anyone come! You knew I would have shouted the house down. Causing these little girls to suffer! For no reason, for no good reason ...'

When Mahmoud made his appearance, Nur stopped talking. He looked scruffy today. Of course, with the nurse gone, he had not been shaved and he was naked to the waist. Waheeba looked haggard. The heavy chores of changing and feeding Nur must have fallen on her shoulders. She sat up when Mahmoud walked in, but maintained a sulky silence, as if she was waiting for him to leave so that she could lie down again. In spite of the fan whirling overhead, the room was hot. The smell of disinfectant tickled Mahmoud's nose. He picked up where Nur had left off.

'I explicitly forbade you from carrying out this barbarity in my house. Time and time again, I told you.'

'This is women's business,' she retorted.

'No, no. Don't use this argument on me. You dragged *my* daughter into this. You were spiteful and wicked and I will not let this incident pass, believe me. Because of this, you are not going to visit your relations in Sinja. I absolutely forbid it.'

She frowned. 'But I have already made my preparations. They are expecting me like every year.'

'I don't care. You have done wrong and you must be punished.'

She looked dismayed, 'What excuse shall I say to them?'

'What excuse?' he bellowed. 'Your stupidity is the excuse! Tell them you disobeyed your husband. Tell them you broke my word in my house.'

'On a day like this?' she cried out. 'You are being harsh to me when all my gold's been stolen?' The robbery had turned her into a victim, and all morning the neighbourhood women had visited to commiserate.

'Shush, I don't want to hear another word from you. I am

here to visit my son and it would be better for you to remove yourself from my sight!'

She stood up, not without difficulty, gathered her tobe around her and waddled out of the room.

The awkward silence that followed was broken by Nur.

'Did the police catch Shukry?' he asked.

Mahmoud shook his head and described the Arabic teacher's visit to the office.

'Ustaz Badr has been very good to me. He spends time with me reading literature and he refuses to be paid. He insists that these are informal discussions, not proper lessons to prepare for an examination, so I hope you will help him with his accommodation problem.'

'We'll see,' said Mahmoud. 'Let's first get your mother's jewellery back and establish that Ustaz Badr had nothing to do with the robbery. Oh, before I forget, I have a letter for you from Dublin.'

He took the envelope out of his pocket. It was moments like these that he found awkward and denting. A part of him still expected Nur to get out of bed, to walk towards him and take the letter. That was what the old Nur would have done, the well-mannered boy who would not remain seated if Mahmoud stood up, who would be the first to put his hand forward to greet his father. Now nature was subverted. When the doctor in London had suggested that Nur be taught how to use his teeth, nose and forehead to be more independent, Mahmoud had rejected the idea. It nauseated him. Waheeba was better than him, in that respect. She was not embarrassed, nor was she overwhelmed. Thank God for that. Mahmoud could depend on her to look after Nur's needs now that there was no nurse. She was the only one able to cope with the boy's moodiness, the days he refused to eat, his migraines, his many minor infections and afflictions. Times had changed indeed; his estranged, unwanted wife was now indispensable.

Zaki, summoned by Nur, came into the room still in his

school uniform. He took the envelope from Mahmoud, placed a large wooden board on Nur's lap and, after showing Nur the envelope, slit it open. The letter was placed on the board within Nur's range of vision. All this took time. So much patience to achieve such a trivial task.

I wouldn't have put up with this, thought Mahmoud, I would have boiled over long ago.

'It's from Tuf Tuf,' said Nur. 'After Victoria he went to Trinity College.'

Mahmoud smiled. It was a pleasure to see Nur animated, even if these happy moments were few and far between. It was time now to head towards Nabilah's quarters.

She would, Mahmoud thought, appreciate it that on the day Waheeba's gold was stolen, he had gone and bought jewellery for her and not for Waheeba. Of course, what had been done to Ferial was awful. Of course, Waheeba had behaved abominably, but there was nothing he could do now. Nabilah would eventually simmer down; she would, sooner or later, be reasonable. He found her in Ferial's room. The girl was sitting up in bed and Nabilah was spooning custard in her mouth. He greeted them and bent down to kiss Ferial. The girl smiled, but her mother was cool and withdrawn.

'Look what I got you . . .' He clumsily pinned the brooch on Ferial's nightdress.

'Thank you, Father, it's very pretty.'

She turned to her mother, eyeing her for a confirmation, but only found a disapproving look.

Mahmoud squeezed Ferial's shoulder.

'In a day or two, you will forget all this pain.'

He slid the box with the necklace across the bed to Nabilah and went to sit in the armchair. He wanted to resolve the situation and eat so that he could have his much-needed siesta. Usually, at this time of day, Nabilah would be bustling around him, ordering lunch and prattling about her day or asking who he had invited for dinner that evening. Today, she was giving him the cold treatment, and she was wearing a plain housecoat. She had not bothered to change her clothes or powder her nose in order to welcome him.

'Aren't you going to look at what I got you?'

She opened the box but hardly gazed at the necklace.

'Is that all you can do? Stop on the way home and buy me a gift. Your own word, in your own house, has no meaning. You have been blatantly disobeyed and you're doing nothing about it! Tell me, you have just come back from there, haven't you?'

'Yes, I went to see Nur.' He folded his arms across his chest.

'And you didn't divorce her?'

He didn't reply.

'I can't believe it!' Her voice rose to shriek. 'Waheeba's going to get away with what she's done! Instead of standing by my side, you are going to let her off. Aren't you indignant on my behalf? On your daughter's behalf?'

'Yes, I am furious. But what good will divorcing her achieve? She is Nur's mother; he needs her now more than ever. I can't kick her out of the saraya.'

'Then I will be the one to go!'

'Nabilah, don't say that. You will feel calm in a day or so. Look, Ferial will get better in no time. Already she has passed through the first difficult hours with, thank God, no complications. Give yourself time. This morning's robbery hasn't made things any easier. That wretched nurse has let us all down.'

'What are you insinuating? Are you blaming me for recommending him?'

'No, I am not. But everyone will naturally ask did you check his credentials?'

'I can't believe it!' she shrieked. 'Look at your poor daughter, look at her suffering!'

He looked at Ferial's peaked face, with the dark shadows under her eyes from the shock and the pain. She would recover and be like any other Umdurman girl. Nur was the one who

207

would never stand up again. Mahmoud felt his body heavy on the armchair, in the lash of her voice.

'Divorce Waheeba or else I am out of here.'

Later he would reflect that he should have ignored her. He should have walked out of the room. But he was hungry and irritable, fatigued and restless.

'Don't threaten me, Nabilah! Don't do that.'

'Listen, it is either me or her.'

When he didn't reply, she repeated, 'It's either me or her.'

'Go!' He waved his hand. 'The door is wide enough for a camel to pass through. Go, I certainly won't stop you.'

She was taken aback. He saw the confusion on her face and hoped that she would back down now.

But she jerked her head.

'So this is how much I mean to you! No, I will not accept this situation. Never.'

She ripped the necklace from its box and threw it at his face. It hit him on the cheek. He blinked, and saw it skid to the floor.

XV

There was a policeman standing outside his house, and the neighbours were gathered. Badr pushed his way through the crowd and found his household in disarray. Two policemen were stomping about, overturning the family's belongings in their search for the stolen jewellery. Hanniyah was standing holding the new baby in her arms, pleading with them to stop. The children looked curious and confused. In the middle of all this, Badr's father was standing, unsteady and drooling. A damp patch spread from his crotch down the leg of his long johns. He was watching the scene, but clearly not understanding its implications. Shukry was nowhere to be seen. Badr followed one of the policemen into the room. He tried to stop him from ransacking the cupboard but the policeman pushed him away. Even Badr's books, his precious books, which he kept up high out of reach of the children's grubby hands, were hauled down and tossed onto the floor. Badr was on his hands and knees, picking up the volumes of *The Revival of the Sciences of Religions*. When he looked up, he saw the policeman grunt and grab what he had been looking for: Hajjah Waheeba's bangles and gold coins wrapped in a brown paper parcel. They were wedged between the books and the wall.

In triumph, the policeman pushed Badr out into the courtyard and called out to his partners.

'You have the wrong man!' Badr struggled to free himself, but now both policemen held him in a vice.

Hanniyah screamed, 'Let go of him!'

She followed as Badr was dragged through the courtyard. He dug his heels in, but his small frame was no match for their strength. It was impossible to believe that they could be making such an error! Hanniyah put the baby down and started to beat her face, the children began to wail. His father was sitting on the floor, gazing down at the children's marbles, oblivious to his surroundings. For once Badr was relieved that he understood nothing.

The policemen barked at the neighbours who were crowding the doorway. They fell back, and Badr was pushed out into the street under their gaze. He continued to shout out his innocence. It was his cousin Shukry who had stolen the jewellery and hidden it in Badr's house! He, Badr, had had nothing to do with it. Ask the owner of the stolen gold, he pleaded, ask Mahmoud Bey.

'I would never take what doesn't belong to me,' he repeated. 'Never! I work all day for my daily bread. I would never reach out my arm to take what isn't rightfully mine. Every bite I put in my children's mouth is halal.'

But the policemen paid him no heed, and none of the neighbours defended him or tried to intervene. What were they thinking of him now? The venerable teacher of Arabic Language and Religious Education, the man who never missed a prayer at the mosque, had turned out to be a thief!

At the station, the English police inspector could not understand Badr's Egyptian accent. Weren't the stolen items found in Badr's house? It was straightforward, Badr was incriminated. Besides, the inspector was more interested in returning the jewellery to its rightful owner. Badr would have to appear before a magistrate. He was taken into custody.

The room he was led into was large, with a high, barred window on either side to maximise ventilation. It had two occupants who looked like archetypical villains and their close proximity made Badr nervous. They smirked at him and their eyes were bitter and knowing. They were the kind of men Badr avoided in the streets and the tram, the kind of men he never met at the mosque or at the school. He felt the cold pinch of fear. This was real, not a nightmare. He did not belong here. He was not a criminal! He was not one of these men. When one of them offered him a cigarette, he declined, and sat further away. He leaned his head against the filthy wall and closed his eyes. Images came of Hanniyah slapping her face, her eyes wild with anxiety, of the frightened children, the lump and responsibility that was his father. A curse on you, Shukry! All this is your fault. Stolen goods in my house! My own house. Bringing sin into the home that sheltered you and fed you. Where was the bastard now? The police must be looking for him. The police will find him, insha'Allah.

He told himself he must be patient, that the truth would be revealed. Shukry would be found, the police would admit that they had made a mistake, and he would return home in time for supper and, like any other ordinary day, he would devour Hanniyah's cooking, supervise the children's homework, and give his father a bath. The house would need tidying up after the damage the policemen had inflicted. There would be things that needed fixing, but he would take all that in his stride. Everything must be put back to order so that they could put this episode behind them and forget all about it. Tomorrow morning he would go to work and none of his colleagues would ever know what happened.

But an hour passed, two hours, four. He prayed maghrib, and a meal was pushed through the door. The room became dark. He prayed isha and the night deepened. The door was unbolted and he jumped up, expectant, but it was an addition to the cell, a drunk, railing and flagging his arms. He vomited, and the stench rose in the darkness, panning itself over the long night. It occurred to Badr – and the realisation was like a slap in the face – that the police would no longer be looking for Shukry. They had found the stolen jewellery and they had taken a man into custody; from their point of view, their work was done. So he was going to spend the night here in this degradation. And what about tomorrow morning? He would not be able to get to work.

Alarm rose in his throat. It was the end of the year examinations and tomorrow the Arabic paper was due for Senior Year Two. Badr had already set the exam and, as was the policy of the school, placed the questions in a sealed envelope. The document was locked in one of the staffroom cupboards. There was only one key and he carried it in his pocket. If he didn't show up to school tomorrow, and he was now likely not to, there would be pandemonium. The headmaster would send one of the clerks or messenger boys to Badr's house because they would assume that he was ill (though he had never in his life taken sick leave and always dragged himself to work no matter what) and come to collect the key.

What would Hanniyah say and not say? What would the neighbours describe? He banged the back of his head against the wall in frustration. What a scandal! Supposing he lost his job? Supposing he never got out of here, how would Hanniyah manage? Four boys and the newborn baby girl, his father ... all of them in a foreign country, no uncles or cousins to help out. A curse on you, Shukry, you were the cousin I took in, but you bit the hand that fed you! At school they would have to break the lock on the cupboard to retrieve the examination paper. Or would one of his colleagues hastily set another paper? One of his colleagues, who envied him his lucrative private lessons and his standing with the Abuzeid family ... Oh, they would be gloating at his downfall. Lord, why was this happening? What if Shukry was never caught? Could he, by now, be on the train, heading for Egypt?

Badr could not sleep with all this anxiety, though the thugs and criminals around him snored as if they had easy consciences. He wished that he had kicked Shukry out of the house long ago. When Madame Nabilah asked him if he knew of an Egyptian nurse for Nur, he should not have nominated Shukry. Shukry was not even qualified – he had only trained a few months and then went off to join the army. But Badr had been eager to find work for his cousin, eager to get him out of the house and the position of nurse came with board and lodging. It was a good opportunity for the lad and yet, like a fool, he squandered it.

Badr was worn out with anger. Earlier this morning, he had been full of optimism, visiting Mahmoud Bey in his office and asking him for a flat in the new building. It was shameful to recall this encounter. You have made my face black in front of others, Shukry. Yes, he had started the day with aspirations and now even the basics were out of reach. But what was the use of all this agitation? What did the Prophet Jonah do when he was in the belly of the whale? He called out to his Lord saying, 'There is no god but You, subhanaka, I was one of the transgressors.'

The dark belly of the whale – that was where Badr was now. Imprisoned and at the bottom of the sea, darkness upon darkness. Why do bad things happen?

Nur had asked him the same question. Why do bad things happen to good people? On that day, Badr had made an effort to bolster the boy's morale and fortitude. Such a young lad, imprisoned in a cell of disability. But Allah does not burden us with more than we can bear. The boy must have hidden reserves that only the All Merciful knows about. And of course '. . . with each difficulty comes ease'. The Abuzeids were in a favourable position to support their son, and the boy had remarkable intellectual abilities. Perhaps these factors were Nur's 'ease'. It had been gratifying for Badr to continue as his tutor, informal though the arrangement was. The boy was a natural learner, bright and quick, and his appreciation for literature was a joy. Badr always looked forward to these sessions, and once he was there, forgot that he was working or helping.

He sighed. After what Shukry had done, would it be possible to face Nur again and continue as his teacher? Anxiety gripped him. Nur had wanted to know, 'Why did the accident happen?'

And now Badr too wanted to know, 'Why am I here, unfairly imprisoned?'

Because Allah is compassionate, there would be, insha'Allah, a release, and it would be wrong to despair. But now, in these moments of distress, the mind drew a blank. Perhaps the shortest journey to Allah is through the disliked, uncomfortable routes. The seeker asks, 'Where shall I find the Divine?' The answer is, 'Come close to illness, poverty and oppression. Dwell for enough time (too long would be counter-productive) in those shadows where laughter does not come easily to the lips.'

Badr was distracted from his thoughts by the clamour of the door opening. Three young men were pushed in, protesting and cursing. From their elegant clothes and the disdainful way they shook off the guard, it was safe to guess that they were not the usual criminals, but, most likely, the sons of the rich, painting the town red, pulled in for rowdy behaviour or just one prank too many. One of them was large and fair-looking, his shirt loose and pulled out of his trousers. He moved away from his companions and slumped against the wall, calling out, 'You don't know who I am, you sons of dogs! One telephone call and I'll be out of here. You'll see!'

He slid to the floor, eyelids drooping. With a shock Badr recognised Nassir Abuzeid. Oh, what a scandal for Mahmoud Bey! Badr felt indignant on his behalf.

Nassir was now staring at Badr across the room with a blank look on his face. Badr hurried over to him.

'Mr Nassir, this is not your place.'

'Here's a fellow who recognises me!' bellowed Nassir in the direction of the door. 'You sons of dogs, you'll rue the day you insulted an Abuzeid.'

Badr went over to the zeer in the corner, filled a tin mug with cool water and threw it over Nassir's head. Nassir spluttered and groaned. Badr wiped his face and started to pat his cheeks.

'Sober up – and shame on you. If your father found out about this!'

Nassir opened his eyes. He recognised Badr and spoke steadily.

'Neither father nor Uncle Idris will ever get a wind of this. Dear, trusted Victor will get me out of here.'

'You think your father's secretary has such influence?'

'Yes, he knows what to do in these kinds of situations. I've already called him. What are *you* doing here?'

Badr explained and all Nassir did was laugh.

'Rotten luck, isn't it.' He stretched out on the floor, taking up considerable space.

Badr moved a little and leaned his back against the wall. He did not know Nassir as well as he knew Nur because Nassir had never been his student. These days, when Badr went over to Idris's house to give Zeinab her lesson, Nassir was usually having his siesta or already out, and all Badr's dealings so far had been with Fatma. He had, naturally, heard the unfavourable rumours about Nassir, but this delinquency was worse than he had imagined.

'What did you and your friends do to end up here?'

Nassir made a dismissive gesture and wiped his face with the edge of his shirt.

'When Father refuses to pay my debts, I'm forced to seek entertainment in the most sordid of places. So what if I rented a villa in Khartoum in the company's name? I can use the Abuzeid name to get doors opened, it's mine after all.'

Badr felt himself hardening.

'I am sure your father has been fair with you. He is one of the most generous men in the country.'

Nassir snorted. 'Not with his son.'

'Shame on you! You're a grown man, Nassir. You shouldn't be dependent on your father.'

'Well, I work for his company, don't I? And all I get is a pittance.'

'Many would be grateful for what you regard as pittance. If you are ambitious for more, then you must work hard for it. For a building to rise, for harvests to be reaped, for wars to be won, some kind of sacrifice must be made. If you strive you will find success. Listen, young man, you are responsible for a wife and children, your brother Nur needs you ...'

'Nur is the one who cared ...' Nassir's voice dropped. 'He would have cheerfully gone to that office at the crack of dawn every day and he would have worked hard. Such a bloody waste!'

'Yes, and it makes it more urgent that you step up and support your father. What happened to Nur could make you a better person, could cause you to reassess your life and leap forward in success.'

Nassir shook his head.

'It's not happening. Not any time soon.' He covered his face with his arm and closed his eyes. His voice was thick when he spoke. 'It still hurts to see him, day in and day out. Sometimes I can't bear it and I want to wipe his misery out of mind. But I go back to him again because I love him so much and I try my best to amuse and distract him. I moved from Medani specially to be close to him – and I would give him my blood, if it helped. I would give him one of my arms or one of my legs.'

Badr was touched by these sentiments, but troubled by the inertia. It was a goodness that neither translated itself into useful action nor helped rein in indulgence.

'Nassir, what we view as a setback might be a mercy in the long run, or a shield that deflects an even greater misfortune. We don't know. Sometimes suffering in this world is a substitute for suffering in the Hereafter. Do you know Maulanna Abdullahi Ed-Dagestani?'

There was no reply from Nassir. He continued to lie with his arm across his face.

Badr continued, 'He is a Sufi sheikh from Turkey. He said that everything in this world, small or large, was created for a reason. Even the smallest mosquito that bites people and makes them itch. There is wisdom behind that itch, in that it can be a substitute for a corresponding irritation in Hell. He said that every trouble we land in comes from a sin which would not be forgiven without that trouble.'

Such purification Badr knew from personal experience. When he was ill with a fever, he would feel as if he were being blasted by the fumes of Hell. Then, afterwards, when the fever abated and left him weak, he would feel cleansed and grateful.

Nassir had fallen asleep.

Why do bad things happen? For pedagogical reasons, so that we can experience the power of Allah, catch a glimpse of Hell and fear it, so that we can practise seeking refuge in Him and, when relief comes give thanks for His mercy. Darkness was created so that, like plants, we could yearn and turn to the light. Badr had observed this in himself whenever one of the children were ill, or when he faced difficulties at work, or when his plans suffered a setback, or when he was thwarted or in pain. He became more receptive to the words of the Qur'an; he became more ardent in his supplications and more eager in his pleas. Now was such a time. In this lowliest of places, where his natural talent to impart a lesson had dimmed, it was time to lift up his palms and beg.

The door swung open and the guard called out Nassir's name. Badr shook him awake. Nassir staggered to his feet, leaning on Badr for support. He was dazed and relieved, eager to get away. His companions were ushered out with him and, although he did not give Badr a backward glance or a promise of help, Badr was comforted by his release. He stretched out on the floor and let his body relax.

The cell seemed wider and airier now. Badr repeated to himself the verse, '. . . *And give good tidings to the patient* . . .'

He was less agitated than before. Soon he was even able to let pleasant images come to his mind. Hanniyah feeding the new baby, her breast taut and larger than the baby's head, her face radiant because she had so much wanted a girl.

'Now I won't be lonely,' she had said. 'Now I will have someone to help me around the house.'

He smiled in the dark; the girl was only a few months old and already her mother had plans for her. Another image: Osama boasting that he had studied so hard for the end of year examination that he would come top of his class. The utter joy on little Ali's face when he saw Badr come home from work. Such total trust. Little Ali was jealous that his older brothers went back and forth to school with Badr.

Badr dozed and dreamt that he was back in Egypt, in the fields of Kafr El Dawar. Palm trees rose high, and all around him was green. His father was ploughing the land, strong and healthy, his sharp eyes missing nothing. Badr was young, but not a child, holding the results of his baccalaureate in his hand. He had walked down to the fields to show the diploma to his father, but now he paused to watch his father's deft movement, the muscles on his forearms and neck, the sweat gathering on his brow. Then his father turned and drew him close. They hugged, and the paper wasn't necessary any more. His father knew that his studious son had passed with flying colours. He was going to the Teacher Training Institute, he was going to become an effendi and wear a clean suit and a fez. People would treat him with respect because he was a learned man.

Badr and his father walked arm in arm to the canal. His father was beaming and proud. My son, Badr, my son got his baccalaureate, he boasted to passers-by. Men congratulated them and moved away. The two of them sat at the edge of the water but in the strange way of dreams they were now in the water, without having moved towards it. His father splashed, his father ducked his head and raised it, the water matting his hair and turning it a darker colour. Badr sat quite still, feeling the warmth lap around him, through to his skin and up to his chin. Water ... Someone was nudging his shoulder, shaking him awake. Badr remembered where he was and sat up straight.

'Cousin.'

The voice was unmistakable, but the face was a distorted approximation of Shukry's. One eye was swollen to the extent

that it was completely closed. The lips were cracked and bleed-
ing, the cheeks were bruised.

'What happened? Who did this to you?'

'Your neighbours. I went home and your family raised a
hullabaloo. The neighbours rounded on me and brought me
here.'

His neighbours believed in his innocence. The Sudanese
rallied at the end, though they were dumbstruck when he was
taken away! Good for you, Hanniyah, that you roused them and
didn't let the culprit get away.

'How could you, Shukry?' His voice was thick. 'How could
you bring stolen goods into my house?'

Shukry spat out blood and phlegm.

'Don't get all pious on me now. I'm in no mood for your
lectures and I curse the day I ever came to this country.'

'You! And what should *I* say?'

'Don't be self-righteous, Badr. You think you helped me!
Was that a job you got me? I hated it! Cleaning that boy's shit
and getting up at night to turn him over so he doesn't get bed
sores. He's a useless pack of bones and it's disgusting. He blubbers
and expects everyone to feel sorry for him. Not me! I'd gladly
put a revolver to his head. I've seen worse in the war, and those
unlucky bastards had nothing to fall back on. Our prince,
though, doesn't even have to lift a finger to earn a living. This
family has so much money, they don't know what to do with
it. That mother of his had more gold than what I took. Double
the amount. I saw it—'

Badr interrupted him. 'Stop this chatter and tell me what's
going to happen now. Did the police tell you anything?'

'You only care about yourself! You're incriminated, though.
They think we were in this together.'

Badr did not rise to the bait. 'Mahmoud Bey and the family
know I have nothing to do with this.'

Shukry snorted. 'The police won't disturb the Bey in the
middle of the night.'

Neither would Nassir. There was no hope in expecting any help from his direction. Badr stood up and looked out of the window.

'I need to get to the school.'

'You'll wallow here for days till someone remembers you. Listen, cousin,' Shukry's voice became sharp, 'I have an idea. We'll tell them that Waheeba *gave* us the jewellery.'

'Don't be ridiculous!' Badr scanned the sky. It was not yet dawn.

'Yes, yes! We'll tell them that she arranged with us to get a cure for her son – we were to recruit a special spiritual healer from Egypt who's been known to perform miracles. She's desperate, she'd do anything! And then, when the healer couldn't fix the boy, she got angry and said I stole her jewellery.'

Badr sat down again. He listened to Shukry's desperate plan, his shrewd stupidity, and he felt no anger towards him, only disappointment. When he was first dragged here, he would have beaten Shukry, if he had found him. Now he was sitting calmly next to him, listening to him prattle and fabricate. Perhaps this was forebearness and turning the other cheek. With an ache, he remembered the flat he had wanted from Mahmoud Bey. A dream, an aspiration that had kept him company for over a year. It would be sensible to bury all hope now, here in the floor of this Khartoum jail.

XVI

Evening withdraws . . .

The poem comes out of him in what is like a sneezing fit;
expectation, tickle, build up, congestion, then burst, release,
relief and, afterwards, that good tingling feeling. Structure and
a play of words, his yearning for Soraya now has a shape. He
tests the words on his tongue. *The stars know what is wrong with
me.*

It is the dark hours before dawn. Everyone else in the hoash
is asleep. Nur had been looking up at the clouds, watching the
night sky pinned up with stars. He had been feeling sorry for
himself, the tears rolling into his ears in the most irritating way,
and then down to wet his hair. There is no need at this time of
night to hold them back or blink them away. But when the
poem comes out of him, they stop of their own accord. They
dry up and do not leave a mark. These tears, he thinks, are like
everyone else's tears, identical. They do not express his particular
anguish or narrate what happened to him. *Travel caused my
tribulations.* It sounds good. It feels different. This is partly
because of its mix of Sudanese colloquial and classic Arabic, a
fusion of formal language and common everyday words. He
had written poems before, juvenilia, imitations of grand words
striving awkwardly to rhyme. But now this, in his mother
tongue. The colloquial words squeezing out of him, out of the
accumulation of the past months, all that he knows so well and
didn't know before. The words are from inside him, his flesh
and blood, his own peculiar situation. *In you, Egypt, are the causes
of my injury. And in Sudan my burden and solace.*

He hears the dawn azan from the nearby mosque, yet there is

no sign of light, no birds singing, no cocks crowing. The prayer foreshadows the day, a challenge to believe that this darkness will soon be chased away by light. The first inkling of dawn is reminiscent of white moonlight, but soon the sky moves from navy to grey, the stars disappearing one by one. Yet still the birds are silent and he waits for them to sing, knowing they will sing. He can now see the neem branches and the corner of the saraya's rose beds, jasmine trellises and eucalyptus trees. He can hear men walking down the alley, coming back from the mosque. The sky becomes pale blue. One bird sings and the others follow. They become loud and insistent, frenzied, as if they had forgotten that they sang yesterday and will sing the next day. The hoash stirs into life: the same noises, the same sights. Someone spitting out water . . . they are making wudu or brushing their teeth.

A cough, a shuffle of feet, a clutter of tin and the thud of bedding folded up for the day. His mother heaves herself to a sitting position, a mound on the angharaib, regaining her equilibrium, before she finally stands up. All this is familiar, the stuff of everyday. The kettle of tea on the coal fire and the sound of the donkey cart which delivers milk. But today is different. Nur has written words, not with his hands but with his head. He has composed a poem and he knows, deep down, he knows that it is a good poem. Very good perhaps; even, if he is lucky, excellent. He likes it. He wants others to hear it and like it. It might look different on the page. It might need bolstering in one end or changing a word here or there. But still, it is good, it is strong. This is the plan for the day then. Before Zaki sets out to school, Nur will dictate the poem to him.

'Who's the poet?' drawls Zaki.

He is sleepy and hasn't yet brushed his teeth. He thinks Nur is reciting a poem from memory, one of the many he knows.

'Guess!'

'I don't know.'

He yawns, and lays the copybook out for Nur to examine.

They are still out in the hoash; soft sunshine, soft breeze. The birds have sung their guts out and settled down. A dove comes close to Nur's bed to drink water from an old tin pot Zaki had left out. The tea is boiling and smells of cardamom. It is the freshest time of the day.

'I thought you were clever!' Nur smiles. The poem, written down, looks definitely like a poem. Raw words made formal and clear in Zaki's schoolboy handwriting.

Realisation sharpens the boy's eyes.

'It's you!' He is wide awake now. 'Swear to God it's you?'

'Don't tell anyone,' says Nur, not yet at least, he wants to savour the moment. 'And light me a cigarette, will you, before you go.'

Zaki dips his rusks in tea, gulps it down laden with sugar and crumbs and rushes off to school. At nine o'clock he will come home again for breakfast. Beans with sesame seed oil, tomatoes, onions and cumin. Nur likes to see him come and go, he likes to go over his lessons with him and hear him playing football in the alley with the neighbourhood boys. But best of all, he likes it when Zaki becomes his right hand, writing down his words and turning pages for him.

The hour after sunrise is not Nur's favourite time of day. He has started to hate tea because he cannot sip it with a straw and it takes too long for his mother or whoever's turn it is to reach the small glass to his lips for sip after sip. The soggy warm rusks, heavy with sweet tea, are easier to eat. Then he is carried indoors for the daily humiliation of diaper change, enema, botched attempts at shaving, water cascading his body for a bath, the drops running unnoticed over his lower body. Only on his face and shoulders, which belong to him, does he feel it as a familiar substance – water from the Nile. He swirls toothpaste in his mouth and spits it in a plastic bowl. No one can brush your teeth for you as well as you can yourself. When the ordeals of hygiene are over – and it feels quicker today, because today is a special day – he is carried out to the hoash again, feeling clean and comfortable. He closes his eyes and sleeps. He sleeps despite the clatter around him, the voices in the alley, the peddlers and tradesmen, beggars and visitors. He sleeps because he had been up half the night working. Working – what a beautiful word, what a blessing! He had been up half the night working on his poem.

Days pass ...

Hajjah Waheeba's gold is retrieved and news reaches the hoash of Ustaz Badr's arrest. After much commotion, the matter is eventually settled. The culprit is sentenced and his innocent cousin is released. But Badr keeps away from the Abuzeids out of shame, and Nur misses his Arabic teacher. He wants him to come back so that he can show him his poem. He has made changes to it over the days. It is stronger and longer. And it has a title now: *Travel is the Cause*, a poem by Nur Abuzeid.

Soraya has seen the poem. He has sent her a copy with Zaki. She is busy studying for her exams and rarely comes to visit. She sends him a note:

'This is the best poem I have ever read in my life. I want to look in your eyes, while you recite it ...'

He replies with lines that do not yet form part of a poem. They are homeless and, in an artistic way, immature. *Your portrait is enveloped in my heart. I remember and I will narrate how our love was struck by the evil eye.*

Zaki carries this fragment to Soraya, running down the alley as spring turns to a scalding summer. He bumps into Idris and, when questioned, acts guilty and flustered. Suspicions aroused, Idris frisks him down and finds *My solace is your dreamy smile, your braids dipped in darkness.* Soraya's name is not on the paper, neither is Nur's.

'Who wrote this rubbish?'

'Me,' Zaki croaks. It is his handwriting and he can't deny it.

Idris gives him a good hiding, one the poor boy will never forget.

'If I ever find you carrying around such nonsense, I will send you back to Sinja, school or no school!'

Days pass, followed by nights . . .

In the battle of the co-wives, his mother scores a victory. It is true – Nabilah has flounced off to Cairo, taking her children. Waheeba beams, smug and triumphant. There is no chance in a million that Mahmoud will ever come back to her, but she is gleeful, nevertheless.

Days pass, days and nights . . .

No secret can be kept in that hoash, even if the secret is a poem. Nassir brings over his friends to visit Nur, particularly those friends who have an interest in poetry. One of them has had a poem published in the newspaper. He recites it, and then it is Nur's turn to recite his poem. He needs nothing written down; it is all in his head. Everyone listens and murmurs appreciation. Waheeba and her girls are flustered at this influx of male visitors who are not family members. They should not be so exposed, but no one has sorted out the logistics of a screen. The women move with their cooking utensils to the dim far corner of the hoash. They fry and stir and Zaki staggers back and forth carrying the dinner trays. The heat is intense, even this late at night. Water is sprinkled on the ground time and time again. It dries immediately, after releasing a tepid coolness. Even the water from the zeer is not cold enough.

Days pass, days and nights . . .

In July comes the first hint of rain and with it news of the revolution. King Farouk has been deposed by an army coup. The Free Officers are keen to resolve the Sudan problem and representatives of the Sudanese parties are invited to Egypt for talks. Everyone who visits Nur speculates about the future. Overnight, it seems, independence is near.

Nur's best friend, Tuf Tuf, is back in town. The last time they saw each other was at the hospital in Alexandria. The last time they played football together was at the season's final in Victoria College. Tuf Tuf hugs Nur. He sits on the edge of his bed and says, 'No one has called me Tuf Tuf since I left school.'

Because he is transparent, he can barely hide his dismay at Nur's condition. Because he is an optimist, he had hoped Nur would be better, despite what others had told him. And, against all the odds, he had hoped that Nur would be able to punch him affectionately on the shoulder again.

It is an emotional moment. Nur is as eager as a child, grinning with joy at his well-travelled friend, his been-there-and-back schoolmate. Which of them is older now? What ages you faster, suffering or experience?

'Look at you!' says Nur. 'You've become light-skinned. You don't see the sun any more?'

'What sun? It's freezing in Dublin, freezing!' Tuf Tuf shivers at the memory. 'I had to move out of the university halls into private lodgings just so that I could get decent heating. And even then there were nights I had to sleep in my corduroys and two sweaters!'

Nur listens to stories of student life at Trinity College, to parodies of Tuf Tuf's landlady and how his allowance dries up days after it arrives and he is in debt for the rest of the month. Nur laughs out loud. Tuf Tuf's charm is in the way he swings from bashful to extrovert. One minute he is silent, sad about Nur, the next he is singing out loud, 'In Dublin's fair city, where the girls are so pretty, I first set my eyes on sweet Molly Malone . . .'

'Confess then,' Nur says, 'confess your adventures with the ladies.'

Tuf Tuf lowers his voice. 'There's a shop girl who's taken a shine to me – she works in the hat department. But I told her upfront, I said I don't want complications, and your people will shun you for going out with a black man and, at the end of the day, I'm going back to Sudan where I will marry a girl my mother chooses for me . . .'

'Coward!' Nur cries out.

'No, I just want to enjoy my life,' his friend protests. 'So I keep everything light-hearted. I go dancing . . .'

'Dancing!' Nur's eyes shine. He grabs Soraya by the waist . . .

'I'm nimble on my feet,' Tuf Tuf boasts, his body loosening up. 'All the girls want to dance with me. I tell you, no one can out-dance *me*. I can keep going all night – and the following morning, how my legs ache! I almost can't get out of bed, I feel like a cripple!' He stops, overcome with embarrassment.

Nur steers him away from this awkwardness, coaxes him back. Nur has his selfish reasons. He wants his friend to feel comfortable, to stay longer and to return for another visit. Too many of the others come once and then stay away. For them, the sight of him brings nothing but discomfort, though he tries to put them at their ease, to laugh and chat about their news and what is happening in the world. He never mentions his disability, he never complains. He wants them around him, their laughter and healthy lives. *Echoes of a vibrant youth.*

'Who are you quoting?'

'Just an aspiring poet no one has heard of. Tell me more about Dublin.'

'The children on the street cross over to rub my hand. Like this.' He leans over and quickly rubs Nur's arm, then looks quizzically at his fingers.

Nur laughs. 'They expect it to come off!'

Tuf Tuf smiles. 'I'm not alone. I'm lodging with an Indian. He's a good sort and keeps me up to date with all that's happening in the world. But when he cooks, oh no. I would not touch that spicy food if they paid me.'

'Eat a lot while you're here, then. We'll slaughter a sheep for you.'

Nassir bounces in, even more upbeat than usual. He overhears the last remark and, after warmly greeting Tuf Tuf, says, 'Now, tonight I've got a barbeque all planned. We're going to the houseboat in Burri. All of us, including you, Nur! And guess who else is coming? Someone you've always wanted to meet? Hamza Al-Naggar himself is going to sing for us!'

Nur is delighted. An old friend – and the opportunity to make a new one all in one day. Tuf Tuf hasn't heard of Hamza Al-Naggar, and so Nur explains.

'He's young, and the first Sudanese singer to use rumba and samba beats in his music. He's also been influenced by the Egyptian singer, Muhammad Abdel-Wahab. During the war, he went to entertain the troops and that's how his popularity spread.'

'You certainly know a lot about him.'

'What else do I do except listen to the radio all day?' There is no bitterness in Nur's voice, just pleasure in talking about what he loves and the anticipation of meeting a man whose voice and melodies he admires.

The journey to the Burri farm has them leaving Umdurman, crossing the bridge into Khartoum and then travelling east. The back of the car is uncomfortable for Nur. Sloped in the seat against Tuf Tuf, he feels constricted, entangled, but this is an adventure, after all. A men's night out and today he is one of them. The sheep is in the boot of the car, its hind legs tied up. Nur can feel its presence, the gentle scratch of its movements. Their party is made up of four cars. The car driven by the driver is carrying the food, a cook and two houseboys. Part of the pleasure of the journey is watching one car overtake another, losing one and catching up with it again. They flash their lights and hoot their horns. Tuf Tuf laughs and Nassir, in the driving seat, says, 'There is going to be a fifth car catching up with us later. I have such a surprise for you!'

'You told us,' says Nur, raising his voice because all the

windows are wide open. 'Hamza Al-Naggar is going to sing for us.'

'Not only that. I have something even hotter.'

'Hotter! You mean dancing girls? But Hamza Al-Naggar doesn't go for that kind of thing! He wants a decent audience. He wants musicians to be treated well. Sudanese society needs to respect singers. I heard him say this in an interview. So once these girls appear, he will not feel comfortable.'

'Don't worry,' says Nassir. 'They will come later in the night. By that time Hamza will have sung to his heart's content. Besides, these girls aren't dancers, they have other talents.'

This is met with hoots and chuckles from the passengers. This is going to be a long night, thinks Nur.

Tuf Tuf leans forward in his seat, squashing Nur's legs in the process. His head is closer to Nassir's now.

'Elaborate, please, on these other talents. What do they exactly do?'

'They box.'

'Box what, for God's sake?' Everyone in the car is laughing.

'They wrestle each other. They've been performing at the cabaret these past few days. They will finish their performance and then come over and give us a private show.'

'Sounds grand to me. You've seen them?'

'Yes, they're a sensation. They dress like professional wrestlers, with shorts and shoes. At first they wrestle properly then – and that's the best part – they go all wild, scratching, biting and pulling each other's hair out.' The laughter in the car is loud enough for Nassir to need to raise his voice. 'Yesterday, after the show, an English lady complained to the Governor and the Town Clerk.' He switches to English. 'She said the girls were revolting.'

Tuf Tuf repeats 'revolting' in his best English accent. It makes Nur smile and remember their days at Victoria College.

'And I'm paying a tidy sum to get them to revolt us!' Nassir laughs.

The car in front of them turns left and they follow, descending from the asphalt road towards the farmlands on the Blue Nile. The gatekeeper recognises them and waves them in. Past the gate, the path is narrow, barely wide enough for one car. Bushes close in on both sides. Thorns brush against the window and Nassir yelps when one of them digs into his shoulder. He closes the window and Nur likes the sound of the thorn branches brushing against the glass as the car moves along.

He is installed on a camp bed up on the terrace. It is a wide, semi-circular, paved pavilion, surrounded by the upper branches of the trees growing below and encircled by a low railing that overlooks the Blue Nile. Nur can smell the river and hear it gushing. It is swollen, this time of year, with the rains that have been falling in Ethiopia. All his senses are alert. The place is full of memories: the front lawn in daylight, and picnics with his father. Now Nassir bustles about, bellowing at the servants, eager to arrange the slaughter of the sheep, the seating for his guests, the drinks and the barbeque. Woe to the cook if he had forgotten the slightest thing. They are too far away from even the smallest shop.

It is cool, compared to Umdurman, and everyone is grateful for that. A breeze blows through the trees. And there's a smell of water and grass. This particular Sudanese beauty makes Nur heave inside, makes him want to gather the place and the mood. It must be a skill, like fishing, to cast your net into a river of dreams and catch a splendid array of words. That first poem had compelled itself into being, thrust itself out of him almost in spite of himself. Words that clamoured to exist. There is value and charm in that, but now he craves ability, a sense of control; he wants to excel at that smooth transition between emotion and art.

Nur had seen photos of Hamza Al-Naggar in the newspapers. In person, his energy is his most striking feature, a radiating vigour and healthy white teeth, a mix of confidence and modesty. He is handsome and impeccably dressed. As if already forewarned, he displays neither surprise nor pity at Nur's condition. When he strums his oud and sings, Nur is rapt. It is the songs he listens to every day on Radio Umdurman, lyrics that inspire and console him. They speak to him of love and he understands. They speak to him of sadness and he understands. Without Hamza's quartet of violin players, without a microphone, accordion or any other oud but his own, Hamza sounds different than he does on the radio. He sings songs that have not yet been broadcast, works in progress that sound urgent and, at the same time, more relaxed. Hamza is repeating and changing, improvising as much as he wants. Nur feels as if he is being given a glimpse into the gradual development of a song in its early, promising stage, the anticipation before it is cast into a black vinyl record.

Hamza stops singing and Nur looks up. Yes, it is late at night and he is lying on a cot on the terrace of the Burri farm. Yes, everyone seated in a large circle is clapping and he cannot. He looks up to see Nassir, concerned and looking at his watch. The wrestling girls have not shown up. The circle of listeners breaks up and their attention drifts off. Chairs are turned and private conversations spring up.

'Nassir, where's dinner?' someone calls out. 'You're starving us!'

The tantalising smell of grilled lamb chops – that tied up sheep who had been scuffling in the boot of the car – is now wafting up from the grounds. All the appetisers; olives, cucumbers and nuts have been eaten up.

'In a minute. Stay put,' Nassir replies. He holds a glass of whisky in his hand and a dark look on his face. He is not sure whether the girls have stood him up or not.

Nur is grateful for this lull. He has ample time to talk to the musician sitting close to his cot, the man who is Sudan's rising star.

'Is it true,' he asks tentatively, 'that Hamza Al-Naggar is not your real name?'

'Hamza is, but I changed my last name. I was afraid of my family's response to my chosen career. I come from a conservative family, the kind of people who think that all musicians are debauched.'

He doesn't smile when he says the word 'debauched'; it is not a joke.

Nur is touched by Hamza's response. He has heard this disparagement of the arts often from the adults of his own family.

'Sudanese society has to change,' he says with passion. 'It has to give poets and musicians, all artists, the respect they deserve.'

Hamza smiles. 'With time people do change. My family now knows the truth. They've accepted me and now even support me.'

'How come you don't write your own lyrics?' Nur blurts out. 'I mean, how do you choose the lyrics to your songs?'

'Poets submit their work to me. If I am inspired by a poem, I compose a tune that goes with the words and then I sing it. Or sometimes I pick up my oud and improvise a tune as I go along, but it remains incomplete until I find the suitable words.'

'I have a poem,' Nur blurts out.

His voice is loud, even strident. Such an opportunity might never come again. Nur, the young man, might be diplomatic and mild, but Nur, the poet, has no inhibitions. Ambition propels him, a new, bold urge to speak out, to show off and share his words. Besides, what does he have to lose? At least he might gain an honest opinion from a professional who has experience and skill.

'Well, let me listen to it,' says Hamza. He puts down his oud and draws his chair closer to Nur.

As Nur starts to recite *Travel is the Cause*, he suddenly thinks that this is not good enough, that these words are weird, that they don't sound like a poem, don't sound like a song. They just sound like me, he thinks. He falters – and goes on. The words lure him and pull him along. The poem is his home – *In you, Egypt, are the causes of my injury* – his own space, and no one else's, his own pain and no one else's. He belongs within its lines. This is his shelter, adorned and unadorned. By the time he nears the end, he is no longer reciting to Hamza Al-Naggar or to anyone from this particular gathering. Nur is talking to Soraya, and Nur is talking to the night, scratching his story on the scrolls of time.

When he finishes, he ducks his head and waits for Hamza to speak, but the gathering is instantly disrupted by the servants carrying the much-anticipated trays of food. The guests of honour, Tuf Tuf and Hamza, are urged to lean forward and extend their arms. The moment is lost. One of the servants (Nassir's houseboy in the Khartoum villa, Babiker, a boy Nur has never seen before) is set the task of feeding Nur. Nur is resigned to this dependence but Babiker, who has never done this before, makes a sloppy job of the procedure and Nur loses his appetite, inhibited by the quick, sharp looks of pity that come his way from the guests as they scoop mouthfuls of meat and bread into their mouths. Nothing disturbs people as much as his inability to feed himself.

Hamza leaves after dinner without a word about the poem or even an acknowledgement. But Nur plans to send him a written copy tomorrow. He composes a covering letter in his head, and then tells himself not to dwell on it too much. He had, after all, enjoyed reciting his poem. And he is now confident again that it is good. 'Where are these girls you promised?' he teases Nassir.

Nassir answers with his mouth full, 'That pimp took my money and then stood me up. Bastard! Tomorrow I will chase him up.'

So this is how the Abuzeid money is squandered. If their father ever hears of this, he will be furious.

Nur feels tired in a pleasant way. His first meeting with Hamza Al-Naggar, this outing, and seeing Tuf Tuf again, is such abundance, all on one evening, all a surprise. So life can be pleasurable, life can be good. Fate, it seems, has not finished with him yet. He dozes, and elation spreads through his incoherent dreams. A world of mist and colours; Soraya's skin and Soraya's laugh … He moves. He punches the air; he runs down the Victoria College track and jumps over one hurdle and another. He lands knowing he has jumped his furthest, his highest yet. His feet on the ground, carrying the weight of his body, he crouches and springs up again. When he wakes up, he sees Nassir and Tuf Tuf sitting side by side. Nassir is holding another glass of whiskey and Tuf Tuf is lighting a cigarette. They seem to have bonded this evening. Nur closes his eyes and listens to Nassir's drunken tirade against the wrestling girls.

'I think I'm going to have to drive us home,' Tuf Tuf says. 'In this state you'll get us all killed.'

Nur joins his friend in quelling Nassir's objections. He, too, doesn't want to die. A new poem is stirring, triggered by this night and this setting, nurtured by the breeze in the trees and the Nile's water that heard him recite his first poem and carried it on.

> *Tomorrow we will be as we want*
> *And walk at sunset by the Nile.*

XVII

It was Time that defeated Soraya at the end. Changes all around, but weeks, months and a whole year passing without the slightest improvement in his condition, or the faintest of progress. She had held on to hope for so long, she had been stubborn and she had been fierce, but Time won at the end. Not what people said to her, and not even when Uncle Mahmoud broke off the engagement. It was the ticking clock. It was life moving forward, and sweeping away her hopes for a miracle. It was how days and days passed, and Nur didn't recover. Now, when they said he was ill, they meant he had influenza or an upset stomach. Now, when they said he was well, they meant he was singing along with the radio and laughing out loud with his friends. Enough of her tantrums and tears, enough of her threats and scenes every time her sisters said, 'You won't marry Nur, you will marry someone else.'

Time tamed her at the end. Not knowing where to turn or what to do, she put her head down and poured her energy into studying for the school leaving certificate. She had always been a good student, but this dedication was new. Sister Josephine was shining a light in another direction and challenging her to work harder. And there was a prize to be won. Unlike Halima and Fatma, Soraya had managed to complete school. Now she could be the first Abuzeid girl to step into university, the first girl in the alley to get a university degree. When the examination results came out, and Soraya's science grades exceeded all expectations, Sister Josephine invited the Abuzeid brothers to a meeting in her office.

Soraya stood outside the door and strained to listen. She

would miss the familiar columns and the blue tiles stretching all the way to the statue of the Virgin Mary; the open, shady courtyard, the nuns bustling and in white. How purposefully they walked! If she never, ever married, she would be like them, forever a virgin, cut off from motherhood and running her own house. The prospect filled her with self-pity. She moved closer to the door of the office. She could hear her father's voice, loud and irritated. Idris seemed to be addressing Mahmoud, '*You* insisted that she be allowed to wear her spectacles and I gave in for your sake. Enough! Why more?'

Sister Josephine replied to this, but her voice was too low for Soraya to hear. Without the spectacles, she would not have succeeded in her examinations. But Idris had not completely caved in. The permission did not extend to wearing the spectacles in his presence. That would be asking too much! On one occasion she forgot to take them off as she was bringing him a glass of water.

'Get away from my face!' had been his immediate reaction.

She could now hear Uncle Mahmoud saying, 'Soraya will not be the only girl there. She will be in good company.'

He began listing the names of their acquaintances whose daughters were allowed to enter university. Idris merely grunted and resumed his predictable objections. No need for university. No need whatsoever. If only Sister Josephine could talk a little louder, but only a few snatches were audible: '. . . instead of sitting . . . let her attend . . . Medicine is an honourable profession.'

Soraya heard Uncle Mahmoud's gentle response, but she could not now make out his exact words. When the meeting was over and the Abuzeid brothers walked out of the office, Sister Josephine looked tired. She put her arm around Soraya's shoulder and said, 'Apply yourself well.'

Soraya knew then that Sister Josephine had won, but it would not be wise to reveal any expression of glee now, because Idris was scowling and in a hurry to get to the car.

'Thank you, Uncle,' she whispered, and Mahmoud smiled at her and winked.

The new academic year started and she was one of the handfuls of girls to enrol at Kitchener's School of Medicine. At first she was in awe of her surroundings, of the lush, spacious lawns of the campus with their tall palm trees, and the young men who stared at her and gave her shy smiles. She had to wear her white tobe every day.

'Don't even dream of taking it off,' warned Fatma. 'One wrong move and Father will put an end to this university business!'

It was a miracle that Idris had agreed to let her attend in the first place. He was even dropping her off every day, driving through the main gate, right up to the quadrangle in front of the library. To become a doctor ... It still didn't feel real. Soraya would do her lab work and study until the small hours, but she found it hard to believe in herself. Campus gossip had it that the boys were laying bets on which of the girls would be married off and out of college by the end of the academic year. Soraya was a strong contender, but she was not the favourite. She was, it was agreed, 'too tall'. When she heard this, she was strangely disappointed. It was not just hurt vanity or a competitive spirit, she genuinely felt bypassed. Such a reaction did not make sense, because, of course, she wanted to continue and had no intention of abandoning her studies. If she was not going to marry Nur, she told herself, she would have a vocation where she could be passionate and useful, respected and more reliant on herself.

It was her old schoolfriend, Amal, who was voted most likely to be whisked off to the marital nest. When the two of them walked together to classes, they provoked comments on how Amal was petite and curvaceous, while Soraya was slim. It was one thing to be tall in a girls' school and quite another matter in university. Here, she was taller than many of the male students and that was something, she realised, they didn't like. No wonder

237

Amal and her dimples were so widely admired. In the girls' common room, which Soraya hated because it was the hottest, stuffiest room on campus, Amal stretched out on a bench and said, 'We need to find you a bridegroom taller than you.'

When Soraya was engaged to Nur, she was flawless. Now that she was available on the marriage market, her imperfections were all on display: short-sighted, loose-limbed and soon to be over-educated.

'How many men,' mused Amal, 'are ready to marry doctors?'

'Well, they could be doctors themselves . . .' Soraya had flung off her tobe and now slipped off her sandals '. . . or so rich and confident that no woman could threaten them. Then, of course, there are the desperate lot. Over sixty, or with a ghastly skin disease, or widowed with seven children, or deaf and dumb . . .'

'Stop it!' Amal laughed. 'Enough! You never used to speak like that at school!'

It was one of a number of things that had changed about Soraya. Her tongue had become coarse, her sarcasm more searing. She developed the ability to pinpoint hidden weaknesses and exaggerate obvious faults. One of their lecturers – Dr Williams – had a limp and a stutter, following a severe injury in the war. When the common room was full of girls, Soraya would mimic his clumsy walk and make fun of him. What happened to Nur had turned her sour.

'I have no intention of getting married unless I'm allowed to finish my degree afterwards,' she said to Amal, chomping through her sandwich, which was the only reason that kept her in the common room. The university might be a modern seat of learning, but the student body was traditional. Coming from an exclusive private school, the two friends hit against incredible customs, one of them being that decent girls did not eat in front of men! So while the boys enjoyed the leafy shade of the student cafeteria, the girls had to eat indoors.

'My brothers are stuffy, but my father's put them in their place. He's really eager for me to become a doctor,' said Amal.

'He will make finishing my degree a condition to my getting married.'

'My sisters are on my side,' said Soraya.

She saw herself in a dress and a white coat, stethoscope around her neck, moving forwards, away from Halima and Fatma, separating from them. They would do her housework for her and look after her children while she went to work. All her future fantasies included a villa in Khartoum, modern furniture like the kind Nabilah had when she was in Umdurman, and daughters who were not circumcised. As for the head of that household, he was faceless, nameless – almost insignificant. Someone who would not insist that she wear a tobe, someone who would leave her alone. Someone who would accept, if not understand, that he had committed the most unforgivable sin in her world, the sin of not being Nur Abuzeid.

She took out of her purse the latest poem Nur had written. It was about a girl who walks towards the narrator, carrying her degree. She's made the whole country proud, and now, with a casual glance, she ensnares the poet. Admiration beats in his heart, he describes the colour of her skin, her supple figure and how the way she walks gives him pleasure. *I will never betray you.* Soraya forgot that she was in the common room. She forgot that it was Tuesday, and that she had just been talking to Amal. She was inside the poem, memorising every line. Nur's own words to her, written, by necessity, in someone else's handwriting. She would buy a notebook with pink roses on the cover, then she would copy out all his poems in her own handwriting. She would put the date next to each poem, the date on which she received each of these precious gifts.

On Thursday night, Nassir, in the role of the dutiful husband, took Fatma and the children to the Blue Nile Cinema. Soraya went along, too, to watch *An American in Paris*. She enjoyed it even more than she expected and was determined that one day, when she escaped the alleys and conventions of Umdurman, she would cut her hair short like Leslie Caron's. Paris, with its exhilaration and appreciation of beauty – Soraya would go there, too, and on the Champs-Elysées they would approve of her tall slim figure. During the intermission, Nassir bought peanuts and ginger ale. Their box had enough seats for the children and Soraya was relieved that she did not need to sit Zeinab on her lap. However, the child came to stand next to her and said, 'Look up, it's a full moon!'

'Did we come here to watch the sky or watch the screen?'

She knew that Zeinab wanted the rest of her drink.

'There is nothing on the screen now.'

Zeinab reached for the bottle in Soraya's hand.

Soraya held on to it tight and put her mouth close to the girl's ear.

'You just had a whole one. Stop being greedy! If I give you mine, you'll pee in your bed.'

Zeinab looked embarrassed and moved back to her seat. Soraya laughed and raised the bottle to her lips. She caught a glimpse of the sky, the wash of clouds underneath the darkness. So much darkness made her uneasy. There was definitely a weight pushing down on the world. Misfortune was always hovering close around people's shoulders. But she would fight it off, and keep fighting with all her might. Otherwise she would be annihilated by this nameless, all-reaching gloom which she couldn't figure out or map. She was eager for the intermission to be over, for the colours and dance of the film to roll again.

Afterwards, on the drive back to Umdurman, when she was going over the last scene in her head and smiling at Gene Kelly, Nassir said, 'Let's pass by Nur. I haven't been to see him today.'

This was a further treat for Soraya. It had been a whole fortnight since they had met. Fatma (and Halima when she visited) had been holding her back, and university had not left her much time or space to battle with them. Tonight, though, because it was Nassir who wanted to go, Fatma did not raise any objections.

They found Nur in his room, listening to the news on the radio. The room seemed to hold more possessions than when Soraya saw it last. The shelves were laden, not only with his sports trophies from Victoria College, but also with more books – whole volumes of poetry – and there was a new record player, too. But it was medical and nursing supplies that dominated the room, and an all-pervading smell of disinfectant. Soraya felt as if she had dropped into a different world, far removed from the Blue Nile Cinema. Nur was propped up in bed, wearing striped pyjamas, and his arms were bent at the elbow like the greater and less than signs of mathematics, facing each other. There was stubble growing on his chin and above his lips, and the sheet was pulled up to above his waist and tucked under his folded hands. He was much thinner than when she had seen him last, the skin stretching over his forehead and cheeks. There were shadows under his eyes, which lit up when he saw her and followed her movements. No one could want to take his place, no one could envy him ... A density filled the room, lulling laughter and restraining exuberance. She wished she had stayed behind at the cinema to watch the second showing of the film. All the gaiety was *there*, not with him. Here the colours were deeper and richer, here the beauty was of a twisted kind. *This* was not going to go away. She was becoming a doctor, she should know. The human body was made for movement, and this stillness was a threat to life itself. Tears came to her eyes. Not again! They served no purpose. She must be sweet for his sake, light-hearted and entertaining. She must share the film with him, make him laugh by saying, 'I want to cut my hair really short, *a la garçon* just like the actress in the film.'

It was not because Nur was gloomy or uncommunicative that his room carried that other-worldly ambience. On the contrary, he was welcoming and friendly, with a cheerful word to each of them. Even Zeinab was given the chance to do what she liked best, which was to climb on his bed, slot a cigarette between his lips and light it up. Because Nur was socially sophisticated, and because of the genuine pleasure he took from their company, he hid from their eyes the persona of the querulous, peevish invalid. Only Soraya knew that demanding, self-centred, almost elderly Nur, in the same way a lover is aware of the naked skin hidden beneath layers of clothes.

'Before the news,' Nur said, between puffs, 'they played a new song by Hamza Al-Naggar.' He sounded excited. 'It was mine! Would you believe it? *Travel is the Cause*. Such a surprise, I had no idea Hamza would do that. I couldn't believe my ears. It felt so strange to hear it put to music, as if it became something else. And then the presenter said: "Lyrics by Nur Abuzeid", in the most matter-of-fact way. My name was said on the radio!'

They all exclaimed in delight.

'Congratulations,' said Nassir. 'And I am not moving from here until they play it again. I have to hear it.'

They did not have to wait for long, as the song was aired immediately after the news. Hamza Al-Naggar's celebrated voice, a gentle melody and lyrics telling a story that was intimate and completely theirs, describing feelings none of them had ever imagined would be made public. Soraya burst into tears and dashed out of the room. She collided with Waheeba, whom she clung to in the expectation that her aunt would offer a comforting shoulder to cry on, but Waheeba shoved her aside and waddled with purpose into the room. Nur, Nassir and Fatma looked up at her. *Like a bird with a broken wing*, sang Hamza.

'What's this?' she gasped.

Nassir was the one who spilled the beans. Waheeba's face darkened. She walked forward to the radio set and twisted the knob to off. The room fell silent except for her heavy breathing.

'Your father will know how to put an end to this,' she said.

To the youngsters' dismay, Mahmoud met with the head of Radio Umdurman first thing in the morning and succeeded in putting a stop to any further broadcast of the song. Nassir pleaded with his father, but to no avail, and Soraya took the unprecedented step of telephoning her uncle in the office.

'Nur needs this . . .' she searched for the right word, a word an adult would understand, '. . . this hobby. It fills his time. *Please*. Let people hear his lyrics. It will make him happy.'

'It's too late, Soraya.' He sounded impatient and busy, with the sounds of the office behind him. 'I can't go back on my word now.'

'Please, Uncle . . .'

'Look, this sort of exposure is not seeming. It is not fitting for our family's name.' His voice became distant as he moved the receiver away from his mouth, 'Victor, I want you to send this telegram . . .'

Soraya pulled out her last card. 'If Nabilah were here, she would have been on Nur's side. She would have approved of these broadcasts.'

There was a click and the line went dead.

'Miss,' said the operator, 'the gentleman has ended the call.'

On that same night, Hamza sang *Travel is the Cause* on the stage of the National Theatre. Never had any of his songs been banned from the radio and his voice rang out with intensity. It was as if he was urging the audience to listen, listen well, for you might not encounter this particular, simple beauty again. Listen, because these words are new. When he finished the last line, *Fly to me, come*, there was a pause, like that of a surprise, before his listeners collected themselves and were on their feet applauding. Encore, encore! Such was the response in the theatre, such were the ripples it produced, that pressure mounted on Radio Umdurman to reinstate the song. And so, when gentlemen of calibre, when high-ranking officials, and men with stellar reputations in the market, pleaded with Mahmoud Abuzeid to reconsider his position, he relented.

It was a victory. The song, unfairly imprisoned, was released and Radio Umdurman broadcast it again and again. And every-one agreed that it was Hamza Al-Naggar's best. His popularity, already strong, was set to soar. Soraya would walk down the alley and hear snatches of Nur's lyrics coming from the houses. She would sit up in bed and sing along with the radio. And every time she heard it, the pain decreased and the enjoyment increased. One day, in the university common room, she heard a senior girl singing a few lines. One morning, during lab, the student working next to her kept humming the tune. Fatma had stories, too, of the neighbourhood women in Umdurman realising that the lyrics were written by Waheeba's son. Nassir's friends wanted to meet Nur and he was more than happy to bring them for visits. Naturally, Idris was uncomfortable, while Mahmoud, after losing the battle with Radio Umdurman, wavered between embarrassment and surprise at the spreading popularity of his son's lyrics. In general, the older generation found themselves pushed into a corner.

A few years ago, in front of Mahmoud, Waheeba and Nabilah, Idris had torn up one of Nur's poems and Mahmoud had urged his son to leave such frivolity and concentrate on his studies. Now their objections were defeated. Now they did not have the heart to chide Nur and found themselves gradually affecting indulgence.

'Anything to keep the wretched boy diverted, anything to comfort him,' they repeated, and in Soraya's opinion they were wrong again. They were underestimating Nur, as if he had not suffered enough, as if he was not deprived enough.

'Poor boy, whinging and making his complaints rhyme,' they said, but Hamza Al-Naggar knew, and the listeners of Radio Umdurman knew, that these lyrics were beautiful and these words were true.

One day on campus Soraya passed a 'Sudan for the Sudanese' rally and stopped to listen. The speaker was adamant in his rejection of any kind of Egyptian influence over a future, independent Sudan. He spoke with passion and serious purpose, then, as if to change tactics, he smiled and said, 'Haven't you heard the poet say *In you Egypt is the cause of my troubles?*'

The crowd laughed and Soraya's heart was beating hard. Even though the paraphrasing was not entirely accurate, it was impossible not to be proud. These people didn't know that Nur was an invalid. For them all that mattered were his words.

At home, Fatma was excited, but for another reason. She paused in the middle of stuffing a green bell pepper and said, 'Halima was just here with good news. You have a suitor! An excellent one, and guess who he is? Your friend Amal's brother! His mother went over to Halima's house to test the waters. If she senses encouragement from our part, the men will come to Father and make a formal offer. I neither encouraged her nor discouraged her – I wanted to speak to you first, before I speak to Father. Then I will answer her.'

Soraya had been about to sit down and help her sister, but she kept standing.

'Don't even mention this to Father! Just tell Halima to tell her no. Say I want to finish my studies.'

'That's what we said to the mother of the previous suitor, and the one before him,' Fatma snapped back. 'This one is your friend's brother. You must give him a chance.'

Soraya walked to the bedroom, tossed her books on the dressing table, and took off her tobe. She switched on the radio. Fatma marched in after her.

'Girl, answer me!' She was still holding the pepper in her hand.

Soraya threw herself on the bed.

'He's not progressive enough.'

'How can you say that? His sister is studying like you are. He himself has a degree and . . .'

'I have specific requirements and he doesn't meet them. I want to live in a modern villa in Khartoum, I want to travel, I want to have short hair and smoke cigarettes. I want to wear trousers!'

Fatma gasped and sat on the edge of the bed.

'Have you lost your mind? What kind of man is going to put up with all this?'

'Exactly! So I'll just stay as I am, then.' She had been waiting for the song and there it was, the first familiar notes of *Travel is the Cause*. It was luxurious to stretch out on the clean sheets, to roll over and mouth the words. 'Fatma, let me listen ...'

Her voice was low and slurred. Already she was intimate with him, in his deep, other world, caught in the pendulum of his thoughts, surrounded by the crystals of his dreams.

The next day at college, Amal was not as forgiving.

'How dare you turn down my brother? Who do you think you are?'

Soraya was taken aback. She repeated the excuse of wanting to continue her studies and hoped that Amal would simmer down. But Amal settled into an aggrieved silence. When Soraya squeezed in to sit next to her in the biology lecture, Amal huffed and moved away. Then the following morning, when Soraya went forward for her daily hug, Amal turned away. And she continued to give her the cold shoulder. The two of them had always done things together; now the university felt awkward and lonely. The breakfast break in the girls' common room became a punishment without Amal to share it.

On impulse, Soraya walked over to her old school. This was a risk, for she had not taken prior permission from her father. Idris, as usual, had dropped her off at university and expected her to stay there until he picked her up in the afternoon. Besides, he would not have approved of her walking in the streets alone without a chaperone. Still, she needed to see her friend Nancy in order to complain about Amal. Nancy was now teaching at the school. She had moved seamlessly from senior student to teacher and the nuns who used to be her teachers were now her colleagues and employers.

Soraya hovered outside the First Junior classroom, watching her friend teach *Little Women*. Nancy's hair was no longer in Goldilock curls. It was in a ponytail and, with her long skirt, she looked every inch the teacher. When she saw Soraya, she smiled and came out to greet her.

'I'll be finished in ten minutes. Wait for me.'

Soraya walked around the empty, shady courtyard. She could hear the faint drone of the teachers in the various classrooms, and the younger students chanting out their times tables. Part of the grievance against British rule, she had come to learn in university, was how they established missionary schools to undermine and lead astray the Muslim population. But Soraya felt comfortable to be here, she always had. She walked to the grotto with the statue of the Virgin Mary dressed in a flowing blue robe and a light white veil draped over her head. Mary was looking upwards. Upwards towards that expanse she understood and loved; that heaven which Soraya was afraid of. During school examinations, the Christian girls would come here to pray and perhaps, she now thought, when they had problems at home they came here, too.

Soraya had never been spiritually inclined. Religious education always made her feel like a child trespassing into adult discourse. It was a language she did not instinctively understand. Besides, life was rich and juicy; it filled all her consciousness, leaving no space for what could come afterwards or what existed before. She did not have an imagination for angels or devils but she was now sure – after Nur's accident – that people were governed by a will greater than their own. It was a power she was wary of – too wary to engage with, or try to understand. Instead, she closed her eyes and ploughed ahead, hoping she would dodge misfortune, trusting in good luck. Underneath her beauty and her sharp tongue, her popularity and social position, there was a spoilt child, demanding and capricious.

Nancy laughed when she heard about Amal's brother.

'Tell Amal the truth. Explain why you rejected him.'

'She would just take it as criticism. If *she* finds fault in her brother it is fine, but the rest of us must think he is wonderful! She is being so unfair to me.'

Nancy fell quiet, then she said, 'Nur is the one you love.

That's why you're turning everyone down. If I were you, I would insist on marrying him.'

Soraya was taken aback.

'What sort of wedding would that be? How would he hold a sword in his arm while I dance, how would he stand next to me for the photograph?'

'The wedding itself is just a formality, just a party,' Nancy soothed her. 'It's not important.'

But the wedding mattered to Soraya, it mattered deeply. She had her dream of more than one party, more than one celebration, traditional gold and African dancing and, on another day, a long white dress like Nabilah's, with a veil and a train.

'You will have your whole life together – the wedding itself really shouldn't matter. So what if he is an invalid? No one is perfect.'

This was not what Soraya wanted to hear. Suddenly she wanted to change the subject.

'Tell me about your news, Nancy. Are you happy working here? You do look happy.'

Nancy smiled and took Soraya's arm.

'Let me get you something to drink, I'm not being a good hostess, am I? Have you already said hello to Sister Josephine? She is so proud that you have gone to college.' They walked arm in arm towards the canteen and it felt like old times. 'I want to tell you something, something I haven't yet told any of my friends.' Nancy's eyes were shining, and her grip on Soraya's arm tightened. 'I've been thinking about this for a long time, have wanted it for ages. And now it's going to happen. I'm going to become a novice.'

On her way out of the school, Soraya met Victor, Uncle Mahmoud's secretary, who was picking up his daughter. The little girl had come down with fever and was being sent home. Soraya hoped he would not, later at the office, tell Idris he had seen her, but there was no guarantee. As she was walking back to the university, she stood on the pavement to watch a woman driving a car. To Soraya's delight the lady waved and stopped her car. It was Sue Harrison, and she remembered Soraya as Mahmoud Abuzeid's charming niece who had accompanied him to their house for last year's Christmas party.

'Let me give you a lift, unless you're going to Umdurman. That would be too far out of my way.'

Soraya scrambled into the car, not believing her luck. For the first time in her life she was sitting in a car driven by a lady!

'I'm going back to the university.'

She had a hundred questions to ask: about driving, about short hair, and all the time she was staring at Sue's bare arms; how tanned she had become since arriving in Khartoum!

Sue drove through the gates of the university and the car had to slow down because a crowd of students spilled from the lawn, onto the road. A political meeting had just broken up and the students were in a boisterous mood. Some of them were chanting.

'Do you know what the occasion is?' asked Sue.

'It must be about changing the name of the university,' Soraya remembered. 'They told us the medical board would approve it today. The Kitchener School of Medicine and Gordon Memorial College are going to merge and have one name – the University College of Khartoum.'

'Oh, what a shame,' said Sue. 'I am fond of these Scottish names.'

The car was almost at a standstill. Soraya could get out now, but even if she did, Sue would still have to drive through to the other gate. She now beeped her horn. A couple of young men glanced over their shoulders but did not move out of the way. Sue blew her horn again.

Soraya felt awkward. She did not know these students personally but they were her colleagues and they were being either very slow or deliberately rude. It was true the road was crowded, but they could still be considerate and make way for the moving car. More 'Free Sudan!' slogans were shouted out. Usually Soraya enjoyed the rhythms and spirit of the anti-British slogans, but now she felt uneasy and Sue was becoming increasingly tense. She did not understand Arabic, but the hostile stares directed at her could not be mistaken.

'I shouldn't have driven in here,' she said. 'I should have known better. Nigel will certainly tick me off for this.'

'Please don't be afraid. They will go away soon,' Soraya replied. 'They are just happy that the university has a new name.'

But it seemed that minor successes, instead of appeasing the pro-independence movement, had the same effect as setbacks. They put the students in a combative mood.

One of them banged the bumper of the car. A voice called out.

'Get out of our way, woman!'

Another, angrier, shouted out, 'What brought you here, anyway?'

There were a few half-hearted jeers, and the car was thumped again.

'Stop it!' Soraya leaned out of the window. 'What are you doing? Let us pass.' When she sensed that her words startled them, she kept on haranguing. 'Get out of the way! You have the whole pavement to walk on!'

One of the students recognised her and laughed out loud and it was this laugh that tipped and lightened the situation. The boys were all now craning to look at Soraya. They made way for the car, amused that she was angry. It was a sight not to be missed; how she was almost standing, halfway out of the window, gesticulating with her arms, her tobe falling to reveal her long hair.

It was a subdued Soraya who went home that day, who lay in bed staring at the ceiling, refusing to study or eat. Nancy talking about love, showing her a new dimension, an altered vision. They had always been different, Nancy nursing a stray cat or reading to a blind child, Nancy not even flinching in the company of lepers while Soraya tagged along, bored and disgusted. Today Nancy's words had affected her deeply. They painted a scenario she had never before visualised: to be the wife of Nur Abuzeid as he was now, after the accident. To nurse him and sacrifice her youth to him, to share his life with all its challenges and limitations, to dwell with him in the twilight between illness and death . . .

Soraya switched on the radio and heard the presenter announce another new song composed and sung by Hamza Al-Naggar, with lyrics by Nur Abuzeid. This song was more searing than *Travel is the Cause*; bolder and more direct. The grown-ups would not like it, not one bit. She smiled, anticipating their discontent – and Nur's further success.

Two days later, as she waited for her father to finish his tea and drop her off at university, he suddenly said, 'You are not going out with me today.'

Soraya was taken aback. 'Why, are there demonstrations in town?'

'No, I have just decided that today you stay at home.' He sipped his tea.

Soraya stared at him in disbelief.

'I have important lectures today. Please take me.'

He shook his head. Fatma walked into the sitting room, carrying a plate of biscuits. She placed them in front of her father and made a gesture to Soraya as if to say, 'I will explain to you later.'

But Soraya was defiant.

'If you can't take me, I can go with Uncle Mahmoud's driver.'

'You will do no such thing!' He dunked a biscuit in his tea. 'You are going to sit in this house today and not leave it.'

'But I—'

'Not a word!' He swallowed. 'Now get out of my face. Go to your room.'

She got up and walked to her room. She felt too energetic to lie down, and too annoyed to change her clothes. What had got into him? Had he found out that she had visited her old school?

Was it Victor, the secretary or Sue Harrison who had given her away? As soon as she heard Idris grab his car keys and walk out of the house, she went back to the sitting room. Fatma was sitting in his place, pouring herself a glass of tea. Her eyes were red and puffy.

Soraya pounced on her.

'So what's the matter with him? Did he find out about the other day?'

Fatma sighed. 'Yes, of course he found out, but he didn't say how. Can anything stay hidden? He took all his anger out on me, I can tell you! He said I wasn't guiding and restraining you enough, that Nassir and I should be living in Uncle Mahmoud's saraya, and that the only reason he wanted us here was that I could keep an eye on you. He said I am no substitute for Mother. Fire begets ashes, he said.'

'This made you cry, didn't it? Poor Fatma. You know it's not true. I am so happy that you moved from Medani and that you're living here. Please, don't go anywhere.'

'I wish he were different,' said Fatma. 'I wish I could talk to him about my problems with Nassir. Maybe if he had a word with Nassir, then Nassir would go out less and stop squandering his money. People borrow from him and never pay him back and he is cheated every single day, the fool that he is! People think we are rich, but I'm at my wits' end most of the time.'

Soraya didn't know what to say. She put her arms around her sister. Tears rolled down Fatma's face and she wiped them away with the edge of her tobe.

'This is what you stayed at home for,' she smiled ruefully, 'to pat me on the shoulders.'

Soraya was jolted back to remembering her missed classes.

'Father is just so unreasonable.'

'He's angry with you.'

'So this is my punishment, then? House arrest?'

She knew why her father hadn't shouted at her or told her off. She was beneath that, not worthy to be addressed. He despised her to that extent! For years she had accepted his treatment, knowing she would one day get away from him to be Nur's wife.

'You know what I think,' said Fatma, taking a sip of her tea. 'It's that new song that's upsetting Father. He heard it again this morning and switched the radio off. The lyrics are shameless. *Her ripe cheeks, her gentle lips. Your beauty keeps me up all night.*'

Soraya laughed. Just hearing Nur's words banished all the badness and put her in a good mood.

'*I want to be alone with you,*' she sang.

Fatma rolled her eyes.

'And then, when Nur says she is slender like the baan tree, Father can put two and two together and of course he doesn't like it. Especially when he worries that everyone else in Umdurman will reach the same conclusion.'

Soraya's eyes were shining. 'Nur will *never* give my name away, and Father's hands are tied. He won't dare criticise Nur now!'

'Yes, but it's your honour, and our whole reputation, which is at stake.' Fatma was serious. 'No one must ever know that you reciprocate Nur's feelings. That would be a scandal. That's why you can't take a wrong step. You have to be above suspicion. Because Nur's lyrics aren't confined to his room. Do you know how far Radio Umdurman's broadcasts are reaching? People from Sinja have been phoning Uncle Mahmoud!'

'Good!' said Soraya. 'I want *everyone* to hear Nur's lyrics again and again.'

'Well, then, you will have to put up with Father's anger. Believe me, he will take out all his frustrations on you.'

Soraya folded her arms. 'Keeping me prisoner here won't solve anything.'

'A husband for you would solve everything,' retorted Fatma. 'Don't you want to get away from Father and be the mistress of your own house?'

'Yes, of course I do.' That had always been the hope, the logical solution.

'Tell me, apart from a handful, what have the rest of your classmates done since they left school?'

'They got married.'

'See? This is the natural thing. So stop being stubborn. When the next suitable suitor comes along, promise you will consider him.' Fatma was looking at her, beseeching. 'Promise you won't dismiss him out of hand. Soraya, you have to look to the future in a different way.'

She knew. At last she knew.

'I promise,' she said, and wondered who he would be.

A few days later, on the first cool evening of the season, the two sisters walked down the alley to Waheeba's hoash. It was the first time Soraya had gone out since Idris sentenced her to house arrest, but a plea for help from their aunt had made Fatma relent. Besides, she did not want to walk all alone in the dark. Nur was inundated with guests, Waheeba had said on the telephone.

'I must serve them dinner and you must come and help.'

They found their aunt and the other women screened from Nur and his guests by several green wooden screens with a lattice design. The coal stoves were lit and Waheeba was sitting on a stool in front of a large pot of boiling oil, shaping each piece of ta'miyyah in her palm and throwing it in. She was pleased to see the two sisters.

'Who are all these guests?' Soraya tried to peer through the screen.

'How do I know, my child? They are all strangers. Ever since these songs have gone out on the radio, we've had men coming and going.'

'You will need to have a separate entrance for them,' said Fatma scooping, with a long ladle, those pieces of falafel that were now a crunchy brown.

'I will talk to your uncle,' said Waheeba. 'Nur needs more

space now – not only his own entrance, but also a diwan, so that we're not so cramped here.

Soraya edged closer to the screen. If she pressed her face close, she could see the whole of the men's gathering. She put on her glasses and saw Nur propped up on his bed at the head of a large circle. One of the men was holding an oud on his lap and an elderly man was reciting a poem from a sheet of paper he was holding in his hand. She listened to the words, and when he finished, the comments of the others held her attention. She heard Nur's voice. It came to her clearer than anyone else's. She liked the look on his face; serious and happy, totally engaged. Some of the men spoke more than others, and some were quietly smoking. She saw Zaki come close to Nur and hold up a glass of water to his lips. Nassir walked in and shook hands all around, touching his brother's elbow before taking a seat. Zaki passed round a tray full of glasses of water. Following a comment made by Nassir, the gentleman with the oud began to play and sing. It was a traditional folk song and the others nodded their heads with the melody.

When Zaki came over to the women's area to refill the water jugs, Soraya called him over.

'Tell me who is who,' she whispered.

They ducked down together, for she had found a spot on the screen where several segments of wood were missing and that gave her a wider range of vision.

'Most of them,' said Zaki with authority, 'are from the Poets' Syndicate.' He named a few names, some of which Soraya recognised. These distinguished poets, when they performed at the university, packed whole lecture halls, and now they were sitting casually in Nur's hoash!

'The one sitting right next to Nur,' continued Zaki, 'is his friend from Victoria College. Everyone calls him Tuf Tuf, but that's not his real name.'

Soraya smiled and took a closer look at Nur's friend. He was sitting with his legs crossed, the back of his hand rubbing against his chin as if checking for stubble.

'Is he always that quiet?'

'No, it's just that he doesn't seem to know much about poetry. He was here visiting Nur and suddenly all these others dropped by. The man with the oud is, of course, Hamza Al-Naggar. He almost comes every evening. It's the others who are here for the first time.'

Hamza Al-Naggar started to sing *Travel is the Cause* and Soraya didn't want to ask Zaki any more questions. She wanted to listen. Nur's song. *Her* song. Nur joined in the singing and Hamza smiled and let him lead. '*Ah ya kanari wa ah ya gamari* ...' and when Nur sang *Ah* the ache was there for everyone to hear, and everyone to share. His passion in colloquial truth.

Soraya wanted this combination of music and poetry to last and last and to become part of the fabric of Umdurman. For every wedding party, for boys to hum in the alleys on their way to school, for schoolgirls to copy in secret notes. For lovers, not yet born, to sing in the style of their times ...

She pressed her face against the wooden screen and listened. Hamza had stopped playing his oud and there was a hush. It was Nur's turn to recite his new poem, in his own voice, his own words.

The prettiest girl in the alley can't stand harsh words

'I will not shackle you to an invalid,' her Uncle Mahmoud had said.

She's pampered, Nur was saying, *but don't ever scold my love*

She could not be Nur's nurse. She was incapable of such a sacrifice. She would feel hard done by and ignored, she who aspired, like her Uncle Mahmoud, to a modern, upbeat life.

This, instead, was where she belonged with Nur, right here, here in his songs. Here within the lyrics they were intimate, caught in the rhythm of his words, propelled by the substance of his dreams.

These songs would be their story and these lyrics their home.

XVIII

The blow, inevitable in itself, comes straight from the source without any intermediaries. It is a direct hit which finds him defenceless, unprepared. Tuf Tuf is visiting him around sunset, a quiet time before Hamza Al-Naggar and the other poets come over for what has become an almost daily literary salon in Nur's hoash. The focus of the salon is the connection between poetry and song, the bonus is Waheeba's lavish dinner. Tuf Tuf is one of Nur's friends who had not stayed away, not said, 'I can't bear to see him like that.'

Now he sits with his legs crossed and his knuckles hovering over his mouth. He is in his bashful mood and blurts out, 'My mother finally selected a bride for me.'

Nur smiles. 'Well, who is she? Have you seen her?'

Tuf Tuf, beleaguered, uncrosses his legs and crosses them again.

'Don't you like her?' Nur chuckles.

Tuf Tuf doesn't smile.

'There is no fault in her,' he whispers.

There is no fault in her. When Hamza sings that line on the radio it sounds boastful and joyful. But Tuf Tuf wraps the words in amazement.

It is a warning, and Nur turns to look away, as if to search for armour, to reach for shield.

'I saw her here,' says Tuf Tuf. 'In one the gatherings, the day you sang *Travel* with Hamza. She was watching from behind the wooden screen. She didn't think anyone could see her, but I did. I walked over to the women's section, never mind if they thought me bold or rude. I reckoned I was here nearly every day and

Aunt Waheeba would welcome me as one of the family. It was like a dream. First, I was hearing about her in your poem and aware of her behind the screen. Then, when I crossed over, there she was in the flesh. I tried to get her out of my mind; I tried hard, until my mother said her name . . .'

'No,' says Nur. 'No! Tell your mother to find you another bride.'

'Why?'

'What do you mean why? You know very well why.'

'Now that my mother is so keen on her, I will have to come up with a reason to refuse. I will have to find fault in her choice.'

'That is such a lame excuse. Tell her Soraya is not your type, tell her you don't want to marry a girl from Umdurman.' A pulse beats in his temple.

'Nur, if it's not me it will be another man. You *know* that.'

'But you're my friend! How dare you? How *can* you?' Tears alter his voice.

'That's why I'm telling you,' Tuf Tuf pleads. 'That's why I didn't want you to hear it from anyone else.'

'I want to punch you. Oh God, what would I give to shove a fist in your face!'

Tuf Tuf bolts out of the hoash.

Later, it is Nassir who seals the bitterness and what is left of the hope. He bears the formal bad news.

'Soraya's engaged. Your friendship with Tuf Tuf must have stood him in good stead because Father and Uncle Idris gave their consent.'

Nur opens his mouth and blackness sweeps up in front of his eyes. He wants to speak, but his voice cannot form words. He wants to scream, and the scream consumes him. He is nothing, and nothing exists but pain. He is trapped; he is squeezed. There is Nassir's dazed, flaccid face, his stupid words of condolence. Leave me alone! Stop taking away one thing, then another, then another. Breathing is difficult and breathing unfurls the foul, ultimate question. Why me? But life still claims him, and he is pulled back against his will. Hamza's voice when he was introducing *Travel is the Cause* at the National Theatre: 'The lyrics are those of a new poet, Nur Abuzeid. I composed the tune in tribute to his talent.'

But I am not a real poet, *Travel is the Cause* was a one-off. There is nothing inside me, because the dead can't be creative. Leave me alone! Let me go on strike. Stop taking away from me one thing and then another.

The doctor diagnoses nervous exhaustion and prescribes sedation. No visitors, he says. A needle is thrust in Nur's arms. He sleeps, but he is still speaking to Tuf Tuf, still locked in the moment he heard the news.

'What about that girl in Dublin?' he screeches. 'The one you go dancing with, the one who works in the hat department.'

He demands an answer; he demands an answer until it hurts. His mind wants to escape towards pleasant, comforting images, while the pain keeps him in one spot, as if a dagger has passed through his stomach and is pinning him down. He remembers the Shakespeare he learnt at school, remembers incidents in the dormitory, the thrill and heave of a football match. His memories of school are crystal clear, but when Tuf Tuf returned from Dublin and they spoke, Nur realised that his friend had shelved these memories, simply because other events had taken place in his life. He had gone to Dublin, sat in lecture halls and made new friends. Not like Nur – Victoria College, Alexandria. Then stop. Nur cries, wrestling bitterness, which demands dry eyes and a constricted throat, choking.

It's past midnight when he opens his eyes. There is no one in the room except his mother and she is silent, not with concern, but with an attitude hovering near disapproval. Nur struggles to understand.

'You must eat,' his mother says.

With her fingers, she scoops kisra and mullah into his mouth. He swallows, and feels the sadness well up inside him. In the days to come, so much will change. There will be no end to the celebrations, and he must live through them. Pull yourself together, he tells himself; this was bound to happen, sooner or later. And, for some reason, he thinks of the day of Eid, and the crescent, which celebrates the end of Ramadan. Everyone wears new clothes, everyone goes visiting; the children play games and eat sweets, and the alleys are alive with celebrations. Friends hug each other while he waits aside for something new or special to lift this day out of the ordinary and make him celebrate.

'Did anyone ask about me?' he asks his mother.

'Yes, Hamza came and he had some young men with him.' She is becoming more comfortable with Hamza now. He comes so often that he is no longer a stranger. 'He left a magazine for you.'

Nur's curiosity is ruffled. He wants to see the magazine, to have Zaki search through the pages for what Hamza would have wanted him to read. But he is too tired now, too drained. Later.

'And your Arabic teacher came too. He said he heard your lyrics on the radio and I said to him it's about time, these broadcasts have been going out for months!'

Ustaz Badr hadn't been to see him since the robbery.

'I hope you were kind to him, Mother. I hope you're not holding a grudge against him.'

Waheeba sighs.

'He is innocent. It was that accursed nurse, Shukry, who plotted everything and executed the crime. Your father said we mustn't lay any blame on Ustaz Badr and he is to be welcomed here. And anyone you value, Nur, I will value and honour. Anyone who makes your burden lighter will find me on his side. But you mustn't let your anger affect your health.'

And that is all she says about how he lost Soraya to his best friend. Neither does Nassir have any further comments, nor does Fatma or Zaki or Batool. As for his new friends – the writers, musicians and poets – they are interested in the final outcomes of Art itself, rather than its ingredients and fuel. He should bunch up his grievances, sculpt them and hone them for his poems. This is the outlet, this is the path; this is more than a dream.

He wakes up to look into his teacher's protruding eyes. He dozes and, when he is wide awake, he finds Ustaz Badr leafing through the magazine that Hamza left.

'Your poem is published here,' says Badr. 'It is part of an article about Hamza Al-Naggar and his songs.'

Badr continues to read and Nur feels young again, a student watching his copybook being marked, eager for approval.

'Is it good?' he asks.

Badr continues to read.

'Or are you a purist?' Nur rushs in. 'I'd wager you don't approve of using colloquial words and phrases.'

'The poem is good but . . .' Badr closes the magazine.

'But what?'

'You can do better,' says Badr.

Nur laughs. He is fond of this man, his tenacity and desperate goodness, his knowledge and simplicity; the strength which floods him like a miracle. Nur hadn't laughed for some time.

'*Travel* is a hit on the radio, your cousin is in prison for robbing my mother's jewellery, you want my father to lease you a flat in his new building – and you sit there and tell me *I* can do better!'

Badr frowns. 'I will gain nothing by flattering you. At the end, what will be will be. So I might as well say the truth. And here is what I think. You will be tempted to write more light verses because popularity is now within your reach, but you can also become a serious poet, a poet others will respect. It is your choice.'

'I will do both,' Nur says. 'I will do both, and I want you to come to me regularly like before. I want us to have our weekly meetings and discussions again. I need . . .' he pauses and swallows. 'I need to be a student again.'

When Nur closes his eyes, there is her image, and every ache and aggravation is aroused, envy of Tuf Tuf and simmering rage.

But a little while ago, talking to Ustaz Badr, he had felt clear-headed and liberated.

A day passes, followed by a night. The sharpness eases and there are stretches of calmness, of leisure, when he does not think of Soraya's engagement to Tuf Tuf. His body had absorbed the shock and the news, like a foreign virus, is now seeping through his system, defeating every antibody, becoming a part of him. There was a Nur before the news, and now, a Nur after the news.

He learns that his reaction to Soraya's engagement is to be kept secret. He will not be allowed to jeopardize her future and so no one will indulge his sadness or publicly acknowledge his loss. The family's honour is at stake, the Abuzeid name. In the days to come, women from Tuf Tuf's family visit in droves. They bring their relations, neighbours and friends to take a look at the bride. They probe and sniff for gossip, but they must not find any. Nur and Soraya's previous betrothal is played down – a formal engagement never really existed, it was just talk, an appealing idea to marry off two sisters to two brothers but nothing came out of it. The bride has no imperfections. Nothing must blemish Soraya's reputation.

> *I feed on bitterness and satiety never comes.*
> *Today sadness has renewed itself.*
> *Let me narrate the story of two souls,*
> *Whose love was struck by the evil eye,*
> *In a twist which Fate had hidden.*
> *Luck won't smile and Time will scorch.*
> *Only the stars know what is wrong with me.*
> *I almost sense them craning to wipe my tears away.*

'Your new poem, *Eid Crescent*, is bleak,' says Hamza when Nur perks up and the evening visitors are allowed.

'So was *Travel is the Cause.*'

'But this one is exaggerated. Such alienation on a day of

262

celebration is not something the majority of listeners will relate to.'

Nur defends his work. 'Are you telling me that no one dies in the Eid, no one loses their job or their money?'

Hamza smiles. 'Look, it's a very good poem, don't get me wrong. But it won't work as a song. Send it to the literary pages of the top newspapers and they will publish it without hesitation.'

'I'll do that,' says Nur. 'And it will go out in my collection when it comes out.'

To get *Eid Crescent* on paper had been a frustrating endeavour. Zaki was at school all morning and even in the afternoon he had to return for an award ceremony. Batool, who took Nur's dictation when Zaki was unavailable, was herself busy preparing Soraya to receive more guests. It was Nassir who had written down the poem. Even this simple task, he had botched. His handwriting was sloppy and Nur spotted many mistakes, which made him annoyed.

'Come on, let's do something new together,' says Hamza. 'Let's write a light-hearted song. Something merry and thrilling.'

'*She's easy and pliant*,' the words spill from his tongue, the most natural response. He can never run out of words to describe her. Her full lips when she smiles, her gentle voice and the way she drawls out certain words. How slowly she walks, how gently she sits and turns to him. And there is more to say, '*Have mercy Angel, your radiance has scorched me.*'

'Perfect!' Hamza hoists the oud to his lap and starts strumming. 'I knew you wouldn't let me down.'

Nur smiles, and instead of another verse, the title of his future collection comes to his mind. A collection Ustaz Badr would approve of, with Nur's name on the front page underneath the words, *Evening Withdraws*.

XIX

Usually, on holidays, Mahmoud slept in late and had the tea tray brought to his bedroom, but today was a special day. He stood on the roof of the saraya and, because it had been a long time since he had come up here, the views captured his attention. The Nile was a pale blue-grey, not yet lit up by the rising sun. On the bank, a few farmers were bending over with hoes. Mahmoud walked to the northern side of the roof, which overlooked Umdurman's Great Square. This was an excellent vantage point, an ideal place for the Harrisons to breakfast, with an unobstructed view of the celebrations. He called the servants and instructed them on how to arrange the seating. The best armchairs were carried from downstairs, the best coffee tables and the newest tablecloths. Once they completed the heavy work, he would release some of them so that they could take part in the celebrations. It had been a remarkable week since the signing of the Self Government Agreement between Britain, Egypt and Sudan. On the day itself, crowds had thronged the streets of Khartoum and people climbed the trees overlooking the Civil-Secretary's Office in order to hear the Governor-General announce the news. On the following day, when the government's official celebration was held, Mahmoud was invited and had a good front seat, but there were as many as fifty thousand Sudanese standing to hear the speeches, punctuated by parades of the guards of honour and RAF planes flying overhead. Today's affair would be more indigenous, a huge, all-party gathering in which the ordinary people of Umdurman would take part. The Harrisons, he was sure, would enjoy the spectacle. He knew them well now and understood the mixture of folklore and personal comfort, exotica and distance that would ensure their highest level of enjoyment.

It was cool this February morning. Once the sun was up, it would become warmer but now he found the breeze unpleasant, even though he was wearing a cardigan. He went downstairs and wandered around the empty house. It was silent and static without Nabilah and the children. They had been gone for months, but he still wasn't used to their absence. Nabilah had packed up and left as soon as Ferial's stitches were removed. He had tried to stop her, but she was adamant. So he gave up and thought, let her mother talk some sense into her, but the signs from Cairo were unfavourable. In the summer he travelled there, as was his custom, but Nabilah was not waiting for him in their flat. Instead, she was at her mother's apartment. When he went to visit, she repeated her ridiculous conditions and did not yield an inch. Most people now thought that they had reverted to their first arrangement of her living permanently in Cairo and he visiting from time to time. Perhaps, in the end, it would come to that.

He went into his room and felt a pang of loneliness; what had Fate given him: three good-for-nothing sons: the eldest undependable, then the wreck, and now the youngest taken away. But Mahmoud was a man of action and not prone to indulging in despair. These moments of introspection were few and far between. Perhaps, he thought now, he should move back to his 'bachelor' quarters in the centre of the saraya, close to Nur and Waheeba. However, that room reminded him of his last serious illness, when he had spent several weeks in bed. For this reason he was reluctant to go back there. Nor did he want a closer proximity to Waheeba. The solution for his loneliness would be to bring Nassir, Fatma and their children to live in the saraya. With Soraya married off, Idris would not need Fatma. If it were up to Mahmoud, Idris would come over, too, but he knew his brother was difficult and independent in his ways. It would be enough for Mahmoud to have Nassir and Fatma. After the wedding he would broach the subject. Already a date had been set, three weeks from today, before the warm weather closed in and made the preparations that much more arduous. He would feel relieved when the girl was finally married off. Perhaps then, Nur would become even more resigned to his fate. It surprised Mahmoud that the boy had reacted so badly to the announcement of Soraya's engagement. Surely it was inevitable? But young people always have difficulty living beyond the moment. That was the excuse he always had for Nabilah. She is young, she will grow, she will learn in time. And then she threw everything in his face without any hesitation or mercy.

'Cut off her allowance,' Idris had advised him. 'She'll come scurrying back to you.' But Mahmoud, though acknowledging the tactical logic of this move, was unable to bring himself to execute it. He was generous by nature and loathed the prospect of Nabilah scrimping and deprived. What bewildered him was how unreasonable her demands were. She continued to ask for the same things, no matter who he sent to intercede with her. She wanted him to divorce Waheeba and leave Umdurman altogether. If she ever returned to Sudan, she said, she would only return to a villa in Khartoum, which would be hers alone. Women were indeed complicated and capricious. There was Nabilah, ready to hand over to Waheeba the whole of the saraya in exchange for a villa in Khartoum, half or even a quarter of its size. How, in God's name, did this make sense?

She was a little girl; that was how he was tending to view her, a daughter with an unhealthy attachment to her mother, a youngster who was refusing to grow up and become a woman. His mouth twisted and he made a face. Everywhere he looked he could see evidence of the comfortable life he had lavished on her, and she had spurned it and gone. He lay down on his bed, fully clothed. Impressions he had overlooked now came to haunt him.

'Let's never go back to Umdurman,' she had said gaily, in their room in the Ritz.

He was lying in bed, watching her sitting at the dressing table brushing her hair. She was in her nightdress and he could see her smooth armpit, the cleave of her breasts, while her hand moved up and down with the hairbrush. When their eyes met in the mirror, she smiled and said, 'Ya Bey, you are a man of the world, too sophisticated for Umdurman!'

Another memory was of him walking in, with tremendous good news, to find her absorbed in some alterations she was making on a dress. There were pins in her mouth and her eyes were focused on the material in her hand. He was happy because Nur, after many dark days, was eating and talking again. He was reading and chatting to his friends, listening to the radio and smoking cigarettes. But Nabilah received the news with a dry smile and a conventional, polite remark. To Mahmoud, an obvious fact was underlined. Nur was his son, not hers, and she was keeping her distance – as if she was holding back so that she would not be contaminated by his bad luck.

In her last letter she had written, 'If you won't fulfil my wishes, then our marriage cannot continue.'

But he had no intention of divorcing her. Why should he give up something he possessed and cherished? She would eventually have her fill of Cairo and return to her senses. Let her indulge herself in her mother's company; let her pique and petulance play itself out. He would be waiting. Certain women in Khartoum were already making advances at him. If he wanted a wife or a mistress, all he had to do was point his finger. But he was waiting for Nabilah. He would forgive her everything if she came back: that she had thrown the necklace in his face, that she had deprived him of his children and that she had spoken to him in the bitterest and most callous of ways. Only one thing stuck in his throat, only one thing would be hard to overlook. She had shared his life and not understood him. Not understood that he could not leave Umdurman, not understood that Waheeba, for all her faults, was Nur's mother and always would be. Umdurman was where Mahmoud belonged. Here on this bed was where he would one day die, and down these alleys his funeral procession would proceed. And every shop owner in the souq, every tradesman pulling his cart, the beggars and the neighbours would know who Mahmoud Abuzeid was, where he came from and what he had done or not done.

Even if Nabilah came back, he brooded, her dismissiveness might continue to rankle, her desire to wrap his Sudanese identity and limit it with spatial classification. From early on she had mistaken his spirited love of modernity for a wholehearted conversion, and she had not taken account of the vicissitudes of Fate. But perhaps he expected too much from her. She was young, after all, and no one should be expected to predict the future. Indirectly, with cunning, Nur's accident had dealt a blow to his second marriage. The ingredients of his life, which he had kept in balance, irrevocably altered. The modern–to–traditional ratio shifted; Nabilah's dining table versus Waheeba's hoash, Cairo's avenues versus the alleys of Umdurman. He had prided himself in harnessing both, in gliding gracefully between both worlds, but now he was faltering; now he was unsure.

'Move to Cairo,' Nabilah had suggested. 'Being away from the misery and backwardness would be better for us.'

But this misery was *his* misery, and this backwardness his duty. She had no idea, nor would she be interested in the fact that he sat nearly every day on one committee or the other: he was on a committee to build the first football stadium in Umdurman, on another to build a charitable hospital and on the board of trustees for the premier woman's college, established by Sheikh Babiker Badri. He did not find these positions tedious, or a waste of his time. On the contrary, they filled him with the satisfaction that he was contributing to his country's progress.

A more intimate gratification was the personal petitions he received, and on which he threw his energy and utilised his connections to carry out. These days it was Nur's progress as a poet that was bringing in the requests. Mahmoud regarded Nur's poetry as a hobby, simply because it did not generate any significant income. He had opposed the early public broadcast of *Travel is the Cause* because he found it embarrassing that his son, who carried his name, should make such a gratuitous exposure of his tragedy. In addition, Mahmoud shared his generation's contempt for popular music and viewed it with suspicion, disdaining the milieu of musicians, dancers and singers whom he and the rest of his class associated with debauchery and loose morals.

'But let the poor boy comfort and occupy himself,' his friends had advised him.

And with time, Mahmoud's reservations thawed. He still regarded Nur's lyrics as silly jingles, but he smiled when his friends and acquaintances mentioned that they had heard Nur's songs on the radio. It was clear, too, that the boy's spirits were lifted with this new pursuit. And anything was welcome as long as it kept the wretched boy amused and out of the pit of despair. It became Mahmoud's duty to help those who helped his son (after, of course, checking up on their morals and reputation). Hamza Al-Naggar's eldest brother was now a new accountant in the Abuzeid office, and today Mahmoud would talk to Nigel Harrison about employment prospects for Hamza's younger brother at Barclays Bank. Letters of recommendation written by Mahmoud had helped secure a position for the father of one of Nur's new poet friends, and for Hamza's accordion player.

And then, of course, there was young Zaki, Nur's right arm, whose further education Mahmoud would foster and finance. As for Ustaz Badr, whose case Nur kept putting forward despite the episode of the robbery, Mahmoud was finally going to lease him a small flat with a nominal rent. Yes, the new building was finally up, the first tall building in downtown Khartoum. Mahmoud felt a surge of pride. There was even a photograph of it in a new monogram about Sudan published by Her Majesty's Stationery Office in London. It was good to build something that was strong and tangible, something that would last. It was an achievement to be proud of. And he would be generous, yes, he would. Let Ustaz Badr have one of the flats. Not every transaction must bring in a profit.

'Thank you Father,' Nur would say, and that was what Mahmoud wanted most of all, that smile and the shining eyes.

He checked his watch and found that he still had time to walk over to Waheeba's hoash and have his coffee. He found Fatma sitting with her aunt while Nur was indoors being given his morning bath.

'He was up late last night,' Waheeba explained. 'He had about thirty guests! Till past midnight they stayed with him. I sent out the dinner and fell asleep.'

'Yesterday's was such a jubilant gathering,' said Fatma. 'Patriotic poems and songs so loud that total strangers walked in from the alley!'

'I don't understand why they're celebrating now, when the English are staying on another three years.' Waheeba shifted on her bed.

Mahmoud smiled. 'It's a transition period. Change can't happen overnight.'

'We've won self-determination,' explained Fatma to her mother-in-law, 'much earlier than anyone ever expected.'

Batool placed the tray with the jabana, cup and a glass of water on a small table in front of him.

'You are always here,' Mahmoud joked with her. 'Don't you ever go to your husband?'

'I'm staying here, Uncle, until after the wedding.' She smiled as she poured out the coffee.

'Of course – we can't do without her these days,' murmured Waheeba.

'We are very busy,' Fatma reiterated.

She looked happier than she had for a long time. Mahmoud knew that Nassir was not the best of husbands and that Fatma's patience was often strained. However, Soraya's upcoming

270

wedding seemed to have plunged her into an array of pleasurable preparations and responsibilities and all her maternal feelings for her younger sister were now concentrated on the details and success of the next few weeks.

'Our bride,' she now said, 'wants to do something new, something extra and special.'

Mahmoud smiled. Soraya was now reverentially referred to as 'the bride' or 'our bride'. She was secluded, so that the sun would not darken her skin, and she was fed on copious amounts of milk and honey to fatten her up.

Fatma continued, 'She wants, on one of the wedding evenings, to wear a white dress like brides do in Egypt.'

Waheeba grunted. 'Oh, these new-fangled ideas!'

'Just for one day ...' Fatma squeezed her mother-in-law's arm. It was obvious she was in favour of this idea herself. 'Soraya would wear a European bridal dress and her bridegroom would wear a dinner suit – a white one, with a bow tie. And she would have bridesmaids, little girls Zeinab's age, all wearing the same dress and walking in front of her in a procession, holding candles. And, Uncle, this is what I wanted to ask you for: could we, please, have a belly dancer from Cairo?'

Mahmoud nearly choked on his coffee. The aspirations these young people had!

'You want me to import a belly dancer for one wedding? Certainly not! It would be too extravagant.'

'Please, Uncle?'

He shook his head. 'There are Egyptian dancing troops here in Sudan. We can hire them. I approve of the idea of the European clothes – and I was thinking of a European evening when I would invite my Egyptian and English acquaintances. I would have a brass band in the garden and a special menu.'

While they talked over the details, he finished his coffee. Fatma was bright with ideas, Waheeba vocal with her experience and Batool an avid listener. But when Nur was carried out into the hoash, they immediately changed the subject.

From the roof, Mahmoud and the Harrisons watched the Great Square fill up. The banners of the political parties were raised high, and tents of different colours gave the square a festive look. But before the speeches, the focus was on the bulls that were being slaughtered for the poor. The slaughter itself proceeded smoothly, but there was a scuffle when it came to distributing the meat. A fight broke out, the women even more strident and determined than the men, and a jumble of skinny arms and colourful tobes in disarray.

'Look at that boy!' cried Sue. 'He got off with the head!'

Sure enough, they could see him on his bicycle, with the head of a bull balanced on his own head. Blood dripped onto his smiling face and sweaty neck while he peddled off in haste. A lorry now drove onto the square, carrying loaves of bread. The driver climbed up on top and began tossing off the loaves in every direction and this caused another scramble, but the bread was more plentiful than the meat and the crowd was less frantic.

Every political party was granted its own entrance and they marched in, carrying their flags and chanting their particular slogans and anthems. The speeches followed, one after the other, while Mahmoud and his guests had brunch. There was on offer fried eggs and ful, a variety of cheeses, sausages and fried liver, and a selection of pastries and fresh grapefruit juice. 'Long Live the Free Sudan!' was followed by ululations and the beat of drums. It was only when the scheduled march through the town started that the roof became quiet and the birds in the garden could be heard again.

'The situation is still confusing,' said Nigel Harrison, sipping his tea. 'The police, the administration and the SDF are up for Sudanisation, but the British officials in the technical departments are to be held. Yet how will they be able to do their work when all the standards decline.' He presented this as a statement rather than a question.

'They will decline,' Mahmoud leaned forward, 'simply because all this is happening too soon and too fast. Do you think the technicians will voluntarily leave?'

'The advice they are hearing is "wait and see". It all depends on whether their existing contracts are legally abrogated or not by "change of master". And again, this is up in the air while the politicians negotiate and negotiate.' There was impatience in his voice, enough for Mahmoud to try and sooth him.

'But you are a private employee Mr Harrison. You need not have these concerns.'

Nigel Harrison crossed his legs.

'It's only a matter of time before the demand for Sudanisation spreads to the private sector.'

Sue spoke for the first time.

'If we leave soon, we can start off somewhere else and save time. We don't have to go home – it would be wonderful to move to Nigeria or Kenya.' She sounded anxious for a change, her eyes on her husband's face.

It must be unsettling, Mahmoud thought, to feel that those below you are surging upwards, crowding you out, waiting and wanting you to leave so that they could pounce and take your place. 'You will be sorely missed if you do go,' he said.

'And we will miss Khartoum too and all our good friends,' said Sue.

'I don't think a move is imminent, dear,' said her husband. 'Not for six months at least.'

'Excellent!' Mahmoud beamed. 'My niece's wedding is in a few weeks' time and you must promise to attend.'

He walked the Harrisons down the stairs and through his empty home, across the terrace, down the garden path, and to the front gate. He basked in their expressions of thanks, their appreciation for the wonderful morning they'd had. He remained standing until they got into their Ford Anglia and drove off. Their admiration for the saraya was gratifying, and he now looked forward to preparing the garden as a venue for Soraya's wedding; especially that European evening when the bride and groom would dress in white. Mahmoud visualised the coloured lights against the bougainvillea and oleander plants, the Sudan Defence Force band in their white uniform playing European music. He would order a banquet with cold meats, salads and fruit. The road would be crowded with the cars of his guests; the red Rolls Royce of Sudan's last Governor-General parked next to the green Cadillac of the prominent Sudanese leader, Sayyid Siddiq. It was high time to start initiating a good relationship with those most likely to form the first national government.

XX

When Nabilah first arrived in Cairo, she was triumphant. Empowered that at last she possessed something tangible and solid against Mahmoud: the irrevocable injury Waheeba had inflicted on Ferial, and his lame response. This was something she could brandish in front of her mother's face, to raise her indignation and rally her support.

'Look, Mama,' she said, swiping down Ferial's underpants to the utmost confusion and bewilderment of the child. 'Look what marrying me off to this retarded Sudanese has done to my daughter!'

Qadriyyah was taken aback. She adjusted her granddaughter's clothes and kissed her cheek several times while holding her in her lap. She said nothing. The roots of her hair were white and she looked run down from staying up late, nursing her husband.

'I am not going back there,' challenged Nabilah.

She felt the change around her; the parquet floor, the smell of polish and the Louis XIV furniture, the crowd of ornaments on the tall chest of drawers. *This* was home; this was Cairo. Outside, the city swirled and she wanted to step into that energy. She wanted to go and come and be part of it. Activity not indolence, civilization!

'He will come after you.' Qadriyyah rested her cheek on Ferial's hair. The girl sat rigid in her arms, alert at the mention of her father. 'He will beg your pardon and you must set conditions for your return. Ask him for a villa in Khartoum, demand—'

'No,' Nabilah interrupted her. 'No. The only thing I want from him is a divorce. I am not going back there. He did nothing, absolutely nothing to Waheeba. I wanted him to divorce her and kick her out of the saraya. I wanted her to be completely disgraced ... then I might have been willing to receive an apology from her. I would have listened to her – but only if she completely abased herself in front of me. But Mama, she had no regrets at all! Instead she circulated all these rumours about how the Egyptian nurse I recommended for Nur turned out to be a thief! On purpose, to taunt me.' Nabilah's voice turned to a screech. 'As if it was my fault that he stole her gold!'

'That is embarrassing, Nabilah. To recommend a servant and then be let down like that! But you must think of your husband, child. Forget Waheeba. Fight with her or don't fight with her – but don't lose your husband.'

Nabilah shook her head. 'He didn't stand by me. He didn't divorce her as I told him to.'

Qadriyyah sighed and gently pushed Ferial off her lap.

'Let's not do anything rash. You need to calm down. Your nerves are on edge now. And my hands are full. Your stepfather is not himself at all. I am truly anxious about him.'

Nabilah cried out, 'It's always Uncle Mohsin this, Uncle Mohsin that! Why does he always have to come first? You always make me feel that I am unimportant, that I am unwanted!'

'Shush,' said her mother, standing up. She was firm again, regaining her authority. 'I have enough burdens without you adding to them. You need to rest after your journey and your ordeal. Take a tranquilliser and go to sleep. We can talk more in the days to come.'

But before they had time to talk again, death intervened. Mohsin had a heart attack in the middle of the afternoon and by evening mother and daughter were in mourning, wearing black and receiving visitors in their sitting room.

'He died of a broken heart.' Qadriyyah twisted her handkerchief. 'The new regime killed him. They took away his position and his peace of mind. And this upheaval played havoc with his health.'

As was customary with funerals, Nabilah met relatives and friends she had not come across for years.

'Alhamdullilah you are here in Cairo,' they said. 'How fortunate it is that you can stand by your mother in her time of grief.'

For the first time in many years, mother and daughter witnessed and shared a searing experience, not an event they would narrate to each other by letters or abridge in telephone calls. The scratch and shock of death overwhelmed them at the same time. And they went over the details again and again.

'I heard you in the bathroom.'

'He made a sound like a cough, a deep cough.'

'He knocked the glass of water by his bedside when he fell.'

'That's when I came rushing in.'

'He looked like he was asleep.'

'No, I knew. I knew straight away he was gone.'

They huddled together, cowed by the proximity of death, their minds on the arrangements and adjustments, who else they needed to call, and would Nabilah quickly sew that button on her mother's black silk blouse. They were jolted against each other and became close, sharing thoughts and impressions. Life stood still; it was just the two of them, all the rancour and exasperation purged away, all the coolness of distance replaced by a sisterhood. Now they would move in step with each other, now the words yesterday, the day he died, a week since the funeral, it's forty days tomorrow – all had a meaning they both understood.

As a new widow, Qadriyyah was subdued and helpless. Nabilah stepped into the role of mistress of the house. When she enrolled the children at a nearby school, a decisive step, which solidified her presence in Cairo, Qadriyyah did not object. Only Mahmoud's visit in the summer stirred her to ask Nabilah to give him a chance and reconsider. To honour her mother's wishes, Nabilah sat stiffly in front of him in the salon and said, 'I can't live with Waheeba in the same house, not even in different quarters. I will only return if we leave Umdurman altogether for a villa in Khartoum. This is a fair and reasonable request.'

Her voice didn't waver; she was beginning to grow up. And, deep inside, she knew that he would not agree to leave Umdurman, not easily at any rate, but she was prepared to put up a fight.

Widowed mother and divorced daughter. There was something compelling and right about the combination. Even though Nabilah was not yet divorced, she revelled in the new situation, a life without the duties and restrictions imposed by men. At last, after so many years, she was finally fulfilling her dream, the dream of having her mother's full attention. The two of them talked and cried. They pored over old photographs, went over old conversations, memories told from Nabilah's perspective, from Qadriyyah's perspective, and then stitched the two stories together. Now Mohsin's widow, Qadriyyah spoke freely about Nabilah's father. He became big again, real again, no longer a secret love, a buried hurt.

'I remember the day your father died,' Qadriyyah would start, and Nabilah would hang on to every word. 'I've been widowed twice,' a rueful smile, taking a drag from her cigarette, 'such bad luck.'

The children were set proper mealtimes, but the widowed mother and divorced daughter ate whenever they liked. Turkish coffee with biscuits and cigarettes would substitute for breakfast. Watermelon and feta cheese would substitute for supper, or else Nabilah, glimpsing the season's first courgettes and eggplants, would make stuffed vegetables for lunch. They would eat them hot and later eat them cold. One day she made koshari, one day she made moulokhia with rabbits. Qadriyyah started to bake again: pies, sponge cakes and jam pastries. Tea and the cakes hot from the oven, irresistible. So more tea and pastries, and peanuts and roasted watermelon seeds as they sat on the balcony. More

Turkish coffee as they listened to plays on the radio and began to laugh again.

On the first day of every month, a clerk from the Cairo Abuzeid office knocked on the door and handed Nabilah a wad of cash. Her monthly allowance continued as if this was an ordinary summer spent in Cairo. Autumn came and went, and it was Nabilah's first winter in Cairo for years. Jumpers and blankets were pulled away from naphthalene balls and carpets spread on every floor; Qadriyyah knitting by the fire; the children's feet in socks and warm slippers. Oh, the joy of sliding her arms into her fur coat, the stove glowing and the smell of roasted chestnuts. The special vegetables and fruits of winter: cabbage, pomegranates, navel oranges, pumpkins and piping hot aniseed, sips of cocoa and sahlab.

Nabilah became plump and matronly while the sky was heavy with rain, Cairo dreamy under clouds, the days short and cold. All her clothes needed adjusting. She needed to let out the waist on this skirt and that dress. So she took to her sewing machine and found herself absorbed and able, her feet on the gridded pedal, which said Singer, her elbows on the smooth mahogany wood. Soon, she was making new dresses for herself and clothes for the children. More ambitious, she made her mother a silk dress in the latest fashion. A dress which the next-door neighbour admired and said, 'Please, Nabilah, make me one exactly the same, but red.'

The neighbour brought her own material and there were pleasurable visits for the fittings, changes here and there to the dress and, at the end, when the neighbour was thoroughly satisfied, she gave Nabilah a gift because it would not be polite or tactful to give money. Grand, bustling Cairo; Nabilah could so easily forget all about Sudan.

The only thing that marred her life was the children. Farouk and Ferial were like lumps of food stuck in her throat. They were refusing to adjust to the move or to embrace their new life.

279

'Give them time,' everyone advised her, 'they will come round in the end.'

But Ferial started to wet her bed and Farouk was doing badly at school. He didn't reply when the teacher spoke to him, just stared back, sullen and dumb. She discovered, to her disgust, that he was cutting the tips of his fingers on purpose, with razors he found discarded on the stairwell or on the road to school. They were small cuts, but the fact that they were deliberate made no sense. It was as if he enjoyed the attention he got when he lifted his thumb up, covered in blood. For then she would wash the blood away, apply mercurochrome and wrap it snug with a bandage. It made her feel pity and contempt for him. He looked wrong, too, walking next to her, his skin too dark and his hair kinky. The man at the haberdashery shop she frequented to buy buttons and tracing paper made comments when he saw them together.

'I don't understand how the mother can be so pretty and the son something else!' he would say, or, with an exaggerated expression of astonishment, 'Can all this beauty have such a dark son?' He was getting bolder with time. 'Why did they marry you off to a foreigner, Madame? What's wrong with your fellow countrymen?'

Nabilah delighted in these comments and considered them part of the amusement and banter of Cairo street life. She would answer back, too, saying, 'It's my fate and my portion' or 'My daughter is pretty, you can't fault her. Thank God, she has smooth hair.'

But deep down, she was troubled about her children. They were like centaurs, neither fully Egyptian nor fully Sudanese, awkward, clumsy, serious and destined to never fit in.

'I want to go home to Father,' said Ferial one day, and packed a little bag.

She succeeded in making her way, undetected, down outside the building and as far as the bottom of the road. Nabilah spanked her and warned her that if she went back to Umdurman,

Hajjah Waheeba would grab her and cut her again with a knife. Ferial became hysterical and throughout the next week had nightmares.

'I want to play in a garden,' she whispered to her mother, 'like the garden of the saraya back home.'

'I will take you to the zoo,' Nabilah said. 'The zoo here is much better and bigger than the one in Khartoum.'

Everything in Cairo was much better and bigger than its counterpart in Khartoum. They must learn to look, these two children. They must understand all the backwardness they were rescued from and appreciate their better life; they must fit in and become normal like other Egyptian children. Their names were not helpful, Nabilah had to admit. The King her son was named after was now deposed and Princess Ferial was out of the country. This was a new Cairo, a new era. Nabilah thrived and wanted her children to thrive, too. Change was in the air, the old order of Pashas and Beys was waning and this suited Nabilah fine. She, too, was an ordinary middle-class woman who no longer wanted her husband Bey.

'This situation cannot continue, my dear,' her mother warned her. 'It is one of three things; either you will make peace with your husband and go back to him, or Mahmoud Bey will stop sending you the allowance or, God forbid, he will divorce you and take the children.'

Sometimes, when Farouk and Ferial exasperated Nabilah, the thought of sending them to live with their father did seem appealing. But she would immediately chide herself. It would be morally wrong to give them up to such chaos. Who would supervise their upbringing in Umdurman? The servants? Hajjah Waheeba? And what calibre of adults would that produce (look at Nassir)? Certainly, Mahmoud had no time or inclination to look after children. And he was a reasonable man. He would want the best for his children, and the best for Farouk and Ferial was to be with their mother.

'There was a time – actually many times – when your

relationship with Mahmoud Bey was warm and strong,' her mother would remind her from time to time. 'Your early years in Cairo, the months you spent in London. Don't let Waheeba sour what was good between you. Don't let her win. Don't leave everything to her and walk away.'

But Qadriyyah's voice was losing its edge. Widowed mother, divorced daughter. They were on an equal footing, now, and Nabilah noticed the changes in her mother; the softer voice, the heavier tread, and a sense of retirement, a drawing back. Qadriyyah resumed dyeing her hair and manicuring her nails; she still made sure that her shoes were polished and would not go out in a crumpled skirt, but she did not shrug her daughter off as she used to. She enjoyed having Nabilah and the children around her. Indeed, she needed Nabilah, and all these speeches urging her to return to Sudan were increasingly becoming earnest but conventional politeness, words she did not really mean.

'Do you want to live your life without a man? Will you be happy alone?'

'I am happy with you, Mama,' Nabilah would reply. 'I am content like this.'

She was making up for the years of separation and even before that. For her hurt when her father died and Qadriyyah remarried, for her feelings of being shunted aside for the sake of her stepfather. She revelled in her mother's undivided attention; *needed* this healing time.

Sometimes, when she couldn't sleep, she would sit at her sewing machine, absorbed and content, her feet pushing the pedal until her mother, at dawn, brought her a cup of tea or it was time to rouse the children for school. Sometimes she dreamt of Mahmoud, or a man who looked like Mahmoud, but might not be him after all. She remembered his passion for the girl he saw in the window of the photographer's studio; how he had searched and found her. She remembered their time in London and how their every activity and encounter pulsed with harmony. She had loved the father desperate for a cure for his son, had loved his gallantry and determination. She recalled walking arm in arm with him to the hospital, conscious of the new hat on her head — a London affectation. Recalled meals they had shared, the entrance to the Ritz, the afternoon they were introduced to the Duke of Bedford. Perfect days, unclouded by Waheeba or Umdurman. Even seeing Nur in that English hospital was not as distressing as seeing him lying propped up in the hoash. He belonged in that English hospital, and he should have stayed there for the full rehabilitation programme, for as long as it took to get him to be as independent as he could. That would have been the modern thing to do; the right decision. But Mahmoud, so enlightened, so forward-thinking, had surprised her by saying no.

'I cannot leave him here by himself,' he had said, 'and I cannot be away from Sudan for so long. So he must return to Umdurman with me. The whole family must surround him and stand by him.'

She remembered how secretly relieved she had been — and still was — that Fate had struck Waheeba's son and not Farouk, how utterly grateful. Time and time again, she thanked Allah Almighty. It was the first and only religious sentiment in her life; that deep gratitude saying alhamdullilah and meaning it. No, she did not want to go back to Umdurman and see that miserable sight again. In Nabilah's mind, religious observance was associated with the rural lower classes; only the poor and uneducated prayed. Her gratitude, though, had an element of worship to it, a step that extended beyond temporary relief and fleeting elation.

The tall, dusky lady standing at the door was difficult to place. Nabilah was distracted by the elegant, obviously expensive, clothes and, instead of searching the stranger's face, her eyes lingered on the silk of the dress, the collar that folded wide almost over the breasts; such exquisite jewelry, such stylish shoes.

'Nabilah, how are you?'

That accent, and the words drawled out, her name bald without Aunty or Abla or Hanim.

'Why Soraya, it's you!' French perfume as Soraya leaned slightly to kiss her. 'I had no idea you were in Cairo. Come in, come in!'

'I am on my honeymoon,' Soraya explained matter-of-factly, as if a honeymoon was neither breathless nor transforming.

She followed Nabilah into the sitting room, looking around with curiosity. Manners were never her strongest point, nor posture. She slumped on a chair, on her lap the boxes she'd been carrying, large parcels wrapped in gift paper.

'I couldn't be in Cairo without seeing my cousins Farouk and Ferial. It's been so long.'

Nabilah still couldn't get over the clothes. They had to be part of the trousseau. Such exquisite taste, and a perfect fit. She could not help but voice her admiration and ask.

'Oh we missed you,' cried Soraya, 'when my sisters and I were getting everything ready. I wished you were in Umdurman so you could have helped me. Instead I had to resort to all our Egyptian and European friends in Khartoum. Here, let me show you a photograph of my wedding.' She was almost the schoolgirl again, peering into her handbag. 'I wore a white dress on one of the evenings, the first girl in the family to do so, maybe even the first girl in Umdurman! Both of my sisters only wore Sudanese traditional clothes and the gold. I did all that, too, but I also added on the European evening and we followed the Egyptian custom of giving every guest a little goblet full of sugared almonds as they were leaving. Everyone liked that so much. I've always wanted to have a white wedding, ever since I was a little girl and attended yours in Cairo.'

Nabilah held the photograph in her hand. Soraya's wedding dress was sumptuous, twisted round the bride's body like a sweet wrapper. The train fell long to the ground and Soraya was wearing gloves and holding a trailing bouquet of branches and flowers. Fastened to the back of her held-up hair was a headpiece shaped like a valentine, from which wisps of tulle fell. Such striking elegance! Who would have thought?

'You were a beautiful bride,' Nabilah said.

She glanced at the bridegroom standing next to Soraya with his bow tie and shining shoes. He was no one she recognised.

'My husband was educated in Britain. He is progressive and open-minded,' said Soraya. 'He has no objections at all to me finishing university.'

'That's excellent. Of course, you must complete your studies.' Nabilah handed back the photograph. 'A gorgeous dress,' she murmured.

'I've always wanted to dress in white like you. I used to enjoy looking at all the photographs of your wedding. Remember when I used to come over to the saraya to pore over the albums?'

Nabilah remembered these visits, which she had found irritating. Soraya would barge in unannounced, then would wander around Nabilah's rooms, fingering the curtains, touching the ornaments, flicking through books and albums, listening to the gramophone and then make snide comments about the children's Egyptian accents or their strict routine. Who would have ever thought that inside the girl's heart was affection and admiration? Nabilah was taken aback. She busied herself with her duties as a hostess. It was somewhat inappropriate for Soraya to trail off alone during her honeymoon. Where was the new husband? When Nabilah was on her honeymoon, Mahmoud had not let her out of his sight; he was too ardent for that. Yet Soraya seemed unhurried; she crossed her legs and chatted, and when the children came home from school, she kissed them and fussed over them. The gifts she had brought, a wax doll for Ferial and a train set for Farouk, were joyfully received, exactly what they had been wanting.

Seeing them together, cousins separated by age among many other things, Nabilah could not help but think that blood was, indeed, thicker than water. Her children were connected to this lady in a way she was not. The physical likeness was there, too, no matter how much she wanted to deny it. It was in Farouk's skin and in Ferial's wide mouth and high forehead. For the first time since she came from Sudan, Nabilah acknowledged the magnitude of what was at stake and all that would be given up.

She cried that night, stifling the sobs, not wanting her mother or the children to notice. Mahmoud had, a number of times, sent go-betweens to persuade her to return to him. They were all Egyptians, the wives of high-ranking officials in Sudan or Nabilah's own distant relatives. None of them had touched her heart or ruffled her resolve. All of them had infuriated her by either hinting at, or pointing out, how much better off she was financially with Mahmoud, and how she had come up in the world by marrying him. They seemed to believe that, by reminding her of why she had married him in the first place, they were guiding her back to her focus. Instead, their visits left her cold, even more rebellious and determined. It was the one person he hadn't sent who had succeeded in unsettling her.

'*I wish you had been in Umdurman to help me plan my wedding.*' So straightforward a sentiment. To help set up the first Egyptian-style wedding in Umdurman, a wedding like her own. This was touching. The girl had looked up to her, even though Nabilah hadn't noticed. And why hadn't she noticed? Because of her own prejudices, and because of the girl's unpolished manners, the fact that she did not address Nabilah formally and wore a tobe and chewed gum and laughed at the children. These were the opaque barriers. Life in Sudan would have had a meaning if Nabilah had been able to make a difference, if she had thrived as a role model, as a champion of progress, as a good influence. She could have taken a younger person's hand and guided them. But she hadn't ... This was the loss that brought tears to her eyes, the loss that would define her children's lives. She had not been able to rise and fill that leadership position. She had allowed

Waheeba, the dust, the heat, the insects, the landscape and customs to defeat her. She had not fought back.

She was softer and more receptive when the next visitor came. Again, he had not been sent by Mahmoud, again he was a surprise. The man standing at the door was his usual obsequious self, crumpled suit and fingers stained with ink.

'Welcome, welcome Ustaz Badr! Children, come and see who is here to visit us.' It was a pleasure to see Farouk and Ferial's shining eyes, to see how eagerly they greeted their former teacher.

Nabilah treated him with full honours. The salon was specially opened for him and the maid was instructed to offer Turkish coffee with cold water, savoury biscuits and baklava.

'Are you back for good? Has your secondment come to an end?'

'No, Madame. Alhamdullilah, it has been extended. I am here for the summer holidays. My family are in Kafr el-Dawar and I came specially to Cairo to see you.'

'That is very kind of you.'

'Madame, I am indebted to your husband. You know the terrible predicament I was in, the shameful embarrassment my cousin placed me in?'

Of course she remembered Shukry stealing Waheeba's gold.

'We all knew you were innocent. We were sure that you had been unfairly imprisoned.'

'But, God forbid, my reputation could have taken a severe blow. It is my incredible good fortune that Mahmoud Bey stood by me and vouched for my character. Not only that, but he has agreed to lease me a flat in his new building. We shall move there, insha'Allah, on our return. Madame, your husband is truly magnanimous.'

She smiled and urged him to have another pastry. But Badr was focused on what he was saying, the reason he was paying this visit, circling delicately around the subject and repeating himself. How the waters must return to their natural course. How the children needed their father. How Farouk was the obvious successor to lead Abuzeid Trading, though, out of politeness, Badr neither mentioned Nur's incapacity nor Nassir's indolence. None of this was new to Nabilah. She had heard it all before; the need for self-sacrifice, the need for compromise, the ultimate future of the children. What was different, this time, was that she listened. Ustaz Badr was not scolding her or belittling her. He was too respectful for that. And it was as if he understood and took for granted her need for Cairo, her love for home. Umdurman was not up to her standards, but Mahmoud was excellent. Umdurman was to be endured, and Mahmoud was to be celebrated. The burden and the prize, the trial and the reward.

And while Badr talked, a sweet memory came to her mind, distinct and sensory, even though it had been just an ordinary day, nothing unusual or special. On a winter afternoon in Umdurman, she had sat on the terrace sipping tea while Ustaz Badr was tutoring the children in the dining room. There was a soft, cool breeze and the enchanted garden of the saraya; the bone china cup in her hand and the sound of the birds. She could hear the drone of Badr's voice, the emphatic rise and fall and the children's squeaky replies. How amused she had been that he taught while sitting perched on the dining room chair, cross-legged and rocking from side to side as if he were still a child, memorising the Qur'an in the kuttab of his village. Afterwards, when the lesson was over, he had stood awhile, chatting to her and reporting on the children's progress. She had enjoyed his formal politeness, his Egyptian accent sharing the news from back home. She had asked him to recommend a piano teacher for Ferial and brushed aside, yet again, his plea to remind Mahmoud of his housing problem. Normal day-to-day life in Umdurman had had its good moments after all.

'Perhaps Qadriyyah Hanim could be persuaded to join you

in Sudan,' said Badr. 'Then she would be close and you would not have any anxieties about her.'

Or perhaps there was yet a resolution she could not see.

'Thank you, Ustaz Badr.' She saw him to the door.

'Whatever for? If only I could be of any assistance to your family!'

It was not the arguments he presented, but the memories he evoked, the confidence he inspired, and the goodness he underlined. Magnanimous and fair. Yes, that was Mahmoud. That was what her husband strove to be, in spite of the backward pull of tradition and the blows of fate. Magnanimous and fair. She should have been his support, she should have understood and appreciated better.

Early next morning she dressed and went out into the fresh air. Here was Cairo at its best and most benign, the bustle of the streets, the cars and buses; the men and women going about their business. Alhamdullilah, she said to herself. She passed a cinema and stood at the bus stop. The bedraggled seller was still there, selling hairpins, sweets and matches. She opened her purse and bought a packet of crystal sugar for the bus journey. The lump of sugar in her mouth made her feel stable again. It was a treat, however small or modest, and this became her outing, her pleasure.

At King Street she got off and walked towards the green curtains that were billowing in the balcony of the second floor, that green curtain that shielded her grandmother from the glare of the sun and the eyes of the neighbours. Her grandmother would approve of her resolution to return. More than approve; she would be pleased and comforted, sending her off with prayers and good wishes, reassuring her that the months would surely fly by and in no time at all it would be the summer holidays and time for Nabilah to return to Cairo once more. She quickened her pace and entered the cool shade of the building. How she loved this stone staircase and the wide, perfect circle of the gallery, spirals all the way up to the sun and sky . . . The maid opened the door for her. They were on friendly terms now, ever since Nabilah had moved to Cairo and become a frequent visitor. Nabilah strode across the hall and the sitting room to the balcony. In the green shade, her grandmother was reading the Qur'an. She closed it and put it aside before opening her arms out wide as if Nabilah was a child.

'Ahlan, Ahlan, what a lovely surprise!'

Nabilah knelt down and was enveloped in lavender and softness; that clear loving voice, saying, 'How lovely you look, my dear. How chic and becoming!' And because she knew very well Nabilah's interests, she touched her sleeves and asked. 'Is that the latest fashion?'

It must be, for Nabilah had spent night after night at her sewing machine, to get the puffs of the sleeves just right.

XXI

After dropping off the basket of food at the prison and spending a few minutes with his cousin, Badr hurried away. Insha'Allah, this would be his last visit. Shukry's sentence was nearly coming to an end.

'As soon as they set you free, you must return to Egypt,' Badr had urged him. 'Spend not a single night in Khartoum. I will buy you the train ticket myself.' Naturally, Shukry was disgruntled at that. He would return to Egypt empty-handed, but enough was enough. His sojourn in Sudan had been a failure and he had no one to blame but himself. 'If he disobeys me this time, I will not host him,' resolved Badr. 'I will not bring him to my house and I will certainly not inform him of my new address.'

My new address. Today was moving day! Today he had hired a donkey cart to move his family and their belongings to the new flat in the Abuzeid building. When he thought about it, he grew light-headed. It was really going to happen, against all the odds. Shukry's crime had brought him closer to the attention of Mahmoud Abuzeid, who was able to see Badr as separate from Shukry. A lesser man would have held a grudge, or feared that forgiveness would make him look weak. For years Badr had prayed for that flat and chased that opportunity. There were times when he had despaired, but today he would walk up those stairs. They would all walk up these stairs, and dear, sweet Hanniyah would have a balcony from where she could sit and look down at the goings-on in the street just like a Cairo lady.

He stepped off the tram and hurried to catch the inaugural prayer at the newly refurbished mosque. King Farouk had been funding this project for almost five years and the prayer hall smelt of paint and the fans that circled overhead were pristine and modern. Badr's bare feet sank in the new, clean carpet. The mosque was packed and Badr could not make his way to the front rows, which were reserved for Sudanese government representatives and high-ranking officials. Naturally, there was a strong Egyptian presence, and among his compatriots Badr recognized the headmaster of his school and the Egyptian Minister. He spotted the turban of the imam who had come especially from Egypt to lead this very first prayer. Badr could not help but note the irony: this imam was the first Minister of Religious Endowment after the July revolution that had overthrown King Farouk. There was wisdom in this, a lesson to be learnt. One could put money and effort into a project and yet not be present when it comes to fruition. Furthermore, death was not the only exit. There could be ignominy – and who knows if the mosque would continue to carry the name of a deposed King? But Badr reigned in his mind from any further speculation when the imam climbed the mimbar and began the Friday sermon.

Hanniyah was frying aubergines when he arrived home.

'Are we moving or are we not?' he shouted, but she was calm in the face of his agitation.

'You must be hungry. The children certainly are.'

She sprinkled salt on the dark aubergines, which oozed with oil.

Badr said to the boys, 'When you finish eating, put some clothes on. You can't go like this.' They were in their underwear as usual. The close proximity to the food made Badr realise that he was hungry. He started to shove bread and aubergines in his mouth. 'The driver of the cart is not going to hang around waiting for us and he should be here any minute.'

'Once the boys are ready they can stand outside and wait for him,' said Hanniyah.

She had accomplished a great deal since he left her this

morning, packing their belongings in crates and boxes. The only things left were the kitchen supplies.

Badr was tense because of his father; he was not sure how the old man would cope with the move. He watched now as Hanniyah fed him: bite-sized pieces and sips of water. She was efficient and matter-of-fact, treating her father-in-law as a child. Yet how remote he was, in a way in which children were never remote, as if he were asleep but still sitting straight. It chilled Badr sometimes, especially when his father suddenly spoke out, random words and incoherent expressions. It was not even worth it to sit next to him now and say, 'Father, we are moving to a wonderful new home today.'

He had passed that stage. Two years ago he was talking lucidly and he had recognized Shukry when he first came from Egypt. Now he was completely detached and it was even rare to hear his voice.

Badr's daughter toddled towards him wearing her Eid dress, which was now too small. He lifted her onto his lap and patted her thighs. She was his joy. After four boys her arrival was exquisite. Every tender feeling in him was aroused and he was more complete as a parent because of her. She babbled now, repeating 'Baba, Baba'. He tried to feed her but she was satiated and wiggled down from his grasp, hanging on to his knees for support. She had only started walking a few months ago. Looking back, Badr remembered that he had not particularly wanted a daughter and certainly never prayed for one. Her arrival was a gift, luxurious and aromatic. A gift that humbled him and made him realise that the sweetest things in life were not necessarily what one strove for and grabbed. Instead, many many times the All-Merciful, the All-Generous would give his servants without being petitioned, without waiting to be asked. And then it would feel like how holding this little girl felt; a surprise, a dreamy blessing.

Badr dressed his father in clean long johns and a grey jellabiya. How loose it hung on him now! This was the man who danced at his son's wedding, twirling his cane above his head while the trumpets blared. This was the man who could wrestle two men at one go, who could swim from one side of the river to the other while holding his breath.

'I always felt puny next to you, Father,' Badr said. 'But instead of making me feel ashamed, you took pride in my love of books. You spared nothing for my education. You did everything so that I could be the effendi in the family, so that I could wear a suit and go out to teach the children of city men.'

His father did not respond or even look at him. He dwelt in a place where Badr's voice was as meaningful as the meowing of a kitten. It was as if he was following an alternative narrative, sights and sounds superimposed over the reality in front of him, his very own script, which absorbed and distorted his senses. Today he could not even push his feet into his plastic slippers. That instinct of sliding one's foot forward had gone.

Time for the farewell scene Badr had ruefully predicted. After nagging him about moving and bitterly criticizing their housing conditions at every opportunity, Hanniyah clung to the neighbourhood women, weeping profusely as if a calamity had fallen or as if they were leaving the entire country forever. In reality, they were only transferring from the outskirts of town to the centre; a few tram stops. It would be a little further away from the school but that was a minor inconvenience.

'Hurry, woman, hurry!'

In her black outdoor abaya she looked formal and foreign. The Sudanese milling around her were in their colourful patterned tobes with bangles on their arms. Sometimes, like now, the Sudan would emphasise its African identity and assert itself as simple and rich, Negro and vibrant, flowing and deep.

The children clambered onto the cart. Don't count them, just say their names.

'Osama, you are the one responsible for your grandfather; Bilal put that crate on your lap. Radwan hold your little sister.

Ali, keep your eyes wide open and watch out in case any of our belongings fall off.'

Now verses to ward off the evil eye. Prayers for an easy, smooth move, for prosperity in that so eagerly striven for new home. Yes, part of Badr's tension was the fear of envy. He could jinx himself if he became exultant. But the greatest danger to come was envy from his colleagues at the school. This was what Al-Ghazali said in his Revival – that we are more likely to envy those who are similar to us, than those who are completely different. Hence, envy is more likely to occur between brothers, cousins and co-workers. This was true. Badr did not envy the rich folk whose children he taught, instead he was more likely to grudge a colleague a pay rise. The cart dipped into a pothole and they were all jolted. Badr turned to glance at his father. He seemed to be soothed by the ride. It had been remarkably easy to persuade him to climb the cart, much to Badr's relief. Perhaps his father was aware of the donkey; after all, he could hear the clip-clop of its feet and smell its hide. Certainly he was enjoying being in a wide-open space and the sense of movement and momentum. Hopefully, he would be persuaded to climb off the cart once they arrived!

Their journey took them eastward, towards the English neighbourhood, though they would not reach that far. They passed the statue of Kitchener astride a horse and went down Sirdar Street. All was quiet on this Friday afternoon, and this made their progress faster. They were in a Christian neighbourhood now, and the buildings were more sophisticated, the inhabitants as light-skinned as Europeans, the women with bare arms and their hair in waves, and men who spoke with the accent of the Levant. Some were Badr's fellow countrymen, Copts from Egypt, and one of them, a parent from the school, recognized Badr and waved.

It didn't embarrass Badr that he was perched on a donkey cart with his family and their motley possessions. He was busy noting that the land on which Mahmoud Bey had built his tall building had been purchased from a Christian, a cautious businessman made insecure by the advent of Independence. Khartoum was, slowly but surely, becoming Islamic. Today the opening of the new mosque, and tomorrow, once the English left, there would be others. A city with a predominant and growing Muslim population had seven churches and only two mosques – only a coloniser would impose such an imbalance! The English would go and take their street names with them – Victoria, Newbold, King and Wingate. They would carry off their statues – Gordon astride a camel and Kitchener on a horse. The cabarets, dance halls and bars that they set up would decay. The prostitution they legalised would become prohibited, and the X signs they unashamedly set up to mark the red-light districts would be pulled down. Anglo-Egyptian rule was over, the proposed union with Egypt had failed, and whatever losses his homeland would incur in the future were justified by its position as the silent partner of the Condominium, the nominal figure which mattered and didn't matter.

We could have done more, Badr mused. We could have spread Islam further, we could have squashed the seeds of religious deviations with more vigour, we could have nurtured and taught Arabic and enlightened. Now it was not exactly too late, but Egypt's influence was stunted. Yet everyone, these days, was keen to stress the friendship of the two neighbouring countries, the two peoples who drank from the same Nile, and thus the decision to continue with the Egyptian Educational Mission. Badr's secondment was secure and to be extended. The miserable night he had spent in custody had not dented his reputation nor jeopardized his employment and he had never felt so grateful in his whole life. It was his biggest, most profound relief. If he spent the rest of his life thanking Allah every minute of every day, it would not be enough. He was overwhelmed by His Lord's mercy and generosity.

They arrived at the Abuzeid building. The shops that lined the ground floor were all closed for the holiday and the offices upstairs, too, were shut. Not all the building was residential; there were placards on the balconies, one advertising a lawyer and another, a procurement business. As Badr had feared, his father refused to descend from the cart.

'Leave him with me and go up,' Hanniyah suggested. Her daughter, dozy from the movement of the cart, had fallen asleep on her lap. 'You and the children go up and maybe I can persuade Uncle Hajj.'

Together with the older boys, Badr carried all the furniture upstairs. The thrill of turning the key and whispering, 'In the name of Allah, the Most-Compassionate, the Most-Merciful . . .'

Their belongings looked paltry in the wide space, shabby against the new flooring and freshly painted walls. Ali started skidding on the tiles, and his older brothers followed. The flat echoed with their cries of delight. This was real. At last, at long last! For the first time since Osama was born, Badr and Hanniyah would have a room all to themselves. He wanted to see her face when she first stepped into the flat. Would she gasp out loud? He would take pleasure in her gratitude, for sure.

Leaving the boys upstairs, he dashed down again.

'Father, you have to get off now. We've arrived.'

There was no response. Gentle nudging and pulling by the arm was met with indifference and then resistance. With the help of Hanniyah and the cart driver, Badr forcibly carried his father off the cart and steadied him on his feet. Unexpectedly, the old man reached out to put his arms around the donkey and almost fell onto its neck, his face against its hide, his hands gripping the saddle. How far he was from his village in Kafr-el-Dawar with all its familiar sensations and characteristic smells . . . Now Badr was going to move him further away, up above street level. More change, more disorientation.

'Come along, Father. The donkey is not ours. It has to go away with its owner.'

The cart driver, a lanky, grumpy youth, was looking perplexed at the old man and was impatient to be off. Badr untangled his father's arms from around the donkey's neck.

He paid off the driver and, with excruciatingly small steps, led his father to the entrance of the building.

'I will go ahead of you,' Hanniyah said. 'Allah only knows when you will get Uncle Hajj up there!'

Her eyes were shining and her cheeks flushed. Yes, this was her day. He said, 'Take the suitcase with you so you can start to unpack.'

She handed the sleeping child to Badr and lugged the suitcase up the stairs. So, baby on his left arm and his right prodding the old man up the stairs.

'Careful, Father, one step at a time.'

Two steps, three steps, they gathered momentum and reached halfway up the stairs. Then his father stopped. For no reason at all he came to a standstill. Badr pleaded and tugged but to no avail. He could hear Hanniyah making her way to the flat up above; he could hear her expression of surprise as she entered through the door.

'Come on, Father.'

He had to be extra gentle. A struggle on the staircase would be unsafe for the three of them. The baby stirred in his arm and opened her eyes. She was beautiful in these waking up moments, incredibly soft, languid and angelic in the clear trusting way she gazed up at him. He kissed her, and she shifted to sit more upright in his embrace.

Here he was with his bliss in one arm and his burden in the other, his pleasure on one side and his trial in the other. Balanced. Striving up with these two attachments. Holding them both at the same time. It was the fresh start of life and the gloomy, narrowing end. Loving them both, serving them both. His father shifted and raised one foot up. How slowly they were progressing! Badr was missing what he had been looking forward to – Hanniyah's expression when she first saw her new home. By the time they reached the flat, she would be engrossed in unpacking and her mind occupied. He would have liked to be with her now, now as she raised her hand to her mouth and broke into a spontaneous ululation of joy.

XXII

Patience, and this is how fame begins. Nur is putting a call through the operator. As usual, Zaki had dialled the number then placed the receiver against Nur's ear. By bending his head sideways he can hold it wedged against his shoulder and Zaki is free to wander off and check that the long cord of the telephone is not entangled in its trip from Nur's room to the hoash. Nur gives his name and the number he wants to reach. Instead of the customary, 'Hold the line, please,' the operator's voice changes and lightens. 'Nur Abuzeid! Really?' He speaks as if he is no longer an operator but an impressionable young man, perhaps a little younger than Nur. It's hard to tell. 'Excuse me for asking, Sir. But are you Nur Abuzeid, the poet?'

This has never happened before. Yesterday he had put in a call to Ustaz Badr at the school and got no such response.

The operator continues, 'I am one of your admirers, Sir. I listen to your lyrics on the radio and copy them down. Your poem *Hope* is a masterpiece in my opinion.'

Nur smiles.

'Thank you.'

The afternoon is different now. He is lying in the same hoash, its uneven floor sprayed with water; he is under the same cloudless sky, hearing the riot of the birds in the saraya's garden and beyond the walls the sounds of the alley: men walking to the mosque, women visiting each other and dawdling, the scuffle and thud of a football game. But now there is an unexpected glow in this wide prison where life ebbs and flows, where others come and go and late at night songs are composed, where young

300

poets come to recite their raw lyrics and leave saying, 'I've attended a literary salon in Umdurman where they serve a good dinner too.' Today Nur is honoured.

'If you don't mind me asking about a specific line in your poem? I dabble in a few verses now and again myself.'

This admirer is voluble. Perhaps being an operator is not suited to his nature, perhaps he should be something else, somewhere else. Nur knows about this. There had been a time too — before the accident — when he wanted to be a poet, but his voice was feeble and the roads were blocked. These days he recites and people listen to the sincerity of his words. They hear a poem tense as a confrontation between bitter and sweet, a story in which the victors are mercy and love.

'Please feel free to ask me anything you want.'

Everyone in the hoash turns to look at Nur. The receiver is sliding and Fatma tucks it back in place. Nassir is making panto-mime gestures of inquiry, which Nur ignores. His mother, sitting on her angharaib is pouring herself a glass of cardamom tea. She sucks the first draught and listens.

'When you say to your loved one *Tomorrow I will put on my best clothes / To go out and meet you by the Nile*, is that a reference to a specific location?'

Nur remembers a family picnic which Nassir had arranged, a whole day out by the river. He remembers the chatter of Fatma and her children, Halima and her children. Nur's cot was carried all the way to the shore and the winter breeze blew through the trees. Soraya sat next to him, and they were both aware of the sound of the water and how special the day was. They talked and didn't need to talk, every little thing they said mattered and was unnecessary at the same time. Later, he sat in his wheelchair and she put on her glasses. She stood behind him, holding open the pages of a magazine. They both looked down and read together one of his poems in classical verse, the one Ustaz Badr rated highly – *Flocks of Beauty*. Nur remembers Soraya's closeness and his words in print, her closeness and her attributes in ink, that mighty, moving Nile, and Nassir with his rod, catching the fish they would later grill.

'The Riveria Park in Umdurman,' Nur replies.

But it was another riverbank which was the trigger for *Hope*, another Nile. It was the men's night out, when they went to the Burri houseboat on the Blue Nile. How can one pinpoint a particular scene, a single place? The poems came from far beyond and deep within, from dreams he'd seen and lines he'd not yet read, from aches and his need to manoeuvre, his need to stretch and reach out, to pull and push and clutch tight, to touch or pinch, carry or stroke, and what must be said to describe her eyes rimmed with kohl and how smitten she is, his own flesh and blood, how tender and smitten.

'I have another question,' says the operator.

Nur is happy to answer. The telephone call to Hamza Al-Naggar, which was important a few minutes ago, can wait. This recognition is gratifying. It fills him up, it makes him feel nourished and at peace. Today his howling demon will be subdued, his rebellious side which urges him to go on strike, will be muted. He had composed his poetry to a void, reciting to a star, reaching out to faceless, nameless strangers and now connections are being made. Balm to his bitterness, the solace he needs, the compensation he ached for when he despaired and asked, why, why me? This is the sort of incident everyone in the family will repeat.

'The telephone operator recognised him!' his father will say at the Abuzeid office.

His father, who was at first ashamed, and now is coming round, because success is much easier to understand than Art. Success carries respectability and draws people near. His mother, too, will repeat the story to that gossipy neighbour and soon, very soon, it will cross the river and reach Soraya's house. The pleasure lasts, settles and lasts, long after the receiver is moved away from his ear.

302

★

Radio Umdurman is coming to interview him. They will use his room because the hoash is too noisy. All day Nur's voice is raised in instructions and requests. The electrician must be called in to tame the creaky overhead fan and fix a faulty wall socket. The room must be tidy, the floors must be cleaned and refreshments must be provided for the interviewer Mr Mu'awia and his crew. Nur had often heard Mr Mu'awia's deep, clear voice on the radio interviewing other poets; now, remembering those clipped tones and direct questions, makes him slightly nervous. Everyone else in the family is on edge; this is a nationwide exposure, which hovers around a sensitive issue. Nur asks to be dressed formally in a long-sleeved shirt and trousers. All his old clothes hang off him in a ridiculous manner which is why this is a brand new outfit, in a significantly smaller size.

It takes an hour to dress him, to manoeuvre the sleeves up the rigid, acute angle of his elbows but he is used to all this now. The white collar of the shirt glows against his skin; his shaved chin tingles with eau de cologne. Nassir snaps a photograph, proud of his new camera. He captures the pure light in Nur's eyes and that graceful smile.

Mr Mu'awia has a smooth look about him, though he is overweight and slightly bald. He had not been informed of the extent of Nur's disability but he hides his embarrassment well for he is a professional broadcaster, dry and slick. It helps that Nur is sitting in an armchair, it helps that he is fully dressed today. The equipment is set up in the room: huge rolls of double-tapes, a record player, and albums of Sudanese songs. Mr Mu'awia orders the children out of the room. They file out, Ferial pulling Zeinab's hand, Farouk dragging his sandals on the tiles. Now a voice check for Nur: he is too far from the microphone, he is too close. Zaki, who excels at being useful, is today in a buzz of excitement. His secondary school exams loom, but intoxicated by this close proximity to the media, all concerns are banished.

Fatma peeks into this room full of men; she is unable to contain her curiosity. Nassir, of course, is clumsy and in the way, babbling about everything and nothing.

'If I could request your silence, Sir, we are about to start recording.' Mr Mu'awia doesn't smile. 'I need complete silence in the room.'

He turns to Nur. 'We will start with a recital of one of your poems.'

'Which one?' Nur looks straight at those eyes that give away nothing.

'*Travel is the Cause*. It's your first composition and we can talk about how you started writing. Do you need the text?'

No, Nur can recite from memory.

'I will introduce you first and then you can start.' Clicks, hums, and the machine is on. Mr Mu'awia speaks and the impersonal voice of Radio Umdurman becomes a human being. 'Nur Abuzeid is one of our most popular lyrical poets . . .'

Nur turns his head to Nassir and Nassir winks. He is beaming with pride, this buffoon brother of his who would not leave his side. Nur had always known that the accident was a blow to his family, too. Their devotion, their being there around him every night and every day. Now his success will be their success, further pride in the family's name. *In you, Egypt, are the causes of my injury. And in Sudan, my burden and solace.*

'Was there a special occasion in which you composed this poem?'

So this is it, the first question. 'I composed it in 1951, when I returned from Egypt. I had finished my studies in Victoria College and I was on the beach in Alexandria . . .' He continues to describe the accident, hearing the waves, the jam of salt water up his nose.

Mr Mu'awia is seemingly unmoved by the tragedy.

'Did you write the poem with the intention of it becoming a song?'

'Not at all! It was a surprise from Hamza Al-Naggar. The radio was switched on – and there it was!'

'How did you feel about that?'

'I found it disturbing at first, then I grew to enjoy it. It propelled me into a new direction. I began to be involved in the whole process of composing lyrics and tunes, even though I do not have a musical background. Hamza and I worked together on *Days and Nights* and *She Reached Out to Shake My Hand*. But that first time, with *Travel is the Cause* – that was entirely a Hamza Al-Naggar conspiracy!' He smiles, but Mr Mu'awia is serious.

'Is that the reason he's been granted the rights to most of your lyrics?'

Nur is taken aback.

'No, he certainly does not usurp my poems. He is a valued friend and a constant visitor; this is why we naturally tend to work together.'

'Who else sings your lyrics?'

'Sayyid Khalifa and Ilyas Hakim.'

'Did you distribute your poems to Sayyid Khalifa?'

'No, he came over for a visit, we chatted about various topics and I showed him my work. He liked *Hope* and *Ya Salaam, Ya Salaam* so he took them. I don't have a specific method of getting my poems to the attention of musicians.'

'It is noticeable that you have achieved outstanding success in the field of the popular lyrical song. What in your opinion is the status of such songs in Sudan?'

Nur relaxes into the interview. Mr Mu'awia plays Sayyid Khalifa singing *Ya Salaam, Ya Salaam*. Nur confesses that his poems tend towards sadness and that he often needs to restrain himself from such indulgence. There is a break in which Mr Mu'awia drinks orange juice and Zaki raises a glass of cold water to Nur's lips. Mr Mu'awia looks away and lights a cigarette, while his crew stare openly. It is always the inability to drink and feed himself which startles others. Nothing else has the same impact.

More questions and it is time for Nur to request a song. He chooses Al-Taj's *Ya Badi'at Al-Loun*. When the last notes die down, Mr Mu'awia ruffles a few papers in his hands and turns to Nur.

'One of our listeners, Mrs Asya from Atbara wants to know to whom these lines were composed.' He begins to read out, '*I want to watch the magic show in your eyes. No one else can sound like you* . . . These verses are, of course, from *You've Cooled and Gone*. Are they addressed to a specific person?'

Nur has the odd sensation of being caught out, of people around him holding their breaths. Nassir shifts uncomfortably in his seat. And out there, through the radio waves . . . is Tuf Tuf listening? The friend who knows and must pretend not to know, the friend who can no longer sit comfortably in Nur's salon and hear him recite his poems. Is *she* listening? Lying in bed in her villa in Khartoum, her newborn daughter by her side.

Anger seizes him; stupid Asya from Atbara, stupid Radio Umdurman, stupid Mr Mu'awia, stupid Nassir, who now looks doleful and wary in case Nur blurts out the wrong thing and stains the family's honour. Some names must never be spoken out loud; some family stories must not be repeated. And Nur knows his duty, he understands the lesson. She is your kin whose reputation must remain unblemished; she is *another man's wife*. He knows all this, and wisdom tells him the strange truth. That easy-going, disinterested Tuf Tuf is a better husband for Soraya than he could have ever been. Through him, she is realising her dreams of modernity, discarding her tobe and cutting her hair short, moving away from Umdurman's conventions, wearing her glasses freely and carrying her degree like a trophy, gliding through the fashionable salons and parties of the capital. Nur would have been possessive of her, he would have held her tight with passionate love, and through and through he was a poet who loved his colloquial tongue, the traditions of his people, the closeness of the Nile and the sounds of the alley. Mrs Asya from Atbara wants to meddle and know; wants to grab and know . . . How different other people are from him! They live in the real world, banal and industrious, while he skids the surface of pain and flutters against sadness. Beauty is his friend; loss is his friend. His is the pleasurable company of writing poems and making songs. He has fewer inhibitions than they do; less time, less space.

'Every word,' he answers. 'Every one of my verses is addressed to the beloved.'

'Abstract or real?'

'Both. My muse and my loss.'

There is a silence in the room. As if noting Nur's discomfort, Mr Mu'awia sits back and changes his tone.

'The unprecedented success of your latest collaboration with Hamza Al-Naggar – reaching the silver screen, no less – tell us more about that.'

Nur breaks into a smile.

'*Have Mercy, Angel* will feature in a new Egyptian film starring the very well known singer Sabah. The song will be performed as a stage duet between Hamza and the diva.'

Nur had been invited to the premier in Cairo. Perhaps he will go. If he can brave the ordeals of the journey and the pity of strangers, he will be rolled down that red carpet to see his name – very small, but nevertheless present – among the credits. It is a pleasant vision.

At last Mr Mu'awia switches off the microphone.

'You were excellent, Mr Nur. Thank you very much.'

He is jubilant and squeezes Nur's elbow. The room stirs into movement. Nassir stands up. Nur feels a sense of relief, a pleasant exhaustion. Mr Mu'awia is beaming; he is someone else, infinitely more approachable.

'We've had so many requests to interview you,' he chats. 'You have such endearing qualities. Remember, we reach thousands, so this will solidify your reputation even more. Let me just finish off.'

Nur watches him as he switches on the tape recorder, holds

the microphone and murmurs in that deep familiar Radio Umdurman voice, 'Dear, esteemed listeners, you were in the company of the poet of love and hope.'

Author's Note & Acknowledgements

Although this novel was inspired by the life of my uncle Hassan Awad Aboulela, I have altered many aspects of family history and inserted imaginary characters in order to produce a work of fiction and not an accurate biography of the poet's life.

I am deeply grateful to my aunt Hajjah Rahma Aboulela (Hassan's sister) for planting the seeds of this novel in my mind and for capturing my heart with her vivid memories and eloquent, lasting emotions.

Thanks equally to my cousin Tal'at Aboulela and his wife Fatma Ezzedin who provided me with materials and patiently answered my questions.

My grateful thanks to Dr Hashim Mirghani El Haj, from the Arabic Department of the University of Sudan, for helping me gain a better understanding of Hassan's work and his position as a popular lyrical poet.

Enormous thanks to my brother Khalid Aboulela for all the generous emails and for finding that tape! And to my cousins Yousra Aboulela and Dr Muhammad Awad Aboulela whose insights and suggestions set me off in rewarding directions.

I am grateful to Mrs Suad Abdelrahman for sharing with me her memories of the bridal dances in Umdurman. And to Jeannine Bardh for help with the family tree.

My beloved late grandmother Haggah Leila Muharram spoke to me often of Cairo in the 1950s and answered my questions in many happy conversations. Also my father's best-friend, our dear late Uncle Abdu Abdelhafiz (may Allah grant them all mercy) shared his memories of Khartoum and Umdurman in the 1950s. In this I am also indebted to *The Sudan Journal of*

Ismay Thomas, edited by Graham Thomas, especially Ismay's entries which describe her encounters with the Aboulela family. *Al Khartoum Ayaam Zamaan* (Khartoum in the Old Days) by Ahmed Abdel Wahab Said also became an invaluable companion.

The extracts of Hassan's poems which appear in the novel are my translations (and sometimes improvisation). I used the texts in the printed tribute *Hassan Awad Aboulela – Sha'ir al-Hob wa Al –Amal* (The Poet of Love and Hope) by Sherief El Fadel Mustapha.

I also translated the poem 'I am Umdurman' by Abdallah Muhammad Zein from his collection *Min Umdurman illa London* (From Umdurman to London).

Other valuable resources were the lectures *Mercy Oceans Book Two* by Sheikh Nazim El-Naqshabandi, the tribute *Saad Aboulela: Rihlat Al-Omr* (A Life's Journey) by Bashir Muhammad Said, *Cairo the Glory Years* by Samir W. Rafaat and the paper *The Sudanese Private Sector: An Historical Overview* by Robert L. Tignor.

It has been a true privilege to have as my editors Arzu Tahsin (W&N) and Elisabeth Schmitz (Grove/Atlantic). I cannot thank them enough for their enthusiasm and excellent advice; their brilliant editorial notes and their unique discernment.

From my early start as a writer I have been blessed with the support of my agent Stephanie Cabot. Enormous thanks to her for her flair and insight and for supporting me for so many years.

Lastly, the two most influential loves of my life, my husband and first reader Nadir Mahjoub and my mother Dr Mona Khalifa – endless gratitude, beyond words, for enveloping me in your wisdom and care.